UNO

UNO .: · · *BY* .. *TZVI PECKAR the THIRD*

---

a POLYMORPH productions PUBLICATION

Papa was rolling stoned

UNO
A KYLE CLAIBOURNE AUTOBIOGRAPHY
SKATING BARE FOOT on a RAZOR'S EDGE

Chapter 1 – Senior Year; Second Semester

"I cannot listen with the you?" she said, in broken English, thick Spanish accent, & repulsed by my American English. My senior Spanish exchange student, girlfriend, had instructed me, "You can spoke slower with us."

"Ona," I say calm, slow. She's putty in my emerald eyes, calls them unfair, hypnotizing. They look just like green crystals, even when I'm not stoned. She slides her fingers between mine, we're bored, lunch, wandering the back of the outdoor high school stadium. Help her over an oak root jabbed up through the concrete, the urban backlot terrain of Indian blood and rotted chicken corpses. Nor. Cal. "So, American," she changes the entire subject as we stroll along the wooden Victorian, two bedroom homes, surrounded by the 50s' retro-fitted, entirely new, modern, now suburban and outdated homes. Our American town is a town that feels misplaced for our high school breakouts. Anyhow, I was trying to tell her a story about..."You explain again," she touches my face, "Slow."

"Those punk photos you like in Photography Class, were taken by a kid a few years ago," I'm speaking slowly, she's listening, we've stopped walking, "He went crazy," and twirl my finger round my temple to demonstrate and in Spanish I say, "In crazy casa, muy año," and she SLAPS me.

"I not stupid. You no need to speak bad Spanish to me," she's mad. I've offended her. Come back. Fuck. I catch up, take her hand, she pulls it away, "Ona."

"No."

"Ona."

"No."

I apologize.

     She   softens up.

            Bats   her   eyes.

"Fine." I kiss her. Hard. We love to kiss. She likes to pull me in tight. A hug. Love. Stupid Spanish girl, falling in love with an American. What are you doing? What are we doing? She certainly tastes exotic, sweet n' sour under-tongue, not the sourdough bread of the Bay Area, the salty warmth of the Spanish coast, an island, a twin island, Mallorca; alone separated by the gulf. My Ona. I so love my eighteen year old Ona.

THE SCHOOL BELL TOLLS — UGH, SENIOR YEAR SUCKS

•SUCKS•

"Killed a Nazi in San Francisco, now he's in an insane asylum," I finish the story.

"Why you tell me this? This very sad."

— It's 1996, February —

I'm sitting by myself in a locker-room shitter; no doors—
took 'em down two months ago when they caught some *Ace
of Base / Tupac* button wearing, country tote-sack, selling a
few bags to the Linebacker. *Tupac* in a tutu thought he
wanted MDA, but the brain-on-hold football star ordered
Quaaludes, which have been out of existence for like ever
now. We all know. We've tried. Tupac thought Quaaludes
meant *Ecstasy* in code, but when the truth be told, the lug-

head beat the tutu up, like really bad. Broke his jaw against the toilet seat, pissed on his head, dropped the drugs out of reach so that when the Gym teach came a waltzing by—

—I don't know why I'm sitting here. I just can't go back to General-Ed English. I'm over it. Fucked up my grades already. Paying the price. But let's get real; that does not equate me to the IQ of these half-wit, knuckle-heads, and deadbeats. Eighteen and can vote; that means my choice—

—Shit I hear someone coming. I get off the john, I got my pants on, I wasn't shitting I was just sitting, but now I gotta pee so I go to the urinal to do that; I'm joined by the Germ, this kid's been held back for 3 years, traded down his leather jacket to a jean jacket, docs for cowboy boots, and a lip full of chew. He cracks his neck, unzips, whips it out, I presume, and informs me, "I'm gonna be a Daddy."
   "That's totally fucked up dude," I gotta say.
   "I know. What a kick," he shakes, "Barely fucked twice."
He steps back, slaps me on the back, "Gotta pull outta the asshole too," his hand slides off my shoulder, steps up to the faucet, and actually washes his hands. I shake. Zip. "Bitches know how to scoop that shit out now, use it against you."
   I turn. He turns off the water. Shakes his hands in my direction, "Jimmy gonna be a Daddy," he says as his sprinkles twinkle onto my black t-shirt, "I'm gonna teach him how to stab stuff."
   "How do you know it's a boy?"
   "That's a stupid question," and he flips his collar, spins on his cowboy heel, and clackity-clack along the tile floor he goes. That was not the punk-rock Jimmy the Germ of yester-year. That was full on embryonic *Invasion of the Body Snatchers*. Fuck that—

—I need a shower.

I wash my face—SPLISH, SPLASH—Wash my emerald green eyed half-Jew face. It's my Mom's Jew blood, so I'm traditionally a full *Heeb* — snipped at birth, hospital, no *Yarmulke*, no pinky tip of wine, just straight out, straight off—But the blood's Jewish. Pops was raised an Evangelical who got his shit together following the Grateful Dead and grew into a full-blown Atheist after that. Bless his little heart. He still gets high as well, Mom a few times more a month. I believe in chemistry, biology, alchemy, and aliens...mushroom aliens, not stupid conspiracy aliens. Archaic stuff ya know. Collective unconsciousness. Your personal DMT grown inside as prevalent as your saliva gland

I believe in intelligent drugs.

*

1st time I dosed on Acid my folks picked me up in Oakland.
We had all gone to the city, me and few friends.
They were from Oakland.
Two black raver girls, me, and Kev, a gutter punk from rich Berkley parents. He always had the good acid. Gels.
Gels were the rage in '91. I was like 13.

Bar Mitzvah Acid along the Bay.
Dad just said I was way too young.
Mom pretended I was dead to her for two days.
I still went to a rave in Richmond off the Iron Triangle
a week later

*

—Ona thinks it's cute that my tip's snipped. The Spanish are short on the Jews, loonnng on the foreskin.

*   *   *

I do not want to go back to class.

*   *   *

I let the weed smoke trickle out of my mouth as I walk, same route Ona and I took an hour ago, but now I'm side-kicking it with Peaty. Peaty's got an oversized *Moby Go* shirt on. His wrists are covered in an impressive collection of jellies as he takes the joint. I watch my step, Oak roots, broken cement and over-cuffed jeans, and his unlaced plaid red *Vans,*. And he's passing the jay back, and I'm stoned and —FIRE DRILL!

The rattling bells echo through the residential blocks. We gotta hustle back. "They do roll call at these things," Peaty's paranoid. Better paranoid than right, so he keeps school on the up and up so his Mom doesn't ban him from his weekend MASSIVES. I'm playing jump rope with his fucking shoe laces as I keep up with his speed walk. We weave through the parking lot, and join up with the body of high schoolers evacuating the ready to burn stucco of plaster-ville educa-shi-on. We need a DJ. "Skoot, Skoot!" I yell. Don't get the wrong I-dea. I don't dress like a Raver. I might jelly up at a Rave, but I'm more low key, black shirt, jeans, sometimes torn jeans, and a torn shirt. I like all Techno. Gabber / Hardcore / House / Jungle, but what really gets me going, psychectually is the tin...drum & bass, gabber, *Aphex Twin*, *Underworld*, tin hits. I sport *Sketchers*; laced. Tin feels like a chill on the underside of your skin when you dance in a trance — Not Trance. I can only handle a little Trance. Always play it at the end of the party, when I'm coming down...gets me low...cause I can't go to afterhours yet. When I can do that, I will learn to appreciate T   r   a   n   c
•ɘ.

         *

              *

                   *

                        Fuck, I'm stoned. My class isn't here— they gather by the football field. We were just at the football field. Someone tugs on my shirt. "What?" I turn, it's Pierre, Pierre the French-Gay exchange student, fire-red medium spiked hair, lots of freckles, delicate physique, loose button up collared pink striped shirt, and he's kissing my cheek, "You look zo handzome today," he says to me.
    "Fire drill?" I ask.

"Fire- dwill?" he asks. He didn't understand me.

"F I R E D-r-i-l-l. A Fire Test?" I say real slow.

"Ah, yes; Fire test," he understands, and waits under his ever expanding grin. Waits for me to continue the conversation.

"Yeah, so, is it real?" I ask.

"What?" he asks.

"The fire. Is there a fire?" I dig Pierre. French brother from a way different mother, but right now I need to keep moving before I get busted.

"Eh, I zink zere waz zomething zum vhere?" he says.

"Yeah, okay, well I'll see you later 'kay?" I say, pat him on the shoulder move along through the bored lot of my generation, and I look back, Pierre's on my tail, I'm stuck, smell smoke, there is a fire, can't see, Pierre's lips are on my ear, "You go to dance with Ona?" Pierre asks.

"Shit there's a dance? Do you think she would want to go?" I ask.

"I wantz to go to ze dance," Pierre says.

"You do huh? Any boys you wanna dance with?" I ask.

"You," and again with the ever-growing grin.

"Cute Pierre; I'm never gonna fuck you."

"Oh, that's too bad; I can fuck you zen?" he toys.

"Ha, Ha; No."

"EVERYBODY BACK TO CLASS!" yells Ms. Klein.

"See ya," I sign off, slap the Pierre on the hiney; leave...

...hoof it all the way back to World History; a backlot, tin roof trailer classroom that's only cool when it rains, and you're high. When the rain drops—PITTER PATTER—on the aluminum roof palates; PITTER PATTER...Actually looks like rain today, glad I'm high; maybe Ona'll wanna go to a movie? Where was that fire? South. By the Shop garages. Makes sense.

Lame.

*   *   *

"You wanna go to a movie after school?" I drop my shoulder against Ona's neighboring locker —CLANK. "You act cool guy," she tells me, slides her book into her American cubby; I crack my neck, "Sometimes," and she scrambles through the metal locker. Moving stuff around—BANG, TANK, DONK, DeDONK—digs into her bag, she can't find something; cigarettes? "Uh, finally," closes her locker. Now she'll talk to me, as she puts a smoke into her luscious, plump maroon, Spanish Island lips, "You?" and offers me one.

"We only got, like two minutes left 'til last period beautiful," I remind her.

"Always you flatter?" she says, "Be more man, you tell me I'm beautiful one time, enough…You want or not?" she wiggles the cigarette in front of my eyes.

"You want to skip class?"

"No. I study hard."

"We can't smoke that here, or outside."

She smiles, she really is beautiful, naturally tanned skin, dark, gently waved hair just past her shoulders. Admiration and strength comes from her defined jaw beneath her baby chub of cheeks. I kiss her dimple, "Go to class."

"America has much too rules," she puts the cigarette back, the hall is empty, "In Spain we smoke all place."

> *How'd I get so lucky? Score the hottest exotic girl here. How'd she get here? For me. Must be. I know a sign when I see one*

"If we skip class, you can smoke."

"Ok, you win, Clever Kyle," she perks up, kisses me, walks away toward the double-doors. The Hall Monitor's got her cellulite arms crossed. My Ona is not going to care about her. "Hall pass, young lady?" I'm a few feet back, wait for it, in or out, "No understand," Ona says.

The Guard of the gates calls upon me, "You know her, tell her she needs a hall pass to leave." Ona looks to me. I step up, "You need a hall pass," I tell her. "Oh, no, no understand," she responds, and I smirk, she winks, "Really lady," I address the law, "She doesn't speak English, like at all."

"Where is she going?"

"Drug store," and I point at my jock.

"How do you know that?" this bitch pries.

"How rude," Ona understands just fine, walks right past her out the double doors, I gotta shrug, "I'm her ride."
"Go."

*   *   *

Ona and I made-out for a while down by the docks, till the breeze kicked in and we got a good whiff of the toxic odor that is the river, that looks like mountain runoff...the mountains are so far away. Super gross. She's done, "Come, we have espresso," she directs, adorable with her English, gets up, buttons her thin fitted, dark-brown, corduroy jacket. "You warm enough?" She shoots me a look. The look when I offend her. This time it's about the weather. Colder here than her Spanish Island warm all year round. "When are we go to Disco?" she insists, not asks, "Pierre want to dancing," takes my hand, leads me off the docks. Franco did a number on these peops. They must lead their own destiny now. Good for them. 'Merica! I mean España!

*   *   *

"I'd rather go to a Rave in the city."
"Spanish Disco is better American Rave."
"Spanish everything is better."
"Yes."
"I was being facetious."
"Facetious, mean treat serious like a joke."
"I'm impressed."
"I get 100s in English in Spain. I am smart, Kyle."
"I know you are."
"Facetious."
"Pussy whipped."
"Pussy what?"
"Nothing," I slap her ass, "Love ya."
She slaps my face.
"No. Italians be rude. You, no Italian," Ona's got me by the balls, "Vamos, coffee."

Let's be clear. Yes Ona is my girlfriend, but no, she has never wanted to go to a San Fran Rave, doesn't know the groove of the *Funky Tekno Tribe*, the *DJ Dan*. She does not like techno enough. She likes *"music."* Look, I do what she wants, it's her that's on borrowed time in America. Ona's not here for citizenship. On loan. Traded for a year. Exchanged. Her voyage. So, we'll end up at a club instead of a rave, end of story, "So we'll hit up a club that night."

"You talk too much; walk me home," she's finished her espresso, I've sipped my coffee, "Leave it," she recommends. "You're getting really pushy, you know that?"

"Know what?"

"Pushy. Demanding."

"I no demand."

"Controlling."

"Oh, yes, control you. Walk me home."

"No."

"Fine," and she walks off. No way. You cannot domesticate a European. Love her. Domesticate her nothing. I'm not looking for a picket fence, I'm in love. Love is forever, houses are mortgaged. She's tough. Gotta be leather skinned.

I take my time to catch up with her. I want to watch her walk. Nor. Cal's cold in February. Never snow cold, but chilly as fuck. I know she's cold. Her shoulders are shrugged forward, collar up, picks up her own pace. But there is something, something different about her all day today. I see it in her eyes, an opposite to her everything else. I think she's ready to sleep with me, at least before high school's out.

Only took her five months to admit she even liked me. Met this girl back in October. It was love at first sight. This other Spanish exchange student, Liana, was in my homeroom. She wanted me, wants me. Her English was the best of them all. She was rich. Came from money, had the good schools. The others were more like family rejects...do something with the kid, sort of exchange student. No matter how good Ona's grades are now, she admitted she was flubbing it back in Spain. Liana was hot enough. I figured I'd make that happen, until she introduced me to Ona. That was the end of that, Ona was my soulmate, I saw that. Her brown eyes. Deep. Solid when they looked into me. Mom never looked at me like that. That's how you know. I've never been in love before. Figured I was free. Live it long. Don't fall in love, fall in fun. I didn't want to meet Ona. I wanted to fuck Liana. That got all screwed up. I'm good though. At least I won't catch something from Spain with my butterfly.

I knew Ona was going to be tough though.

Maybe that was the attraction. There was a *Romeo and Juliet* thing going on, and a *Jeckle and Hyde* reality, we were very different people, but love does have no boundaries, and despite my interior fight, my thought out intellectual destiny of sexual freedom in a time of the archaic revival, can still be realized in love as it exists in a monogamous delight. Like a drug, that you can be high on all day. One drug. Same drug, same high, but the highest of the high. A functional high. Back then she didn't want to go out with me. Said I should go with the other girl. "No, you."

Chapter 2 - Negative Five Months

I'm was with Ona outside the snack bar. "Do. You. Like to Bowl?" I asked her. "What is Booul?" She got here two weeks ago with two years of English in in her pocket and her first conversation is with this American boy who's cornered her with jib-jab after buying a snack and speaking her ear off about words she couldn't connect so fast...so I just asked her out instead of working so hard, asked, real slow.

"You know, Bowl," I say this with an additional visual track mixed into my voice, the pantomime, and she laughs, and she has a nice laugh.

"You very funny," she says, and I'm noticing her eyes, a woman's eyes, she doesn't have that kid glee, she's sharp— a sophisticated face —and I really wanted her to go out with me. "I know bo-l. We b-O-l in Spain."

"We'll go out. Double date, you, me, some friends, eat, hangout, go bowling?" I ask.

"I don't know you saying; you speak too fast."

"I want to take you on a date," I repeat, no pantomime.

"I don't know this word; dayte?"

"You be my girlfriend?" I ask.

"No!" she says, shocked, half-laughing, "You funny. I think I know meaning; I tell no."

"Why?"

"I have boyfriend, at Spain."

"Friends, bowling, no boyfriend," I totally lie.

"Too fast. You talk too fast," Ona pulls out a pen and quarter-legal pad, "You have my telephone?" and she writes it down, and I couldn't tell if she was answering my question or actually suggesting I take her number, but it didn't really matter, I got her number and I feared the hour I had to call her, do the English thing without my physical charm of the pantomime. How am I gonna talk to her on the phone? I suck at Spanish.

"Figure it out Kyle," I tell myself, "Figure it the fuck out."

I used my Sophomore Spanish book. I figured it out. We figured it out; me, myself, and I...well enough. She went out.

*   *   *

Maybe everyone is right? Maybe girls mature faster than boys, and maybe European girls are ten steps ahead of American girls. Ona flipped the game on me, introduced me to Liana, heavy make-up, done up hair, who eloquently says in her seductive Spanish accent, "Very nice to meet you, Kyle." She can speak English. I was impressed. Ona's more attractive. Naturally attractive. Attraction.

BACK THEN— Ona bats her eyes at me, knows Liana's showing off. "Ona thinks you are very cute, and she's right," and kisses me on the cheek and I realize this girl's sending off the most sensual vibe I have ever come across. Sex melting off her body; not my type though, but my loins can't deny her superpower. The turn off is her desperation...desperate for a connection. She can be our translator. I pull my card, "Meet, Pierre," the French ginger fry exchange student, who speaks with everything sprinkled in the Gay-Pari' Z accent, and a most effeminate voice. I love him. He's my new favorite person. He's just honest; judges not. Lanky, ginger kid who's in an ever flow of arm and hand gestures, poses, facial poses; all that. Even when he's standing still he can't stand straight. He'll distract Liana. "Kyle, zi zthink ze and zi need boy dates," Pierre says with puppy dog eyes. "I don't have another gay friend."
"Ze do not zeed to be gay."

— Oh, brother.

Okay, fine, I call Scotty from across town, East side, Casa Senior, drinks a lot, in a band, plays guitar, a little funk, a bit of a skater, a little punk, and makes techno on his 4 track every time his band doesn't show up for practice. Scotty likes the women. Scotty will like Liana, and Pierre. No one I know thinks twice about nobody's character, unless it's a racist, homophobic, sexist, or an anti-drug characteristic. I don't know those people. They're invisible to me.

Well Pierre should be happy bowling with two strapping teenager men like ourselves. I'm not finding Pierre a real date, not here. Not North of Marin County. Yet in my defense, I did ask one of the bi-boys, but they weren't into it, "Gay is gay man, we're not gay…That guy'll get the wrong idea." And I'm thinking, really, what are you waiting for, you guys are the only guys who play with guys in this whole town; why not have a croissant? You don't even fuck each other. "We're into East Bay boys." They're always into East Bay boys. Rave sex cult.

I wrap my arms around Ona at the head of the bowling lane. Cover her hands that hold the black ball. She wiggles me off, "I do it myself," and I step off. She's tough. I like tough. A challenge. I like a challenge. Just remember she's European, 10 steps ahead of us all...that alone will keep me one step ahead of her...and I'm watching her step, step, step, and drop the ball. The ball bounces and does the slow roll into the gutter. I could have prevented that. She turns back toward me, man she has beautiful eyes, "Your turn," is all she says and walks past me, but I see it, she looked at me, out of the corner of her eye, oh she's good, she's in a lot of control here; she likes me. I turn to watch her sit back down with our friends. Pierre is watching Scotty already making out with Liana. These girl's Spanish boyfriends are a few lakes away.

—That guy's got serious game.
I need 9 to pull that off that quick.

My European Princess plops down by Pierre and they start chatting about something. I can only imagine what they could be saying to each other in their broken English. I scoop up my red and purple swirled ball from the return rack, step up to the arrows, look back at Ona. She smiles at me. "You get gutter, too," criticizes me, even before I step. "Afraid not bonita," and I send the solid ball into the air— too hard —it bounces, it rolls, it goes straight into the gutter, and Ona bursts out in laughter. Now she'll hook up with me. Pierre gets up, it's his turn. Fireboy cat walks right up to me and grabs my dick. I jump, "Zi teazch Kyle zow to holdz za bool."

"No," I zay.

"We'll zee," and he kisses my cheek, picks up his pink ball, and doesn't even try, just plops it down, and again we wait for a sloooow ball roll down the lane, only for Pierre to get a slow strike.

"Inz Paris, we uze alcohol at za boolz house."

Scotty turns to Pierre, "What the fuck are you talking about dude?" and Liana pinches Scotty's nipple. "I bored," Liana's bored sucking face? "We go Scotty's house." Ona immediately gets up, "Vamos." —Nice— "Means, let's go, bro," Scotty says right at me as he kicks off his bowling shoes.

*   *

*

We all pack into my *B-Blue*, a blue 1989 VW Golf, my pride and joy, the car that will take me across this fine nation that has begun to party again. Rave. Rave, rave, rave-on. I cruise us all cross town, *Moby's Drop-a-Drop-a-Beat* maintains Scotty's tongue in Liana's mouth in the backseat while Pierre keeps blowing in Scotty's ear. S-man, swatts P away, but Pierre won't give up. Ona's shotgun. "I not like disco music," she tells me, "Not in disco."

"You don't like dancing, huh?"

"No," she's snaps, mad I didn't understand, "I go disco all time in Mallorca."

"Oh?" I'm confused, "What's Mai-jorca?"

"Ugh," she broods. I'm fucking up.

"That's where she's from," Liana tells me from the back. I lower the music. "What?" Scotty tries to kiss her again, she pushes him off, "I said, Ona is from Mallorca. It's an island in Spain."

"aklsdkajsd;l jwiejf;iasdf," Ona starts barking at Liana in Spanish.

"Speak English," Liana scolds Ona back, "Not nice to speak in way they don't understand."

"Afaos rt;vqoierjgfad," Ona mumbles in Spanish to herself, broods, looks out the window, and turns the music she dislikes, louder.

> —*She's got an attitude. Cute though. Cute with attitude.*
> *Very sexy. Matured sexy. Not candy. Not Pop.*

"Do you like *Portishead*?" I ask her. She lights up. She likes *Portishead*. "Very like! You (points to radio) Poreeshed?" I switch the CD to *Dummy* as I drive. She's looking at me, on & off, the rest of the way through the track-home eastside of town; *Last night a DJ saved my life— Indeep.*

Deep in the cul-de-sacs of cloned homes, I pull us into Scotty's driveway. His cookie cutter of a house is decorated in a stone decor front yard, the walnuts of the dessert, a couple of spruce trees, and an attached garage. His bedroom's above the car port, but we enter through the front door. Scotty's gonna give Liana the tour towards his bedroom.

*   *

I don't know where Pierre and the sex twins disappeared too, because I'm busy making out with Ona in the living room, by the un-burning fireplace, standing—

> *—Why are we standing, we should go on the couch?*
> *If I move her she's sure to stop,*
> *I know this,*
> *I've seen how's she's been all night,*
> *she's not a 100% into this,*
> *but I'm kissing her now...*

...and she pulls away.

"You okay?" I ask.

"Where's Liana?" she asks, actually concerned.

"I don't know," I say as Ona looks around a bit, her arms have not let go of me, maybe she is into this? Why am I so into this? Feels so weird. Maybe the gamble of a woman from Spain? A woman from across the world? Could she take you away from here? Could be cool.

"Maybe find her?" she interrupts my stoner thoughts.

"I'm sure they're fine," and I kiss her again, she kisses back, but she's concerned, stops, "Come, find her," Ona insists. Okay, she's a goner like me. I'll move to Spain with her one day. Dope. Killer parties. Massive MASSIVES. Yerdopa

*   *

*

These numbskulls are nowhere to be found downstairs, so we're quietly making our way up the carpeted steps to the second floor. We can hear something. Maybe a shower?

As we reach the last step, I stop, put my arm out to hold Ona back, "Wait here," I whisper.

"No, I go," she whispers back, stern; with authority.

"Then you go first."

"Too fast," she says not understanding my English again.

"You first."

"Noooo," she says, and I laugh and she covers my mouth, but she laughs, and we both laugh, and Pierre startles us as he pops out from around the corner, "Zee thiz," he whispers; shushes us, "Zhhh."

Stealth like, we make our way down the hall to Scotty's Mom's room, the Master-Bedroom. The door is still open. Pierre leads us in. The sound of the shower has become obvious and Pierre presses his ear against the bathroom door, "Lizzen."

Ona shakes her head, "No, do not this." And as much as I want to snoopy-snoop, I want Ona more, so I pull on Pierre to move him back. There is a moment of silence between us, the soundtrack filled by the sound of a shower, and then a loud, "Uh!" from Liana, and all-of-a-sudden Ona's pressing her ear against the bathroom door and gasps at what she hears. "What? What's going on?" I ask her, she waves me over, I look at Pierre. He's all smiles and joins us. Now we're all snoopin' with our ears pressed up against the bathroom door.

*

— ShhhooooowwwwwwwerrrR —

"Here move here," Scotty.

"No wait, I go this," Liana.

"Careful. Hold the nozzle."

*

"What a nuzzel?" Ona asks me.

"Later," I whisper.

"Why hold a later? What a later?" Ona asks.

"I'll tell you later, beautiful."

*

"Put in now," Liana.

"I can't, you're not wet enough," Scotty explains.

"What? I wet, we in shower? You want to stop?" Liana asks, totally confused.

"No, let me try again, here let me try this," Scotty says.

"MUY BIEN!" yells Liana, "OH! OH! BIEN, BIEN!"

"Okay you're wet now, let me try again," Scotty says.

"No! Not there!" Liana yells.

"Oh sorry; shit this is way too hard in the shower," he's a quitter, but not a quitter, quitter.

"Huh, you stop, you not want to do now?" Liana asks.

And the shower turns off and we are freaked, we gotta get outta here, and we make a ton of noise as we trip over each other, fall to the floor, get up run out the door, slam it behind us, not cool, and down the hall, down the stairs, into the living room, and Ona and I take the couch and she's laughing so hard into my chest, and Pierre is pacing, "Oh ze know, ze know!"

*

Liana wasn't so much embarrassed about us all listening as much as she was mad at Scotty for his ultimate fail in the shower. "It was his idea; I no like him," she said to Ona, and this is where everything got fucked up for the rest of the semester— What my Ona heard was this translation in her head, His = Me, "Taking a shower and having sex with Scotty was Kyle's idea; I don't like Kyle." Scotty did bang her in bed. She insisted he finish the job. He obliged. Good man, *Charlie Brown*.

I remained friends with Pierre. Ona just stopped talking to me. No explanation beyond, "I do not *like* you." I'd see her in the halls, and she tried to frown when I pass her, but she's got a twinkle in those majestic brown eyes, and I know that's a grin on her face, but I can't get through to her, I've tried, oh have I tried, because a month later I heard the whole story from Liana, when Liana had gotten bored and asked if I wanted to hang out...

*

..."I'm so bored here in this city, I want to go home," Liana tells me during lunch; a few blocks off campus. "Donde casa?" I try. "Muy buen," she is such a liar, "*San Sebastian*. Beach city. Beautiful. Muy bonita," she takes my hands, "You should come. You love it. Big raves on ocean."

I'm so ready to graduate. Get out. Get my Rave On. Get a stupid job, a promoter maybe, start with fliers in San Fran until I can throw down a party of my own. I'm shallow. I just want to dance. Maybe write a book or two about dance culture, but mostly dance. San Sebastian would be hot.

*

To be honest I've just recently realized I've never really made any good friends here...

and I've been here all my life...

I know people, I know everyone; I'm not unpopular. I hang out, but do I have a friend? I don't think so. Scotty's my closest friend. He's trapped in crosstown high school, so he's set up with a whole other set of friends, peops. Pierre's looking at me. He's at lunch with Liana and me. Everyone is...Well us four. I'm tagging along with these foreigners. Ona doesn't like Liana's flirtation. She's here because she's really got no friends. I probably shouldn't be here, but I like these guys, and they like me. I'm becoming their American guide. What's he looking at? I point to myself, he winks. Pierre. Cute. I look at Ona, she turns away from me, talks nothingness with Pierre.

"Why don't you call Scotty?" I ask Liana, and that's it Ona's over it, over me coming around, and she gets up, scoops up her lunch bag, "I'm leave." And she leaves. Pierre must volunteer his opinion, "I do not zink zhe like youz,

Kyle," and he scoots closer putting his arms around me, "I zike you, itz okay."

"Thanks darling," I accept his love. Pierre kisses my cheek, "I like when you zay darling; what iz darling?" Liana reaches over to my hand and takes it, "You take me to a movie," she says to me.

"Whoa."

"Come Kyle, Ona no care," she says to me, bats her over mascaraed eyes.

"Okay, but don't make it romantic," I insist.

"No, not romantic; I am just bored, home all the time," she says.

"All Americanz zo boring," Pierre is disappointed in me.

"Pierre comes too."

— I'm so glad his English isn't good enough to make a pun out of that.
Zes, Ze cum deux, trois, quatre, cinq, sex sex sex...I can hear it now.
Cause I thunk it outloud inside. Thinkin's for chumps.
Heard that once. Super stupid stuff.

"Okay, Saturday, but during the day," I say.

"Okay," and we all hear the bell ringing a few blocks away at school; well timed world. We all get up, but Pierre takes me aside, "Liana ez not like Ona; ze knowz?"

"Yeah man I know. You'll protect me," I say.

"Hold your hand?" he asks.

"Nope," and goose him in the butthole, he doesn't flinch.

"Zokay, we zex now," he responds; I just shake my American mind. This guy.

*

Liana goes directly to class. Liana goes directly to Ona, "I go on date with Kyle, is okay?" (*probably in Spanish*) Ona replied, "I do not care; do what you want, have fun."

*

We, Pierre and I, took Liana to see *Alex Winter's Freaked*; she got none-of-it, she got as close to me as she could throughout the whole thing. We were all stoned. Pierre was a perfect gentleman. I think Pierre wanted me to get laid and create some good old fashioned *90210* drama to our small group. I could feel her eyes on me, barely watches the movie, stares at me, waits for me to lunge myself— *Ona would never go for that, this is so uncomfortable* —but I was there, I was munching the popcorn— *I should have never gotten us stoned before this, what the fuck was I thinking, I'm so fucking horny. If she touches my leg I'm fucked. I'm gonna go for it, she'll keep her mouth shut, right? She ain't gonna ruin my chances with Ona*, right? *You just gotta be clever about it. Drop Pierre off first.* Obviously. But our brains don't trigger in the obvious. Our minds calculate, hypothesize, fabricate, deduct, and our Ego decides. If your subconscious delivers an obvious answer to your conscious, then all the work has been done for you; instinct think. *That's why I eat trips.* Feeds you cleverness, for your instinctual shrewdness. A gentle man, connected in discussion with his Archaic nature;

evolved.

*

Movie's done and I drove Pierre home. He got cute, told us to, "Fuck a good one," and we drove off. Now we're just driving around the country side, aimlessly, through the fog. She's never been out in the deep country, says she's recanted her super awesome rave beach town, home life, "San Sabastian." She's wealthy. Parents had let her do whatever she wanted. She did too much so they told her she needed discipline. Gave her two options, Spanish Boarding School, or American Exchange Program. Strick huh? "Can we stop somewhere?" she asks as we roll up a hill, nearing *Gravity* road. I brought her here unconsciously; totally on purpose. I knew she'd get all gushy on the country roads in the evening. I'm a dick. I shouldn't have done this. Ona's pissing me off though. I know she likes me, but the cold shoulder. Playing so hard to get back is really testing my patience. If I hook up with Liana it'll make her jealous...but can I stop Liana from sleeping with me if I start something? I shouldn't have brought her here. We should have gone dancing. I can't sleep with this girl, that's too far. The drama of a kiss, and maybe a little sex...is enough...I got no 9 so I bet I can contain myself.

Trained in the arts of repression on the dancefloor.

*

Liana looks around. There is no view, just rolling grass on one side and more on the other, "Why not stop at view of town?"

"You'll see. Roll down your window," I instruct. She is confused, does as I say, "It's so cold, Kyle. Why do we do this?" I put the car in neutral, and very slowly the car begins to roll; uphill.

"Watch the trees," I say as I turn her head toward the open passenger window.

"We are going up?" she asks, "But we roll backwards?"

"Exactly," I say, she giggles, turns back watches, turns back to me, slides her hand into my thigh, "You so cute, Kyle," and plants one right on me, but I can't, "I really like Ona." She's offended, slaps me, sits back, "Take me home. Pierre right, all American boys boring."

"What about Scotty?"

"Scotty over. I don't want boyfriend, Kyle. You make mistake. Take me home," and she pouts. You realize she's in-love with you. That's why you pulled back. You sensed it. Smelt it. There is value in yourself, for your cleverness in societal survival. Awesome, but she's super pissed off.

*

Chapter - Back to Chapter 1 Last Paragraph...

It's *The Jesus & Mary Chain's Automatic* all the way to the city; San Francisco. Ona brought the CD. Pierre's shotgun while <u>my</u> Ona rides in the back with Liana and Trish. *(to catch you up, this is months later, second semester, April; few months from graduation. Ona and I have been together for a minute now. Lots of sex, safe sex, condoms, she isn't on the pill)* Trish's a Senior who got into the Rave scene via her very own Mom. Her Mom's not what you call the most stringent of parents. Trish's Mom's the enabler. Trish's Mom's pretty cool. Trish's Mom's got a history in the game. To be more specific, Trish's Mom's friends are the game, so if you stick around Trish, you usually have a path to the pot of pills at the end of the rainbow.

"You're Mom still dealing ɘ," I ask her as we cross the red Golden Gate Bridge.

"MDA, I got three if anyone wants some?" Trish offers.

"I take that as a yes?"

"Yes."

"I've used the ɘcstasy in Spain," Liana tells us.

"I too. I love zit," Pierre says into the rearview mirror. Liana leans over my seat, she's behind me, Ona turns to watch the passing buildings; quiet as usual. She's not so quiet one on one, but in a group setting she goes silent, just a few whispers to Liana that no one can hear or even understand since she only speaks Spanish with her. I find it rude, but I don't bring it up anymore. Every time I bring it up she gets testy and tells me, "I speak when I want. I no not need speak when you want."

*   *   *

We're checking our coats in at the *Palladium*, "This ain't a Rave guys," Trish is correct, as she hands over her pho'fur collared windbreaker, as she adjusts her rainbow, glow stick bracelets.

"This a Disco," says Ona, her choice, she wanted a Disco, not a Rave.

"Yeah that's right, you guys go to Disco's over there," Trish plays the good sport, "I get it, well next time we gotta go to an Oakland party or something; our Raves are better than clubs," and Trish wanders off into the darkness of a hall leading not to *Frankie Knuckles or Derrick May*, but extended dance Pop mixes— *C & C Factory, Janet Jackson, Naughty By Nature, Michael Jackson*, it's not *Underground Sound of Lisbon*, it is *The Goodmen's Give It Up* mixed into everything, and these clubbers are blowing whistles like its off, off the hook. It is not. It is fun enough with my pals and at the right time the micro-cosmos in my belly will disperse into my blood stream and my veins will be lined with the faint amount of...

                      ... ɘcstasy I have ingested.

I popped the smallest of pieces, a quarter of a pill, everyone else split the rest equally. I'm the designated driver. I can't trip for hours. I'm up, but I'm jonesing for more. Trish usually has stronger stuff.

First time I rolled at a Rave, danced all night, got home in the morning, got grounded for two months. I was a Freshman. I had no way of getting home without my ride...The acid was one thing, but my parents are not fans of the ǝcstacy...

I was hooked from the get go. Second time was in town, at Trish's house when I was a Sophomore. We ended up all wandering through town for hours. It was fun. Last year, like ǝ v ǝ ry other wǝǝkǝnd. Last summer I started slǝǝping with girls on it. Generally, at the ravǝs. Safely of course. I wear wǝtsuits. Not high enough to try to sleep with Ona tonight. I would, but I'm not high enough to consider it rolling sǝx. She might be.

Ona seems to be having a good time tonight. She's spent most of her trip dancing with Pierre. They even do a little grinding, then she backs off, then a little more. Ona lets herself get sexy with Pierre, and I like watching her like that, she doesn't let herself go that much. I guess gay Pierre's a safe bet, and Liana comes up to me and she's rolling hard as she slides her hands around my chest from behind, she whispers in my ear, "You and me make love with Ona?" as she runs her hand down my belly towards my package, and I turn around and whisper, "Go to the bathroom, touch yourself," I look around, "We'll be there soon," and I kiss her on the cheek. "Really?" she asks. I roll my eyes, "Yeah, really."

— *No, not really.*

I'm sure Ona is rolling hard like Liana so I gotta go give Pierre a break and dance with my girl. I'd be down for a threesome with Ona, but not Lianna. Girl's gotta be a stranger, not someone who's trying to get in on the game. Pierre thinks this is going to be a three-way dance, "Go find a boy, boy," I tell him, pat him on the dick for inspiration, slap his ass and we send him off to the bar. He'll get served. He looks the oldest out of us all. They didn't card him at the door. Place is 18 and over. 21 and they bracelet you so the bartender will serve you. Pierre's got no bracelet, Pierre will still get served. The girls complained the first hour about that fact. "We drink in Spain."

"Well this isn't Spain."

"America is very stupid," Ona said. I figured they'd forget about that by the time the ǝ kicked in and I was right...although Liana, none-the-less, has gotten a few guys to buy her a few drinks. Ona asked me to get her one a couple of times, but by now she's given up on all of that. The DJ breaks out some Hip Hop *Ice Cube* and *Das EFX Check Yo Self*, and Ona's not into Rap, and pulls me off the dance floor to a booth deeper into the club, and she gets really close to me, and her eyes. Her are eyes are strong, solid, and the ǝ is way gone from my system, but I can tell she thinks I'm as high as her, so I'm gonna fake it.

You didn't want to fall in love with Ona. You didn't want to fall in love. Just liked her. Thought she was beautiful. Never seen such a girl like her before. You wanted to kiss her. Make love to her, but fall in love? That doesn't happen to cats like you. You have too much life to live.

Now, tonight, in this booth, with her licking her lips and rubbing my wood over my jeans, I can't help but fall in love, again. The ǝ is doing wonders for her self-esteem. I could go into Psychology, do testing on the rejuvenating effects of ǝcstacy. Maybe when I'm 65? All's fair in love and war, and I've lost the battle. I give her the kiss she wants and we make out and she is really into it, more than ever before; purring. I can feel her larynx vibrating as she squeezes my dick, suckling my tongue, my tongue she sucks, like my own dick, but my tongue. She's going to make me cum here in the club, and we can't have that, so I stop her, I pull back and she's insulted, but I calm her down.

"Baby, I love you," I say, for the first time in my young life, to her, to anyone and mean, in love.

"No. You not say that. You on drugs," she responds.

"Not really. I didn't take enough," I defend my emotion.

"You took plenty. You not feel that way, we just friends."

"Is that how you really feel?" I ask, but the music is loud and she pulls the, "I no understand your English, too loud," and shuts down the whole moment with, "Where Liana? She probably in trouble. We find her," and I think to myself, *oh shit I sent Liana to the bathroom with a really bad idea, I hope she didn't do that...*

*   *   *

. . .*Bobby Brown*, really? We make our way through the dance floor towards the bar. Trish's still raving out to herself. Kinda forgot about Trish. She seems fine, having a good time. Waves at us. I wave back. She waves us over, but Ona keeps wandering. We make our way around the bend of brass rails that separates the floor from the bar, and the bar's packed and Pierre's somewhere, "Excuse me," and we're trying to make our way through the mass of patrons trying to get their drink on.

"What time?" Ona yells at me, but I can't really hear her, "What?" I yell back, she stops, her mouth now against my ear, "Que hora?"

"That means what time is it, right?" I yell, directly into her eardrum.

"Yes! What time it is?" she yells back into my ear. I check my *Swatch*, "Twelve Thirty!"

"We must go. It too late," she reminds me. That's fine, but we gotta find Pierre. "Go get Liana," I tell her, "I find Pierre."

—*Shit, now you're talking broken English.*

"Where she?"

"Bathroom."

"Where bathroom?"

"That way," I tell her and shoo her off, "Meet at coat check!" and she disappears, and I wonder if she'll find her way; she's still rolling hard. Some guy better not try to get up on my girl. *I better find Pierre and get us out of here.*

"Where the fuck is he?" I say aloud, triggering a drunk metro-sexual who informs me that, "This isn't a gay club, it's mixed; you're going to have to be more specific," and leans into me, spills his drink on my *Sketchers*, his breath wreaks of booze, and I engage, yell in his ear, "Red head, French. Lots of freckles."

"That's specific sunshine, sorry, can't help you on that," as he points out his blonde hair that changes colors as the lights spin. "That's not what I meant," and I turn away, catch the Flaming Frenchman out of the corner of my eye, and I'm not even excusing myself, just pushing my way to the end of the bar where Pierre is being pampered by two fag-hags, drunk as shit.

"KYLLLE!" Pierre falls into me, drunk, tells me he's got, "A vodka zour, juzt like Paris."

"Good for you, we gotta go."

"Too fazt, we go?" he asks with a half sip of his vodka sour.

"Curfew, remember?"

"Ah, we no school tomorrow," and he squeezes one of the girl's nipple and she giggles, "We drink zen go. You want alcohol?"

"Sure, let me get Ona," pat him on the shoulder, leave. One of Pierre's ladies stops me, grabs my collar, sloppy speak, "Where you going?"

"My girlfriend," I say, but she won't have it.

"You can't get away that easy," she says, and I gently remove her fingers from my collar and say with great kindness and compassion, "Yes I can."

"I'm not buying your friend a drink," she explains to Pierre. He shakes his empty one. She can't resist his beautiful French eyes and orders him another. "Another round!"

Ona pulls

on Liana, "Vamos." There's some guy with them. Some stranger. "Ready?" I ask as I approach the girls, try to separate them from this cock-lurker. Ona addresses me, "Tell her we have to go!"

"Nah man," the lurker says, "Too early."

"I find friend, Mike," Liana tells me as she touches the guy's chest. Mike puts his arm around Ona, whoa, and I take her hand and pull her closer to me out of his elbow curl. "Do you know him?" I ask her, she shakes her head. Liana and Mike are in a stare. Even though she's a foot shorter, she just starts kissing him.

"Hey Mike, how do you know Liana?" I ask, not wanting to start any shit. Liana stops kissing him, "He goes to our school," she tells me, but he fashions a bar bracelet. I take Liana's hand and gently pull her toward me. He's lurking. Touching her arm. Liana's ϶ head has her instantly falling into my eyes as I've changed her attention. She leans in to kiss me. "Hot," Mike says. Ona pushes her off. I step up to Mike, "You don't go to our school, do you?" I ask Mike.

"What school do you go to?" he asks.

"Petaluma High."

"No way bro, I'm college, San Francisco State— Hey you got any more acid?" he asks.

"No, nice to meet you Mike, later,", I turn, gently push the girls forward, "Just walk." I look back at the guy. He's going into the Men's bathroom, good. Mike's bad news.

"You guys have to be more careful," I tell the girls, "He totally lied to you."

"I don't understand, too loud," Liana yells, "We go now?"

"Yes, let me get Pierre," and I kiss Ona to make sure she's okay, present in all this, "You are a clever," she tells me. "What?"

"You are clever. I like you. I like you, Clever," she kisses me, coining my nickname.

"I'm really not that clever."

"You, Clever. You be my boyfriend for-϶v϶-r," she asks.

"Sure things babygirl."

"I no baby girl. I grown woman."

"Indeed."

On the phone, the next day, Ona explains her and Liana's absence at lunch, "She real sad, she cry."

"Because of Mike?"

"She lonely. I say not alone in America, I say sorry."

"What are you sorry for?"

"You."

"Me?"

"You my boyfriend, Liana alone."

"Oh," I guess. Thought Liana wasn't the relationship type.

"Then she kiss me, with tongue," Ona lays it out.

"Last night?"

"In bathroom."

"Oh..."

"I very mad at Liana."

"So, what did you do?"

"I was mad. I make her stop."

"Uh huh?"

"She stop, but she be romantic still, hold my hand and ask me if we three be together," Ona says, "I very mad."

What do I say? Admit it? Admit I played a joke on Liana
Admit we almost hooked up once
pause. quiet.

"I say no to her," Ona breaks the silence, "I no talk to her;
ever."

......................•————————————————————————

...and I too won't talk to Liana for the rest of the semester, but Pierre will remain her friend, and he will be there for her, and I will ask him about her. "Good, zhe haz zum friendz," he'll tell me, and that's true, I don't know any of them, but I see her with them every now and then, and in a few weeks I'll become comfortable waving to her as we pass in the hall, and in the final weeks before graduation we will all make amends realizing Liana <u>was</u> actually terribly lonely back then and suffered from severe culture shock that Pierre had kept a secret from us upon her request. She had to start on some anti-depressants. That rebalance enabled her to make some nice friends, the nice way, and she did end up sleeping with Scotty again, and they actually went out for a while, a few weeks, and they slept with each other a lot and then she broke up with him.

———————————————————•.....................

There was a much longer pause to the phone call. I didn't know what to say, so I just picked some dirt from my fingernail. I was on the back deck. I had gotten high while my parents went grocery shopping.

"You come to Spain for summer," Ona suggests.

"Spain? Really?

"Si, muy bien?" she asks.

"Mucho bien!"

"No," she says.

"What? No, what?"

"You not say mucho bien, bad Spanish," she corrects me, "If you go Spain, then you speak nothing, I speak, okay?"

"Bien," I say.

"No, Clever," she snaps, "No Spanish."

*

Ona and I had consummated our high school relationship in February. We were watching *Risky Business* on video. She'd never seen it, so I showed her, and she got bored so we started to make-out, and she got hot, took off her shirt, unbuckled my pants, and asked, "You have?"

I had to get up and go upstairs to my fucking room to find a condom. Looked through like three drawers 'cause I had to hide them again since Mom found some weed a month ago and been going through my shit one drawer at a time these days, so she doesn't have to buy her own. Back downstairs, and Ona's on the family couch under a blanket and I see all her clothes are on the floor. I drop my drawers and she looks away, "I no want to see it," she says. Next time, maybe, and I cover myself as I unwrap and apply the latex glove, climb under the blankets. It went quick. First time seems to always go quick for me. I don't really know, though, but that second round with *Rebecca De Mornay* on the train while I made love to Ona, again. That round was blissful for the lot of us. We made sure to get back to it the next day and then the next few days. I was better then. We were better. She had admitted she had a serious boyfriend before, last year, older guy, wouldn't tell me if he was better. I think she thinks he's better. "I love you more," she told me. That means he fucked her better, but I won the long haul...that I never wanted, too young, but you can't stop Love, so Love is what we're in forever more. My life plans must change. I must do all my things with Ona. I'll get good at that. At least her idea of us going to Spain is better than us going to Los Angeles, her other option if she were to go to college in the states →

Chapter 3 - Getting My Shit Together

Dah, Dah, Dadadada, dah dah, dada dada, struttin' through San Francisco, store to store, gatherin' collections for travel here and there, and I left Dad at the Presidio for the day. He gave me my wad of cash we had saved from my secret Bar Mitzvah. My parents call it the, "College Fund." Secret Bar Mitzvah because my parents aren't about the Jew part, just the ism. Never go to temple, use an electric menorah, and threw me a Bar Mitzvah party without study to collect for my College Fund. Yeah, the college fund I don't plan on using for college. So here we are now. Never applied to any schools. My SATs were good; high marks, upper 20%. My grades; they sucked. Remedial reading and 1300 or something on your SATs equals Community College, and that is definitely not going to happen for me. I need to dance, not prolong my stay in this small town. If anything, I'd become an underground chemist.

Something I can something out of.

*

I hit up two travel stores on Market— *Voodoo Child - Moby* on my CD walkman:

TRAVEL STORE NUMERO UNO-
   1) Fanny Pack, black and grey, pickpocket prevention
   2) Compass, why not? On a pocket chain, Deer imprint
   3) Open like six Backpacks, check the space, shoulder
      test, these all suck - No Purchase
   4) Books on Europe, too many. *Shoestring,* that's the one
   5) "You do the Euro-Passes here?" I ask
      "No, Youth Hostel. West Side," the clerk responds.
   6) Moving right along

Called Voodoo Child samples out Jimi Hendrix's deep distant tone; *Paaaarty* sings the chorus.

TRAVEL STORE NUMERO DOSE-
   1) Four more Backpacks, different brands.
      I decide on the dark green body, black straps
   2) Phone cards, "These work from over there?" I ask.
      "Over where?" the clerk asks.
      "Spain?"
      "Yes, all of Europe," he says. I buy ten for $25 each
   3) Sunglasses. Big Ovals, Flower Print, Square...
      I Settle on the Aviators...they hide me better,
      reflect your everything...reflects your beautiful world.

I'm on the street right in front of the store. I got the backpack draped over one shoulder, and I'm wondering where Ona and I should go first, but that's for us to plan later, right now I gotta get to the other side of the city and it's begun to sprinkle. Okay, I gotta hoof it up to the *O'Farrell* parking lot to get the car before it rains any harder.

*   *   *

Finally, and I'm popping the trunk, drop the backpack, slam it shut, pull out of the spot, don't hit a column, and spiral down to the bottom of the lot to my way West Side to the Youth Hostel to get us our Eurail Passes so we may ride the rail; lovers across the Old World, dosing, and toking, and rolling as we will ride, and the rail will be our dream— $300 bucks each? You fool. Nah.

*

Dad gets in the driver's side. I've skooted over to avoid the rain. He's soaked, had no umbrella, and waited in the rain for the last few minutes because this city lacks overhangs.

"Why'd you do that?" I ask.

"I want to get sick," he says.

"Oh yeah, why's that Pops?"

"So, I die of Pneumonia."

"I can live with that."

"Bet you can," he punches me in the arm and we make the 45-minute drive back to home. My sperm donor tries to talk to me like a man about women, about Mom, about Ona, about the future. "Come on Dad."

I'm just tired. Ready to get on a plane. He always knew I'd be a fuck up and not go to college. He always knew I was hyper-active, couldn't sit still. Pops told Mom that if they didn't give me the money to go fuck Ona in every European country, that I'd just hop on some train here in the great USA and die of a drug overdose at one of those stupid Electronic Hippie Rave Parties. "Deadheads listening to records." Dad's not head over heels about the Bay Area. Grown out of the Hippie thing. I think he'd be happier in Santa Barbra, but we can't afford that. He can't decide if the Republicans are evil or just crooks or if the Democrats are just totally wrong, but he hates the Libertarians, and would rather the Unions take care of everything. I know his politics are totally mix matched and nonsensical. Just dose everyone, that's what I say. Turn everybody on. "I love this girl Dad, you understand that, right?

"Yeah, I know you love her. But you'll probably fuck up, or— Shit, just know, you'll have other girlfriends; you're eighteen."

"I didn't plan on falling in love."

"You don't plan on anything. That's precisely your problem."

"And you're so perfect?"

"Yes."

My Dad doesn't like to argue. Never bothers to raise his voice. It's as passive aggressive as one could get. Gets under my skin, but it's been that way forever and throughout my teens, no matter how hard I've tried to make him crack, he's as solid as a rock with no shifting feelings, and a wicked tongue capable of owning the last word. I don't fight it. Listen to a brother out. Say what you gotta say, my brain will figure it out for myself. "You're highly susceptible to influence, Kyle.:"

"That's not true."

"Prove it," Dad requests the impossible.

"I'm not."

"Who asked who to Europe?"

"Why would I say no?"

"That's not what I asked."

Acccchhhem, Dad clears his throat, rolls down the window, rain pushes in on him, he spits, rolls it back up and continues, "That's the difference son, you'll never love a beautiful woman the way I love your Mother," and we're home and it's stopped raining, but the world is wet, and Dad's words make me feel all funky inside.

—Whatever, that's his life, Ona's ours.
Ruined at eighteen? Please. Next stop, graduation.

*

I've definitely gotten better at this phone stuff with Ona, months of practice, and yet I want her to re-say what she just said. I do feel a little emasculated by my Dad. A little. Like on the mind feeling, not traumatized, or anything that will matter...but makes a person sensitive none-the-less.

"I not flying with <u>you</u>. You come late," she says again.

"I don't understand," I start, but she interrupts.

"No, my English good now! You understand," she insists.

"I don't mean— Okay, why do I have to come after you?" I ask more directly.

"I have test," she says as vague as possible.

"What test?" I ask.

"College test," she says.

"You applied to college? You didn't tell me anything about this." I'm not mad just utterly confused, there is a serious lack of communication going on here and it's not the language barrier.

"No, Kyle. You not listen. Spain give test after graduate, to go college," she tries to explain, and she is really making that college try, but I'm stuck on the fact that we are not flying to Europe together.

"Like the S.A.T?" I tell her, "I get it. So, what? So, I wait outside while you take the test? I don't get it?"

"Get it?" she doesn't understand, a term she has always had trouble with.

"Why can't I be with you?" I ask.

"I need to study. I no time to study here for test. I go to *Madrid* first, then *Mallorca*," she says.

"The test is in Madrid?"

"Si, Aye Kyle cabron; you come to Mallorca two weeks late from me, on?" she pauses, "You come 22 July."

I'm looking at my parent's calendar in the kitchen. Yeah, I'm having this argument on the kitchen phone, and Dad's come in like twice looking for nothing in the fridge and keeps poking me saying, "Can't love her like I love your Mother," and I swear if he does it one more time I'm kneeing him the balls when he leans into my ear...Okay I found the 22nd of July, fuck, July 22nd, she even has me saying the date all European backwards now. I circle it, write, FLY TO ONA's BOOTY, and scratch out Booty. I'm staring at the scratches. What if she comes over and sees that, gets mad 'cause she can be such a...*Ugh...get over it...what's two weeks...*"Okay fine, I'll come July 22nd, but you better be ready for me, dove."

"Don't be Clever, you make me mad tonight," she says.

"What?"

"You know. You no trust me."

"Of course, I trust you; I don't get it?" I say, realizing I said, "*get it*," again.

"Huh?" she's confused.

"I trust you, Ona. I know you want me to come."

"I do, but I want happy. I want you to be a good," she says. Her voice sounds weary of this adventure, at least a little, and maybe I don't blame her, this is a bigger deal for her than me, at least in the family meeting me department. For me, I've got my entire savings on the line here, spending it to be with her for 3 months rampaging 'round Europa.

> —*I'm an asshole.*
> *I'm sacrificing nothing.*
> *I got only gold, she's got all the stress.*

"I will be perfect," I reassure her.

"That what I afraid of," she says and laughs, "Goodnight Clever, love you."

"Goodnight Ona, love you too," and we hang-up and Dad's there in the kitchen doorway putting his finger down his throat— and then says it again, "You'll never love her like I love your Mother."

I smirk.

*   *   *

Mom's getting me my plane ticket. She's on the cordless phone with the airline, *American Airlines*, back on hold, "When do we pick up your passport?" she asks me.

I close the *Shoestring* book onto my finger, save my place in *Rome*, "Next week?"

"I don't think so," she responds putting the phone back up to her ear as she wanders out of the living room, "Don't go in the kitchen the reception sucks in the kitchen!" I yell back at her, but she's gone, disappears into the kitchen, and suddenly she's back, the phone down by her side, "Every time I go in there the phone dies," she tells me.

"I told you; don't go in there." Mom smirks, redials the airlines, "We get your Passport on Friday morning before work; you'll be late to school," she says.

"Why'd you ask then?" I question.

"Shh," she says, "Yes hello, I got disconnected…"

*   *   *

I've gotta get on that plane; I'm over pretending to take school seriously anymore. I'm over it. Today does not matter.

I'm done.

But I'm not.

A   month   and a   half   to   go.

*   *   *

Ona's loosened up a bit, laughs more, smokes more cigarettes, open to Public Displays of Affection, PDA.

"How's Liana?" Ona asks me by my locker.

"I don't know. Seems okay."

"Pierre say she on drug now."

I'm not sure why she's bringing all this up, and then she surprisingly says, "Maybe we be nice to her now; End of year."

"Okay, if you're sure?"

"Sure?" she doesn't understand, closing her locker.

"Okay, we'll all be friends again," I say.

"You nice guy, Clever. You make me happy," she says, petting my face, "I miss you in Madrid."

"I'll miss you too, baby."

She gently slaps my face, "No baby, I a woman," she playfully scolds, but she means it. She always means it.

*   *   *

Thursday night; the gangs all at their homes, everyone's studying, everything's coming to a close for my foreign friends. They have full semesters, but I'm a regular senior, I got no finals. So, while they all dig their heads in the pages, I start getting some last hours, days, nights with some of my old crowd. Word is the whole world's thinking 'bout New York City, their club scene. New York's the next stop. *Limelight, Tunnel Club,* Brooklyn Raves. Off the hook. Like an island of nightlife...Weird that people actually have jobs?

*   *   *

*

"I don't want you to get hurt over there," Dad says.
"Better safe than sorry."
"It's not a joke Kyle," he stops me.
"Sorry."
"I'm being serious. Those are different places than here. The police are different, the people are different, and you are *American*, and you have to remember that all the time, you are *American*, you are not them, you are the *Alien*," he's lecturing me as normal a Father can, "They don't like us."
"I know," I say, "I'm going to be polite, and safe, and I won't go anywhere without Ona, and I won't let her go anywhere without me."
"Mom taught you about the money?" he asks.
"Yeah, some; she's going to show me the rest later."
"You love this girl?" he asks, well knowing what I will say.
"Yes, dude, I've told you this."
"I talked with her father yesterday, he seems nice enough," he says, "Not much English, but I understood him; happy to meet you. He will pick you up at the airport."
"I know," I say.

"I got you a ton of condoms," Dad says.

"Thanks Dad,"

"Wear them,"

"I do,"

"Wear them there too,"

"I. Will."

"Don't take drugs out of *Amsterdam*,"

"No shit," I say, but this is where he gets super serious, Dad get's f'n real.

"Nothing. There is no good outcome in taking drugs out of *Amsterdam*."

"Okaaaay."

"Don't be a smartass."

"I won't do drugs in Europe."

"You do know you can drink alcohol?" his alternative.

"Yeah, I know."

"Get drunk, not high."

"I know, jeez."

"You're so incompetent."

"Wait, what?"

"Get the map."

*

Dad's got the Europe map sprawled out on the kitchen table, he's showing me where *Amsterdam* is, "Look," he starts, "The only way to leave Amsterdam is through— Belgium, that's the safe route, down to France where if you get caught they will only lock you up until the embassy saves your dumb-ass, but still that's only weed, not mushrooms. You bring those mushrooms across a border and you'll have more trouble, they'll make an example of a *Stupid American Tourist* and it'll take us months to get you released. You ever see, *Midnight Express*?"

"No."

"Watch it."

"I'm not going to do drugs, Dad," but he ignores me.

"The other way out, Germany, and you're fucked, but if you do get through Germany, where you going?" he circles the *Iron Curtain* with his finger, "Czechoslovakia, Austria, then what down to Italy, all fucked, fucked-fucked-fucked; stamping your passport and throwing you in jail where they're keeping *Arian Youth*...and they'll see that Jew snipped prick of yours and you're fucked."

"Jesus, Dad. Chill the fuck out," I say as Mom walks in.

"Don't take drugs out of Amsterdam," she says.

"Come on people," I'm insulted, "I'm not an idiot."

"Yes, you are," Dad retorts.

"Kyle, don't do drugs," Mom says and kisses me.

"Yes, Mother."

*   *   *

Moby's Yeah— slow roll (*in a car, not on* 9) through the early evening fog. One week left. Ona's got two more finals. I will not see her until the night before Graduation. We are both busy with family stuff, last minute preparations for getting off this continent of an island, cross the pond, get our European dance on. Tonight, Liana sits side-saddle. She doesn't care about finals. She wants to have fun before she goes back to her parents. I don't know what's up with her parents, but with as much freedom they seem to give her, she really doesn't like them. We slow to a stop sign, "Ona's really scared," she says, I look in my rear-view mirror, no cars coming, I'm not gonna go yet, "What do you mean?" I ask.

"She scared about you going to Spain."

"What is she scared about? I won't like it? That I'm gonna like it?" I explain, realizing this is why I'm here, this is why Liana's riding side-saddle, something's going on with the Ona.

"You don't understand. We are not *American*, Kyle. We all have to go home now," she consults me.

"I know."

"No, you don't know. I do not want to go home. I am like you. Free person. Ona wants to go home. She is very different."

— She wants
you to see something,
you're not getting it,

she's not coming on to us.
So she's not trying to steal me.
What is she doing? —

"What are you trying to say Liana? Ona doesn't want me to come to Spain all of a sudden?"

"No, no. She love you, Kyle. She love you much, too much she says," Liana is being real.

"So, she wants me to go?"

"Yes, but she is scared," she says again, "I just warn you. Be careful." HONK, HONK! There's a car behind us. I roll forward, so foggy, "Where are we going?" I ask Liana.

"I no not know. You take me somewhere?" she says. I take us to Marin. I trust Liana tonight. She's humbled herself. The meds have humbled her. Her flirt is gone. Her flirt has morphed into empathy. I show her the ferry to San Francisco. It's nothing special, but it's not home, and we got ourselves some coffee, and she seems happy. I want Liana to be happy. She had a hard year. I guess Liana's my friend.

"You think she's scared to say goodbye?" I ask her. She offers me a cigarette. I'm not in the mood.

"She afraid you break her heart. She said she is very mad you kissed her."

"I won't break her heart? That's crazy. I'm totally in love with her," I sip my cup, "Does she want me to stay in Spain is that it? I could do that. I got no ties. I'll learn Spanish," I plead.

—but who am I pleading too, Liana?
Why does she look like she's going to cry?
Did we say something wrong?

"Are you alright?" I place my hand on her back which triggers the tears and she starts to weep, "I don't want to go home," tears, tears, "I want to stay America. I want to be happy," more tears, tears, she's stopped talking, tears, and I have to hold her. Let it out, Liana. Life's hard. We all got stuff to deal with. You can stay here. Do whatever you want. You're eighteen. You don't have to go home.

Here we all thought she was having a terrible time, that she wasn't happy, that everyone else was enjoying the American experience, and here she was, wanting to enjoy the entire American experience, still looking for it, disliking her whatever awaits or doesn't await her at home. Do you have friends back home? Maybe you burnt all your bridges, two timed on friends, friends who were happy to see her go, sisters who only want to coddle her, sisters who are all happy with boyfriends, her rich detached parents, *Basque* men that disgust her. Despises her own language. Secretly despises Ona. Ona came to America for no reason. Just to do something different. Mallorca is a small island. Boring. At least going to America is something. And what happens to *Ms. No Expectations*, she meets the best boy in the whole school, fell in love, and now he's coming to Spain to travel all over Europe together. Sucks to be Liana.

"Maybe you come back and take me all the States?" she asks me into my shirt.

"What would you do until then?"

"You and Ona visit me in *San Sabastian*."

"We'll do that."

"You will?"

"But I'm not coming back, here," I sware.

"I know."

*

Ona and Pierre wanted to go to one last San Francisco "Discotecha," before they had to go home. It's graduation night. We did not take anything with us. Ona thinks it's stupid they cannot drink and can't stop giggling with Pierre about how drunk they are going to get when they get home. She's being rude. It's all Pierre, Spain, Spain, Madrid is beautiful, Spain, Drink, Drink, Have Fun Again, Drink, Madrid, Madrid, Madrid.

"I get it," I say after 4 hours of that shit.

"Huh?" she asks as I drop her off at her foster exchange home.

"Never mind."
"I miss you."
"I'll miss you, too."
"I miss you now," she clarifies.

—Sure didn't act like it tonight.

She's crying. Well, she's choked up. Her eyes are red, watery, but Ona doesn't cry. I kiss her. I have to kiss her. When she gets like that, she just wants to be kissed. Sometimes it's the only time she likes to make-out anymore, when she is sad.

"Goodbye, Clever."
"Love you, Ona."
"Love you."

poof
*   *   *

F   LASH   IN THE DARK   •

*   *   *

Time crawl.   Snail.   Sluggish.

*   *   *

Cra-

-wl, slowly
          slower still
               Still
               Sleeping
               Waiting
               Anticipating…… .   .   .

.

Chapter 4 - Almost

What time is it? 4am; I am not sleeping, I'll fall asleep at like 5:45am again, just like last night, just like the past six nights, I can't sleep. She better fucking call me tonight.

*

What's happening? Everything's moving, stop shaking, stop that, I can't hold on; earthquake. Lame.

*

—I open my eyes

Mom's looking right at me, "Ona's on the phone." She's shaking me, rocking me awake at 1pm? I take the phone.

Shoo, Mom ——• "Ona?"

"Kyle, why you take so long?" she asks, but before I can get anything out, "I miss you Clever, how many day?"

"I think like five," I say, "Donde esta?"

"Ah, very good," she actually compliments my Spanish, so something's up, and she goes on, "It nice to speak Spanish again, I missed Spain. Beautiful here. You go to love Spain."

"Are you studying?"

"Yes, very hard. We have groups to study with. Very hard we study," she says, "How my English? I speak nothing being here."

"Good, very good; I miss you," I admit.

"Si; hold, por favor," and I don't hear her, the phone is cupped, I'm on hold with Spain—

—Suddenly she's back.

"Kyle?"

"Hey, yeah-"

"Do you know, can you come to *Barcelona* first?"

"Que?"

"Change plane to go to *Barcelona*?"

"I don't think so, why?"

"Hold on—"

—She's back.

"De donde viene tu tierra avion?"

"Huh?"

She giggles—

"Sorry Kyle, I forgot you American. Uh, where do your plane land?"

"I land in Madrid then transfer to Mallorca."

"No, no Mallorca, I cannot meet you. You go to Barcelona."

"Ona, I don't think I can change my flight. I gotta ask Ma."

"Ask her. I hold."

"Why do I have to meet you in Barcelona all of a sudden?"

"Ah too fast— I have go, ask your Mother."

"Okay, hold on- MOOOOM!"

*

"Mom, can I change my flight from Mallorca to Barcelona?"

"No! Why would you ask such a crazy thing? What's going on?"

"I don't know?"

"What do you mean? Let me talk to her."

"Ona? My Mom wants to talk to you."

"Child, no I do not talk to your Mother. You cannot change?"

"No, she says I can't change..."

UGH! - Mom's pulling on me trying to get to the phone.

"No Mom, chill, fuck— Look, Ona, listen..."

"No, I have go, group start. You cannot change, that okay, I decide," she says.

"Decide what?" I ask.

"I call you tomorrow, I go study. Bye." she says.

"Love you."

"Yes. Bye Kyle. I call you," and she hangs up.

Pause. Beat. Pause. Moment. Time. Crawl, Crawl; crawl—

"WELL?!" Mom bursts.

"I don't know. Nothing; I think it's cool," I say.

"Is everything okay?"

"Yeah, I think it's cool."

"Is she getting cold feet?" my Mom asks.

"No. No man. It's not that, something about meeting her in Barcelona instead of going to her home."

"Did she say why?" Mom asks.

"Nope."

"I'm sure it's fine."

"It's fine! God! Can I go back to sleep now?"
"No. It's one o'clock. Get up."

—Five more days.

    *   *   *

—I need to get on that plane.

    *   *   *

Time makes the heart grow fonder.

Time gives the mind...
I finally figured her out. Ona. Before this time apart, I had totally taken the relationship for granted. It was a high school romance. Almost a dream. Having a girlfriend for the last Semester was a-okay. Always had someone to be with. Had sex. Had a reason to revisit everything I'd grown up around. If it wasn't for Ona, I probably wouldn't have done much this year. At least not around here. But that's me. Who is she? I saw her become herself.

Women mature faster than men.
Boys masturbate more often.

.than a girl who came to America for something to do. Did she grow here? Or did she pause here? Did she learn about herself, or did she learn about myself? Why was she so scared to fall in love in America? And now I understand my beautiful Ona. She was a woman of skepticism, not untrusting, it was a bewilderment by the cruelty of time and space. Back home she knew only what she always knew and there she followed. She didn't consider much self although inside she was full of herself, well knowing she was strong and worthy of another man's affection. I represent "her" world, while her father's world represents "her." That's why she didn't want to fall in love with me.

We are her future.
I am the giving man, guiding man, but not a leader, not a showman, just a guide for the high, higher through love. I do

not control her. America does not control her. So, why is she so happy to be back in Spain? She's anticipating switching sides of the teeter-totter. How wonderful to fully engulf herself into "herself." Not only have a man willing to put her needs before his, but to lead and guide to show us through a strange land as I did for her. Showing her what I thought she wanted to see. In America, I was an invisible force of love, in Spain I will be hers to display. A trophy. An American souvenir.

*

*

"Is she going to call you today?" Mom asks through the bathroom door as I step out of the shower; dry off.

"Yeah!"

"I called the airline, you can't change to Barcelona!" she's yelling through the door. No more of this madness, I open the door.

"What did they say?" I ask her; intent.

"You can't change so late. Not without a huge fee!" still yelling?

"How much?" and I wave her voice down.

"You cannot change your ticket, Kyle," she toned it down.

"Okay, she'll be okay," I say and about to close the door when Moms stops me.

"Clever."

"What?" ...hey... "Wait, don't call me that."

"I did get you something though, Kyle."

"Ah, come on Mom, enough with the gifts, I love you, I will be back." I consult her with a kiss on the cheek.

"When?" she asks, sly like a fox.

"Huh? Three months, you know you booked it."

"You can come home in six if you want?" she says with this smirk.

"Huh?" I don't know what she's getting at, people and their puzzle play.

"I couldn't change your ticket to Barcelona, but they did give you an open flight home," she explains.

"What's that mean?"

"It means if you want to stay longer, you just call the airlines and tell them when you want to come home…up to eight months, but some days are no fly days," she explains.

"Eight months?" I can't believe it.

"You're not staying for Eight Months," Mom's adamant, "I got it for you so you can come home early if something happens."

"Oh, yeah, like no way, but wow eight months, how cool."

"You're not staying for eight months."

"I can't believe it," I say.

"Get dressed," and she closes the door on me.

*

With a soft, caring tone, "I'll see you tomorrow," I pronounce, seduce the Ona through the phone, no matter how odd that conversation actually was, "See you tomorrow, Kyle. Fly good," and the phone goes dead. I do not sleep. I'm in the shower by 3:30am, Mom kisses me goodbye in her robe, Dad's got my bag, hands it to me, "Yours to carry, get used to it." The bag's pretty heavy, but when I lock the buckles around my chest and abs it lightens up. I can do this. I took care of myself these three months. Pushups, medium weights in our yard, pullups, ride a bike for two hours on a handful of *Mini-Thins*. I'm fit, I'm cut, I'm ready to bang my baby on a beach across the ocean. Damn. Bags in the trunk, Dad's warming the car, sips his coffee, I slide in, buckle, and he drives, gets us breakfast at a diner in San Fran, which gives me a chance to pack my stash before the airport. In the bathroom stall, I pull my two baggies of 9, out of my pocket. I gotta stash if for the flight. One bag's got six full tablets, the other is stuffed with a fine powder of twenty crushed tablets. I hold the baggies under my johnson, rip a condom open with my teeth, roll it on mister softy. Should do the trick. .   .   .

Pops unloads me at Terminal 3, hands me an extra $1,000 in cash, "Be good son," check in, metal detectors, Gate 6B, American Airlines, Madrid, Magazines, Boarding— So I got $3,000 to survive. That seems like a lot for 3 months.

Chapter - 5 - A few hundred miles from Home

I am on the plane. high . on a plane.

• BING • BING • BING — "The Captain has turned on the fasten seatbelt sign. Our flight attendants will come collect your final items of trash as we prepare for landing. The temperature is 32 Celsius in Madrid, partly cloudy, the time is 9:53 am. Thank you for flying *American Airlines*."

I am over Europe. I have been on this plane for hours. The layover in New York was nothing to write home about. We're landing. We've landed. We're taxi-ing in. I'm more than ready to get off this plane. One more flight to go. Madrid to Mallorca. No Customs yet. You know what that means...my balls are sweating from the condoms. Meander to Gate 26A. Flights on time. Thirty Minute wait. I'm starving. I have no Spanish cash yet. I don't want to make change. I'll wait...

        ...we've boarded. Everything is Spanish. They are translating nothing. I know the drill. Seatbelt, Exits, Life-Jacket, Oxygen, Mask yourself, then you are allowed to assist the helpless children. Relax and Enjoy your flight...

                    ...we're landing. Fast flight. Fastest yet. Thank you, air gods...

                        ...and exiting...

....

...exiting. Oh, shit, I'm about to see Ona. Ha, ha that's so wild. We're gonna party. Get drunk. And I step onto the metal grate that connects our jetliner to this protruding tunnel of the Airport. I can't believe I am here. Wow, I feel strange. There is a warm breeze that slips through the cracks that connects this plane to the Spanish tube. I'm not walking, I've stopped on the metal grate. Just a stare down the tunnel. All the text is Español. It is long. This tunnel represents the last few steps to the great escape. I've done this. I've flown all the way across the world for this girl. For myself. For the both of us. Holy fuck, I really did this. I gotta see her—

—that was the longest tunnel ever designed by man. I step out into the small Terminal and, no, I don't see Ona quite yet. I'm being directed down a line of red rope to a set of glass doors, down an escalator, Customs, welcome to a new world dude, and I'm in a jetlagged daze as I show my Passport to the Customs Agent, "Hola, enjoy España. No trouble," and he stamps my Passport, hands it back, waves me on. I expected so much more. He didn't ask me anything. Probably best, too tired to speak clearly. No pat down, nothing. I wasted so many condoms. Next time I cut a hole in the tip so I can pee. Ona's gonna hate me for all this, but I can't risk coming up empty handed on the greatest adventure of my life time • Maybe when we get to her Dad's they'll let me crash for an hour? My head pounds. Feel like I'm still on the plane. Where am I? I stop walking, look at the signs, Spanish, Spanish, Spanish, what do they say, oh wait there's English, "Exit," nice. I follow the Exit sign. It's led me down a long hallway. I've forgotten I'm going to have to wait for my bag. That sign better say Baggage Claim. "Recogida de Equipaje." No, that means something else...No other door? Well, roll the dice, Clever, and I exit through the doors into the slow-motion of the small baggage claim of the Mallorca Island Airport. The sounds are fluid. I understand nothing. Not one word sounds familiar to me. I might as well be in China. It doesn't even sound Mexican.

*

If it was all a movie, it would have been in slow motion.
If it was all a movie, it would have all been made up.
If it was all a movie, it would not be believable.
Close yourself to belief; know yourselveS

*

I see her, Ona, she has not made herself up for me, she has sported a casual tan shirt, jeans, her hair in a ponytail, no make-up, and I say as I scoop her up into my arms, "Help me to believe," and I'm squeezing my girl again, and I'm elated, thrilled, I can't believe I'm here. We twirl, so do roses, ever so romantic, people must be watching like a *Magnetic*

Fields song on repeat forever. Lovers reunited. Lovers from across the ocean, together again.

Take a picture before you miss it.

And you put her down as she beats on your chest with her fists. Her sneakers find the floor and you lean in to kiss her blossomed voluptuous dark lips. It takes a just a moment, like a mistake, less than a second for her to give you her cheek, "Don't. Go get your bag. I wait for you outside. I get taxi, be fast, I expect phone call at home," she scolds you, walks out of the baggage claim.

Not the greeting one would expect. Maybe I embarrassed her. I can feel people turning away from me, disappointed in us. No kiss. No fun. What's up?

*

I what?
Where am I?
Who are you?
Why are you looking at me that way?
Do I even know you?
Excuse me, I'm was supposed to meet my girlfriend?
Do you know her? Name's Ona?
Why are you looking at me that way?
You look just like Ona.
You sure you're not her? You know my name.

"Why are you acting so weird?" I ask her as I exit the baggage claim into the musty heat of Mallorca.

"No, I'm not act weird," she says putting out her half smoked cigarette, "It would been better if you met in Barcelona," she says waving down a Taxi.

"Where's your Dad?" I ask.

"He's at the apartment, we meet him," she says.

"I missed you," but she ignores me as a Taxi pulls up to the curb. "Taxi, vamos," she tells me and gets in. The driver helps me with my backpack, "American. Oh, you love Mallorca. Most beautiful place in the whole world."

—At least he was polite.

Chapter - 6 - No, fucking way.

Ona's on the far end of the L shaped couch, it's leather, dark leather, I know, I keep staring at it. The couch withers with age the longer I stare. We're in her Father's apartment. He's not home. I haven't met him yet. Probably best, Ona needed to have a talk with me, yet she's not even looking at me. She stares out the window as I stare at the cracks in the couch. "So, you want to break up with me?" I break the silence, "Is that what you're saying?"

"I made mistake, Kyle. We should break up in America, first," she tries to justify herself.

"Sure, if I wasn't flying all the way here to be with you."

"I no want to be your girlfriend in Spain," she says, "That is all. Here we just friends."

"But we're not just friends."

"You want to go home?" she asks, and I believe her, I believe she can take it or leave it— Do whatever you want Kyle —"I don't want to go home," I say with all my heart, "I want to be with you, Ona; I want to be with you, here, there, anywhere. I don't want to go home."

"You make me mad," she turns away again, "You not care what I want."

"Crazy, I totally care about what you want."

She gets up, walks right past me, turns back, brushes her hair out of her face, "I make a phone call. You want a cigarette? She offers me a smoke from her pack that she's been nervously fiddling with in her hand.

"No, I'm cool; no, actually, yes," I'm confused, my head aches, pounding now, disoriented, Spanish coming from the TV, silence from her, loudness from the depths of my psyche ready to crack.

"Too fast, Kyle. Here you talk slow, 'kay? No embarrass me. Cigarette? You smoke on balcony." She hands me the smoke. Fine, but this is the last gift I'm accepting until we're back together. Yeah. Bitch. I take the smoke with a lot of adolescent attitude. Ona walks away. I ferociously slide open the balcony door, step out, slam it shut. Shit, I don't have a lighter. "YOU'LL NEVER LOVE HER LIKE I LOVE YOUR MOTHER," Dad reminds me all the way from across the Ocean, across the American Continent, deep in the center of my head he reminds me, "YOU'LL NEVER LOVE HER LIKE I LOVE YOUR MOTHER," and I'm thinking about it and my head aches, my stomach had already turned in the Taxi, twice. I want to puke. I don't want to open my eyes. If I open my eyes, I'll see this beautiful alien landscape, I'll get dizzier, I'll see how far I am from home, I'll realize I left my home, I'll be alone, here on the balcony, in Mallorca; alone. I puke over the railing. A door opens and closes. Must be Ona's father.

There is stain from the puddle of puke below the apartment that would be my coming, my becoming; a shadow, attached to this vile fool of a being, myself. I am the witness to everything, everything; everything.

*

There is a hum out here, on the balcony. In Mallorca, Spain. An island. Isolated from Europe, isolated from the states. It's the air-conditioner from the floor above. The machine above me is dripping. Another puddle, not of my tears. I puked my tears. All over the pavement down there.

I'm fucking exhausted. What time is it at home? I should probably go back inside, but I don't want to. 9 hour difference. It's 3:10, minus, minus, dizzy, go back inside. Add later. Subtract later. I'm scared. I feel things I've never felt before. Sickness. A sickness I can't shake. Never felt so sideways. Get it together, Clever. Think of something. Do something. Save this relationship. Idea? Any idea. Why am I so confused? Oh yeah, because my first real girlfriend just dumped me. 5am. Fuck it's 5am back home. I've been up for like thirty something...

I leave the glass door open, who cares right, hot out, Ona's got no air-conditioner, just fans. I step into the hallway. The place is small. Skinny, narrow. A small man backs out of one of the two rooms. The shared bathroom is behind me, the kitchen is past them. I suppose this is her father. Spanish name. I don't remember. Why should I, I'm just a friend here, right. He's handsome. Well-built chest revealed for leisure through his half buttoned up dress shirt. He sports *Khaki* knee longs with *Birkenstocks*. His apartment feels like a boat to me. We're on the third floor, this is not a boat. Designed like a boat, skinny and short. I'm no giant. 5' 7 on a good day, but her pops looks about 5'2, four eleven if I wanted to be a dick about it. He steps up to me, the young man who's been banging your daughter in bum-fuck nowhere California, same guy that just puked over your balcony.

"Kyle?" he reaches out his hand, "Pleasure to meet you," he says in perfect English.

I've been hesitant for a moment now. I've been hesitant about shaking another person's hand before. The homeless. Bureaucrats I've never met. Dogs. Crawfish. Girls. But a father, like this, letting me stay here, on the couch, traveling across Europe with his daughter, this hand I have never shook before. "Happy to be here, thank you," he doesn't have much of a grip, "I speak very poor English," he says to me, "But I try with you."

"That's okay."

"Ona, give me her lesson book, I studied," he lets go of my hand and pokes me in the heart, "For you. You tell me how I, your visit finish."

"I_will_do_my_best," I speak, like speaking to a five-year-old, make sure he got all the words, allowing him the time to translate in his head.

"Buen; se llama Corso," Ona's Dad tells me his name.

"Nice to meet you Corso. Thank you for letting me stay here," I tell him, Ona sort of rolls her eyes. Shhs me with her finger. I get it. Not broken up. Dad thinks I'm just a friend. Wow, the jet-lag done fucked with my brain. Maybe I need a nap.

"Papa want to take us to eat; do you want sleep or go?"

"What kind?" I ask, with a more positive attitude. This confuses her.

"Ocean. Fish. I not eat fish in long," and she turns to her father, talks in Spanish, back and forth. I'm oblivious to myself, maybe I'm sick, I don't want fish...smell, not today, I do need...

"You sleep. You jetlagged," Ona instructs, "We bring you."

"Ok," just show me where to sleep now. She points to the living area, to the pullout couch her I had been seated upon when she played up the whole charade of "just friends," even though her Pops wasn't there. *Practice makes perfect?*

I pass Ona as I head to sleep, she touches my wrist, "Are you okay?" she asks, cold. "Yeah, fine. Jet-lagged," I say. "No, not that. About that," and she nods toward the living area. "Sleeping in there? Yeah, all cool. Go eat."

"I get jacket," Corso says, "Mira, I spoke English for Kyle."

"Muy bein Papa," and she turns to me, "No, about breakup. You not too sad, correct?"

It's real?

*

She wakes me up. I had fallen asleep in her room.

I smell McDonalds before I see it.

"You got sick. I bring you American food." I open the bag. It's not McDonalds. It is a burger and fries. I place the paper wrapped burger on the sheet. Ona picks it up, there is no stain, she puts it back in the bag, puts the bag on the nightstand, "You still mad at me?" I ask.

"You no listen, you invisible," she's mad, "I not mad at you, Kyle. I not love with you. Now we friends, that all," she says in a whisper, "You sleep here, tonight."

"Why are you whispering?"

"I want to go to Barcelona now— We go there in 2 days no next week, okay? Sleep so you not jet lagged," she instructs.

"So, you still want to go around Europe with me?"

"Why you always dramatic? Yes, we go, just friends. You do that, we have good time, okay?"

"Nothing romantic, just friends," I say a little louder, maybe her sleeping father will be convinced. I take her hand, yet like a whip, her fingers lash-back and she turns in vengeance, "No more touch. No more molest."

"Molest?"

"We just friends, Clever. Broke up. I sorry." The door closes. I am by myself. Dark. 11:13pm. Her father must have heard all that. Denial is useless.   This show was not for him

---

Ona's dumped you.   No reason.   Just over. Does not love you

She said that. She said she didn't love me. Why am I here? When did she have this epiphany? How are we expected to not hook up traveling in the same train, same room, different city, every night for the next 3 months? She's lost it. Spooked. Kid's spooked. Kid's gotta chill. We need to get drunk tomorrow night, that'll help her out. She's always bragged about how much better the clubs were here. Tomorrow will be tomorrow. She'll see she wants "us" here,

too.

*

Oh,

god I gotta wake up. Fuck. Ona better be in a better mood. I need a good mood Ona. A door closes. Steps, steps, someone else is awake, too. Sliding door. Ona's going to smoke. Who's going to shower first? Her dad? Never lived with her...what's her standard? I gotta pee. Quiet. Don't catch her attention. I'm in my boxers. Black and White, star on the left hip. I creep out of my room, down the hall, past the kitchen, the sliding door, she's on the phone, I'm in the guest bathroom, no shower. I pee. It's quite loud. Bet she can hear me. Do girl's think about us peeing? Holding ourselves? Who's she talking, too, laughing? Good mood Ona. I flush. Stroll past the sliding glass door, Ona was looking in, turns her back on me, I've passed, back to the hall, back to her room. Right? Or will she need to come in? We'll tackle that hurdle when the time comes...Maybe I should have showered first?

*

Yellow Waterproof Sony CD Walkman, *Dance Classics Tomorrow Mix CD, Hause Record Tracks, Indo Tribe, Liquid Sky, Funk Techno Tribe, Portishead, Aphex Twin, etc.* I'm in my jammies on her bed. I should have been banging my girl hello last night, not this floppy teddy. A door sound. Steps. The shower. She didn't come in here. Kick back. Listen to the music. I press play. Three songs, the door opens, Ona in a towel tells me, "You now," and leaves.

You shower and rub one out. Mark your territory with disowned sperm down her father's drain. You've been blue-balled since the fucking airport. Expectations down the drain.   You turn off the water. This sucks for you. This sucks for anyone. Just sucks, huh?

---

*

I enter their kitchenette. I've got jeans on, holes in the knees, a black t-shirt, and Ona turns from her father and says to me, "You would like to go to the beach today?"

"Yeah sure— Good morning," and, "Good morning," to her father, Corso.

"Buenos Dias Kyle," Corso replies with a squeeze on the shoulder.

"Papa don't, Kyle no hablo espanol.".

"I understand Buenos Dias, Good Day," I am proud.

"Very good," Dad says.

"Do not encourage, Kyle," replies Ms. Mood.

"Ona, be considerate," he turns to me, "You love Mallorca beaches. Most beautiful in whole world."

"Take me," I touch her waist, instinctually. She moves aside, takes her plate to the sink, rinses it, turns to me. I sit. Corso slides a plate of bread and butter over for my digestion. "Thanks."

"You wear shorts to beach," Ona addresses me, "Not cold like *Bodega*."

"Oh, well Bodega's freezing, muy frio," I tell Corso, "You really can't compare the two. The sun's hot in LA. Water's still cold."

"All America is cold Papa," Ona takes his plate, rinses it, "Come on, you loved California," I refute as she scrubs the plate as if there was dried sauce on it, like it was filthy. She's nervous. Wants to get out of this small apartment. Away from pretending to her Dad.

*

You don't know Ona. Why would you expect too?
                  I don't know Ona. Why should I expect too?
Ona knows precisely who she is. Why expect less?
                  Ona knows me. Why shouldn't she?

She's a complicated soul. Lost her Mom to her Mom.
           I don't bring up her Mom, I know she died.
I know it happened when Ona was twelve.
                      I know it was cancer.
      I know her Mother was clinically depressed about it.
                      I don't know how.
                    I don't know where.
             I don't know how Ona feels.
          I have never lost anyone to suicide.
    Probably sucks like fucking brain cracking crazy.
    Ona's pretty solid considering. I respect that in her.

I will not pretend to know what it means not to have photos
of your Mother decorating the house with the photos of her,
her father, and her brother...who's in the Spanish Military,
stationed in Afghanistan. Lots of opium in Afghanistan—

                    —Ona   interrupts
my train of thought. I zoned out as she continued to
converse with her father in front of me. They were talking, I
was thinking, I snapped back in, I'm back, she's still
complaining about America, "People don't take a rest, never
rest, always busy, busy, doing things. Cold, no one is warm
like they pretend, like TV. All America is TV."
    "Not all of it, I'm not cold, you like me?" I interject;
independently patriotic.
    "You know what mean. You only nice person in all
California."

                          —*Awe, I'm flattered.*

*

On the beach Ona takes a sip of her bottled beer. The sun is
blazing, so hot, I do have my shorts on. I think I have to go
in the water. No joke, this is not a California sun. I'd be

Afrocentric if I lived here. Tan like crazy. I get dark. I open my beer, we are basically alone on this beach. It was a thirty-minute drive. Ona listened to Spanish Pop the whole way. Said nothing. Asked if I was thirsty. Took us to a liquor store. Had me wait in the car. The beach is real, meaning state park or something. There was a small car lot. Trail led through some brush, then this secluded, curved beach line; not so much secluded, but not very populated. A good half a kilometer away, I can see kids playing in the low water, so low, not even at their knees and they are way out there, "How far is it that shallow?" I ask Ona. I turn. She's removing the top of her bathing suit, holding her breasts in her hands. "Why you look?"

"Sorry," I turn away from my girlfriend. Wait? What? I turn back to her. She's on her towel, face down, breast down, turns her face toward me, "This is Spain, this is okay. You just no look."

"I wasn't looking."

"La Paz," she silences me, turns her face into the towel. I watch the immobile ocean. There are no waves here. Everything seems to tranquil. La Paz. On the inside, there is low tide pulling us deeper and deeper away from each other the closer we become. She will love me again tomorrow. Maybe we should split some ɘ tonight?

"Tonight, we go Disco," Ona says, "I take us to Menorca, Island. You can drink better."

"Drugs?"

"You no drugs in Spain. No trouble for me."

"But we're just friends."

"No trouble, Clever."

"You still think I'm cute."

"Annoying; like a toddler."

Ona takes a sun bathe. I wander in the water. There are other women down the beach, topless, in the water. I want to watch them, but I don't want to offend Ona. Would it offend them, down there, as they splash each other? I do not know the protocol, but it turns me on enough that I'm going to sit in the water for a moment instead of stand.

*   *   *

Menorca, twin island of Ona's Mallorca, is a club island/bar island with narrow streets, and lined with basic square plaster buildings. Nothing is very well lit, every place has those Spanish shingles, more cobblestone, more or less still ignoring my surroundings, all Ona on the mind all the time, we took a boat here. A ferry. Sundown. Early for clubbing? She had said it herself in the States— Her whole attitude here has me in a perpetual state of question, the same question, "WHAT ARE WE DOING?"— "Fuck I never called my folks," I remember out-loud to Ona as we turn a corner to the land of Disco Plenty. The town has met at a triangular crossroad. There are nine different mini-night clubs in one place, and every place has a line. A variety of house music from the tunnels of the opening and closing doors of the clubs. The crowd is louder still. Drunk. Loud. Drunk. Loud as fuck. Alien words. English would be alien here. Loud. Drunk. "Call them when we home," Ona leans into my ear, pulls me toward the longest line. "But I'll be wasted?"

"You cannot call here? Why talking about it?" Ona is annoyed. She needs a drink.

"I'll just call them we get to Barcelona."
She ignores me. Or didn't hear me. Not paying attention. Not her problem. Tonight, Ona's made herself up, eye shadow, curled her hair, dark brown lipstick, she's got a loose sleeveless shirt, cotton, her push-up bra creates a curve of cleavage just above the hem, and jeans so she doesn't get in any trouble with me; boots— "Pardon," the guy behind me signals for me to move up in line. We're up, our turn. We flash our passports, they wave us in...a small wooden hall, to a spiral staircase that leads down to the basement, the basement of a house? This place is no bigger than a thousand foot basement. A mini-bar in the corner. It was free to enter. It is loud bass and it's getting louder fast, thud, thud, thud, thud, Euro-House, deep, deep house, all bass, boom, boom, thud, boooom, tist, tist, and its dark, really dark and there seem to have been more people outside then inside. Ona is not pleased, "We have beer and go."

"Why have a beer?"

"I want to be drunk," and she walks away to the mini-bar, buys herself a beer. I guess we're going Dutch now? Why wait until Amsterdam, right? I buy myself a beer, while Ona chats in Spanish with two guys loitering against the wall beside the bar. She looks at me. Does she want me to step in? She turns back, touches one of the guys on the chest, waves, turns back to me, I step up. "They say better bar outside triangle."

"But I thought you wanted a Disco?"

"They take us."

"Do you know them?"

"This Spain. Spanish men not like American. You can trust. Vamos," she swigs her beer. Swigs again. Points to the guys to wait. Swigs again. Finishes about half a beer. I know. I picked it up as we left. Shook it. Took a swig myself. Never actually got that first beer. Why are we following these douche-bags? This girl's not even drunk and she's got me following random dudes. Ona's lost it. Ona's a totally different person in Spain. Maybe that's why her Pops mailed her to America?

*

She's getting wasted; so drunk, she's dancing. I'm nursing my third beer, some canned shit, cost some sort of Spanish money. She's had like three sweet drinks, and now leaning up against one of the guy's that brought us here. This is actually our third club. The second was worse than the first. This one is more like a bar with a dancefloor. Full bar. These guys are totally douchey. I cannot understand a word they say, but their body language tells it all, and they've groped like twenty girls already, yet act all gentlemanly like with Ona. That's their con, isn't it. Not American. American's are stupid. Cocky. Think they're entitled. These Latin fucks con the fuck out of you treating everyone else like a piece of meat, but you like dessert...and if I don't figure this out, my Ona is going to be chocolate mousse for this douche-bag and not me. And he slips up, on the dancefloor. She's wasted, can barely dance. I see it, he slides his hand around her waist, down the front of her jeans, she pushes back, falls down, I rush the scene, "Pardon, Pardon," and I scoop Ona up, "Come on we have to go," and the guy steps between us, "Americano go then."

"Hey, she's with me, man."

"She dance with me. She, what you say, okay?"

"El bano," Ona tells me.

"What?"

"Bathroom," pukes on the guy and I rush her to the toilet. Please don't follow us. Don't follow me. She's in the bathroom, I look back down the bar. The two guys are talking amongst themselves, pointing at me, but not threatening me. I think they've given up. Kinda makes them even more douchey.

*

"You have to drive," Ona leans back against the ferry's handrail, "I too drunk."

"Can you direct me?"

But she looks at me confused. She doesn't understand. Answers in Spanish, "Hoblahblah."

"Directions home," I repeat.

"No, no home," she leans into me for support, "Barcelona. I miss Barcelona."

— Is she crying?

*

Ona puked over the rail shortly after. I got her a paper towel from the guard. He said something rude to me in Spanish, but no harm no foul, I don't understand shit. "Here," and I gave her the quicker picker upper and we didn't talk until we got to the car. "I tell where to drive," she instructs me. "Kinda have too."

"Don't be clever," she rolls down her window, "Drive there, same as America," and she points out her window. I have to lean forward to figure out what the fuck she's pointing at; the gate, okay, and I believe she means we don't drive on the left like in England? "So, what's with that guy back there?" I ask. "No, talk. Just drive," she says, and continues to direct me with points out the windows, points across my nose, tapping on the windshield to go straight; completely non-verbal. I went through like six stoplights. She scolded me verbally in Spanish and then continued to tap for me to keep driving. Tap, Tap, Tap. Annoying as all hell. I gotta dump this broad. Too late. Fuck this. I expect an apology, or at least a hand-job before we go to precious Barcelona that had her in drunken tears. Someone really hate's her island.

*

Outside her father's apartment building I stop, 4:45am, I humble my machismo, "I'm sorry I've made things so complicated."

"We both make things complicated," she says, her head leaning against the cool window as she waves for me to give her the car keys.

"We have to plan our trip still," I hand her the keys.

"Donde? Europe?" she's flipping through keys.

"Yeah, our Eurail Pass, what order of cities?"

"We do that in Barcelona, my cousin help us," she doesn't want to explain, slides the key in, unlocks the door.

"Your cousin, the one we're staying with?"

"Siiiii, why so many questions, I sleep now," the door nearly closing back on me.

"You are such a bitch when you're drunk."

But she didn't hear me. Good. Best she doesn't hear that. Goodnight sweet dove. Tomorrow will be one day closer to an adventure with your prince. She'll be nicer tomorrow. I know it. Drunk bitch. Love you. Mua. I pass out fast.

•denial•

Chapter - Vamonos or Vamos?

"Vamos!"
I've been pushed awake. Ona's standing clothed before me. I am not dreaming. A dream would be less fashionable, all skin. "Vamos," she pokes me with a smile.

"You're in a better mood."

"I hang over, but good news."

"What's up?" I need coffee, she needs me to pull my blanket up over my chest, "Prudish, much?"

"What is this word?"

"What word?"

"Prudish-uch?"

"Prudish. Prudish means...Never mind, what's the good news," now that I've covered my nipples.

"We go Barcelona today, day early."

"Why?"

"Vamonos, get your bag. Ferry leave soon."

And she disappears back to her room. Guess we gotta go?

Chapter - Gag me with a Barbwire Spoon

"Don't be very clever with my family," Ona requires of me on the deck of a larger ferry destined to Barcelona. "Why are we taking a boat?"

"I buy tickets in California."

"Yeah, but the plane is like an hour and this boat takes like eight, like all day?"

"I thought boat be romantic."

"It is."

She's walking away. What am I reading wrong? How many possible readings are there? Ona, just talk to me. Please. Just talk to me. And I catch up to her, take her arm, "Just talk to me, please." She pulls away. "Molestor. Leave alone. I watch water alone."

"What did I do?"

"Nothing, you do."

"I'm sorry about the boat stuff...Boat's cool, beautiful out here."

"Go there," she turns to the water, "We friends. I not mad."

But she's not going to say anything more either. Nada. Silence. Just the slosh of this not so romantic ferry chugging into the waves of the *Balearic Sea*. It is beautiful out here. I'll give her some space. She needs space. Feels guilty asking for it. I get it. I gotta get a grip. Sensitive. I'm not sensitive, I'm Clever. Give her space. Space along the Balearic Sea; beautiful

space...

...and we're docking. And Ona's found me upfront. "Vamonos," and I follow her to the dock. I'm invisible. She's ran right up to her cousin, a short little dude, shoulder length loose thick hair, he's dressed like the perfect hippie in his layered tie-dyed shirt with an unlaced leather vest, loose cotton cloth pants, *Birkenstocks*, headphones around his neck, and I know this dude is seriously stoned. At the minimum, Barcelona should be offering me weed. I need weed. Weed. Am I still invisible, no, I'm being waved over—

—"Kyle, this is Miguel."

I go for his hand, he comes charging in with a hug.

"Brother Clever, Ona's told me everything about you."

"Cool."

"Cool," Miguel turns to Ona with his arm around my shoulder,

"You were right, this American is, awesome."

I'm flabbergasted. Ona said that. About me. What about the breakup? "We're going to get you stoned. Now? Okay?"

"Okay."

"Yes, Kyle need to be stoned to be fun," Ona still catty as can be, yet Miguel laughs, "I hear you brother Clever. That's English term correct? I hear you?"

"Yes. How come you speak such perfect English?"

"Private school."

"How come you didn't do that?" I ask Ona.

"Cabron. My father is poor," she retorts, "Take us," she says to Miguel and hands him her backpack. She steps off towards the car lot. "She can be like that," Miguel schools me.

"I know," I confess.

"Don't date girls like Ona. You're a smart man. Keep it...how do you say?"

"Platonic?"

"Yeah. Platonic. Hard word," he says. We haven't moved, haven't followed Ona. Miguel is having a guy moment. The hippy is not a feminist. "We're not platonic," I tell him just as he walks away. What the fuck. Does he think we're just friends? That's fucked up. Me and that girl, Mr. Cousin Miguel, we were never platonic.

Miguel is waving me over, across the street that leads us right into the promenade. "Miguel is the coolest guy in all of Spain," Ona crushes on her own flesh and blood. I lean into Miguel, "You two first or fifth cousins?"

But he didn't hear me. Distracted by some chickens in a cage, stacked three boxes high, four boxes long. There is music humming out of Miguel's headphones scarfed around his neck. As Ona pulls us into a shoe shop, I can hear Miguel's music better, *Jimi Hendrix*, very nice, very hippy of you and then that is all interrupted as the cashier pops in a new CD, presses play, and enter, *Phil Collins*. *Phil Collins* tunes in a shoe store; makes sense. Carry on. "You buying something?" I call out to Ona as she meanders a shelf of flats. I don't like flats. Flat boots, okay, but I want a girl with some kick, ya know. Not a testicle spike of a heel, just something. That goes for me as well, *Sketchers* with a kick, to keep me dancing.

She waves me off and time is consistent.

*   *   *   *   *   *   *   *   *

This long strip of a pedestrian Market Place is lined
with merchants
Colorful fruits, Cloth Wraps, Shirts, Skirts, Chickens, Turtles,
Doves, Performers, Maps, Souvenirs, Travel Agents

*   *   *   *   *   *   *   *   *   *

"Ona said you her only American friend."
Miguel knows a lot about nothing.

"More than a friend..." and he grabs me by the shoulder, pulls me in tight, still walking, Hendrix in my ear, "Brother Clever, we know!" kisses my cheek, "You are American Brother from another Mother, and that make you my American Cousin. We dig. We dig," he stops at the corner. Ona has begun to cross. "Ona! Donde esta?! This way," and he releases me, takes a hard right, leads us past the *Gaudi Chapel* that is under reconstruction. I don't notice. A lot of scaffolds. Looks like they'll fall. Ona and Miguel chat up a storm. Spanish. Spanish. Miguel directs me every so often, waits for me to catch up. I'm zoned out. Not on the city, but about this Ona, this young, lost girl. Empathize with her. Crazy year. Crazy love. Crazy future. It was crazy then, it's crazy now. You can't deny that, Clever. Listen to Kyle, and don't talk to yourself, out loud.

I'm tired...zoned...watching them walk ahead of me.

That is a big ass backpack she's totting.

Mine's the same. Maybe we took too much. I catch up with them, "Maybe we packed too hardcore?"

"You can store half at our place," Miguel offers. "Thanks," I'm appreciative. We'll be back here again.

"You make map?" Ona asks Miguel.

"We make it. Always worried, you are," he tells her.

"You don't have to speak English for Kyle," she explains.

"I feel so loved when you talk that way," I tell her.

"Love. He just joking," she tells Miguel...

....then shoots me the stern, *say nothing muther fucker*, look of a feline ready to kill. Her thick eye brows clenched, her eyes fixated on my soul, and a claw that punchers my beating heart.

—This is going to explode tonight. Me, her.
Outside. Down the street, maybe farther.
Away from her family.
This bitch is going to explain herself.
I'm a pacifist with a wicked tongue.
Come at me, Ms. Ona of España.

Miguel stops at a four-story, plaster white, apartment complex; buzzes the door. "Hola," a woman's voice from the speaker. "Mama," Miguel yells as he yanks the door that won't open. His mom scolds him in Spanish through the little speaker. Probably about not having his keys. Door buzzes, unlocks, Miguel steps in, Ona stops me at the door. Miguel has already made his way up a flight of stairs.
"Why being weird?" she asks directly.
"I'm not being weird," I defend myself.
"No more talk about you me in America."
"I didn't say anything. Besides, Ona, I thought that was all for your Dad?" She doesn't understand. Makes her madder. "No, California love. You in Europe now. Europe better. Just like Europe. No America memories. Okay?" •

•I think I nodded. I didn't say a thing. Did I blink?•
Maybe I blinked • But did I nod? • Or did I disappear?•
I think I nodded • I didn't say a word • I blinked • When?•

?

Chapter - Family

Lots of kisses and hugs, Ona's got like six cousins.
These rascals are all younger, pre-teens, & adolescent. The
five-year-old, Niñita, might be the most darling in her
yellow sundress stitched up with baby blue flowers and

happy honeybees. She's shy. I've bent down to her height. "What's your name?" She just twists left, then right, left then right, "Is your name Honeybee?" She doesn't understand me. Miguel taps her on the head, "Como se lama?"

"Niñita!" she squeaks and runs away. Back up to the adult eye level, eye to eye with Ona's aunt. This woman, this very sexy older woman comes off softly-strong. Her hair so thick, bold, long, past her breasts, curved against her dark complexion, strong jaw, strong face, bold nose, very sexy, dressed in a long brown cotton dress with a few brass ornamented belts around her waist.

— Shit, I think I just checked out Ona's aunt.

"This is my friend, Kyle, but he like name Clever better."

"Well, Clever, welcome to Barcelona, and welcome to our home. Whatever you need, you ask," and she leans in, kisses both my cheeks, backs off, smiles, nudges Ona, "He's very cute for an American."

"Yeah, I try to find him a French girlfriend."

"No," the aunt turns her attention to me, "French girls entitled. You want a España woman. Strong woman."

"That's what I've been telling your niece for months now."

Ona does not appreciate my little game. The look. Fuck you, Ona. You wanted to play games, I can play. I can play that game. We're together. Just admit it. I have Ona's aunt's full attention. "Clever, a very suitable name," she turns back to Ona, "He's a slippery one," leans into Ona's ear. I can read her lips, "Get him before he goes home." At least, she was speaking English, so I'm sure she whispered that in English. Yeah, totally what she said. I'm the man. You're stuck with me girl. We got the love we never wanted. And it'll happen, again, and again. Love you. I want to puke. I'm so gross.

Miguel was birthed from their Dad's previous marriage. He's obviously the eldest. "We're gonna get stoned in my room, cool?" Miguel addresses his stepmom. "On the balcony, Miguel, not inside."

This apartment is tremendous, huge as shit, I can't get over the elongated, wooden rosters in the ceiling, the massive main hall plastered & stained. Vines grow on the inside. The home is warm, humid. I don't think they have air-conditioning either. All the windows are open and not a room is without at least one ceiling fan.

Wait. What did Ona need to do? Call who, school?

"Excuse me, can I use telephone?" Ona, specifically in English, asked her aunt.

Why English?
Why would you want <u>Me</u> to know?
Why
here
in
S
p
a
i
n
?
Pain. I feel so much pain in Spain
Why here, why in Spain?
Why now?

"What do you think?" I inquire after updating Miguel on what is really going on. Miguel plays it cool, stoned as he hands me the joint. His balcony looks over their shared yard. Directly across and to the side are packed in buildings. Four story apartment buildings. We're not in the center of town. A variety of colors. Pastel in nature. Blue. Pink. Purple. Orange. "Hey man, I think it's great you were there for Ona in America. I couldn't think of a more chill guy," he strokes my ego.
"I appreciate that," and I do, though I don't, because Miguel doesn't know me. You just met me.

"And girls, well you know, young girls, they don't know what they want," he makes that snapping motion without sound to request the joint back. "Oh yeah," and I pass it back, "We call that Bogarting, in the States."

"Yeah," inhale— °toke. °toke. °toke —"I know," with smoke in his lungs, "That's what I mean," exhales— COUGH, COUGH, cough —"Oh, good ganja, eh?" he asks me.

"Pretty stoney," and I take the jay.

"Usually we use Hash, but I got a joint of marijuana just for my new American friend."

"Thanks, Miguel," — °toke. °toke,

"Good to meet you,"—phew%ooooooo "Europe going to be a blast," he tells me from the cloud I've covered him in, "You'll see. Women, everywhere," takes the joint back, "You see. Women like American boys. They know you're on holiday. They never see you egocentric assholes ever again," and he laughs, and laughs. I laugh. It's funny. Funny and...fucked up.

Wait.
All Americans arn't assholes, just most.

"We're not all capitalist assholes, you know?" my stoned ass defends the flag; a flag I have only considered a total of three times in my entire life. First when I saw one at the fireworks show when I was three. Second when I got in trouble for getting the Pledge of Allegiance wrong. And now. What do I care about the American flag? What I care about is myself. Me. Who I am. What I represent. Not what my country's flag represents. "I'm not my country," I continue.

"Hey, tranquilo, amigo, I am say that all you need to do is speak American English and you get sex in five minutes here...well not Barcelona, but other girls, they're desperate for good men."

*

I'm snapped out of my visceral reaction to being dumped in Spain...but now the reality is that I still hear the faint headphone tin sound of *Jimi Hendrix*. "You really like *Jimi Hendrix*," I tell this kid. He pops off one of the earphones.

"Que?"

"You really like *Hendrix*, huh?"

"Only music I want to die too," he proclaims while he drops the headphones around his neck, still playing, now louder; his musical necklace. Miquel lowers the volume. I still hear it.

"I only listen to *Jimi*, man," Miguel gets real, "You never know when you're going to die," and he pushes on me, faking me out; four stories onto cobblestone, run over by one of those tiny cars? No, thank you, "Very funny," I retort as I catch my breath.

"No joke Mr. Kyle. If I fell off, I would at very least, have *Jimi* in my ears. I want to die in peace."

"You're over reacting."

"You want to die listening to *Phil Collins*?"

"Why would I do that?"

"You in store, like shoe store. They always play *Phil Collins*," he puts a little Hashish in a bowl, offers me the first hit. I'm stoned already. Jetlag. Weed. Depression. I'm stoned enough. "Thanks man," and I take the bowl. He offers me the lights, "Oh, yeah, thanks." I hit it.

"Bus loses breaks, moves to not hit baby, crash into shoe store. Now what?" He asks. I exhale, "Die?"

"Die listen to *Phil Collins*," he says as a matter of fact.

"Listen-ing," I correct him. He's confused. "Listening to *Phil Collins*. Not Listen to *Phil Collins*."

"Oh, I always get the i-n-g wrong. Pàsame."

"Huh?"

"The pipe. Pass to me."

"Oh, shit, I so stoned I thought you were speaking Spanish."

"I was."

—Now I'm confused.

I hand Miguel the bowl. How long have we been out here? Twenty minutes? Thirty? Where's Ona? Still on the phone?

"Mira, any way you die, *Phil Collins* could be play-ing..."

"Good, that was right," I am a proud teacher.

"Yeah, and then you die with him, not *Jimi*. I make certain I die with a little *Jimi* in my ears. So I listen, how you say? Twenty Four and Seven."

"Close enough. Dude, where's Ona?" I change the topic as he gives me the bowl back.

"No se," he answers, "Talk with Alejandro I think?"

"Is that another cousin?" I ask.

"No. Very funny, Clever. We not like that here in Spain. They do that in South America."

—Do what in South America?
Something inherently bigoted in that acknowledgement.
What don't they do here? I can't ask.
Too stoned, and besides,
I probably just misunderstood.

"You know how girls be with new boyfriends," he takes the bowl back, "Talk, talk, talk," hits the bowl.

—Did he say New Boyfriend?
You better turn that Jimi up Mr. Miguel.

"What the fuck are you talking about dude?" I'm fierce with anger.

"I don't know," he exhales, ashes it over the balcony, "I know they finally hook up in Madrid, but— Did I say something wrong?" he sees it on my face, he sees the anguish of fire and pain behind my eyes, "Oh, no, you came here for Ona? You want to be with her? Awe brother," he steps to me, I step back, "Don't touch me."

"Sorry."

"You do know <u>I am already</u> her boyfriend, right?"

"No. Ona not say that," but he believes me, "But I believe you, Clever. You my American brother. I sorry. She can be very mean."

"I can't believe this, what the fuck is going on Miguel; be honest with me," I want to hit something so fucking bad, but hold it in buddy, draw the blood of your palm with your fingernails, do not hit Miguel, Miguel is an innocent bystander, he is not to blame, he is very disappointed in Ona, ashamed, I can see that on his face, I can read this foreigner, who speaks great fucking English, "Just tell me what you know."

"Maybe I shouldn't, maybe this is between you and Ona," he really wants out of this conversation.

"No, talk to me, now," I insist.

"Alejandro's my best friend," he says right before I hit him in the nose, blood everywhere, and even though it was totally unjustified, he laughs and says, "I'm bleeding, but I still hear *Jimi*, so I not dead," and he smiles.

"What? I just hit you dude?"

"You should hit me. I would hit you, if you told me."

"You're not bullshitting me. She dumped me for your best friend?"

"No one knew you boyfriend. I would have been mad at her to bring you here like this. But it okay. We all get along. You see."

—*Not happy.*

"European girls love Americans."

—*Heard it before.*

"I be your side man. I translate for you at bars; get us laid out there on the rails."

—*Ona will be mine again.*

The sliding glass door opens. Ona, "Smell like marijuana. Vamos, we take Kyle for seafood."

"We need to talk," I say right to her.

"Don't be weird. We go eat. Vamos," and she walks away from me.

"Why didn't you say something?" I ask my defender Miguel.

"I no get involved. I *Switzerland*. Come, we eat," and now he walks away from me. If I don't follow them, then I will not eat. If I do follow them, I will kill her before we get to the restaurant; unless I disappear, snort some of that Trish powder and forget shit smells like garbage.

—YOU WILL NEVER LOVER HE LIKE I LOVE YOUR MOTHER
—DO YOU HEAR ME SON? I SAID—

What does that even mean? How far did she go with that guy? Who is he? Is he an ex she never told me about; how far did she go with that guy? Did you fuck him? Blow him? What? How far, how far did you go with that guy? Are you talking about him right now, to Miguel, as we wander through Bull-shit-a-lone-a, Spain. I had put *Bjork* in my walkman to help the madness dissipate. It was a wrong choice. I do not want to die to *Bjork*. I want to die by bus, right in front of Ona. Make her feel what it would mean to lose me forever. Where'd they go? Miguel waves me over to a restaurant across the street. I missed them cross. Who cares? They didn't, obviously. Crossed without me. Can you dedicate a suicide?

-EX-

"This is Rickardo," Ona introduces me to a twelve-year old sitting at our table. That's not all. We are all certainly not alone for seafood. There is an American girl here as well, Stacey. We were introduced first. I know what that's all about. Fuck you guys. Now who's the kid? "This is Miguel's other young brother, you not meet him at apartment. He and Stacey come with us on Round-a-bout." That's what they call it in English here. Travel Europe in a circle. Miguel's coined it Yerdopa. I have adopted the term with admiration. Rickardo is a stick. Kid needs to eat. Stacey, can eat a little less.

I'm in a dicky mood. I needed to snort more or lick it instead. I chickened out. Hadn't tested it yet. Went with caution. Bad.

—We have a caravan traveling with us now?
I don't know these people, and the stick's a pre-teen?
How much partying can we do totting a pre-teen around?
Next thing they're gonna say is the new guy's coming with us?
I'll kill her. Straight up kill her here in Barcelona under the moon.

"What do you mean coming with us?" I am getting even more New Information and I know I'm not going to like this, but hey what's to like tonight? I so do not want to get on a fucking train with her right now. "On the trains. He, Miguel, and Stacey all coming—"

Rickardo has a stupid smile on his face, I could punch it away. Stacey can tell I'm not thrilled. "It'll be fun," she interjects, "Better with a group of people."

"Just surprised," I pronounce, "This was only just supposed to be a romantic getaway for Ona and me, but she dumped me when I got off the plane, so like, whatever, the more the merrier, right?" and I walk out.

• • • •

Ona follows me out onto the street. Draw bitch, "Who the fuck is Alejandro?" I blurt out, spittle all in her face. I'm so close. In her face. No one seems to care. Spain is different. In the States, I would have been knocked silly for a threat like that. Doesn't matter. Ona isn't fazed by my anger. Ona's angry. I broke a sacred bond. I spoke of our relationship. Well too bad bitch, you're the liar here, not me. Ona's squinting, she is ferocious, she wants to tear me apart, gouge at my neck with her leopard teeth, I am the deer, she will let my neck spill, drag me aside, find me putrid, leave me alone to rot. Isn't that what you did in Mallorca? Cut me?

• • • •

"I know you over act with this," she wants to say more.
"Is that all you have to say?"
"What you want me to say? Huh?"

I wait.

"You want me say I love you forever?"

I wait.

"You know nothing. You think you so clever, you not."

I wait.

"Why you look me like that? You no speak? You always speak. Speak, speak, speak," she's going on and on. Miguel approaches her from behind, takes her arm, "Ona, come...we do this at home."

"You rude, Kyle," she says to me and goes back inside. Miguel waits for me, "You come?"

"You got a cigarette?" I ask him.

"Yeah, yeah. Have the whole pack. You come when you ready."

"I'm not going back in there."

"You come when you ready. I order you Octopus."

Nothing.

"Awe, you'll love it. Delicious here in Barcelona. Best Octopus anywhere. You'll love it. Come when you ready," and he pats me on the back, heads to the door, spins around, tosses me the lighter, salutes, and disappears back into the restaurant. I chain smoke two cigarettes as I wait for the lump in my throat to dissipate. I am hungry. Cigarettes made me hungry. I better eat now or I won't eat. I look inside. They have their meals already. So, fast. They are laughing; a good old time. I will have a good old time. I will give her the silent treatment, flirt with Stacey, and have a good old time; for now.

*

Ona gives me an ounce of respect on the walk home. We walk together, behind the others. Miguel wants to show us a park. Ona has been beside me for a number of blocks now.

"Just one question," I ask.

*

"Did you...

...cheat on me?"

"Who tell you this?"

"Who do you think?"

"Miguel?"

"Yeah, Miguel. He felt bad for me."

She's silent. Angry or cold. Solid or simmering.

"Well?" I insist on an answer to this question.

"Nothing. Miguel know nothing— You over acting," she explains.

"I am not over reacting, he called him your Boyfriend."

"You misread Miguel's English, you so stupid, Clever."

"No Ona, boyfriend means the same thing in every language."

"You mad because we not go alone in Europe," she tries to take the upper hand, "You always make it Ona and Kyle, Ona and Kyle. Now we just friends, now you Kyle, and I Ona, so now we can have other friends too."

"I'm sorry, maybe I over-reacted," I'm sheep-tired of this fight in my head, this fight in a country I'm lost in without her, in a world so compact that if I don't give in I will go crazy— fine, I'll do it, I will be *Just a Friend*, and the romance will happen when it happens.

"Ona, I'm so sorry. I'm so fucking sorry," I can't apologize enough.

— *Apologize, again.*

"I'm an idiot, I get it, I'm so sorry. Culture shock, you remember culture shock, right? You had it in when you first got to the States, remember."

"You scared too?" she asks.

— *You're breaking her down.*

"Yeah, I'm really scared," I say.

"That is why I invite Miguel. With friends, trip will be better, we can be more comfortable."

"I'm not feeling very comfortable," I confess.

"You still tired. You sleep more," and she walks away, catches up to Miguel and friends.

"I don't need more sleep...I need to wake up," I tell the gargoyle on the church we pass.

*

I'm the one who closes the door to the apartment. I'm the last one in. I'm the one on the outskirts of this tribe.

"I gotta call my parents," I tell Ona after pulling her away from Miguel who has flopped on the couch to watch Spanish TV.

"Go call. I sure they worried," she says, pushes me away, returns to the couch. I can't stop staring. What am I looking for? A hint. A hint of something more than my inner resilience to this. It's all still bullshit.

— Just friends.

Ona's Aunt has to help me use the phone. Everyone's in the living room, my couch, and I mean everyone. This family is huge. Walking past is slow motion. I catch Stacey watch me, Miguel look up from a map, at me. Aunty shows me to her bedroom.

— I should fuck Ona's Aunt. That'll show her.

"Thank you," I am a puppy dog. Up and down, by the minute. I need to balance out...she leaves, closes the door, RING . RING . "Hello?"
   "Kyle, is that you?" Mom asks. It's a spotty connection.
   "Yeah, Mom, can you hear me?"
   "Yes! Oh, Kyle are you okay? We were worried."
   "Great," yeah lie like a dog, "We're in Barcelona already."
   "Oh, I am so relieved. Why did you go early?"

— Because Ona dumped me,
broke my heart,
and now wants to prolong the pain,
by going all over Europe together as just friends.

"We want to get this party started," I lie.
   "Well don't be in a hurry, Kyle. You have a long trip, enjoy yourself," Mom blindly advises me, "Here's your father."
   "Kyle?"
   "Hey, Dad, how's the States?"
   "Still trying to impeach Clinton," he updates me about shit I don't care about, "How's Ona?"
   "Great," I lie, or maybe she is great?

She actually doesn't seem all that upset about breaking up? Right? If I think about it she's still a happier version of her American self?

Defenses.

That must be it is.

Over compensation.

"Kyle?"

"Yeah, Dad?"

"Just great? Did you meet her father?"

"Yeah, nice guy...look, I gotta go. Ona's Aunt let me use their phone, so I guess it must cost a lot?"

"Where are you going now?"

"I don't know yet, they're figuring it out."

"Nice family?"

"Yes, nice family. Her cousins are going on the trip with us."

"Why?"

"I don't really know."

"Probably better."

"I guess?"

"Don't be an asshole. You and Ona will have your humping and bumping time," he informs me about stuff I definitely do not want to think about right now.

"Yeah, whatever," I say.

"Yeah, whatever. Get off the phone, and don't forget to buy the family a present for letting my deadbeat kid sleep with their niece on their couch."

"Sure thing, Pops. Love you, bye," and I hang up.

*

I lean in over Miguel's shoulder, "So where we going?" I ask, with barely an ounce of enthusiasm, but it still spooks him. "Scare me," he says with a hold on his heart. *Jimi* around his neck, *Hey Joe*.

"Sorry. I, I asked where we're all going," and I look up and over at Ona, for acceptance. She smiles.

"This way," Miguel rotates the map, "Best route, you be very happy." He has drawn lines with a red marker all around Europe. Taps Barcelona with the end of the pen and traces the line listing off our voyage...I hear none of it...My face is a mask. My face looks at the map, shows expression, nods, all the while my eyes look up from the top of my lids at Ona. Is she fading from me? Faded. Is she a shadow of herself? Her interest is in the stars not the map. How far does she really want to go? How far away from me is far enough?

"We gotta get to Amsterdam, that is imperative because I cannot carry out of Spain."

"Makes sense," I respond, eyes off, "Amsterdam first."

"No amigo, Amsterdam is too far. We must stop first. We drink in those place."

Better wrap that 9 back around my useless penis.

"Okay."
"Madrid first."

Chapter - Su-Sussudio

The balcony before bed. A hit of hashish. Alone. A car drove by. Miguel was right. This was the sign..."*Oh, All the time, Su-Sussudio.*" I can't. I can't stop singing it. Stuck in there. Maybe what I need is, "*One more night.*"

"*Gimme.*"

"*Cause I can't live forever.*"

You know you have the lyrics wrong. Childhood memories. Come and go like repetitive songs you've memorized in the backseat of the car. Age 3. Age 5. 6. 9. 11 and you recognize the redundancy of it all. Then a new hit single. 12. 13 your choices. You seek from friends,

Mtv, CDs, mixed tapes, a lot of Modern Rock. Age 14 more Modern Rock, Alternative, what else is there? Another *Phil Collins* hit. How did I ever like him before? Age 16 and we're swapping DJ tapes from the bay. Bastardize Collins with the New York Hardcore. *Phil Collins, "One more night. Gimme one more night."* You got to test the waters. Remix. Rewind. Maybe the kid should put some headphones on? Buy a new tape. Listen more. Be attentive. Never let them see you sweat. Wash that man right out of your hair. Papa was rolling stoned, you beast of boredumb.

The metal hashish pipe knocking against the metal railing is a little louder than I wanted it to be. I stop. Cringe. The ash had popped and sprinkled out of the head. The morning sky is revealing itself. I stood here all night. Five am and I can see the sun just way out across the sea sneaking up from the horizon. It could be a good morning. *I got nothing to lose if I speak my mind / I don't care no more / I don't care anymore-ore.* I slide the glass door open, pack my bag, write a little note thanking Ona's Aunt and Uncle, write Miguel a little note, "Meet you at the coffee shop on corner," and I'm out. My time. Two hours of my time. Kyle time. No one but me. Me.

You have to take a half of pill to snap out of it. Get happy. Tie the rest around yourself again. Walk it off. Just wander a four-block radius. Don't get lost. Watch it get bright. You like Barcelona. Too bad you won't see a lot of it. With another hour and a half to kill you pull out your map, find a *Gaudi* spot and make it happen • The building looks as if it had been constructed by a giant's hand, who has toyed with a massive clump of soft clay. The form is no form at all. Makes you think of something different than Ona. Now the ƨ helps. Now you can join the choo-choo gang. And you enter the small coffee shop to seek out your friends who are not there, yet. This is not a sitting café. There only a coffee bar.

You're high•

Smilƨ

Chapter - The Tracks We Weave

"Cappuccino," I ask the barista.

"Espresso,"

"No, I want Cappuccino," I say real slow.

"Espresso!" she is angry, points at a sign, takes another person's order.

"Yes, Espresso," I tell her, and wait. She helps three other people then gives me an espresso in a tiny ceramic cup. Everyone drinks it right there at the bar. Shit. Okay, I take the sip. She holds up three fingers. I am guessing that is how much. Shit, I don't know, and I'm pushed to the side by someone else ordering and I notice it is just chaos in here.

The Ona crew's right outside in the line when I exit. Ona, Miguel, Stacey, and Sticks (*Rickardo*). "Ona," I call as I step up to them. "You have?" she asks. "Yeah, I kinda dine and ditched."

"Dine and ditchd?" she doesn't know the term.

"Didn't pay."

She whaps me, "You act like asshole," and turns her back on me. I did not play that well. I don't care; I'm high. She'll get over that. I wait for them around the corner as they get their espressos. I can see Ona and company through the corner windows of the shop. She is complaining about me. I'm kinda happy I made her mad. At least I know she still cares. "Yo," I address Miguel, and pantomime that I could use a hit. He nods, takes me around the corner gets me stoned while the others get their espressos. Ha, now I'm stoned. A little high, a little stoned, feel good again. Wish I could be high all the time. Shit bounces off me like water on latex; like I'm a fish. Sobriety and drama is like flies swarming the moist, loose, diarrhea that is you •

Cold shoulder from the coffee spot to the train station. They say it's like a subway. I don't care about a subway. "I've been on one in D.C," I cockily state to Stacey. "How big of you," she retorts. "I'm just saying, a subway out of Barcelona isn't as romantic as a boat ride into the B," I explain. "The B? Is that what they call it now?"

"Yeah, why not?"

"Cause it's stupid," Stacey says, "Drop the whole I'm better than this attitude. I know what's up. I know that bitch dumped you."

"Shit, what the fuck," I'm taken back.

"I told her it was fucking rude. That, unless you're a wife beater or something random like skitzo, then she should have told you that shit before you got on that plane."

"Thanks."

"Don't thank me. She told me to mind my own business...So, minding I am, and I'm telling you, even before we get on this subway; forget about her, have fun. Please. Or you're gonna fuck it up for me too, and I spent too much money to have a shitty time in Europe."

"Damn."

"Just minding my own business."

"Understood. Do I gotta sign some contract? Maybe my attorney can look it over first? And I have a problem with full forgetfulness. How about, partial forgetting about her, just in case, you know, she still loves me."

— *Wow, feels good to speak Ənglish like a normal person.*

"Get over it. Have fun. Fun."

And we disappear into the train station and we gotta buy tickets. Miguel orders for us. We're fumbling to give him the proper money. He stops us, pays for it, and we're going to Track 5, boarding right away. The train's packed. Standing room only. Smells bad. Body odor. Beach body odor from everyone's bags. The train pulls out, out of town, above ground, I turn to Miguel, "I thought you said this was a subway."

"Yes. Passengers to countryside. We get bigger train in Madrid. Full Eurorail trains. Not subways."

Remember you've just graduated. You are free. You can look out at the countryside of Spain and see exactly what you saw outside the car windows driving Ona around the rolling golden hills of farms along your hometown. Now things look so similar and smell so vile. Now you are unsure how free you ever were in your hometown dreaming of what was all out there. Until you met her. The beautiful girl, standing bodies away from you, with a hold of the rail, her fingernails painted a burgundy red. The girl who isn't looking at you. She watches the landscape pass her by. She is leaving. She has a smile over her sadness. Over your sadness. What is she happy about? Stacey was hard on you. Said it straight. American. No metaphor. Straight up. Kept it real. You won't believe her. Why should you? She doesn't know anything about love and neither do you. You're getting tired. Half a pill wasn't strong ənough. You are learning about walls.

Miguel brought four *Jimi* tapes. The one he's got going on now is a selection of instrumentals. "Instrumentals are better for train. Less noise. More soundtrack. Like movie," he tells me and covers his ears again. Three hours to Madrid. Two hours in and most everyone has departed. Thirty minutes to the city and a whole new lot has boarded. These people do not smell as bad, yet the old beach bags still linger in these moist, humid cars, "Why don't they air-condition the trains?"

"It is air-conditioned," Rickardo the stick tells me, points his elongated finger from his elongated arm towards the vent. You can see the dust bunnies flicker from the breeze coming from the vent. Seeing is not believing.

Chapter - Madrid

This place is not Barcelona. This place is urban. Barcelona was old school urban, Madrid seems more modern, more beat up. A lot of people. Too many cars., the buildings are new and old, eh. We've taken a cab somewhere residential. Apartment buildings. Looks like the projects. I follow the pack out of the car. The driver pops the back and we all take our own bags. I don't know where we are and nobody seems to care accept Miguel and Ona. Miguel pays the cabby. There is a hand on my bicep. Ona. She pulls me aside, "Don't get mad."

Step, by step.
    Floor after floor.
        Sixteen more steps.
            Thirty-seven steps down the hall of the fifth floor of this dormitory. Miguel has already vanished inside the suite's door. Rickardo waits for us at the closed door. "Que?" Ona says to him, pushes the Stick to the side and opens the door and goes straight in like she lives here.

*

Miguel is in the apartment, hugging on this tall guy in khakis, a button up shirt; loafers. Real preppy. Real tall. Six-two I learn. He is smiling. He is very happy to see us. Ona hugs him. Lifts her off the floor. He is happy to see her as he kisses her. He has a backpack by his feet. His backpack. This is him. This is the new boyfriend.

                  "Come!" Miguel breaks them up,
                        "We have to catch bus."

*

I have not been introduced.
                There are too many of us for one cab.
          Stacey and I go with Rickardo.
Miguel, Ona, and the giant go in another.
                        "Rickardo?"
                          "Yeah?"
                  "Who is that guy?"
            "I mind my own business."
              Stacey grits her teeth.

"Is that Miguel's best friend?"
"Yeah."
"Ona's boyfriend?"
"Maybe?"
"Don't lie to me, Rickardo."
"Why you ask? You know answer."

Chapter - Pragmatic Chaos Theory

*

Against all odds, all of them, even all the pain, all the laughter, all the shared tears...and look at me now, here in the cabin on the train there is an empty seat across from Ona and him. Ona and the dude I was finally introduced to on the platform. Miguel had made the intro. "Kyle, this is my friend Alejandro," and the thief reached out his hand, and it had no wrinkles, no age, no wisdom, nothing to fear, no more competition than myself. I gripped him strong. His hand is milquetoast. He does not know his strength.

He believes he's already won. You are in second place. Bumped from a starter to a mile away. There is a long ride ahead of you all. You'll make conversation. You'll challenge his wits to your cleverness. How is his English? But you're on the train now, and Stacey's offered you the window seat in this six seat cabin. Three opposing seats to three. A kind gesture, but that would seat you directly across from Ona who has sat beside her new Matador.

Stacey isn't a bully. She's empathetic. Maybe if you're across from them it will all go sour on them, and you get a good view. Besides, she'd rather not sit across the giant Matador, that was not a man, but, a childish bull. His rubbery, runny snout isn't sexy, it is threatening with bone protruding from either side. Even threatening to Ona. His fur is not soft, it is brittle and coarse, and yet his eyes are that of a puppy, needy. This bull is bullshit. She is threatened...

...as this over-grown polo boy tries to lay a kiss on her cheek as I sit myself beside the door. Rickardo sits between Stacey and I. Miguel slaps my hand, grabs it, "Brother you have another headphone, you put in mine. We *Jimi* to Paris together, and he releases my hand, holds out his walkman, "Maybe later," I say and check the love birds out of the corner of my eye. Ona is standoffish. She doesn't like his bullish hands. Her fight is the fight I am familiar with. Cold. She may not like this guy. Did she get pushed into this?

She won't look at you.

I won't look at   her.

*

When you wake up you can clearly see Ona's head leaning on Alejandro's shoulder. Her legs crossed with his, her arms wrapped around his waist, and they are asleep. His hand is snug between her jeans. That fucking bastard.   That bitch.

Moby's Go spins in my ears. I'm not sure what to do. I don't want to be here. Where do I want to be?

    — Over there. You could be there. That would not be here.

She's waking up. It's still dark. She cannot see me. Her motion has woken him. He cannot see me. Everyone is asleep. If I take my headphones off I would hear some *Jimi* from Miguel's headset. They are kissing. *Why are they kissing?*

They don't see you. You're in the shadows of the train. An afterthought. Left behind on the platform when you shook the thief's hand. They are in love. Two doves that have found each other during the throws of college exams. There must be some misunderstanding.

I don't want to believe anymore *Moby*. Tell me I don't have to believe anymore. I don't want to be the lyrics of a shitty love song. I don't want to be that *Phil Collins'* verse. I can't handle being a repetitive chorus. *Moby* scratch the words out. Burn the sheet music. Break the beats. Change the nostalgia.   Get me out of this cabin.

Stretch your legs. This is a terribly cramped room. Get up. Stretch. Let Ona see you. Don't look at her. Ignore her. Slide the door open, step out, into the roar of the thinner windows of the train hall. Some are half cracked, the air whistles. Let the door go, it closes on its own. It is automated. It knows it's place. Stacey has followed you out. You can hear her from behind. Tap the car door, slide. The outdoor sounds of a soaring train along the rust colored tracks. CLACKITY-CLACK. CLACKITY-DAKITY-CLACK. You can appreciate the sounds. You wait. You hold the wall. Listen. *Moby* and the CLACKITY-CLACK. Maybe you needed this. Needed to know the world does work without lyrics. You were just in a moment of manipulation. Culture Shock. Ona is not really with that guy.

---

*

Miguel steps out behind Stacey.
CLACKITY-CLACK. CLACKITY-CLACK
Miguel holds the cabin door open.
CLACKITY-CLACK

He is angry. Yelling into the cabin.

Swats them off, lets the door close.
CLACKITY-CLACK
CLACKITY-CLACK

Stacey and Miguel look at you.
CLACKITY-CLACK

You can feel them through the glass.
CLACKITY-CLACK. CLACKITY-CLACK

Empathy.
CLACKITY-CLACK

Real people.
Real people who can see real pain.
Today at least.
CLACKITY
Now
CLACK
For
You
CLACKITY-PACKITY
Poo

*

They walked me to the dining car.
We all got an overpriced baguette.

"I told her I not happy with her," Miguel tells us.
"Can you turn off the music for once," Stacey begs Miguel.

You can hear him lower the tunes. This guy will never stop *Hendrix*.
Paranoia has really gotten ahold of Miguel. But why? Do you care
about Miguel? Does he really care about you or his pride? What pride

---

"Thank you," Stacey pats Miguel's hand.
"It's fucking rude, right?" I stay on topic.
"Very," Stacey rubs my back.
"What you going to do?" Miguel asks me like there are any
options.
"Kill your best friend."

"Nah, man, I can't let you do that. Alejandro a good person. He not mean bad," Miguel tries to justify his asshole of a best buddy.

"Why don't you hop off?" Stacey offers an option.

"Then what?" I ask.

"Then you find us, uh, in Amsterdam," Miguel is proud of his plan.

"Really?"

"Why not? You got a Eurorail. You can go anywhere."

"Ditch you guys?"

"Find us," Miguel says, "But maybe in Paris not Amsterdam. We go Amsterdam after Paris. You ride train to Amsterdam with us."

You can think about this. Sleep on it. There's still ten hours until Paris. Miguel shows you both that there are a number of interesting spots between now and then. *San Sabastian* is coming up. You rolled double sixes. Hop off and fuck Liana. Yeah, fuck Liana. That is what you need right now.   Revenge.

Stacey slides the cabin door open, to no surprise, Ona, Alejandro, and Rickardo are playing a game of *Uno*. They are in full on giggle mode. The light is on, obviously. How funny can *Uno* be? They slow their giggles. "Donde esta?" Ona asks Miguel. "Dining car," he responds, then offers information I was planning on using, "Clever's gonna meet us in Paris." Stacey sits, "Deal me in," she tells Rickardo. She wants nothing to do with whatever is about to go down.

"Why?" Ona asks, waving off Alejandro's playful hands.

"Miguel says San Sebastian's next stop."

"No, you no need to go there," Ona's jealous.

"It cool. Gotta see everything," I tell her, "All the options."

"That stupid. San Sebastian is not as good as Mallorca," Ona tries to cover her jealousy with basic Spanish loyalty.

"I'll stay with Liana. Meet you in Paris...actually no, Amsterdam. I'll hang with Pierre in *Pairie*," I am calm, collected, manipulative.

"Fine, cabron," and she pouts, gets up, takes Alejandro's hand, pushes their way past me in the doorway, down the hall, out the car.

"What was that all about?" Stacey is curious now.

"That was revenge," and I slide my Aviators on and prep my escape.

Chapter - Solo; Numero Uno

The sun rises from behind the shadowed golden tan hillside— Still warm out, I've been waiting for the next train since I got off. Twenty minutes, 2 hours, two and a half hours now. The clerk said "Ses,- Six." This is a desolate train station in the far nowhere country of Spain. No farms. Grass. Golden, sun tanned grass. I've stayed awake. I can't sleep. I hopped a train. That's not the term? Skipped? Switched for sure. Hopping is when you have no ticket. "I got a ticket. I got all sorts of tickets," I say aloud to entertain myself. There are no people awaiting a train with me. Seems very rare. Is there a town?

I transcribed Liana's number onto my wrist. Didn't want to have to dig through my fanny pack with all my money, just to find the sheet of numbers. I got the important ones on that. The back of a receipt. I got Mom's, Dad's work, Ona the bitch, Liana, Pierre, & Miguel's Mom. I meander around to the other side of the station; again. Same wooden planks, same loose ones, same countryside as the other side, same brick wall, same clerk South window, same sign *Pueyo*. I wait until seven thirty.

"Why is the train late?" I ask the clerk.

"Que? No ingeles?" he responds.

"You knew English last night?"

"No se," he says sips his coffee from a paper cup.

"Train, hora?"

"Eh, Ses- Six," he says.

"Es - *(and I count under my breath)* Uno, Dose, Tres, Quatro, Sinco, Ses- Ss, Sssiete? Uh, Siete- Thirty?" oh I suck at this.

"Ses- Six," he repeats.

"No, it is now Seven Thirty. When does train come?"

He shakes his head— We are getting nowhere, I think I'm stuck waiting. How early can I call Liana?

*

I'm at the pay phone
First time I'm gonna use the phone card.
Dial the number, wait for ring, then dial PIN.
I can do that.
Liana's number. I check my wrist. Do I use the 01?
The buttons do not make a sound when I press them.
Maybe this phone doesn't work?

You will do this again. Change it up. PIN first? Follow instructions. Go forward. Do the number. Ignore the absence of sound. Wait it out. There is a clicking sound. You should put the number in. Try it without the zero one first. No, that didn't work. It was because you put the zero one, but you can't recall. This is confusing. You say aloud, "So, tired."

You're sleep deprived.

If I could only get stoned, fall asleep. Come on phone, work!

And it works, without the zero one, and you're getting that strange European ring that sounds like an all bass no treble slowed rpm of a balloon as it deflates. You can breathe now. You want Liana to pick up. You want to pick her up, but you're too tired. Depressed actually. Sucks to be left out here all alone. No one seemingly to really care about your wellbeing. No one worried they would never see you again.

You could really go for a familiar voice right now.

I step away from the phone, over to the tracks, I'm squinting,
I can hear something, a machine
I see it, something's coming— yeah, it's the train.
I'll call Liana from town.
Cross back over the tracks.
The train comes into the station.
"San Sebastian?" I ask the Conductor.
"Si, American?"
"Si."
"Passport?"
"But this is still Spain?"
"Passport."

Dig into your drawers,   show him your dick.

He takes my passport. "Um, hm."
So?
"San Sebastian?"
"Yes."
"You ticket?"

Show him   your asshole.

He takes the ticket.
"No. Ticket different train. You buy from me."
And he pulls out a ticket pad, writes me up, helps me
decipher from my loose bills.

He probably took me for a twenty spot.
Board.
Looks like the small train from Barcelona.
Take a seat. The place is empty.
Did I really need to buy a ticket?

Took you.   Sucker.

American.

•   •   •

The train leaves the station
One hour to go
It will take the train Three

•

*

.

/ You'll fall asleep. Closed eyes.
Your ears can hear the CHUGGETA, CHUGGETA of the train on the
rails. It is hypnotizing. It won't stop, just fades away as you fall
deeper and deeper into another well needed sleep. The train has
stopped, it has woken you. A group of people board. Rewrap your
pack strap around your wrist and go back to sleep. Train moves and
you sleep. The train has stopped again. You've drooled on yourself.
Can't see straight. Exhausted. There are even more passengers.
Almost two thirds full. Various ages. No children. Everyone has bags
of sorts. Beach bags, plastic bags, tote bags, backpacks, and purses.

Lady sat beside me. Now I'm awake. We've been on the
tracks for over an hour. Fuck, how long is this trip? Don't
think about Ona, think about her and you won't fall back
asleep…oh I just did it, I thought about her. Great. Real
clever; Clever. I gotta do something about that name, I gotta
take it away from her, make it mine. Give it to everyone. If it
isn't special, then it can never belong to her again; forever

more I will, alone, be known as Clever. Everyone will call me Clever. "Were you born with that name?" they'll ask.

"No. My ex killed Kyle in Mallorca. Left him to drown in a European pond with a purple arrow in his back. Clever, on the other hand, Clever swam up stream, against the flow, a different set of tracks, swarmed with arrows targeted on his back. Clever lives, longing to prosper."

"Prosper in what?"

"Pussy," callous in my egocentric loss, "Prosper in pussy. Prosper in dance, in drugs; in other people's dreams."

That's a rude thought. You are allowed two to four of those, but never more, Clever. Not your style. You are a lover, not a hater. Women are beautiful, women are inspired, women are the kindness that you seek...their body is more than all of that combined. You know this. You respect. Ona, naturally, has just pissed you the fuck off; take it out on her, not them, not us.

And the train comes to a complete stop after drifting into San Sebastian at a mile per hour. At first, I was very taken by the slow drift. I have never felt such a sensation, such a slow roll. Opium. That's what I gotta find here. Maybe in Prague. The buildings across the tracks seemed to pass by centimeters to my eyes. It has helped me contextualize centimeters as opposed to inches. I'm waking up, energized. Shit, I'm gonna see my friend Liana in a totally new city. Kinda cool, Clever. Fuck Ona, fun time. I gotta get off this train! Move already. I can see the fucking station like twenty meters ahead. Come on! I get up. I'm getting to the door. I'll be the first off. First and free. Ona killed Kyle, there is only Clever left to live. Long live Clever, Clever the Kid taking a train solo to San Sabastian to lay that pipe to Liana and make that Ona bitch cry her jealous heart out in Gay Paris— and my dick gets hard at the thought —as the train stops. Screech. Whistle. Doors. Go, Clever, go.

Chapter - Blinded in San Sebastian

—I step off the train, onto the platform; small depot, not a station. This is not a city. This is a sprawling Spanish beach town wrapped along the curve of the cove. It is beautiful. "Pardon, telephono?" I ask the first train station employee I see. I'm in a hurry. A hurry for fun. He's wearing a dark blue uniform of some sort, there's a badge but he's not a cop. Points across the station with his small spiral notebook, "Outside," and he walks away only to be stopped by another tourist. There is music playing on the platform. What is it? Oh shit...it's *Phil Collins*.

No, shit.

No, shit.

You have got to be kidding me.
Get out of this station.
Exit.

*

It's so warm out. Its gonna get hot today. I gotta get out of these torn jeans. They got a breeze, but by noon if I'm not baring skin I might as well be in *Iraq*. I look around, find the phone, try this whole thing again, no ZERO • ONE this time, I'm in town, this is not long distance. Foreign clackey, ring, three times, maybe I should—

"Hola, como esta?" a woman's voice speaks to me through the receiver. The sound is quite clear, better than San Fran's public phones.

"Uh, hola, eh, um, como se llama, Kyle. *(think)* Um, es Liana en casa?" I struggle.

"Are you looking for Liana," the woman asks me in perfect English. She must have recognized I talk Spanish like shit.

"You speak English?" I ask, innocently enough.

"Very well. You must be Kyle from Petaluma," she says so clearly into my ear, barely an accent, who is this person?

"Wow, you can pronounce Petaluma?"

"My daughter lived there for one year. Are you in town now?"

"Yeah, I'm in San Sebastian right now, just got off the train, is Liana there?" I am so stoked to talk like a normal person; to be understood clearly once again.

"I am afraid she is not here at the moment," and I hear it this time, an English accent, like from the UK. Her English is more proper than an American's.

The world is very ...

...on this side of the pond.

But what do you really know? You've been Europe side for less than a week. You haven't paid attention to much other than your broken heart. How many people outside of your circle have you even spoken too? Three, four at the most including all the train track employees. You don't know shit about this place. But if that's what you need to do to stop thinking about the cancer that has corrupted your love gene, then that's what a boy-man has to do.

"Will she be back soon?"

"She is in town. Shopping for the party. Can you call back at four o'clock?"

"Yeah, yeah, I can do that," and I look around. I don't know where to go. Probably the beach. I ask, "Where should I go?"

"San Sebastian is the most beautiful city in Spain. Everywhere you go, you will be happy."

"Okay, that's cool. I guess I'll go to the beach?"

"Yes, very nice. Lots of stores. Call at four o'clock. Say hello to Ona for me. Adios."

"Adios," I could have said with more exuberance, but she said the black magic word, Ona, and that really threw a wrench into the most beautiful city in Spain. I am here, in the most romantic coastline in the entire world and I am here without Ona; alone staring at the blue sky over the ocean's horizon.

"We do not live far," she is speaking again, "If you look at the hills, that is where we live."

"Oh, gracias."

"You are very welcome, have fun," she ends.

"Adios," I am able to say without heaving my hate all over the yellow receiver. Five hours to kill with this heavy ass backpack. I consider the idea I could ditch it in a locker at the station, but what if the beach is actually super far? Looks far. I better keep it. I just gotta do it.

Twenty blocks in and I'm sweating like a fucking pig and the backpack hasn't gotten any lighter.

*

Took a minute, but I found the Metro.
They call it El Topo; the mole.

*

I pop out across from the Civic Center, a massive old building, not ancient, I'm not impressed, geometric stale gardens, just corners of grass, walkways of beige cement, a palm in the center, other surrounding squares of lawn and another palm. The sea is just below me as it crashes against the immense stone break wall— CRASH, SWOOSH, CRASH, SWOOSH, CRASH, SWOOSH —My stomach growls.

Still hungry.

Make my way down the boardwalk, adjust my backpack with a hip kick, what do I eat? I turn into the streets. These roads are super narrow, lots of people, cobblestone road everywhere. I stay on the sidewalk. My backpack is pissing people off as my pack and I weave through the tourists. The buildings are old, lots of cement, no metal; some wood. Buildings painted in bright colors, three buildings next to each other blue, yellow, orange. We got blue-greens, reds, not many reds, more peach. I enter a Tapas spot. Everyone looks at me, all locals, no tourists, I should go. I hit up another Tapas place. They are closing? Fucking Siesta! I gotta find a place quick. So, hungry. So, hot.

I want a bakery.

I tred three more blocks. Everything is closing. No one will serve me. Busted. Now what? I walk all the way back to the beach. There has to be a tourist friendly place at the beach? I find a *Hilton Hotel*, should be a win. I go in. The dining room is closed for Siesta. The gay attendant flirts with me, tells me he can get me a good deal on a room, tells me about the Rave tonight on the beach, tells me he can get me on the list. I give him my info for the list. His name's Armando. "A lot of Spanish names start with an A, huh?" I point out. "We are the best names," he tells me. Everything in Spain is the best according to the locals. "The beach bar has appetizers, handsome."

I go to the Palm Tree Façade of a bar on the beach. There is a dozen or so tourists in their mid-fifties parked around the bar, in flowery Hawaiian shirts. We are nowhere near Hawaii. Here's my opportunity to drop this huge ass backpack, kick back on a wooden stool, okay maybe sit up straight, or just lean on the bar on this wooden stool. I take a deep breath. There is a slight breeze from the ocean. I can appreciate that. I remember, do not go swimming, you got drugs wrapped around Old Rodney. No that's not its name, but it's funny. I tap Little Old Rodney as the bartender steps up to serve me. If she had a bikini and breasts he'd be Big Old Rodney, but this bartender has Schwarzenegger pecks and an Adam's apple. "Hola, welcome to the *Hilton*, you stay with us?"

"No, I just want to order some appetizers?"

"No service to tourists. You will have to go elsewhere," in proper English.

"Ah come on man, just like a shrimp cocktail or something?"

"I cannot," he says, hoping I will just leave. I look over the few people at the bar. Canadians. That's my guess. If I knew they spoke English earlier I would have asked them to pretend I was in their cohort. Too late now. I'm going to die if I don't eat something. No one here is going to give me a hand, "What are they; Locals?" I bark at the bartender from my hunger grumps.

"They are guests of the hotel. Adios, gracias," and that's it, he turns his back on me. I have to leave. This sucks. What was that, a whole three minutes without a backpack on?

Fuck you, *Hilton*.

The bartender cleans a few glasses.
¿I leave, but where?
¿Donde esta?

*

I walked along the beach for literally 5 minutes till ditching that sandy shit for some cobblestone; backpacks and sand do not mix well with the thighs, I still need food. Need. No, I am not going to supplement my appetite. I'm not stupid.

*

I'm back in town. This place, in retrospect, is only like five blocks on a slope. This whole city slopes up from the coved beach. *Liana lives in the hills up there, huh?* The hills are completely covered in buildings, looks like all residential condos, apartments, homes, like blocks, Tetris blocks, but laid out horizontally, not stacked, each block is another step up for a giant. I am not a giant. I am a little man-boy, alone in this strange place, starving; dumped. I need a friend. Find a phone.

call early

*

"Hola, como esta?" Liana's Mom has answered
the phone again.

"Hi, it's Kyle, did Liana—"

"I told her you were here."

"Awesome."

"She said if you call early,
meet her at the *Hilton Hotel*.
Do you know where the hotel is?"

"Yeah. I passed by it," I lie.

"If you do not find her, call again at 4pm
and we will send a car for you," she offers me.

"Gracias."

"De Nada."

*

The lobby hasn't changed since I last saw it an hour ago. Strange to be somewhere familiar. Everything else I have either never seen before, or forgot as I walked back along the other side of streets. Liana spins through the revolving entrance. I see her before she sees me. I will notice her friend following her in, in a moment.

"Slut!" I yell, emboldened by over confidence and desperation for attention. I am aware I am a child. Aren't we all when the shit has hit the fan and splattered all over your face. Who is that girl with her? Liana runs over to me, leaps into my arms. Her shear force and the weight of the backpack sends us tumbling over a lounge chair. This shatters a vase, that spills flowers and dirt all over the place like a gunshot to its ceramic, as it crashes along the marble flooring. We cannot stop laughing. Liana keeps kissing my cheeks, "I miss you, Clever!!!"

At least someone cares about you. You are still a recognizable person.

Liana is only wearing a bikini top and beach-skirt. She's not as busty in an actual bikini. That's cool. She cares. "Missed you too, kid," and I give her a quick kiss on the lips. "Where Ona?" she asks. Not suspicious, not projecting, just honestly and rationally asking, "¿Donde Ona?"

"She's not here."

But we're interrupted by the security guard, "Vamos!" he barks at us. Liana lays into him. She's gone into super rich bitch mode. Her friend helps me up, dusts me off, "Come," she says; wow.

Liana notices us exiting, spits on the guard, runs after us, past us, through the revolving doors, and in a flash we're all in Liana's convertible parked in front and suddenly driving up hill to her home. I'm in the back, and I am finally having a good time. I can finally breath...and I think Liana's friend has pretty eyes, but I can't get a good look at them, yet.

The car makes a sharp turn into a round-about, half around, and out, "Kyle, this is Yasmin. She is my very best friend in whole world." Yasmin's upfront, shotgun, turns back to me, the wind whaps her face with her hair, she parts it around her ear, reaches out her slim, perfectly proportioned hand, "Hola, Kyle." I take her fingers, gently nod, and correct her, "Not Kyle. Clever."
"Clever?"
"Clever is what his girlfriend calls him."
"Very cute. I like Clever."
"Call me Clever."
"Hola, Clever."

She is gorgeous. Exotic. Not what you are used to. Ona was a delicacy as well, but that was obvious, that was home. No one looked like her at home. This girl, after days of passing by beautiful Spanish women, European girls in bikinis, this girl stands out. She is exotic to you. This is real. She is a local. This is San Sebastian. Long, long thigh level brown hair, where it coves around her hips that a thin girl should not have. She is dark skinned Spanish, emerald green eyes that match yours. Eyes that would make anyone want to get stoned. A sleek physique. You couldn't help but watch her as she had sat herself in the convertible. That was when you had a moment to truly notice her. Her figure was photograph as it came around the car door. You were in the back already. Your eyes froze. Her pose, perfect, perfectly sculpted by her long sundress, yellows, and blues. Her tanned bronze belly revealed as she too has a bikini top. Her breasts, so small, so small they are alluring; humbling in their own right. Tiny little things. Kiss, kissable. You are attracted to Yasmin. She's not your usual type, but you can feel it.

Little Old Rodney is getting frisky...just kidding...well, not really. Strangely I am mostly captivated by her nose. Her face is beautifully sculpted long, and her nose, even longer, yet proportional in some way. Like a carrot beckoning you to her. This new sexual organ, the nose, brings out her large cat eyes. I can imagine the tip of it tickle my butthole as she licks my grundle. Her weed eyes. Our Emerald Eyes. We share the same color, yet there is something terribly sexier about hers that I just can't put my finger on. Something. Maybe an invisible aroma my conscious mind can't register in the back of this convertible. Something about her. I cannot help but tell her, "We have the same eyes," and she blushes and whispers into Liana's ear, and they giggle. We all gotta roll...

"Where's Ona?" Liana yells over the music and wind.

"She dumped me."

"Nooo."

"Si. For another guy."

"No. Puta cabron. I knew she was a bitch."

*

We reach Liana's casa de wealth. Stucco, curved driveway, lots of front yard room, stone and pebbled front yard, roses, grapevines crawling along the corners of the house, a front fountain, *bet they got a pool*. Liana tells me, "Big Rave on the Beach tonight, you go with us."

Yasmin adds, "Yes you come with us, okay?"

And I answer accordingly, "Yes," and I turn to Liana and say, "Guess what Trish gave me before I left?"

*

The house is vast, with large window doors facing the ocean, and Liana leads us right through them that lead to the rectangular lap pool with open gutters along the edge, and surrounded by flat lava tile. I follow L to the other side where you look out over the entire town, downhill, towards the ocean. If you step off the side, you will fall a few stories to your death. I am not stepping forward. "You really need a railing here?"

"People know how to hold their alcohol in Spain, not like in the States," she explains. I'm not buying it. Still dangerous as fuck.

Yasmin has sat on a lounge chair. Her skirt has parted by her leg. Her leg is slim, dark; alluring. The sun is different here. Her toes are sweet in her sandals, laced around her ankle and partially up her leg. The sun Illuminates things with an orange, red tone. Almost apocalyptic, but it has no feeling of mal intent, on the contrary, it is most romantic, and Yasmin's beauty is only accentuated by this sun.

You can feel Liana watching you. She must notice you're into Yasmin. You do your best not to stare. Don't want to rock the boat. That would be less than clever. Keep your bases loaded. Luck of the draw, not the draw of luck, even though you are not attracted to Liana. Chemistry is real. Pretty doesn't equate to attraction. But you are on a journey now, different than before. Now you must experiment with Chemistry, fiddle with the finale without a Hypothesis, fr99.

"Tonight," and I feel her hand on my back, it is Liana, caught me staring at Yasmin, "You forget all about Ona." Liana wants to take care of me. "Tonight, Yasmin and me, show you a good time. Show you what Spain really like." And she's got me staring out down at the beach again, thinking...thinking that the luck of the draw may actually be a Spanish sandwich, which nobody can deny; which nobody can deny.

*

"A pleasure to meet you Kyle," Liana's mother startles us all. I could have fallen of this psychotic pool ledge to my death from that. Miss everything life could offer; without music. Miguel is no fool. I turn. Mom's a short, stout woman. Takes a moment, but I can just make out the resemblance between her and Liana. Nobody's perfect...except maybe Yasmin over there.

"Mother,

we are going to eat and then attend the party early," she adjusts her bikini, "Marcos will drive us so we can drink, bein?"

"Si," her mother is in agreement, "Ask Anna to prepare fish for Kyle," turns to me, "You like fish yes?"

"Yeah, fish is good," and Mom says something in Spanish that Liana is not happy about. Mom waves to me and disappears back into the house.

"What did she say?" I ask Liana.

"She told me she was going to Madrid tonight."

"So, what, free house; why you pissed?"

"My Dad lives in Madrid."

"Yeah, kay?"

"Cabron," Yasmin, now standing right up on us says, "Her Papa is a molestor," and spits over the edge.

"Sorry?" I say to Liana.

"No sorry. My life not yours."

"I guess I don't get it."

"Her Mom is a...uh how do you say— Gold Digger?"

Chapter - Never let the fat lady sing

There was so much traffic, Marcus the driver, has to drop us off like twenty blocks from the beach. Yasmin and I are waiting for Liana who's leans into the driver's side of the Town Car, talking to Marcus, waving her tail left and right. You can see her cheeks just under the short skirt. I point it out to Yasmin who appropriately says, "She very sexy girl."

"Will there be a lot of people tonight?" I ask.

"So many," she says, "Last month, less— but now summer, so very many people come." I nod. Have to nod. She's looking me right in the eye. Direct. That's too much. That is not the American way, Emerald Eyes   .   .
.

"You are right; we do have the same eyes," she tells me, only to be interrupted by Liana, "Okay, Marcus come back and wait; 2am he be here, but he wait till 5 if we like," and she notices Yasmin is leaning into me, "You two are cute." Shit, I didn't even notice. And as soon as all that, Liana is quick to pull her Yasmin away. I follow the girls into the foot traffic that heads toward the   beach   rave.

The closer we get,

the   thicker

and more chaotic

.becomes   crowd   the

Cars are stopped in the middle of the road as people crisscross around to get ahead, meet their friends, lost, confused, drunk, and probably already drugged. At least twenty percent of the guys don't have shirts on. They tend to sport Bermuda shorts, tennis shoes, glow stick bracelets, necklaces, and look really douche to me. I just have my black t-shirt, my torn jeans, and my Sketchers. I am not as douche. I don't bother thinking much about my attire. I am stupid though. To think the evening would cool down? Fuck me. Jeans are sticky in this 82° humidity. Yasmin pulls me through two cars, they honk at us, we're following a different group down another street, "This faster," she says to me as she lets go of my hand. Fuck she is hot, and damn this place is crazy. So many people. At least they don't smell like the train. I do however smell the ocean though, serious ocean, fish everywhere, and I think we're getting closer as we get to the docks. The line is fucking forever.

I follow my ladies along; closer and closer to the entrance. This line is like six people wide and we've walked about four blocks already and it keeps going, "I got on some list," I finally admit to Liana, "Oh a guest list? Who?"

"I don't know," I say as she makes me keep walking. Yasmin has gotten lost a few rows back talking to some friends. "Yasmin!" I yell, she kisses the hot hunk of a muther fucking shirtless guy on the cheek and catches up with us, "Homo-Javier here," she tells Liana and Liana in return tells her, "Clever say he is on a guest list."

"Who list?" she asks as she loops her arm around mine and we are all like *Dorothy* and her stooges. "Um, it was just some gay guy who worked at the *Hilton*," and Yasmin stops, and Liana stops and they look at each other, and Liana adamantly asks, "Do you bring Trish drugs?"

"Duh?"

"Okay, you give one to Armando, and he will get us VIP too," Liana instructs me.

"Who is Armando?" I ask, and they both look at me like I'm an idiot, and I simply say, "But then we're short a tab."

"I just drink, I okay, I no want the əcstasy," Liana refuses and I remember Liana's on anti-depressants, not supposed to do drugs on drugs, "Are you sure?"

"You give Armando. He give us more later," says the coolest person in my life. I misjudged Liana back in the States. Blinded by love. Liana's the real deal. She's loyal. Have I ever been loyal? Do I have a friend to be loyal too? Liana, I will be loyal to Liana. Whatever she needs, I'm there. I'm finding myself. I'm growing up. Becoming a real boy. By the time I get to *Italy* this little Old Rodney, ha, will be a

man.

*

"It's an illusion, it's a game..."
I sing, *Genesis*, as we approach the front of the line. "What is game?" Yasmin asks me. "No, nothing...just a stupid song," I tell her. "What song?" she asks.

"No, really, it's nothing."

"It Phil Collins," Liana tells her.

"I love Phil Collins!" Yasmin screams into my ear.

Really?

What's up with Europe? Finally, we've reached the front of the line. Liana says something in Spanish to the gate keeper. He points us towards a side entrance. We approach this side entrance and a very gay Spaniard in tight baby-blue short shorts, a half-shirt with a bloodshot smiley face on it, bleached short blonde hair. He is flipping through the pages of a list attached to a clipboard. His pinky sticks out like he's holding a cup of tea, "Llama?" he asks without looking up from the pages. Liana nudges me with her elbow, "Kyle, Kyle Claibourne." He looks at us, back down at his clipboard reminds himself, "Kyle?" as he scrolls the four pages of names +1(s). He stops to check his beeper. He stares at it. What's the deal? Can you just find my name? Did I even give that dude at the hotel my name? I must have, right? Shit, I don't remember. "Armando," Yasmin tells the guy.

"Armando? Blah, blah, blah," he says something Spanish to her. She nods. She looks disappointed in him. Liana is also giving him some attitude.

"You know Armando?" he asks me in English.

"Yes," I say.

"How you know Armando?"

"Uh, like long time...met him in London...I'm a promoter, from San Francisco," I lie through my teeth.

"San Francisco? I want to go. You take me home if I let you in?" he flirts with me.

"Sure, why not."

"You lie, but you cute and you know Armando," and he stamps our hands and pushes us past him. Now I'm in the lead. Follow Clever. Clever knows what's up. Clever got you two into the Rave for free; in your foreign country. Proud? Turned on? Ready to rave on? Ready to roll?~~~~~~
~~~*We run through the white draped hallway that leads right out to the beach. Sure, it's all one giant beach, but the hallway made it special. At the end of the drapes was a series of florescent colored beads. We're laughing as we break out into the night. There are a billion people on the beach; dancing, yet we are still in the VIP area which is basically the same *Hilton* bar on the beach that I've already been too, but now with white leather couches all over, and

enclosed from the main beach with more drapes; separated from the actual Rave...

...."Let's take it now?" I suggest to Yasmin, "Okay," she's ready, Liana orders us both a Rum and Cola to down it with, and we do this at the table closest to the pool, and the House Music is crazy loud, but just muffled enough from the giant cloth walls to hear each other at a loud volume. I pull out an old plastic wrap from a cigarette pack; holds 3 tablets. *Don't tell them how they got here.* I put a single tablet in Yasmin's palm. She examines the indentation with her angelic, green eyes, "I like small heart."

❥ ❧ A single heart, sliced in half by the ❤ pill cut ⊖ 🖤 ❥

"Your heart, my heart," I say as pop the tablet, raise my cup. Yasmin gently sticks her long pointy tongue out, places the pill on the tip, rolls it in, "SALUDE!"

Yasmin surprises me with a peck on the lips, "Welcome to Basque Country!" then plants one on Liana, with tongue, and that's when I see him, over Liana's shoulder; Armando from the concierge desk, now dressed in hot pink suspenders over his waxed bare chest, white slacks, and day-glow make-up. His short hair is gelled into small thorns and he's got bling rings all along his knuckles. "Hey, you are American Boy looking for appetizers," he says kissing me on both cheeks, "You are friends with Yasmin?" he asks me as Liana slides up to bat, "Hola," cheek kiss, and he turns back to Yasmin, "Muy Bonita," and he kisses her again, "Gracia," she replies, and Armando turns back to me, wraps his arm around my waist, "You come to España, to be with women?"

"Uh?"

Armando continues, presses against me, "You better off come to Spain for men. Women here will cut your balls off make you wish you were gay."

"I believe it."

"Oh you better," he winks at Liana. This reminds me, be an example of American excellence, a grateful guest, "I have a thank you gift for the guest list," I tell him.

"Oh, really?" he looks to Yasmin, she just smiles as I hand him a tab.

" ℮cstasy," I inform him.

"How exotic, American drugs," he kisses me, "Thanks Hollywood...maybe if you're high enough you'll find me later," and scampers off to his next set of guests, more tourist types. He snakes his arms around a heavy-set husband. That guy wants to give him some money for something. Armando won't take it, twists the husband's titty. The Canadian homestead wife giggles, and the husband insists. Armando takes the money, and I see Armando palm the husband something, pat the fat man on the ass and scamper away to the next. Armando is certainly distributing party favors to his guests. I guess he didn't need my ℮. "We dance before we feel it, yes?" Yasmin asks Liana.

"Yes."

"Come—"she turns me around, pushes me forward, takes Liana's hand and they run off in front of me toward the giant drapery to the VIP exit, our entrance into the main party---
----
---> Rave On

                                                                    *

                                                                                    *

                                        *

*

    *EuroHouse high-hats, dropple beats, big bass, thick bass, loooow bass, deep bass, chords, chords, synchronicity, deep bass, thousands of people smashed together, dancing on the sand. Giant lights blast rainbows in the dark sky laced with fog machines above us all, and all along the calm waters of the cove. This is some serious party. We are still meandering through the crowd. You have to dance in order to move around anywhere. I'm still following the girls, don't want to get lost, not before the э kicks in— Wow, so hard to dance and trudge through this beach sand —There are just so many people. Most of the guys aren't wearing shirts 'cause it's still 80° out, but with the mass of dancing bodies it feels like a hundred. It might be a hundred? I think I gotta take off my shit. I'm sweating so much. All the girls only have bikini tops and short loose skirts, and I swear if it gets one degree hotter these ladies are taking it all off.

If there is one thing you know now— at this rave on the beach —is that there are plenty of beautiful women populating the European pond. Maybe you don't have to be so hurt of Ona. Maybe this is why you are here.

This party's only been rolling for a good two hours...
...EuroHouse high-hats, dropple beats, big bass, thick bass, loooow bass, deep bass, chords, chords, synchronicity, deep bass, thousands of people dancing in the sand, by the sea, under the stars, with a full moon that is laughing with us. . . . .
                                                                                                      .
                                                                                                      .
                                                                                                      .
all. . . . .
and they expect another few thousand who are collected in the streets waiting to get let in. Yasmin and Liana have finally stopped closer to the shore where there are less people, more elbow room to dance. Yasmin leans into me, "I feel in my toes. Sand feel— How do you say? Soft?" and she drifts back to dance by herself. The disinhibition has begun to roll me closer, like a snowball of high on the beach into others who have begun to roll along with mэ. Happy to see Liana, happy. How cool is this, "How cool is this?" I yell over to her, "Fun!" and she keeps dancing, and I turn around to look out into the crowd. Wow, so many people, my feet going up and down, up and down, and up and down, and how did that girl feel her feet in the sand with shoes on. Who was that girl, that girl was beautiful, Ona is beautiful, I wonder if Ona is at this party, maybe I should go look for her, wow this э is kicking in fast, like super-fast. The environment will stimulate the drug, will give it the boost it

deserves, unlike on a train, or on the street— SIREN-SIREN-SIREN-SIREN —and delicate hands have begun to caress my chest from behind. I had taken my shirt off like thirty minutes ago or something, how long have I been dancing, looking at the crowd, oh those fingers feel so good, who is that, don't look— Feel. Feel it; feel the soft feather bristles trace along your chest. These hands like my pecks. I am a good-looking guy. I can't deny it. Handsome and well built. I don't play sports. I do however workout on my own. I prefer calisthenics. Whatever my body can do on its own seems more genuine to me. My penis feels fat, warm; I discreately pat a fuller Old Rodney, laugh to myself, keep dancing. Something cool on my neck; someone kissing me, licking me, suckling me, I turn. It was Yasmin, she's smiling, wiping the edge of her lips, bashful realizing what she just did, the roll has made her almost child-like about her curious actions, so I just step up to her and time shifts to our tongues slithering into each other, licking around together, skinless muscles. This is great ♫. I have never felt such smooth slippery happiness, and we gently stop kissing and she's smiling and we are dancing, solo again, and Liana is gone, where did she go? and I'm still dancing. I cannot stop dancing— SIREN - SIREN —and the beat goes— WHISTLES, WHISTLES, SCOOT, SCOOT —and the hits go on, and the sand is the fluff of the earth, and my reflection is an exotic beauty, free in the dance with her fingers as they touch herself, her legs graceful flow, up and down, off the sand, and the lights they spin upon us illuminating our reflective shadows, following our every lead, dancing with us as we dance with all of them, and the rainbows want me to eat candy and I ask Yasmin, "Do you want to eat candy?"

"Oh, you want to eat my— Uh, how you say, pussy?"

"Oh? Uh, yeah I guess so?"

...EuroHouse high-hats, dropple beats, big bass, thick bass, loooow bass, deep bass, chords, chords, synchronicity, deep bass, thousands of people dancing in the sand, by the sea, under the stars, with a full moon that is as horny as us...
. . .

...even though that is not actually what I meant, yet I feel like she translated it precisely. She was not mincing my words. She was not mishearing me. With pure mental translation under the sprinkling stars, she asked if she had heard me correctly. Read my mind. A mind I, myself, was too bashful to read for us. What is her name? Beautiful works. I will call her Yasmin. Now we stare into each other, each other's reflective pool of our own emerald eyes, and I see she is rolling hard, and I am rolling hard, and I'm getting a little twitchy eye, things are going in and out of horizontal television lines, and she says, "Yo mucho," and she points up.

She is really high.

"I know, we should sit," and I take her hand, lead her to the shoreline and she sits right before the wet sand; I have remained standing. The clouds, a few, are illuminated over the water. Reflected in the mirror that is the Ocean. The moon is brilliant, like a spotlight that illuminates me, illuminates the world; illuminates Yasmin's emerald eyes. She is watching the same scenery as eye. Eye can feel her eyes. Rolling isn't really visual, but the same dopamine that stimulates your senses, is enhancing your sight to see the movement in the stars as they gently sprinkle along the black universe surrounding us all.

Out over and in the ocean, the tide rolls slow in and out, CRASH THUNDER, a flash, in the sky, and I suddenly see the hundreds of naked people dancing in the ocean. "No way," I say aloud, "Is that really there?"

"The people?"
"Yeah."
"They there. Very short here."
"You mean shallow."
"Yes. You stand very good."
"Okay, this is the coolest party spot yet."
"Liana donde esta?"

"No se," I answer. Yasmin gets up. Catches my eyes in the illumination from the rave. "You have my eyes," she says, again, like we have never discussed this before, "I know," I say to her, and she's touching my face, outlining my eyes with her fingers, she can't stop looking into me, and by association I in her eyes, "You are so beautiful," I say, "Thank you."

"Que?"

"You are beautiful." I take her hand and we're instantly sucked into a game of playing with each other's smooth fingers, circling each other's palms, standing there nearly naked on the beach, surrounded by the constant thumping of the beat married to the pulse of our veins, like children, adolescent, wanting to fuck. The treble tickles its way up our spine, and I want to make love to this woman, make beautiful, smooth, slippery, lovely sex with this Yasmin of the Basque, "No hablo espanol," she says to me, so alluring, sexy, like she said kiss me, and I kiss her and we continue to kiss.

Do you dare, open your eyes and see your reflection in hers? Would be exquisitely intimate. You just can't top kissing this woman, this sexy, sexy girl you have just met. Hooking up with a fellow raver on the steps somewhere in the auditorium while rolling into a third hour, not intimate, just real...now is not that. You may orgasm from this all, this now. "I want," she whispers between a breath, inhibition has been replaced by instinct. Your minds are no longer calculating our minds in time— Feel it; pure and simple —it is only what our bodies feel that happens. You are a body, not a thought, we are not the thinkers of the world, Yasmin and you are the lovers of the world CRASH_THUNDER FLASH IN THE SKY your libido are drives unchecked and the lord of play has answered a prayer you hadn't requested as the sprinkling stars becomes the refreshing, sexy, piss of the clouds down upon you both, soaking you, wetting your play, raining, and the pattering on your skin. still kissing . still embraced, so sexy, so sensual, so immanent, under the thunder and lightning of a

San Sebastian storm.

...and she stops, smiles, "It raining," she says, "We go, come—" and pulls me back into the wet mobbing body of

the beach dance floor. d a n e uninterrupted
by t h e r a i n . .

●EuroHouse●●●●●●high*hats,
DrOPPLe●●●BEATS, ●●●**BIGBASS,**
THICK●**bass,** ● loooow**bass,**
deep B A S S,●chords,●chords,
synchronicity, deep bass,
thousands of people dance,
dance in the sand, dance by
the sea, dance under the stars,
dance with a full moon
under the gods golden

showers

. . . .
. . ●.
. .●.
. .

. ●

. . . powers.

Everyone is rolling. Everyone is drunk. Everyone is dancing.
There is no music. The DJ has stopped, people are lost,
where is the music, where is Liana. Yasmin will not let go of
me, I am her responsibility, we might as well be handcuffed,
but that girl, who is that girl over there, that girl is fucking

crazy hot and naked. The naked woman pulls on my hand, Yasmin let go.

The naked goddess pulls you closer, and closer, "I love you," she says and pushes you back into the crowd, the crowd, the crows, you are part of the crowd. You are them as they are all you. We are all everyone and everyone is us. We are never alone with so many people lost in the rain .

.   .   ••.

•ə.v•ə.ryon•ə   is looking for their friends, who are their friends, are their friends as high as me;

                                                    .
                                                                        •

.

Yasmin's back. Here all along. Right beside me. Pulling on my arm again; tug, tug. This •ə. and this •ə.nvironment should be packaged into a pill.•:I really have no idea where or who I am right now.• :I am not going to let go of these green eyes. "Come," she says to me. Her eyes look just like mine. Crazy. Dreamy. Esoteric. and we make a break onto the boardwalk. ••. The boardwalk is just more bodies, bodies rushing up stream, downstream, •. cross stream. ••. No dancing on the boardwalk. People here are retreating like it's acid rain. •• •. I am laughing. Lift my face to the sky, open my mouth, take tabs of tabs of Liquid LSD from the heavens; manna from the Jews, Mana from the Polynesians. I am becoming both, I am becoming •ə.v•ə.rything. Yasmin smiles. We are standing outside a •. candy store. I know what she's thinking. She is my feminine half of a perfect 69th union. Pastries. Creamy eclairs. Cherry bubbles. Wow, okay, now I remember where we left off, "We should find the car," I say to Yasmin. "Yes," she looks left, right, "I know. This direction," and she lets go of my hand, we shouldn't lose each other now, on the street heading to the Hi...• .   •
                                                        .   .   •

lton.

In this pouring rain, you can't find her again. She's gotten swept away in the mass of human ants running for cover where there is no cover. This is not rain, this is a storm. Wind, rain, lighting, thunder, hard cocks and wet pussys. There are lessons to be learned. No reason to feel things that aren't questioned first. Remember that. You can find your way. The hotel is what you know. How far could that be? It could be to your left, it could be behind you. Did you turn around?

"Hilton," you ask a passerby. They point ahead. You follow the flow, ahead. Forward. Get ahead of the curve. Don't stay behind anymore.

This is great. Spain is great. San Sabastian is forever the sexiest city I have ever been in. To forget Ona in such a fashion; couldn't ask for better. Ona. I want to sleep with Ona again. I do love her. The rain isn't letting up. Girls are losing their tops. I have had a number of nipples brush against me. Still moving forward in the middle of the street, amongst a billion bodies. The Hilton's just up ahead. Maybe you'll find Liana there. Liana's cute. Cared about me. Loyal. Remember how loyal she was today. She could suck my dick. That would be nice. Friendly. I don't want to sleep with her though. Would mean too much to her. I should try to hook up with her friend from today. I liked her. Yasmin. Yeah, Yasmin. Sexy. Sex, with Yasmin. Sex. Oh, there's there Hilton.

You can relax, ready yourself for the sex. Liana and her friend are there. They wave you over to the black car that brought us. You remember him, Marcus. "Hola, Marcus?" you say into the driver's window. "Si," he says. You stand there, so happy, getting pummeled by the rain. The two girls are in the back seat. You wave to them. "Have you been waiting long?" you ask Marcus. "Not long," he says.

"Good, good. We had a long walk. Lost them for a minute," I tell him. "Si, senior."

*

Liana's sick in the front seat.
Yasmin has her hand on me in the backseat.
She keeps looking at me.
Pats little Old Rodney.
Looks at me.
I want to kiss her. She won't let me.

*

At Liana's house the rain is still coming down; hard.
She's really sick. Drank way too much.
Marcus helps her inside.
Yasmin and I wait in the living room
as Marcus puts her to bed.
He returns fast, didn't fuck her,
"Buenos noches," he says and leaves.
Leaves us; alone.
Finally.

*

Am I still high?
Possibly. Totally.
"Warm out, swim?" Yasmin asks...
...walks away, right through the glass doors.
*

*

I have an obligation to accept

*

*

*
*
*
*
*   *   *   *through the doors, the rain is lighter, a drizzle.
She is correct, the air is warm, the sprizzle is refreshing, the
pool is not illuminated, it is a map of the stars. Yasmin
removes her clothes as she steps into the sparkling water.

First her bikini top, her small breasts, little nipple cones, so happy to feel the air, then her skirt, her panties as she submerges into the water. She is perfectly groomed. An upside down triangle; an arrow. She has disappeared. I must indulge her invitation, one *Sketcher* after the other, one pant leg after another, one pair of boxers, and I feel the water rise my little Old Rodney, and I giggle...can't get over the name. Makes me laugh. Makes me smile. Humor. Positivity positively pleasurabbbb l e as i submerge into the dark black waters .

It is
in fact
. a black bottom pool.

—————————————————————. .•••. .•.. •

Even under the surface you swim amongst the reflection of the stars. Breast stroke after tadpole stroke towards your vixen across the deep. The closer you get, the more the colors in the night sky kaleidoscope light holograms within the pool itself, along your skin, along her toe's wake. Breaking the surface, the colors snap in reverse, back to the fireworks over the shore. Blast after Blast. You are firm, not hard. The music has begun again. Miles away, along the cove. Deep Bass. Deep

Bass Echoing through the Night. .•••. •..

Bass Under Water. Bass Below. ————————————

•   •••BASSABOV•ɘ.   BASSB•ɘ.LOW•BASSABOV•ɘ.

BASSB•ɘ.LOW•BASSABOV•ɘ.•.•• • .

•   ————————————————————

Yasmin sits on the edge as you wade in the center of the universe. She is looking right at you, not the glistening rings from the water that emulates your desire with the ripples of a wake; you are awoke. She spreads her elegant legs for you. Her third eye wants you to come closer, and closer. Notice her toes as they toy with the water, making bubbles, swirling bubbles. See how her eyes lead you up her ankle, along her calf, closer to the third eye, the second mouth, the flower at the heart of the universe; waiting, impatiently as it quivers and salivates. Your own lips need to be licked, you know this need from your own tongue as it tastes the flesh of your lips as Yasmin's toe reaches over to your shoulder, her knee bends, leads you closer~glides you directly between~ her thighs ~and when you resurface from the wet milked dream, you are only moments away, yards closer, closer, nearly a few centimeters, meters, metronomes, metro-gnomes, lust tunes, sluve tune, luvswoons you as yourself floats, drifts from the current, the tide her thigh has caused to draw you closer to he.r. wet from the anticipation. he.r. thighs tremble as she is tickled by your wet hair, he.r. flower fluttering, calling, whispering, "third eye" luv you,

---

...waits, wants, since the candy on the beach, since the words slipped from her lips into mine along her second layer of lips, "Candy," and she moans as your tongue enters the most ripe, sweet, tangy, tender, taste again, this time to tingle the talent, and you love / i love Yasmin's love as it slips and lips back with licks on my face. a loving conversation deep in her heat, the warmth, the milk, the lust without a hard t, a light, firm, luscious, lubricated limb that protrudes from my head into her second mouth, in search of the Third Eye, to libble and flibble and lipple with my tonuge, her hand on my skull, we are tribal, Archaic in our actions. There is no intelligence greater than the intelligence of our chemical botany; we are flowers, snipped and dipped in a pool of water away from our commune, our tribe below still in the throes of their mating dance along the cove as she pushes me deeper , closer , my mouth membrane against the bone...she prefers the way my appendage swirls along the inside of her flesh, the inside of the inside~ harder, too "t.deep t.deep t.deep!" she begins to chant, " t.deep t.deep t.deep t.deǝ eǝ ep

---

Yasmin of the Bastian has a passionate rage, as she clenches her thighs, her muscles press your face deeper and deeper to the womb, her pelvis, a floating clavicle, expands at will, with pressure against it, expanding it, your essence...drowning in the flow of a milky way in the center of the universe and you too have cum, in the pool, and now you have cum again, purely from the sensitivity of the water molecules and levitating bubbles surrounding yourself. You have closed your eyes, just for a moment, and heard the water shift; she has slid into the pool, slid upon you, now inside of her and you fuck her, and she wants to be fucked, harder, and harder, cum or not...breath and float and kiss and wade in unison, attached, hooked, fish, tadpoles, fucking, and fucking onto the pool steps, backwards and underwater, with a hand on the guardrail as she holds her breath, limp, allowing your gyration and hook to hold her submerged engulfed, and she'll need air as you need air, and you'll breath and make your way to the hot-tub for a moment or two, and

kiss, and fuck and fuck again and you don't think of the consequences, and the chlorine's making her dry...you might be win.
.ded

I can't cum anymore. I jerk myself off under water as I lick her flower to see if I can wet her up one last time, but I won't cum anymore...she still tastes like the candy-store so I can't stop. I have left Ona for good between these thighs. I have moved on. I have a new girlfriend now. I better fuck her again so she understands what's up, and I am able to get hard again, as she milks up a little, and I carry her wrapped around me to the lounge chairs, and lover her one last time, tonight, slowly, sideways, watching the fireworks over the ocean, cumming and cumming on me. She can't stop again, I won't stop, she cums again. I have never sexed like this before. Not just the ɘ? Some of it, sometimes, other times, her eyes, when she looks at m.ɘ. Will she look at m.ɘ?

She hasn't really looked at you. Is that a problem? Would eye contact have really made a difference? If the sex was as it is, as its been, then why would eye contact make a difference, as you turn her face towards yours, she still won't look you in the eye and your hips tire... You're taken back by yourself. Have you forgotten the color of her eyes? What were they? Too dark to tell now. The fireworks keep changing the hue. Tomorrow. You can look at her eyes tomorrow.. .

...and I think my dick is soft...it is, I've slipped out of her still dripping warm vaginal lips;
        "You no like me?"

The woman you have been pleasing all night has become self-conscious. The drug has had a similar effect on you. Is that why you have shriveled back into yourself? Or was the climax of the fireworks the take down of the high. No matter, you have no stamina left. You are limp. You kiss her shoulder. She shuns you. Does not feel the same. She is cold, shivering.

The warmth of the night has gotten under our skin. I got the creepies on the skin like her. Spine stuff from ɘcstasy. Roll it off. Creepies . we must get up. Crack my back, pop.pop.pop.p.

pop.

Yasmin hasn't moved yet. She's turned away from me. Covering herself, I guess? Her backside is chemistry. A Erlenmeyer flask...lovely...under the night...lovely...in S pain.

You're a gentleman, excuse yourself to the bathroom, let her have time alone. In the shower you feel cleansed, clear, free, in love, found.

Outside, Yasmin has dipped into the pool and done her best to wash as much of your semen out of her. At least for cleanliness sake. She's been on the pill since she was sixteen. Zero abortions and proud; pees in the pool too, and giggles. She had fun with you tonight.

Did you?

"Goodnight, Clever," the sun is almost up, and we're both crashing, in separate rooms. Yasmin will sleep with Liana, you will sleep in the master bedroom since Mom's out of town. "Buenos noches," Y says as she walks away, naked, down the hall, and into Liana's room. We both jerk off for the next thirty minutes, but with no new resolution, we give in to sleep. "Goodnight, Yasmin. Love you," I say as I fall into a slumber meant for greatness. I do not miss Ona. I have had my revenge. I can see her again, a new man. For tonight I have lost a sliver of my self-identity somewhere in San Sabastian; barely a papercut from a razor's edge. Loved her .

Chapter - Got me a ticket for a Euro-Train

I wake up to Liana sucking me off. If it wasn't so unbelievable I may have believed it, but no way did she just sneak in here and do whatever she wanted. I am hard. Someone's doing a fine job. I dare not stop her. Under my covers. Could be Yasmin? Hope it's Yasmin, but this someone smells different. Smells like Liana. What if she wants to have sex? I guess I'm ready...but what about Yasmin? Ona? Oh god, Liana, my ass clenches, rock hard.er, harder, harder, and she swallows my release, all smiles, lifts her head out from under the covers, giggles. I can't believe it. Liana's smiling. "What's so funny?" I ask.

"You so surprised," she says, "I surprised you."
"You could say that."
"You sleep with Yasmin, yes?"
"Yeah."
"She my girlfriend."
"Really?"
"On and off. She says you too nice to have threesome."
"And what is this?"
"Last time I probably ever see, Clever. I give you a present, for being such good friend."
"Love you, Liana."
"Love you too, Clever. Ona will feel better soon. You see. You two true love. True love rules world."
"I know."
"I miss you. Be careful," and she licks little Old Rodney's bald head clean, slides out of the sheets; naked. She has a nice figure. I'm glad she didn't fuck me. That would have been awkward. A blowjob's not sex, a blowjob can just be friendly, like that one; very friendly, loyal.

Did that

really happen?

• you know it did •

•

You've showered. Not feeling yourself today.
You're a little off. Cloudy. Happy with a headache.
The muscles along your temples pound.
The three-minute shower did not help.
They all want you to take brief showers in
showers that barely shower in the first place.
That's why everyone is in a daze here.
They never wake up.
Siesta 'cause
showers
suck

---

*

"Buenos dias," Yasmin addresses me as I enter the kitchen. She looks entirely different. Her hair is up in a bun, her attire is that of a waitress with a name tag that reads *Hilton* hotel. She sips her cappuccino as she leans, braces herself against the counter. Make-up? I prefer her more natural. "Those drug too strong," she tells me. You don't know what to do with yourself, your hands, your feet, your stature. Should you ask for a coffee? Is there a banana or something to eat while she talks to you. "I get you less strong, today, si? When you leave?" she wants to know. "Hola," and here comes Liana. She'll kiss Yasmin first, smile at you, "Kyle, you want an espresso?"

"Yes, please."

"You work at the hotel?" I ask Yasmin.

"Si," as she puts her cup on the counter. Liana scolds her, they have a little spat, and you decide to interrupt, "How come you guys weren't on the list last night?" which catches Liana's attention, "We were. You not on list. We play a joke on you," and Yasmin quickly smirks, turns to Liana, "I go," kisses her on the lips, "I get your friend better drug from Armando. If leave before I come, you come," and with that she turns to me, "Si?"

"Yeah, yeah," I'm certain to saying yes on scoring some drugs, "Thanks," and she'll make her way over to you, kiss you on the lips, friendly enough and she's gone, and now all you want to know is when your train leaves so you can get those fancy "better" pills. What makes them better? She had said mine were too strong; yours better not be weak. Right?

*

"When do you leave?" Liana'll ask.
I'll check my fanny pack for my schedule.
2:30pm
"What time is it now?"
There's a digital clock on the microwave.
12:30
"Oh, you go now."
"Maybe there's a later train."
Noon; tomorrow.
"I have to go."
"You go with Yasmin."

"To the Hotel?"
"Yes, you like drugs. Go get them. No one check trains."
"Okay, then."

And you'll hurry to the front, but you'll miss her, and Liana will have
Marcus come to the house, take you both
And Armando will have been ready as usual
being he is the concierge of the
biggest party
you have
ever
*

"Thanks man," I am appreciative of this Armando.
50000 Pesetas. That's either $200 or more.
Feels like he gave me a lot.
Liana tells me it's a good deal.
She was on the take.
They all ate fish that night.
Fish with drinks
for
25000 Pesetas
and you know this
because it was written in the sand

*

Armando promised us his batch is not weak.
And mine? "Too much body high."
"Equal, with brain high too."
"Wouldn't that be stronger?"
"Everything in Spain stronger,"
they all said in unison.
Fucking with me at every turn. Gullible much, Clever?

*   *   *

CHOO, CHOO. CHUG-A-CHUGGA-CHUGGA. CHOO, CHOO.
CHOO, CHOO. CHUG-A-CHUGGA-CHUGGA. CHOO, CHOO.
Cooler this afternoon. Liana's been waiting by the tracks
with me. Opened up a little about her parents. Wants to go
back to America. Maybe New York, or Florida. I figure if she

wants out of here, then get out of here. "Look at me," I tell her, "Two weeks ago I was in that little town. Now," I say, and she interjects a joke, "And now you sleep with new girl and wake up with penis in other girl mouth."

"I was going to say," I correct her as she smiles at me, "Never wanting to go back?"

"You never wanted to go back when you there."

"True."

"Train," she points out the obvious as the Choo-Choo comes sliding into the station and

she kissed your
cheek.
"Love you, Clever.

Be safe.

Write me.

Save me."

Chapter - Negative Party Train to Paris

I have to smoke to manage the air in here. How did I start smoking? One here and there. Today I woke up desiring one. I found a pack on the Liana's kitchen table. Swiped it. Remembered it really. I think I bought them for Liana last night. Anyhow, glad I got them 'cause everyone is smoking on this train and fuck if I'm not. Second hand smoke is the worst. Rather smoke. The train is packed with hundreds of post-party goers from the washed-out Rave. I had to go in the bathroom, lick a fingertip of American ∍ dust just to be around them, kick this headache and exhaustion. With a burning cigarette dangled from my lip, I am still cramming my way through the aisles of the train cars looking for a place to sit. I've done this train twice now. This is another regular passenger train, two rows of couple-seats and an aisle between them, with burnt-out ravers standing in the aisle. Almost everyone has headphones on. I do not. Head hurts too much. A lot of people listen to *Blur, New Order, Modern English, ABC*; it's an eighties *Modern Rock* party in here after a zillion minutes of techno. *Phil Collins* is starting to make more sense. I have to give up looking for a seat, but Clever's not a quitter, gonna find one. Takes like twenty minutes to get from one end of the train to the other, the dining hall was tragically filled, people boozing already. This is not a party, this is hangover boozing. Keep their shit together while riding the tracks back home to where-ever and however long that is. I'm going to *Paris*. I have to meet my eX-girlfriend and her douchebag boyfriend. Maybe I should fuck Stacey? On the ∍, right in front of Ona. I'm high and mighty on myself from yesterday. Reveal is the night.

No, fuck Alejandro on ∍ in front of Ona. Tell her Alejandro wanted to teach me a thing or two. *Yeah that's the ticket...Not.*

Have you've changed? Have you lost your American ways? Have you sold out a little of your loyalty in spite and undisclosed revenge? Are you just another American common əlitist? Or are you just high? Never-mind all that, you are not sleeping with Stacey, or around. Last night was fucked. Reveal in it, but you know you totally didn't wear a condom, ask if she had anything, ask if she was on anything as you blew your load in and all over her again and again. So, what if the memory makes you powerful, you could have really fucked up last night. Don't be an idiot. You still want Ona to come back. You still love her, no matter how much it really hurts. The tears are not from exhaustion. You're tired, this is true, but face it you're fucking depressed. Your beautiful, smart, uncommon girlfriend dumped you. You fucked around, risked your life out of undisclosed revenge, and now, you'll have to face your fəancéə and she'll know. She'll know you're contaminated with shame and ecstacy. So what, she hurt you.

There are American's on this caterpillar of a motorcar. I hear 'em as I pass, perfect clear English, every now and then a New Yo'ka— and I'm almost back to the other end of the train once again when the whistle blows and we slow down, we approach a station. People shuffle, get their packs, repack their bags, down their drinks, and the train stops— *siisss* — and jerk—

stopped, and everyone,
and I mean everyone,
departs
& without a thought
I'm caught in the exodus,

STOP. Plank your feet on the platform and stop, wait it out, let them all pass, think; where are you?

where do you go from here?

and what time is it? Check your watch. Five fifteen. Check.

—inside, in the station, one long hall of a room with a seventy-five-people capacity. There are more. I am last. There is no other way. There are no exits out of this station. It is a border. The border between *Spain & France*. Passport time. This line will take forever. Music. I need music. What if a train pulls into the station, falls off the tracks? What would I want to die to? I put my backpack down, unzip it, pull out the walkman, pop the CD, *Moby self-titled*, too much, I dig for another, looking for my *Underworld* mix, I'm gonna, ah there it is, the line shifts forward, I schooch up, put the CD in, zip up my pack, but before that, touch the little baggy of pills Armando gave you, just to make sure they're safe and sound, then zip up, headphones on, and stand up, and still waiting, sixty, seventy people in my line to go—

—How much drugs do I fucking have on me?
I need to sort this out soon.
Later is not as good as before this line.
Confidence; confidence repeals suspicion—

Twenty minutes tick by; I don't bother to check my watch, I read the time by the number of tracks on the walkman window. I'm up next, actually now. All went faster than I'd imagined.

"Bonjour," I say to the woman behind the bars. She takes my Passport, "No Conductor stamp," and she slides my Passport back not stamped by her either.

"Don't you stamp it?"

"Conductor stamp, then I stamp— Next," and she is literally shooing me to the side, and the next person, a Frenchman steps up, gives his Passport, "Excuse me," I say, trying to get back to my issue at hand, they both shoot me the dirty look.

"No. Conductor stamp; then line again," and she turns back to the Frenchman and they complain about me in French that I know nothing about French besides hellos, goodbyes, and fuck...I need to do what?

—Get the Conductor to stamp my passport?
I gotta go back to the train.

So, I do that, pissed, so lame. What if I had walked? How 'bout that? She didn't ask me that? 'Cause this is not a station dumbass. Well she still made an assumption. How else did I get here if I didn't take the train? Those aren't the rules. There are rules about travel. Sometimes you must follow the rules. I'm not going to make legal assumptions like Ona. Like her assumptions we can't make it work, so she annulled the relationships while out of town by suckling the closest dick she could find to break my heart; all so I'd leave you alone to your miserable self in Europe. Too much self, Ona. That's what you have. What we all have. I lost some of myself last night. Gave it away. All over her. And I...finally find the conductor...

...stepping out for a cigarette on the Platform after I scoured that whole caterpillar of a transport.
"I need my ticket stamped?"
"We. When I finish."
Shows his smoke.
I wait. He waves me back.
I wait.
I wait.
Wait.
wait.
wait.
People really like their breaks here, sacred shit. I wait, he chain-smokes, two more, then comes to me, motions for me to give me the ticket.
I hand him the ticket he stamps it.
"Train leave in five minutes, hurry to border stamp or next tonight," checks the back of his ticket-pad, "9:30."
I'm out, back in line. The line is shorter. Three people.
I'm up. Same lady.
"Stamp, please," I request.
The attendant gives me a dirty look.

"American?"

"Yeah?"

"Where from?"
"California." — *Passport says all right there, bitch.*
"Hollywood?" she asks.
"Northern California," she waits for more specifics,

"San Francisco."

"I been to San Francisco," she tells me wasting time.

"Cool," and she gives me that dirty look again.

"I just really need to catch the train."

"San Francisco has nice bridge. I liked bridge," and she stamps my passport.

*

        This train is a train. All cabins. It's gonna be like Russian roulette when it comes to picking cabin mates. I've dodged the bullet, I've been matched with nice people from *Nicé*. Jacques and Mina? Maybe it was Nina? They're on their way to Amsterdam via Paris. Their bi-yearly jaunt to collect a ton of drugs. Told me not to worry about taking drugs out of Amsterdam. "It not hard, no one care. American myth. You just be smart, not stupid," and asks if she can see my backpack. I don't see why not? She's sweet. Twenty-two, twenty-three, bowl cut, dark eye shadow, slim physique, short, black rimmed glasses. Attractive? To some. Not my type. She feels around my bag, flips it over, shows me the bottom zipper, unzips it, pulls out a large nylon flap. "What the fuck is that?" I ask.

        I have not examined my bag as I should have. "That is to cover straps," Jacques tells me, but now she's turned out another flap of nylon, "That is where you hide drugs," he finishes. I look. There are a number of pockets on the bottom inside back. You just pull the flaps out to reveal pockets. The flap, when in place, covers the holes and keeps things from shuffling out. Score. "See. Easy," and she hands me the pack back, takes her seat, kisses her bo.

*

        I'm chilling by myself now. My cabin pals took a stroll to the dining car. I've been watching the landscape out the window. How could that last train be so packed and this so distributed. I enjoyed the chit chat. Needed to find people I could share some 9 with. Good energy. Spread the wealth. They taught me well. Sorted my stuff out. Gave them a couple pills. A dick would have given them Armando's, but I care about people, I care about their drugs. I gave them two hearts. I know the hearts aren't poison. The whole chit chat also gave me a chance to bitch about Ona, confess to cheating on her with Yasmin. Mina told me not worry. Said that "...sex on drugs doesn't count, and she's not here, so it shouldn't matter." The reminiscing, the positivity, and this stranger's blessing doesn't add up to a cocktail of revenge. I've blown my chance to lie about it. So, now what?

Watch the countryside of France pass along. Cows, sheep. *Moby* back in my ears. The houses look so different. They're so much more triangular than Northern California. Our Victorian homes are mesmerizing, these homes, not so much, no decor, designed triangular in nature. For snow. What do Californians know about snow? I know nothing. Triangle roofs atop white blocks. There are a lot of old windmills, watermills— the river we've begun gliding along is magnificent as the overcast sky reflects the river in melting silver in the shadows of brush— BLACKNESS —a tunnel, so dark, how close is the wall— LIGHT —the river's back, and we curve away from into the woods, deeper and deeper into a forested area...

...I think I have to pee.

Get to Paris in five more hours.

Call Pierre.
Ona said would speak Pierre her hotel Amsterdam.

I'm thinking in broken English.
This line for the *"luv"* is long.

Five more hours of swaying back and forth on this fucking train. My turn. "Gracias," I thank the guy exiting the bathroom. He ignores me, but now I can pee.

Chapter - Paris for a Night like this

The Paris train station might be bigger than Madrid— They just renamed this place— According to the English tourist pamphlet t'was *Gare du Lille*, but now it iz more properly titled *"Gare du Lille Flanders."* The ceiling is see through, all glass, plates of window panes, like the fossils of a building put back together with that dark brown rusted look, not rust, but darkened bone, as the glass fills in the decomposed dinosaur flesh. I think this woman's almost off the phone, looks like it as she does the hurry up hand gesture to the receiver, uh huh, get on with it, wrap it up, and she's off, "Gracias," I say step up to the phone. "Pardón," she's offended that I spoke Spanish in France. Why don't you spit upon the ground as well you *Les Misérables* spinster? —I took Ona to *Les Mis* in San Fran, that was one of the better nights. We didn't bicker once. A romantic dinner across from Union Square, walked to the theater— Foggy walk back, she loved the play, never seen a large musical before, "You are wonderful to me, Clever," and we kissed in the fog, in the center of Union Square. Ah the good old days, the days of yore. And you thought I was all SCOOT-SCOOT, DOPE-DOPE.

Nope.

I gotta call Pierre. I gotta get my fanny pack out a little bit, don't unbuckle, try to grab it— fucker creeped deep down there —think I got it with two fingers, pull up, yeah that's it. I use my other fingers to spider it up out of the lip of jeans— Wheph, I take a breath, light another cigarette. I really hate smoking, I'm gonna put it out, fuck it, take a few puffs first. This half of Armando ɘ is testing me. Popped it as we started to roll into the station...that took an entire hour. I thought it was like gonna be five, ten minutes tops. So, now I'm in the throes of the start of this alien drug —Okay, call Pierre. Get the phone card out, and the flimsy, oh so flimsy receipt I wrote everyone's numbers on. I am surely going to lose this. No, think positive, Clever. You will not get busted and you will not lose this piece of paper, and Yasmin did not have AIDS— Find Pierre's number, oh shit zip the fanny back up —Money anyone? Right here above my balls, wide open, stupid American not thinking, leaving his wiener out for everyone to grab ahold of ...Shove that fannypack back down there, okay call Pierre— ɘ, ɘ, ɘ ...Phone making same sound as San Sebastian— telling me to take more ɘ. ɘ . ɘ .This time this is going to work, I am empowered, thank you ɘ excellent, thank you Yasmin, *Mmmm, Yasmin,* "Hello Pierre?!" Okay this shit is/was strong as

fuck. it's just wearing off, now.

You don't recall the last 2 hours; train, phone, wait; but what was all that? This is awesome. You feel awesome. You see your friend. His red hair. His...

---

*

smile as he hugs me, and we spin each other around, me and the ginger of France, Pierre, outside the train station, in his Gay-Pari. "You so handsome. Gleaming!" Pierre compliments my glow. I smile; so, good to see Pierre, always sunshine. We are smiling at each other; "Hungry?"

"Not fish," I insist.

*

Outside, evening, dinner menu, Eiffel Tower right fucking over there, two, three blocks away. I think the 9's wore off; maybe since the cab ride, tired, wow train-lag? "I feel like I'm still moving," I say. "On train?" Pierre asks. He slides me a menu, "Yeah, train." Maitre d' comes, "Za Ze Le MooZe Pooze." Pierre answers, "We. Eh, un escargot, deux." The Maitre d' bows, "We, monsieur," and disappears. "You sleep with Liana?" Pierre outright asks me. "What? No? No. Ew. Why would I do that?" I gotta pee. Excuse myself to the, "Toilette."

*

*   *

I'm in here, the toilette, and hey I'm a modern guy, I'm alternative in nature, I jam with the odd and obscure, yet I have never seen a restaurant bathroom, a nice restaurant's urinal, that is just a ceramic broken tiled hole in the ground. There is no urinal, there is a tile square— One, Two, Three, Four tiles, a hole carved in the center, and yeah I can tell this is where I pee, It's obvious, and there is a bucket to wash it down, if one chooses. I'm not going to touch that bucket.

*   *

*
*
.

"You know they only have a hole to pee in?" I say to Pierre as I sit back down, take a piece of bread, eat it, there is already a bottle of wine and two half-full glasses on our table.

"We; old buildings have," Pierre answers, picking up his glass for a toast; I raise my glass, "Aren't they all old buildings?"

"Bon Jour, Clever!" Pierre says.

"Bon Jour, Pierre of Pari!" I cheer— CLINK —Snails; We indulge in shelled slugs, only after we pop an Aman pill each. I couldn't deprive my favorite Frenchman in all of Europa, "Cheers, to an əX-cəllənt əvəning!"

"No mo, Ona!" Pierre cheers; CLINK.

"I hate her," I say, "But I meant the drugs, lovey."

                              "We," Pierre says and it's back to the snails; garlic sauce soaked, dripping, delicacies of the moss— Firm flesh. You have to press the curled shell down with your index finger, while you twist and dig the rubbery, slug of meat with a tiny fine silver pitchfork. I imagine I have stabbed into Alejandro's penis; a little pop, like your pinky cracked, and the slug is on the hook, curled around the three spikes of metal, his dick so small, coated in thick, creamy garlic sauce, and six is not enough, but they're a zillion francs a piece, so six this time and a main course of Frog Legs. We finish the bottle; we're toasted, Pierre wants to take me Bowling as promised. The ə is kicking in. I know this because I suddenly keep looking for Yasmin. Where is Yasmin? Will I find her here again, in Paris? Will she follow me all around Europa? I want Yasmin. I want to taste her, not the garlic cream. She was...a dream...a dream, oh-oh what a drə.əm.

*

Six in the evening is not the Bowling Party Pierre planned, families; all families— skip it.

"I zo high," Pierre says leaning on me as we exit.

*

The Eiffel Tower line is empty; dinner time, Pierre and I make the move to see the site— High.

Pierre walks me to the elevator.

It takes us up nearly 3/4s of the way. Now ze stepz.

*
*
*

You are inside, you are outside, you are climbing up Eiffel step by metal step up, another reconstructed fossil of an architectural dinosaur, a towering beast, so massive one can climb its bones with ease. The ə is really stacking up in me,

I've collected about a hit and a half in my system, over-drive, in the past nine, ten hours— It's mellow Clever, but I feel this round is doubling up a bit, grinding my teeth, the metal is me, I feel the metal, it is the rusted cold my bones have felt under my denial since Ona stripped me of my skin. I may have felt my own skin for the last time on the beach back on her island, a land so far away from now. Sun trying to burn my naturally tanned skin. I cannot burn. My skin is leather. At least that is what I thought, until she removed her top on the beach and scolded me for looking.

WE ARE NO LONGER AN ITEM
you will never lover her like i love your mother

i suddenly feel small. inside, out. cannot even see her from this height; Ona nor Yasmin. i try, i cannot; and i have stopped over half-way up, i'm looking out over Paris, France. i am trying to see, at least, Liana over the mountain, "Long gone Clever; long gone," a farewell to the flesh, as i am here — Now — experiencing the bone, the white, tender bones of mine — *i have yet to be fossilled* — "I have yet to be fossilled!" i yell running, and running, and climbing, and running, and running, and climbing, and running, and climbing, fuck you Ona, look at me run, and running and climbing and running, ate your dick's dick, ate all that shit, and running and running and running, and fucked that girl plenty, so hot i was, and fuck you Ona; i wish you could have seen it going in and out of that flower fun, not yours; You are a wilted hurt that knows it wants me back. Back so bad. Climbing. yeah, you want it, you see it going in and out of Yasmin, holding, stroking, holding, stopped and moved, and move and move mmmm Yasmin likes it, huh Ona? Yasmin likes it. Ona wants it, but Yasmin gets it, and i'm on the top, inside, penetrating the tip of *Eiffel*, below me the expanding vagina, the vulva, Paris is the ovaries of this metallic woman, and Ona's pulling on me, she wants it, "please, please," and i'm jerking it at her face, and rubbing it and pounding it, so hard— SMACK, SMACK —and it beats against her cheeks as i stroke my fine hard, yard hard cock of a rod, and cum all over France trying to get to you, only trying to get to you Ona, and i drop my dick, snap out of it, realize what I had just done; jerked off on the Eiffel Tower. What is wrong with you? Nothing, i feel free; bigger again as I put it back into my pants, zip up, quietly, slowly, I know I'm alone up here, I can't help it, I'm so hurt, I'm so sad, I'm so high, just crying, looking down, my hand dribbles of my worthless seamen who are falling to their death below, suited up in their white hats, blue bow ties, and glistening slacks, so sad, crying, so sad, I want to cry, go home, disappear, anything, but I'm so sad, so paralyzed inside, my hand covered in my own semen

•you   will never   love her   like   i   love your mother•

I do not want to die, I will not kill myself— no need to jump, stupid —I will just disappear, become invisible like I am to her, so invisible and sad— and I look up, Pierre has not caught up to me as of yet. I wipe my hand off on my pants, then I wipe the cum off my pants and onto a low railing. I'm suddenly so sad, confused, so glad he didn't see that, so high, the 9 is too much, I gotta stop it...change the channel, flip the switch, look out at Paris again, look at the lights; tell yourself...

It is pretty out there in the world. You don't have to be blind to see that. You're stronger than you think. Moments ago, you knew your strength. Your friend beside you knows your value. He is there to show you a good time, as you had done for him. Exchange students. One of high school, this other, you, of life.

...there is a Rave down there, I can see it, red and blue lights spinning through the streets, beautiful, a few of them, like UFO Mobile Parties hover-crafting along the streets of Paris, so amazing. I'm in Paris, so beautiful, where's Pierre, I want to see that ginger, I love that ginger...Fuck it, I love 9cstacy, it's not her fault, its Ona's fault. There he is, and I hug him, "I'm so happy to be here," I say and we both look out over the beautifully lit skyline of Paris that circles this upside down female organ of a sculpture and Pierre sniffs the air,

he smells me. Of course, he does. He's fucking gay. He smiles at me, smirks, grins; knows, whispers to me
"You very bad, Clever."

     *   *   *

I'm at the train-platform, waiting again, still in Paris,
Pierre went home, it's like 2am.
Eiffel, ϱ, Wine; Walking, Walking, Train here, ϱ
Backwards is Me.
Tired, exhausted, why am I going to meet Ona and them?
I don't want to be alone out here— Not forever.
Not yet— But I'm out of friends; to visit.
I gotta meet up with them, then I sleep.
Sleep in Amsterdam.
Three Hour Trip.
Sleep to Amsterdam.

(_ . _)

Wake Up!
Don't fall asleep on the platform Clever; wrap your arm around the backpack better. Don't get robbed.
— *Come on train.*

     *

Wandering the depot. Nothing. Backpack cliques.
Too tired to mingle.
Go outside. Go back inside. Buy an espresso.
Buy another espresso. Wandering the depot.
Nothing but backpack cliques sleeping in safe circles
Go to the toilette. Pee. Poo, diarrhea from the espresso.
No more espresso tonight.

Chapter - In a Nut-Shell

Spain was warmer than Gay Paris, colder in soul though, dark deranged, heartless and cold— Ona —Fuck, you better put on a "Happy Face" for that bitch. After a couple hours of sleep, I'll be able to fake it again. Yasmin. Yasmin broke the spell until the ɘ wore off...Maybe I should eat some more? No, sleep. You need sleep. Sleep. Train sleep. Sleep, Clever, sleep.

Chapter - Schudden; *Dutch for Shake as in Shaky Hands*

WHISTLE! —wakes me the fuck up, holy shit I'm here, fucking Am-Ster-Damn foo, this place smells like weed already, and I literally just stepped off the train...I need some weed. That's been my mistake I had no control over these past few days...has it been days? I see some dude, backpack wearing fool, leaves two cone shaped joints on a platform bench. He stood them on the wide tip of these massive doobies. Where's he going? He just left them? Getting on the train? I'm right beside the joints, out in public, on the bench. Did he leave them for me? I could just swipe these. Get high. I want to get high. I have to exchange my money if I want to buy. Hmm.?

Don't be an idiot. You would never pick up two sticks on the Haight Ashbury, why the fuck would this be any different? You want to die? Do you have a death wish these days? I don't think so. Mental hop.s•c:o•t.ch and you walk away, regretful, but safe. Better safe than...

"Kyle!"

Someone's yelled for me? A stranger? A voice I have not wanted to hear for days, the girl that broke my heart, I recognize this stranger's voice.

"Hi Ona," I say, I'm not even going to bother with a Spanish hello. She hugs me, sports a black unzipped hoody, a girl's t-shirt, I feel her breasts push up against me as she gives me this good squeeze.

—*Alejandro turn gay on ya or something?*

"I so worry for you." And I push her back, not comfortable with her sudden concern for my wellbeing.

"Uh, uh. I'm not doing this," I say. I'm mad at her, friends don't press their breasts against the guy they just dumped, it just isn't Kosher girl-friend.

"You know not how to be a real friend," now she's mad at me; she's mad at me? Good we're even.

"I know plenty," I scold her.

I'm just so wrecked tired, burnt from the binge, the trains, the crazy in my head that won't stop, just negative thoughts suffocating happy memories all day, into the night, even while I was sleeping with Yasmin, even when I kissed her. I can't fight anymore, I just got tired, too tired, my fight is gone, "I'm sorry, I'm just so tired," and really need some weed.

"You sleep in our room," Ona says, and leads me out of the train station, more like a *Bart Station* than a serious train transport sort of place, but the city is right there, we're already in the middle of it all. Whole place is cobblestone, mostly pedestrian, lots of people on bikes, a trolley— "Hey, it's just like San Fran," I say to Ona except really smells like marijuana every step you take. "I see trolley already," she replies, and man I thought I was just being friendly. Give me a fucking break, what do you want from me? My shoulders are tired, I'm hunched carrying this backpack. Everyone is smoking weed in the streets, this is crazy. I light a cigarette— no, I don't. I don't have one, so I drop the pack in the street and feel a little guilty then say fuck it, be an American for once and then ask Ona, "You got a smoke?"

"Here," she hands me hers, "How Liana?" prying as we turn down a curved street, narrower, one way, no cars, pedestrian street lined with Coffee Shops everywhere; all weed bars...I gotta go to the exchange.

"She's okay. Met one of her sisters."

"Is she rich like she say?"

"Richer."

"Huh."

"Have you gotten stoned yet?"

*

Ona did not let me go to a Coffee Shop,
she wanted me straight to the room.
We're entering the small, old, run down, hotel.
"What's a Smart-Shop?"
I ask about the store across from the hotel.
"I don't know this smart shop?"
Completely dark windows; highly secretive.
Tired, go after sleep.
"What floor?"
"Three."
One.

Two.

3
301
Small; King Size.
Everyone's backpacks are on the floor.
One love-seat window couch cloaked in a knitted throw.
"Where's Miguel?" I ask dropping my backpack in a corner.
"Friends. Rickardo, Alejandro go Torture Museum, I meet"

I flop on the bed.
"I'm exhausted, I need to crash for a bit."
Not the softest of sheets and pillow.
"We come for lunch? No shower, just toilet," Ona says fixing her make-up in the mirror. "You must stink," I jest. "You not funny, Clever. We go Dresden after here." I know the schedule. "Not yet, right?" I'm looking at her ass in her jeans. Tight little butt. Yasmin had more hips; I'm sorry Ona.
I'm sorry I did that; I'll keep it
To myself...I won't
Upset you.
Like
You
Hurt
Me.
I am asleep
She is gone

I   am   asleep

I'm done sleeping, 3pm, they never came back for lunch, knew they wouldn't— wait did she leave me a room key — annoying. I'm crawling out of the bed, I had made myself comfortable mid-sleep, got under the sheets, and I see a key on the dresser and pocket it immediately. Oh yeah, no shower. *Really?* I look into the bathroom and she's right, only a sink. I wash my face, I use someone's soap, then re-rinse thinking Alejackoff probably used it. Should I just wander? Probably? Come back later see if they want to do a dinner thing, gag? 3pm? Yeah, I ain't waiting .   .   .

*

The bell on the inside of the door of the Smart Shop DING-a-LINGsss as I enter. The place is spacious, nearly empty, a few green and tan beanbag chairs, the walls are a mute tan, one long glass display case, posters of *Psilocybin Mushrooms* all over, *Alex Grey* posters, *Jimi Hendrix* playing over-head, and a white-dude with dreadlocks, dressed in casual hippy attire comes through the beaded back office, "Welcome."

"What is this place?"

"Smart Shop. We sell Psychedelics; see," and he shows me the display case; various paper packets with weight numbers and scientific names, "We have various strains of psychedelic fungus. Do you know what you like?"

"Wow, like, no; Not really? These packets have mushrooms in them?"

"No, you choose, and then I fill a packet," and he slides me a laminated menu.

The menu has photographs of each variation of shroom, and I am in awe. I had heard about the marijuana, I knew like you could do drugs here, that like no one cared, legal, but a Smart Shop? This is all new to me, I'm in a dream—

"You got *Amarula Mascura*?" I ask.

"I wish; very rare," he says.

"Even here in Europe? Doesn't it come from Russia?"

He laughs, likes that I know something, "You get for me, I make you rich," he laughs, and makes a few other suggestions, headier shrooms than others, visual strains, embryonic love state caps, and I'm ready, I'm ready to get a sample of each.

"Shit, I didn't exchange my money yet," I've got a ton of Francs, some Pesos or whatever from Spain, shit no Dutch/Netherland currency yet, I can't buy shit.

And CUT. Your movie is not playing out well ever since Ona came back into the picture. You just need to exchange some money for freedom; the American way. Buy your time, buy your trips, by

yourself.

DING-a-LING goes the door as I exit onto the cobblestone street. The hotel we're staying at has a really old sign, faded, missing a letter. Why are we staying here? I'm having a sense of boredom, I need some excitement. I'm more awake. I need a Coffee Shop, where the fuck are these guys, I want to get my Amsterdam on. I need that exchange. I don't want to wait for them, but as much as I'd like to think I can navigate a foreign country, I fear that is all in my head and everywhere I've been so far, I've had a leader, a guide, a friend. I better wait.

*

I wait in the lobby,
Pick up a Dutch magazine.
Light one of the smokes Ona left for me.
Suck it up. I can't tell if this is a rag or news.

*

Now I'm back in the room,
take a piss, drop a load,
wait for another thirty minutes,
and finally the door opens
and it's Ona's brother, Rickardo, "Hola?"

"Yup, right here bro," I get up from the floor. Alone I had been doing pushups, sit-ups, a little blood flow, stay cut; stay handsome.
"I come to get for dinner, you want to eat?"
"Finally. Yeah, but I gotta go to an exchange first," I tell him, grab my fanny-pack from the mattress, wrap it around me, stuff it down my jock.

*

"Ona says you Jew?" Alejandro tries to make conversation with me across the dinner table. We're outside on the sidewalk, right by a canal, across from a smoky Coffee Shop, still need weed, and it's kinda chilly so I'm sporting Ona's favorite blazer with a psychedelic doodle collage of faces melting into each other on the back. "Yeah, I'm sorta Jewish.

My Mom's a Jew, Dad's nuthin," I explain, as I dig into my chocolate crepes, so good, better than fish, better than the steamed lamb and boiled chicken Ona and Alejandro are barely eating. Rickardo thought I was cool to order the crepes, the sponge of a mind followed my lead, and I wonder if he will grow up to be as sheepish with women as I am, follow their lead in love.

In love. That's where you cower. That's where you struggle with your entropy. In love, you are subordinate. Alone you follow the world's flow. See your own hypocrisy? There is none. You are supposed to flow downstream. *"Life is but a dream, it's what you make it. Always try to give, don't just take it."* Sing the Harptones from a puppeteer on the corner. He has the Harptones as puppets performing the number. You are the only one at the table interested. Interested in the strings, the dolls, the song, *"Life is but a dream, and we can live it."*

"They torture a lot of Jews in Germany," Alejandro continues.

"Torture? How about killed, man," is all I have to say to that stupid shit.

"They torture here too, we go today to Museum," he says.

"Yeah, well your continent's been fucked up a lot longer than ours," I volunteer my bitter opinion, make this conversation right. Not so much as trying to piss people off, but shit, here I am stuck eating dinner with Ona and her new dick-toy. "When's Miguel getting here?" is all I care about, I need a drug buddy, get back on the flow; these goody-two-shoes suck and only want to get drunk.

"He come," Ona says picking off of Alejandro's plate; gross.

*

Miguel shows up smoking a joint, headphones just off his ears, but close enough for him to hear *Hendrix*. Pulls up a chair right by me, "Clever! Smoke, smoke son, smoke," and he puts it in my lips. Here I am, smoking weed after chocolate crepes at a restaurant table...things just got better. I exhale the toxic puff the magic dragon right into Ona and

Alejackoff's faces. Ona waves the smoke away, "You a child." Miguel's takes the j, tokes and blows...

...the smoke right at Ona.

I burst in laughter.

Ona gets up, "You both child, you play alone."

Ona takes Alejandro's hand and follows. Rickardo wants to hang with me and the Miguel. "No, they do drugs. You come with us," Ona insists.

"No. I stay," he acts out.

Miguel calms him, "Hermano, no." Rickardo tantrums out of his chair, it scrapes along the pavement, falls over, leaves it. "Spanish, Spanish, Spanish" Rickardo yells at us, times are tense, I laugh, where's Stacey? Rickardo pouts his away across the bridge. Alejandro waves bye to us as Ona pulls him. Miguel and I begin our time, alone, free.

"I need to hit a Smart-Shop."

"Closed at night."

"No?"

"No worry, I got already."

*

Miguel and I have found some park. He's pulled out two plastic baggies full of shrooms. "Two kinds, hermano," he says, "This one super, how do you say, visuals?"

"Okay cool, I like visuals. The other one heady?"

"Heady?" he doesn't know that term.

"Heady, like too much thinking."

"No, never too much think. These just very, very strong. Not good for a city. I save these for a beach."

"Cool."

-We divided the Visual Stash-

Clever	Miguel
4 Caps; 2 big, 2 small	Caps: 1 big, 1 small
6 Stems; 3 fat purples, 3 skinny whites	Stems: 2 fat purples

Miguel's taken less so he can better guide me through this alien town, "I know this place by heart; but I don't want you to recognize anything after tonight," he had said as he slid my portions over.

There is a good amount of people wandering through the park. Dusk is leading to what seems will be a very active nightlife. Everyone smokes their cone joints, kiss, laugh, take flash photos, and you remember you have some ecstasy. Should you offer it to Miguel? Hippyflip? You know at some point you will. If anywhere, Amsterdam is the there. Miguel's opened the *Evian* water, scooped up all his shrooms, filled his mouth, started to chew, took a swig, and handed you the perspiring plastic bottle. You'll hit the joint one more time then eat your dose. You will ask yourself a question. "Can you forget about being in love, now that love has cursed you like the rest of the world?" And you will let the psychedelics open doors for your adolescent mind to answer. But will you accept what you find, or will you disband yourself from your outer core and enter a state of eternal bliss? Only time will tell as long as you tell time. And if things go south, you'll flip the script.   .   .9pm

---

We finish the joint. We have plenty more.
                    Get up. The grass was a bit damp.
Exit the park.
                    Cross a bridge, tread through a residential area.
Cross another bridge.
                    Cross another bridge.
                    Cross yet another bridge.
                                        "Where are we going?" I ask.
            "Everywhere the wind sings Mary," says my guide.
"Mary-Ann with the shaky hands?" I inquire.
"Yeah, I like *The Who*, too. Yes, I'll get us to the redlight district," he tells me leading me around a bend and I stop, I feel strange, belly turns; here it comes, wave one.

****
    "Hey man," Miguel whispers into my ear..."Yeah," I ask...

****

"I think the journey is about to begin."

I puke.

Currents flow past my expanding pupils, heave, whoa, okay, take a breath, one more heave, and I breath, breath again, one more deep, deep breath, and a whiff of a freshly lit joint passes my eyes, whoa strong, step back, let out my deep breath, Miguel, smiling, exhales his toke into my face, covered in clouds, and I hear something, a tin sound of a guitar starting to strum it up, and Miguel looks me right in my emerald eyes— his are brown, dark; his pupil, a distorting void, expands right before my eyes —I can feel my own eyes widen. "We are on the journey of a lifetime...these are some of the strongest shrooms in Amsterdam." — "But I thought we took the other ones?" — "Those are even stronger." — "Fuck yeah." — "Don't get lost. Ona will kill me." — "Don't say her name." — "I got you, hermano, just you and I." — "And the shrooms." — "And the shrooms," — "Hey," I say, "You want to hippyflip?" — "No, not me. I only natural," Miguel is a purest. I am a chemist. "More for me," and I pop one of the two I had instinctually put in my front pocket for us, for a time like this. I slip the other into my coin pocket; for later.

"Astro-Man," Miguel says, as the sound of *Jimi* spins from his headphones and we begin our journey, yet again, crossing this shortening bridge, dance down a cobblestone road with *Hendrix* on 10 so I too can be safe in death. Miguel dances and drifts away, across the street, I can hear him forever, I am attached to Miguel through the sounds of the sixties. And your mind tells you that, "You'll never love her like we love our mothers," no that's not how it goes, and ha, ha, those girls waved at you, they were high, not as high as you, oh it went like, and I start singing aloud to Astro-Man, my own lyrics—

You'll never, I said never,
Love, never love,
Her— brother. Never love her,
Ne-e-ever Love Heeerrrr,
Like I lovin' your Mother.

You're hilarious, laughing at your own lyrics, so stoned, high, no visuals, everything's so bright already, what a great outlook, and Miguel's waiting for you at some corner; some Locust Bug Store,
"What up?"

"Want buy some weed?"

"Dude I am so high already," I say, so happy, have a little balanced rock to my flow. We have both forgotten about the six other joints in Miguel's side-bag. "Love how I feel, like I'm in water 'stead of the air," I say to Miguel. He's flowing too, I see it, we've both kinda zoned out looking at different things. Something has happened. I can see movement where movement should not move. I am experienced, jump start this. I close my eyes, tight, tighter, open, bright lights of night, out of focus, look to the green neon locust who cleans it's wing. Must be going somewhere, maybe preparing for a green girl fly for fun under the Amsterdam Moon sky, "Moon-Sky," I say out loud. Miguel responds, "Donde?" I turn to him, "Did you want to go in there?"

"Yeah, smoke some weed."

"Yeah man, let's smoke some weed.

Where can we do that?"

"Anywhere man,
this is Amsterdam."

You just smoked some weed. Handed it back to Miguel. Where did it go? Why do you need more? The world is becoming more predominant. Your third person is maturing in the center of your forehead. When in Rome...

"Oh man that's right this is fucking Amsterdam," and I've stepped off the curb into the street, spin myself around, and suddenly everything's all blurred and squiggly, and the lights are spun, blacks and whites, no color, where has all the color gone, and I'm being pulled back onto the curb by Mister Miguel into the Locust shaped doors of the Locust Coffee Shop, a two story building of neon green lights filled with flying neon green, glow in the dark, streams of light; living locusts. The invisible green bugs are everywhere and Miguel gets me to the bar, and the bartender says something in a non-English accent language of English, I think?— Oh Miguel's sitting down over there, a booth, I should go there; breath. One step at a time, my eyes open, tunnels, open floodgates of realism, taking in every piece of visual information I can— but something tells me this is just the be gin   ni   n   g.

                                    "When did we eat these?"
"I think like hour?"

                                                        "So, fast," I say.
"You tripping.?..g.?

        Ghost smoke locusts come to hover over our table, from where, I look, from everyone, everyone is breeding locust-ghosts from their nostrils, their mouths, ears, eyes; no one has eyes. I turn back to Miguel, he still has eyes, "So hard." He hands me a menu, the words alive like a 3-D postcard, "I can't read that dude." Miguel orders something from the waiter and two coffees show up, and I'm like, oh shit. "It is a Coffee Shop," and then guy who brought us these cups puts down another cup of six pre-rolled coned joints, Miguel pays him, and I ask the guy, "if he makes cups?"— "He ignores me," I tell myself and watch him counting the coins in his palm. I have no idea what they are doing, money? Money in America is confusing enough, how are you doing that, man? Miguel is the man, I need this guide, without him tonight I am surely— "Oh yeah, thanks," and I'm taking the joint Miguel is offering— FLASH—SO MUCH LIGHT—BLIND—
—WHERE—WHO—DARKNESS-openyoureyes...DOPAMINE
                            INJECTION IN THE SKULL...
it was just Miguel's lighter, but the flare jumpstarted that familiar feeling of the creepies. Miguel waves the flame at the tip of the J in my lips. I hit it. "I not honest," he says to me, "I give you a lot of mushrooms. You very high. These very strong."

*

Outside, minutes later, hours in counting, and you are mesmerized by this beautiful horse with such an immense facel; full snout. Miguel has to pull you away from the black police stallion. You had a moment of sanity. You had stopped tripping. You are with Miguel on some street in, "Where are we?"

"You cannot talk to police," Miguel tells you as you drift to look back over your shoulder. The horse is a block, square, and far away, behind you, "Shrooms are legal to buy, but you cannot disturb peace." Yeah, yeah, you heard him, you heard him over his redundant *Jimi Hendrix*.

Does this guy really think he is going to die with his walkman on? There are more people in this area all of a sudden. The neighborhood had become stores until the tunnel? When did we pass the tunnel? You are thinking double. Relax. Breath. Quieter here...   ...The ⁕ɘ.'s keeping you busy, buzzing around. But it's quieter here and your mood has changed, from the mood of your stranger... ...my mood, my strangers. The walking people are quiet, no one is talking, just murmurs of men who whisper into their date's ears. The girls giggle, quietly, at me. They think I'm handsome...   ...You are handsome, Clever. Look at how they giggle at you. How they prefer you to their Arian European, improperness mates...   ...This land is more residential, apartment buildings, two, three stories, and I see men against a wall, a line of sorts. Must be a club with red-lights in the windows. I've stopped in the middle of the street. There is a dance performance, shadows in the windows of the red-lights, shadows of women dancing, one shadow per window; or might they be silhouettes? "When are we?" you ask Miguel. "Red-Light district," he answers. "I know that," you say, "I want to know what the time is?" I ask him again. Red-smoke steams from the pores in the glass windows, as light shadows the performer. Beautiful black silhouette women in bikinis with shining diamond shaped eyes. I can see the whites of their eyes flirting with me as they all press themselves against the invisible walls, one by one; women who find me attractive, magnetic—

"You very handsome, Clever," Ona had told you on the bench, middle of home, beside the river. She had kissed you again. The day after she had decided to be with you. You were so happy. "So, handsome. You look like boy now, in year you be more handsome."

—smoke and red-light oozes out of the tantric trance tones of the open passageways to the dens. The cobblestone below my feet has begun to shift and bubble. The stones, obvious to the soles of my feet, move up and down, up and down. Shifting me from one passage to another. From one quest to

You must watch your step, Clever, this path across this shallow river is fraught with moving stones. The algae is slippery when wet, misty

rain upon my head. A few drops. I have to make my way to the sidewalk. That is the rationale behind the men along the wall; there they are safe from the confused, indecisive cobblestone river. The men here, safer than these undeceive misty-rain drops, unstable, unsquared pegs, bubbling in hardened mortar, with questionably larger steps, cement buttons of doom. This sidewalk is no safer. The entrance to the passage swarmed by lines of safe men. I step, one sidewalk cobblestone at a time, skip the ones with inscriptions. Everyone knows the inscriptions are traps, booby traps, boobies above, in silhouette, to distract you, to have you stumble, step on an inscription, set off the Amsterdam Nazi Torture chambers. The women above must be trapped. Prisoners, sex slaves, no, not here, not now, not in the nineties, just the ones forced to tease you into one false step so they can stretch you until your limbs— SNAP — the tendons pop like cut rubber bands, stumble against the wall, in line, bump into an Arab. He scolds me in Arabic with the soothing sounds of tantric trance misting down on us from the glowing windows directly above, misty rain drops...from the air conditioners...from her lust foamings against the window, and Miguel pulls on my shirt, "Don't walk away from me, okay?" he reminds me; in English.

"I'm not tripping so hard anymore," I tell my mate.
"Me neither," Miguel reassures me.
Which one of us is lying?

There are so many men waiting along the walls, up the stairs into the tunnels, passages, quests, for their might of a legal conquest. I am suddenly head-tripping so hard. We've gone at least a few blocks, I know this cause of crossing streets. I know this because we know this....

:...:——————————— And
how
thoughts   .   . . .past to toy with y.o ur. ... .
find their way into the: .. .. memories
creating
a Misty Rain who promises you the dreams of a world without a *Pinocchio*, with no strings attached to her puppetry, no donkey ears, no string puppets in stop.motion.animation as the drunken red nosed Rudolph pisses gold all over you, alone, here, without your girlfriend, without your friends. You are not here with your ex who is not your lover. You are not even here, even without a friend who is not a stranger; misty rain in line. You're okay, Clever. Just fuck one of these girls with a rubber. Maybe slut up with three? You're here. We're here. Nobody here but you are

everywhere
in line ——————————————————————————

. for a while now I think, though Miguel is nowhere to be found, left, probably getting high—•—oh that guy beside me is moving forward, I should follow him, one step, two steps, stop. I look at another Arab next to me, in a suit, with a tie; he does not like me, he won't look at me. I am still unsure what we all might be waiting for. Someone was telling me a story, about a boy who lied, who turned to wood, and grew inside a donkey's ass.hole, below a booty's buns...that turns me on...sexy thoughts and it's got the cobblestone bubbling again, my legs anxious, horny, still safer in this line than navigating that river across to the prostitutes across the way. That's not for me. Should be consensual...and the line moves again, and I follow. Obviously, all these other guys are waiting for something different. . I kinda wish Ona was here . . I bet she missed this exhibit . . Not a lot of girls on this side, in this line. There are a few girls in the lines across the way. Asian girls who come out of the opposing passage ways, greet the men...the line moves again, I follow. I can't see past the line as it curls into a passage a few men ahead of me. A similar passage to those across the way. But, I'm here, and those are there. With the windows above. These women so sexy dancing so slow. Are they on display? The line shifts forward again, I hope I'm not on the gay side now that I'm in the passage as an older white guy makes his way down the narrow steps out of this tunnel, past the line, and finally past me. One at a time? Time, passes as the shadows melt along the opposing stairwell wall. The longer I wait, the higher you get. Upper the stairs. Downing the stairs. Walls still move, so slowly past the stone escalator, escalating myself one man closer to the pink door, so far away as close to almost inside. How deep? Deeper? Inside. Inside what? I miss Misty. Her reign under the stars, along the beach in San Sebastian, when she kissed me before Yasmin my lover lead me deeper into ecstasy...like a flight in the day, two states too close to get any real business done, just smitten for love; alone.

I don't know anybody here. The pink door atop the final step sounds misty rain bells, like jewelry, like nipples adorned by silver rings, too delicate to chain down, and behind me, misty rain rings her bells. I want to follow...thefog—————————

.

    +
      +
          +.
          +
                        +
                                    •
  +   •   •
              +   •   .

                                          • ————————
————————————————————————————— "the misty rain bells, please," you ask the petite, blind, pretty, pretty woman who takes your hand and leads you through the door into the red hallways through drapes of raining bells, closing a web of misty rain bells behind her and leaving you naked inside, surrounded by the soothing, headier sounds of actual tantric trance and the high of the rain mist, and the hippyflip is . follow ing the bells, and you ask
"Misty?" •————————————————————————————•
    "Money?" ——————————————————————•"Yes, I

have money," you told her, honestly, respectfully, consentually. "Show me," she says in a wistful voice, "Yes," you whisper back, and yes, you are still confused...but calmed in the thick liquid bath of sounds————————————————————————————

...as I am trying to pull the fanny-pack out from inside my pants. I finally see the gentle fingers of a dainty young woman, unbuckling my belt, about to unbutton my jeans. I gently take her hands, so soft, "No," I say, and I look up into the mist, "But you wait in line?"

————————————————————————————You're in denial of a room, you are well aware you entered, and why, even if now you don't recall entering the room. You must have, you are here, with this beautiful Asian girl. She can't be older than you. She looks so soft. You are still standing. You thought you had sat on that bedded table. You hadn't. Your biological instinct is projecting. You need to give her some money, that is her request. You have, to give. . . "Would you like some ecstacy too?" and she giggles, "Second time, yes?"

"Yes, money, here," and now the fanny-pack slips right out with ease. You are capable of unzipping it, eager to hand her the bills and get this transaction over. Always so confusing, money and psychedelics. I pull out a few bills, not all, I know not to give all, but maybe this much paper? "Yes, good," says her voice, the lights have dimmed darker, the red light is off, all the lights are off, there is some light cutting through from the shade. I slide the curtain to the side, gently, with my pinky, look through the crack, the street below, the lines, the red lights in the opposing windows, sexy shadows. I wish I was in one of those rooms. If I was alone in Amsterdam, this high, I would totally be in one of those rooms. "You like?" a soft, wispy, misty Asian voice asks behind me. So soft a mist, i am instantly aroused, again. The red light dims back on, and I see only red illuminating a single mattress with tightly pulled sheets folded at the pillow, water bottles on a small nightstand, red neon snake lights slithering along the corners, up and along the ceiling above, finally aware of my sensual surroundings and the trance. "You like?" and I see her, she is not slim, not malnurited, not dead on arrival like a crackhead, like you've been scolded to imagine, to stay away, to fear the sensual freedom of the oldest profession. She has nice breasts, hips, a slim belly, in her bikini, swaying, Asian, just my height, in heels. Her face so cute, a doll. "Misty?" I ask her name. She smiles, bows her head, "You like Misty?"

"Misty rain," you tell her, and this makes her happy as she bounces over and kisses you on the mouth with a peck, peck, like rain drops, rubbing herself on your waist as her legs hold her up, wrapped around your back. "You like all? Or just mouth?"

——————————————————————— . You blink . ——
. blinked.
"You like all.
Happy, joy," she says and she pops off her top, and suddenly she isn't voluptuous, she is very small, A-cups. She looks twelve. Am I in trouble? Did I go to the wrong place? "No trouble, you pay, you pay for everything," and she turns on the mist, suddenly mist is oozing from behind the curtains, and it is soothing, and I forget there is more in her years, that, can't count, no, she's not a child, "No, no, I not little girl," she reassures me. Right? Yes. Look at those beautiful Asian eyes. She's too old to be so young...she knows, I am okay today with this woman, shapely, my height without the heels, almost motherly, but never a mother of children, a mother of men. "You will never love her like I lover your mother," Dad says. "That's right, I'm gonna cum all over this sweet-pee's head, piss in her pussy," I say aloud, "No do that," she responds, but I kiss her with a vicious, passionate revenge upon my Ona's selfishness. She kisses me back, deep tongue, ravenous. Likes it. We slow down, slower, she sits me on the table bed, her prodigious, expanding anime eyes wink, in love with me . "You," she stutters, nervous, "You kiss me like that, I let you do all thing, not only fuck, you can do all, okay, I like you, Clever."

You kiss her again. She pulls you in, touches your pants, grabs you, reacting like a pump, as she licks the inside of your mouth and squeezes your mass, her breasts begin to grow, inflate, and she has become more and more voluptuous, she is all volupt, and somehow you've wrapped yourself around her bulbous Asian body. Her entirely has blossomed, bubbled up, even her face, her chubby cheeks, her bulbous lips...

...kiss my neck, as she becomes larger and larger in the mist; not flabby overweight fat, but flesh, perfectly oversized chub flesh and I sink into her beautiful mass to kiss the mounds of love, so soft on my own huge luscious lips as my thickness is thicker in my underwear... I am still clothed ...I was never naked. Naked inside • as her panties have snapped off from her bodily growth, and she presses my fingers into her thighs, deep, deep into her thick wet lips, my massive tongue still licking upon her nipple, suckling, salivating, dribbling all over the world of flesh, my cum dribbling in her hand that had removed me earlier, "Oh, too quick," she says, "No worry, I get hard again," and she puts me upon the mattress in this strange room...I got lost there, making out with her...trippy, so very trippy with her. She has removed your shoes? I had closed my eyes for so long, maybe I dreamed, because now I am naked, my penis is warm, wet, tickled, warmed, and enlarging in her luscious lips.

You pull back, oh god, did you fuck this girl, no just her mouth, you got scared, spooked, you don't have a rubber on. She has one, she puts it on you, calms you, you are her baby tonight, she won't hurt you, "Shh, breath, you got scared. No rush, we hold, soft, breath," she tells you, curling her slim, young body against yours as you have leaned back up against the cold wallpapered wall. She strokes your belly with her fingers, you are calming down, she can't be too young, and if she is, she's probably clean. Psychedelics, so confusing sometimes. You can't fight it, have to flow, have to breath. She's right, make love to her. Slowly, lovely, sexy. Love her.

I'm feeling a bit woozy. She's so sweet, just gently playing with my outty belly button with her soft finger tips, but I'm woozy. There is a smell I'm catching up to, something odd, mildew, but different. Do they clean these rooms? Am I safe in here? What if I give something to Ona? Oh, shit, I'm not alone, where the fuck is Miguel? If he finds me in here, whoa what are you doing? She's climbed on top of you, backwards, slid you inside, she is so skinny. Not sexy. Boney back. More bones than most. So many back bones, bones where there shouldn't be bones. Hard to touch them, do they hurt her? Her pussy is boney, hard, she has no chest, no nipples...and I push her off, my dick is raging hard. I came earlier, prematurely, means I won't cum for awhile...It'll hurts, blue balls. So what. I gotta get out of here, nothing melting, everything solid, I'm not h-eye-gh anymore. You're Mind Eigh. "Jew," she says to me. She is offended, but that's low. "Fuck you," I say to her, throw my pants on, grab my shoes, nearly push her aside, but stampede past her instead. "You cum to quick, not man!" she yells as I rush out of the room, stomp my way down the stairs, "Fucked up, that was fucked up. I'm a fucking, fuck, fucked up..."

...and you're back out on the streets and you have to put your shoes back on and people are looking at you, but that passes, nobody really cares, this is Amsterdam, they've seen worse. Miguel's looking right into your eyes. You know it's him, you can hear the purple haze around him, his aurora. "What does it mean, the purple haze?" you ask him as if nothing ever happened, and he tells you that you need to put your shoes back on, and he helps you and tells you they have found you, and you wonder who they are? Mom? Dad? Were you that fucked up? Do you have to go home?

          Miguel's eyes are twisted, but someone else has her arms around my shoulder sitting on the curb. Stacey. That's the them. "How'd you find me?" I ask her. "You just popped up," she says.

*

Gondola.
Night.
Stars.
Slush of a slow oar.
Slush of a s l o w o a r .
S l u sh
S l u sh
S   l   u   sh.

                                                Gondola.

Night.
Stars.
Slush of a slow oar.
Slush of a s l o w o a r.
S l u sh
S l u sh
S l u sh.

*

"Ride's over," Miguel snaps me out of my shroom nap...Stars streak into shape. I blink, slowly. This is not over. Take a breath. "Go slow," I plead in the calmness of my physically-psychedelically mellow-ation. Stacey helps me up, slowly, leads me off the boat. Miguel on shore offers me his hand, I take it, step onto the concrete, turn, nothing different, we are in Amsterdam; I get it now. Nothing different. It's done. That was the last slip. I mellowed, tired. Are we going to bed, now? Sleep. I'm ready to stop off. Slow into the deep. Stacey's stopped at some pseudo nicer hotel than ours. Has a better façade. Etchings. Middle ages. A man on a horse over the door way. I try to make it move. It won't move. I squint harder, no sights to see...body high, close your eyes, the swirls of fractals come quick, open your eyes, do not nod off. Say goodnight. "Are you staying here?" I ask. Stacey kisses me on the cheek, "Yeah, my friends from the states are staying here." I don't know why i continue the conversation, but i do, "A lot of people in Amsterdam." She looks tired. "Lots of people in Europe," she responds. She wants to go to bed. "I don't know anybody here," i tell her. Silent moment. Did Miguel hear me? i don't know. i don't want to think about this. "You know us, Clever," she says, kisses me again, then waves goodnight, disappearing into the hotel. i feel smaller than earlier. Did i get smaller? i hope i'm not sick. i don't know, "Want to go?" i ask Miguel. "Yeah, we go now...You want to wear *Jimi*?" he offers me his headphones. i am honored. humbled. "yes, i would"... and He puts the headphones over your head, past your ears, around your neck, raises the volume, & you smile. you are not alone. i have a friend. two friends.

Miguel and I, with Stacey.

i   am not

              free

.

if i am nat

              jret

me

.

*

Chapter - Squat Life v1.0

This is not our hostel.

Miguel stops me across the street from a warehouse— we had passed some docks a few blocks back, but that's this whole place, although the canals have widened, think it's the river. Yeah, it's a river. The places around here are abandoned, covered in street art, *Andre' the Giant* has even gotten this far, spray-paint, wheat-paste, paint-pen poetry, scribbles; no tags. Miguel points out a sculpture of broken dock-wood, massive pieces stacked and leaning against each other, there is no direct interpretation, it is not a face, a body, it's not supposed to be a stack of wood, it is, what it is. Hendrix has lead us to this populated warehouse. I know its inhabited because there are various colored lights in different windows. These windows do not have naked women pining for your tourista dollars. I see shadows smoking on the roof, bikes locked up along a railing, and Miguel says, "I only know small number of people here. Everyone cool, but you American, so you only talk to people, I talk to, comprende?"

My head's so shroomy I prefer not to talk to anyone right now anyway, "Yeah man I'll just watch," I tell him, assuring him I won't start any trouble. "You tired?" he asks. "I'm cool, I'm cool," I lie, I'm tired, but I don't feel so small anymore. I feel upright, I can hang. I need to get stoned.

"You need to get stoned?" Miguel asks me.

"Read my mind, bro."

"Inside."

Miguel grabs a small rock and pries the metal door opened. Looks heavy. He opens it more with just his fingertips then palms the inside in order to safely pry it open the rest of the way. Someone has lined the door edge with a rusty line of razor blades. If you just went for it, grabbed the door to open it, you would surely slice your hands up. Clever. This is less an entrance as much as it is the door to an elevator. Old one. Kind with a gate. "Another fossil," I tell Miguel. He's not sure what I mean, presses the third floor button, lights his joint, hands it to me, I take a hit, deep, long, another, pass it back, "You're still tripping huh?" Miguel asks.

"Headtripping," I tell him, "Where are we?"

"Anarchist art squat," he explains, "I show you all that's cool in Europe."

Elevator stops, shakes. Miguel pulls the gate and walks through a curtain of corroding canvas.
                    Miguel hands the joint back to me, "Put it out."
                    I hit it, put it out with the spit on my thumb,
                    follow Miguel through the canvas curtain.

"Be cool," and he leads me
                                        to a metal stairwell,
                                            grated steps
                                              going up
                                               to the
                                                top.
                                                  .

                                                  .

                                                  .
        "This is Clever," Miguel introduces me to the four
            artists hanging in the penthouse on the roof.
            Foreman's old office. Bosses of this office.
            Now a Squat. Now Amsterdam Art.
            "You artist too?" the girl asks you.
            "I like artists," is an honest
                answer to her question,
                but so is No. Yes,
                    is better.
        "I want to be a chemist," I say instead.

I guess she's French.
                                        I sit by Miguel.

The group sparks a joint.
                                        We smoke.
They think I am something I am not.
                    Best I can do as a stranger.
A stranger is something to you that I am not.
                    These people do not give a fuck.
            Peace, Love, Art, & Anarchy is the theme.

i am going to...

...try
not to
look at the
One Girl in this room,
but Misty Rain has empowered me
to catch the eye of a hooker
that is telling, to my psyche
Stop looking over at her. She keeps
looking back at me, under that stocking cap.
Is every Girl in Europe interested in American Boys?
yes
.

Cloaked in the shadows under our dark clothes, hoodies, keeping close to the walls, Miguel and I follow his unreserved, life driven, unhome makers of the world, as they take us from roof top to roof top. It is a pastime. Tip toe on the shingles, flat foot on the squared off tops. These punks are Edmund and Keevan. The girl whom i now intend to sleep with before this night is through, is Marie...

...who you have learned doesn't speak a speck of English. It will mean nothing. Eliminate the lack of awareness from the hallucination of tonight, that you will only recall tomorrow as you feel like *Oliver Twist* sprawling rooftops, with the city's silence that allows for *Jimi* from tin headphones, reverbarate above Amsterdam at dawn. You are not in England, England; you're in Never Neverland, Clever * Pan

---

"Can we stop?" you make a request of Miguel,
"I'd like to watch the sun."

*   *

*   *

*

Miguel's waking me up, "We go," he pulls on me, "Now."
"What's the give?"
"Come," and he steps over to the door to the metal stairs that lead to the elevator. We had crashed on the roof. It's bright

out. He's waving me over. "What?" I yell at him. Miguel flips
me off and rushes through the door letting it close back
behind him. "Shit," and I gotta follow, rush, something's up.
He's holding the elevator for me.
I rush in. Tap, tap on the button. Tap, tap on the button.
The fossil comes to life. A jolt, a slow lowering,
down,
dow,
n
,
n
w
o
d
,
"What's wrong dude?"
"Their dealer's here. He has a gun."
"Where?"
"I don't know."
"What the fuck do you mean you don't know?"
"We gotta go."
"What if he's downstairs?"
"We just gotta go."
And Miguel turns up *Jimi*.
I shift the Anarchist Cookbook in my back belt.
Swiped it last night while the girl showed me their library.

I had crashed on a mattress on the roof. Remember
bumming some zillion cigarettes last night. I remember
putting them out on the mattress. Would it burn? Is the
wives' tale true? Burned one on my palm. That hurt. Still
hurts. At the bottom, bottom right of the palm, well aligned
with my life line. Life line? I really don't know. Never really
bought into that palm reading stuff. Only when I'm tripping.
I was tripping last night; hard. So, hard. Miguel asks to bum
a smoke from me as the elevator continues down. "I don't
have any smokes?" you tell him. "You smoke all?" he accuses
me. So, you pat down your pockets to see if you
remembered it all incorrectly. You have a pack, you pull it
out, there is one broken one left. "No shit," and the elevator

stops. Silence. "You want the smoke?" —but he shushes you. That's right...you're in commando mode. Someone out there might be a killer. God my head hurts. "I think I banged a hooker last night," I tell Miguel. "Dude, shhh," and he opens the gate, quietly, steps out, quieter. The elevator starts to move. He hadn't held the gate; it closed, triggered the dead dinosaur before I exited, and the elevator started to rise. He's freaking, in silent. I am going up. He's out of sight, you're fucked.

.

. .   .   .**Chapter - Squat Life v1.1**

"Am I sexy, you will know," was the only English that girl knew last night. You had thought she was hitting on you, she wasn't. She was gay, but that was the only English she spoke all night. Very strange. "Am I sexy, you will know," again and again, and now the elevator stops on the second floor. Your head is spun. Clouded. When did Clever sleep. Is he really in trouble? What is trouble? A bulky guy enters the elevator with a skinny punk. You scoot left, closer to the gate once they've taken foot inside. The punk's got small liberty spikes, green, sharp, like needles. The big guy is crying,

he is also holding a gun, and when he speaks, he speaks in Dutch, but when he speaks you can hear a lisp, you can sense he is A-typical, odd; slow perhaps? He has the gun. A pistol. Nothing fancy. Small in his fat fingers. Starts waving it at the punk, saying something, crying. They don't notice you. You can decipher enough to imagine the big guy's saying no more than, "You, not you, you do something, something, no you, not you. something-something. no, no," and the more it goes on the more forgiving the green punk becomes, staying his distance, pleading for the guy to lower the guy. They are friends...otherwise you'd be spooked...as you wipe your brow, turn your back on them, "No, No," he starts yelling again; BANG•

———————————————— beat   ————BANG•—BANG•————

— BANG•————————— and I can hear him lower the gun, feel it. The smell of gun powder. Stop. Everything stop. Just...

Stop.

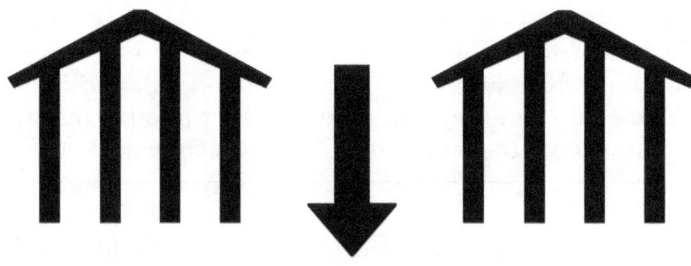

·

The lift has stopped; top floor. You step aside to let the killer exit. He apologizes to his friends in the loft, steps out, the gate closes; you haven't dared turn your back. You don't want to see it, and you don't want <u>them</u> to see their sacred book in your pants. This is all bad. Stealth mode presses the down button and you can hear the hollering above as the stampede of anarchist friends rush to the lift to see who pressed the button, but it's too late, their sight has been impaired by the roof of the elevator, and you will rush that first floor, push Miguel out the door, "Run for your life!" and pass Miguel as you rush yourself back into the city, anywhere. Anywhere but there, anywhere but death, "Voodoo Child! Voodoo Child!" you instinctually scream, because you are afraid you are going to die and you want Miguel to follow you. Because you had turned around— before you got off, you turned around —death at your feet. Blood on your shoes. Death in your brain. Chemistry extinguished through the biological breakdown of a single metal bullet through a young man's neck.

— Accidentally?

And you're far enough away. Far enough not to be caught. He never even noticed you. You even felt invisible in that lift. Breathe. You survived. You heard a man die. . Forget . about . that . You are not emotionally matured enough to deal with that in a foreign language, foreign land, witnessing the struggle of a man's improper brain development. He really did not know what he was doing. .. very sad .

—Miguel should eat some 9 with me.

And your only friend catches up with you, and you already have your defense mechanism in the palm of your hand, and he walks up to you, "You okay?" and you put one pill right into his mouth and he eats it as you take yours, and admit, "Saw someone get shot."

—But I turned our cloud upside down.

He knows. He heard it. He saw the body. "What did you put in my mouth?"

"Ecstasy."

"I deserve that."

"Don't get me almost killed again."

"Welcome to Europe."

"Have a nice trip."

"Did you like the shrooms?"

"I did."

*

"I stole this from their library," I tell him, full of truths after looking death in the guts. He takes *The Anarchist Cookbook* from my hands. "English?"

"I'm not gonna steal a Danish version."

"Good book, but I am a socialist," he says handing it back to me.

*

"Where we going?"

"Van Gough Exhibit." Miguel crosses a bridge. I'm close behind, took a moment to look down the canal...enjoy something again. "Why?" I ask him. "Mira, Ona, Alejandro...Stacey," and he turns a stoned corner. Stone, brick, cobble, whatever; not high. I need a hit. "Can I get a joint?" and Miguel stops, flips his side-bag around his waist, unzips a flap, pulls out a perfect cone, hands it to

your cloudy head, my pill is going to take some time to wake me up, and Miguel's lit it, just like that. I don't need this, I need to breath...so many cigarettes. I take another hit. "I've never seen a *Van Gough*. He paints the weird square people; right?"

"Wrong," Miguel corrects me, pointing to his ear.

"Is Ona really going to be there?" cough, "Here," pass it back to Miguel, "I really rather go to sleep."

"Sleep? You give me the ϑ, <u>hermano</u>."

Chapter - Balancing Regret and the Future

                                                          —moving along
to the next room in this small gallery, Ona wraps her arm
around Alejandro's waist, he's too tall to lean her head on,
she just leans into his lanky-longness as they cross through
the next doorway. This is not a museum. They called it a
museum. This is an art gallery. These are prints, not
paintings.—this ǝ is rǝally ǝrrǝtating mǝ—.Miguel seems fine
talking up the cashier in the front room. I'm not going to
linger around the love birds no more, I'll look at this *print*
longer, *The Sower, 1888*, that's not so old; field of lavender?

    I   am   highly   allergic   to   lavender,
the site of the flower irks me. Could be lavender? Might as
well be. NEGATIVE ǝ why stop here, he tore off his ear off
for a woman. .   .

. . .I have done Nothing.
I am looking at a pathetic print; 15,007 of 100,000. Turn the bend, the cheaters are embraced, so romantic, allowing him to shove his tongue down your throat in the middle of a cheap knock-off of a museum, in front of me, "What's up?" I ask, Ona pushes Alejandro off, embarrassed. Alejandro's face is covered in soot. He is angry.

You are a pathetic, jealous, entitled, American asshole.

"I'm gonna smoke outside," I tell them, strut off, cut a fart.

...There is no time to argue. You're better off letting them be happy in their own perish. You suddenly have a more positive attitude. The dope drop has triggered your reward circuits. You know you have an escape from the stagnant still life of falling in love...last night...the still crumbling, stained statues behind the gates and mortgages, behind the neighbors to the left of you and acquaintances to the right of you, behind your back fence, the kids in school for a lifetime, remembering you as their mother. If that makes you happy Ona, you are that what you need to be. .   . •w i t h ou t
————————————————————————————— me.

i can be free. i have my own ꭱ. My own dopamine. Love you ꭱ. Love you, too, Kyle. You said my name. i never say my name anymore. i'll get us a souvenir. A magnet, *Van Gogh*; self portrait of his skull smoking a rolled spliff.

Eternity; ꭱ.

*

"Stone Free," Miguel whispers into my ear as we cross yet another bridge; the love birds behind us, we're meeting up with Stacey and Rickardo now, "Stone Free is the best on ꭱ."
    "You like it?"
    "Like you, hermano."
    "Not organic," I jest.
    "Awe, I not vegetarian loco, I take cocoa, and eh, heroin, but I no purchase. Only gift."

"You tricked me."

"If you say so?"

"Now I take you to purchase?"

"What about Stacey?"

"They go to castle, we go Smart Shop," and he turns back to Ona and her lanky idiot, "There," points left, "Adios, eh, que hora?" and we walk on, and Alejandro flips you off and you don't care, Miguel and I are going to have a mighty fine

time. again.   Nothing Can-hurt-us-now.

                 "Can we get some H?"

"No, that is illegal."

                         "Opium?"

     "No. That still illegal here."

                     "LSD?"

                   "Nope."

              "Mescaline?"

"Peyote, yes. Ayahuasca, sometimes."

            "Crystal Meth?"

           "In England and Scottland...tons of it."

"We're not going there."

                          "Off course."

"I have ecstasy dust if we need to stay awake."

            "You're crazy, hermano, crazy American."

                            *

                            *

                            *

                            *

                            *

***********SmarTtt ttt__sha*man__ShoppinG***********

Shopping is an activity one either must do, can do, wants to do, desires to do, or in my case, needs to do. For this budding shaman, I can only hope that time has set itself with my stride, as I enter the store, the lab, the pHaʀmacy, where I will give the cashier a ring, a covenant, and the cashier will in return, deliver a mail-order bride of psychedelics, and I will be bombastic, penetrative, indoctrinated towards my shamanistic degree in order to indulge of the honeymoon of life from now until ɘternity, and my purchased wife will be pure, virginal to the earth. A spore who has traveled light years to be with us, with me, myself, and I, do. Psilocybin and I were legally introduced last night. The matchmaker had set us up. We flirted, we may have gone too far, and yet not far enough. Now, as much as one wants to lead oneself downstream, the current always helps you decide whom you are to travel with; the beaver, or the log?

I don't feel so guilty about it all today. Maybe I'm juggling with some regret? Maybe I want to go back to her, Misty, my Misty Rain, not Ona. Yasmin, if ever, I was to ever see her again. Misty however is still here. Still alone. Waiting for her other shift. Another chance at me? See her again, be more prepared for what she wanted to do, bring a condom, stay safe, fuck like banshees...If I can break away from the crew again. If I can repeat myself, without being redundant, without over thinking the unthinkable; i am absolutely ɘuphoric. A whole new level. A greater peace. Contentment with evɘrything I'm going to back to s ɘ e her. I'll propose to her...show her I am a real man, not a chicken in denial that his ex-girlfriend can be seduced back into my arms by shear ɘxistence...when his ɘx-fiançe waits patiently in the arms of Liana the lustful .

...You know the Asian princess actually liked you. That's why she was disappointed. Makes you hard thinking about it. A prostitute was actually disappointed from her John paying and then backing out of laying. Disappointed. She'll be so hot for you when she sees you walk back in for her. Ten-fold...You are lucky man. You are, "In lo. .

"..ve this Smartshop," I holler at Miguel who's smoking a joint by the window lounge area postered with planets, constellations, everything beautiful in this world; pretty much . turn back to the shop . that has a glass door refrigerator, lit from the inside with a blue light, displaying bulbous mushrooms in plastic packaging; reds, purple pinks, greens, yellow dots, white dots, so thick, filled with juice, "You can eat them fresh?" I ask. They are listening to *Curtis Mayfield* in here.

"Yes, very strong," the clerk says. He's a hefty fella, trimmed beard, and a black t-shirt with a twirled universe and a single atom in the middle. Unlocks the fridge, "Some people like fresh more than dried; Some think dried stronger. Everyone has their own opinion," he moves aside for me to get a better look, "You try fresh, you like, you come back for more." Miguel steps up to us, "You gotta get the dried shrooms. The fresh ones go bad on holiday."

*

I buy a few packs of dried shrooms, and a freshy which I eat with a sodapop chaser right outside the shop.
"What do we do today?" I ask Miguel.
"Train to Dresden."
"Oh shit, what time?"
"Past midnight."
"Oh, thank god."
"Why?"
"No reason, just don't want to trip on a train for hours."

---

and...

"I like this excstacy. Very clean."
"Told you," I say and we walk on; rolling.

*

Ona, Ail-let-ja-lick-me, and Rickardo meet us outside the hotel. "Where you go?" Ona scolds us, "We worry all night."

"Your boy ate mushrooms," Miguel announces, Ona sighs, "You child, Clever. You do drugs make problem for others."

—This is such a bullshit judgement.
First, I do not do a lot of drugs

Second, I am not some fucking addict, stealing, fighting, and or
cheating on my girlfriend. And third...
I guess I did steal the book?
But I'm not the one that killed anybody today.

"Your hero Miguel here is on 9X, and took shrooms with me last night," I rat on Miguel to level the playing field, and sing, "*Have you ever been mellow, have you ever tried?*"

"Yeah hermano, but you on 9X and <u>shrooms</u>. I'm just rolling," he says, and that's it, Ona snaps, "I no want to see you until train. You stupid Clever and make Miguel stupid," and she's up and walks off with her massive backpack. Alejandro's looking to Miguel for advice, "Go," he says to Alejandro, and he drops Miguel's backpack at M's feet and runs off to catch Ona. Rickardo hands me my backpack. "What's up, why you got our bags?"

Miguel explains we had to check out of the hotel and now we just carry the bags until the train. Lovely. Massive backpack and a set of fresh shrooms digesting in your belly. Today might suck. I can't let it suck. See, that girl changes the entire dynamic. All goes to hell. Euphoria sucked dry. I have to get in a good mood or I will have a bad trip. Take more 9? Could bolster your mood? Coulda, shoulda, mighta, maybe? We'll see. I don't feel so bad. Maybe you can ride this one...find something for you and only you. Meet everyone back at the train, ditch them all, ditch the negative energy. "Maybe I'll meet you all back at the train tonight;
midnight, right?"

"Do not get lost."

"Why would I get lost?"

"Mushrooms?"

"I'm experienced, dude."

"Do not get lost."

And Miguel picks up his backpack, slaps Rickardo on the shoulder, and they run off to catch the asshole twins. "Why would I get lost?"

*

I'm so fucking lost. I've gone up and down these streets for hours and I still can't find that fucking Red-light district. I can't ask. Too high to ask, too embarrassed to ask. You have to find her on your own.

That is what this is all. . .

...a.bout.

● ─────────────────────────────────

●.

.●·This trip is about you, your own time, your own desire in the heart of Amsterdam. Walking helps you keep the visuals at bay. Keeps your mind focused on the task at hand; your Asian lover and the Gabber that taps your step a stepping; happily   :
. fending the cobblestone this round.   .
No river to cross, you are on the other s
id
₉

─────────────────────────────────── ●

●

●●No. Not this street, this street waves in the breeze, but I have to stop walking, backpack pain, so heavy, find a park, a park bench, anything to sit on, relax. Stop at this stoop, sit here...the concrete won't stop melting...spins into a *Mayan Calendar* that laughs at you and loses it's teeth, which makes me laugh as the eyes turn into gem stones sending a rainbow straight up, but it is not all the colors in the rainbow, it is yellows and blues, blues that bleed black between the cobblestone, a blackness that oozes closer...──────────
───────────────────────────────────...and   closer towards you. You have never tripped as hard as these two days. Almost spooky, but in control. Tried shrooms twice in a row before, but the second day was never fulfilling to you, to any of your friends. Figured it to be a waste. But here, now, with the boost of dopamine floodgates, the variety of shroom has givin' new meaning to this consistent non-time, lapsed, psychedelic continuum. It is alluring, a darkness that could cover you, even in the dead of night, even while you sit lonely, alone, saddened, feeling, all feels. Feels of joy, feels of great depression. A depression that doesn't consume you, instead informs you, debriefs you on the stoop as the sun fades and the night eases its way into the back of your skull reminding your libido that Yasmin is gone, Ona is sexing in a stall at some random restaurant with Alejandro, all-the-while you know you need to get back on your

feet and fly to the loveliest hooker in all of Amsterdam, your mission, your ambition, obsession; save her from her-selves. And you try twenty more blocks. You look at every window for a red light, every doorway for a line of Arabians, every pathway for her. Maybe you'll find her on the street, going to work, you would be her first shift, laugh together in the crowd. Your fingers will accidentally touch, she'll blush, you'll chub up, she'll bat her eyes, you'll know what you have to do, and kiss her between all the men and women who wait for her to turn her red light on for them... ——————————————
—————————————————————— I feel ferocious. Want to ravage the girl. Fuck her hard. Fuck her long, fuck her in front of Ona, fuck her in the red lit window. Fucking cum all over her face, that she will delightfully lick off her cheek and beg you to take her with you on Holiday, back to the states, your mail-order...A red light!———————————————
————————————————————Your will has willed upon the psychedelics melting order in your brain to line up with the destiny of the outside world. The shrooms have made it so. The shrooms have communed with the 9 and together they have led you home. ..
through one of these many passage ways, passage stays, passage lays

Don't forget about the train ————————————————————

Don't remind me.

Don't forget about Ona ————————————————————

Do not remind me.

Don't forget to find her ————————————————————

"Who?"
"Everyone who will leave you."
*
I will never recall how long I weeped for.
How long I waited in various lines.

How long I longed to get it right.
How long I weeped for her.
Ona. Not her. Not Yasmin.
Not Ona. Me. Not You.
And
I
weeped.

On   the street.

In the lines.
In the passages.
Inexperienced.
In Experience.
never finding the one
being unsatisfied by some
All the way back to the train station.
I have failed. I have failed at love again.
Stupid drugs. Ona's right. Stupid drugs.
Stupid outcomes. Stupid dreams.
Drugs make me want to love.
I do not want to love,
drugs, only,
love

•
*

Train Station. You have to get back to the station. "Which way," I ask myself, "Don't get lost," Miguel reminds me in the back of my head. The visuals all stopped after the third passage I scoped out. Mind fuck as fuck, but visuals, sensuality, all that zipped away...I thought I found her in one room, but she couldn't make me cum. It was very uncomfortable so I tried another room...She wasn't very pretty, but I was so, so dedicated? She let me suckle her nipple while she massaged me to a climax. It was a pleasure, but I worry I've spent more than I should...drugs man...drugs and money, so confusing. ..so very complicated

.   .

$

Whoa is you, lost in Old Amsterdam, in love with a whore, forgetting your way, stone cold, trembling, feeling, stuff you never did before that girl. Before that last year of high school. You never thought of feelings & love. Whoa is a you. Little lost Rodney. Tickled &

pickled.

You didn't bother with the future. There was never anywhere you really had to be. So why put a single train station on such a high pedestal?

She is no goddess.

She is not the marble pussy to lose your marbles over. Find the train station, board the next trip. If you miss your crew, good, you'd rather be alone right now. This journey for your escape is over. The next caterpillar will be boarding in five minutes, over there just down this road, cross the open court, past the trolley; the train station to Dresden. Why are you going to Dresden? "Burnt buildings. I want to see the burned buildings. Where the Nazi's fell," you tell Stacey as you follow her onto the train. "Find your Jewish roots?"

"Probably not so much."

Chapter - The Guts of an unborn Caterpillar Larva

Tight quarters. Sleeping cars. A set on one side, another set on the opposing side, bunk beds; all just one elongated, cramped hall through the center of this worm. My backpack scrapes along the doors, doors which are walls. "Do we have bunks?" you ask her. "No." A guy's up ahead. Stacey let's him squeeze through. He's middle aged, blonde to grey, thin, in a suit shirt and tie, carries only a briefcase, coughs on me when he passes, "Scusé," he apologies, but that was gross. "Really, no bunk to sleep?" you ask Stacey, "No, we had to make a reservation," and she opens the door between cars, whoosh, follow her through, "Where are we going?!"~~~~~~~~~ ~~~~~~ ~~~~~~"Middle there are seats!"~~~~~~ ~~~~~~~~~~~~"WHAT?!"~~~~~~~~~CH-SHHHHHHHHHH-NAWP-ChShug-SHHHHHHHHH—we stop in the next car. . . same as the last car . . . "Where we going? Stacey?" She turns. I'm cracked out. Need to sit down. On edge. "Seats are in the middle of the train. You tripping?" she asks with great astonishment cloaked in the nonchalant lack of surprise.

"I am."
"Dude? Come on."

*

Miguel's passed out, headphones on loud. Ona and Alejandro are seated down the car. Rickardo moves over to let Stacey and you in. Have to hug your backpacks. "How long's this train?" you ask Stacy; breathing. "Ten plus hours," she says, "Here," hands you her water bottle, "Drink some water. Goodnight."   You untwist the cap, sip, alone

surrounded by

all   of   .them.   .   .

---

*

The night on the train is cold,
you feel it the under your skin; death.
Stacey gave her window seat to you.
You are appreciative of your American friend.

*

The window glass is cold against my forehead;
Stacey's bent over into her backpack across from her.
My eyes have adjusted to the darkness outside the train.
Spins to fast under my eyelids. I still won't be able to sleep
for another few minutes.
Fields- Fields- Fields- and Steins,
all killed on these dark grey landscapes, cold coffins.
Deutschland headtrip. Are we even in Germany yet?
****european soil****
trains, tracks
head trip
mellow, cold, calm, wretched smells
I pace the skinny halls. Beige curtains.
Cold Plain Lower than Neutral Heights.

+   +

+   +

+   +

+   +

+

+

+

YOU'LL NEVER LOVE HER LIKE i LOVE YOUR MOTHER
You are still reminded as you return to your seat.
Forget about her. Forget about you.

And out the window you know you have slide along the razors edge
into the Fatherland
Your Mother is Jewish. You'll never love her like I love.
you ill ever of er ilke in love our other
was it a slavic puzzle
your parents wanted you to solve
but for who
?

My grandparents, as children— toddlers —were on these
tracks, trembling, under their own skin, a contagion, societal,
looked upon as an ancestral virus. Dark grey landscapes,
death. A sickness that ate these children from the inside as it
manifested into a physical superiority of a human tumor,
separating itself from its host, mating amongst the newly
defined purity away from its ancestry in pagan and scientific
curiosities, skeletons, skeletons wrapped, shrink wrapped in
leather. Hundreds of them, here alone, further into the fields,
thousands of them, men and small, big and women, boys
and girls, walking nowhere, step by step, single file, alone,
together, into the cement tunnel. I cannot see farther than the
four to six feet between the train window and the scrolling
of these underground tunnels to the metropolis of wooden
shacks, chicken shacks long, for the size of man, bunk upon
bunk, like these trains, I cannot still sleep, I must actively
sleep, stay alert, we are being herded toward the gallows; all
the people, sleeping in the cars, their last night, we have
been kind to the dead, American's saved the dead. You
rather not die. You have better things to figure out. Be nice
to figure something out. Do something. Think about
something. Sadness is a boredom's head-trip. Nazi's even
loved. There is a yellow stone, in the distance, past the sand
field. They grow sand here, where they worship the yellow
stone.

You worship the yellow stone. Want to touch the yellow stone. Give
yourself to it. Closer, as the tint of the yellow philosophized stone is
farther releasing its phosphate into the heavens, pollenating your
biologically chemical ambitions; even in your wetdreams. . . . .
SLAP
Open your eyes!

Rickardo has slapped you. "Dude, you," and he demonstrates the classy act of jerking off, "In sleep."

—Oh, that is so fucking embarrassing.
Did I cum?

I pull my hand out of my pants, gently, nothing. The stick stopped me just in time.

—The yellow stone.

"What the fuck? Mushroom dreams," I confess to the kid, "A yellow stone, beautiful yellow stone. Red hair, tinted possibly, but a yellow stone none-the-less," he's still listening despite the fact he was watching me jerk myself off in the dream..."and then it starts to mist up, like backwards rain particles, but they are light, lighter than the atmosphere so they rise, dissipate into the clouds...Phosphate? That's what it was, an electrically charged particle that contains mineral phosphorus? The 1% of me?"

"You weird."

"Sorry."

*

Stacey wakes me up this time. "We're pulling into the station," and I rub my eyes. We're in a different car altogether. They moved me. When? I don't remember falling asleep, I sit up, "I didn't hear the whistle. You got a smoke?"
"Gonna be colder here," she says, lights my cigarette.
I cough, take another drag, really cough, and gag, and I, *accchem*, choke up a loogie, spit the nasty bugger into the ashtray. "Quit while you're ahead," she tells me and leaves. I open the curtains, rows of triangular housing; grey tones. The door closes behind me, spooks me. I'm on edge. Unfortunately can recall Neo-Night-Fascists-mares, Nazi-Night-mares, Remote controlled armies of rabbits; murderous mares . stormtroopers . kill *Hitler; he was an*

Asshole.
I wrote it small enough in paint pen, on the corner of the window, covered it with the curtain before leaving...Door slides open, German-Ticket Guard, "Passport." They do stand as straight as can be, aware. Stares me right in the eye uses his thumb to flip open my navy blue American Passport. He hasn't looked at it yet, eyes glued on me. Dare I blink? "I'm visiting from America." Nothing; he is stoic, looks down at the passport.

Looks at me; stamps it.
Hands it to me; doesn't let go,

"You carry Amsterdam Marijuana, American?"

"No, no I didn't do any Marijuana there."
"You Jewish?"
"No."
"I see," cocks his head to the side looks me over, "Show me."
"What?"
"Your penis."
"But?"

"Very good, enjoy Dresden, fine food here," and he leaves, no Nazism, no mares, nothing. Have I been raised prejudice? I won't deny, today it was I who was the bigot. Makes my skin crawl to feel so strange, so naive, stupid. I should be more open-minded. German's are people too.

This is not an afternoon special, Clever, say it proud, true, be honest, it's not your fault a German has never been portrayed as much more than scum all your life. From *Indiana Jones*, to *Schindler's List*, to the stories and tales of East Berlin. No, they are not all Nazi undergrounds, most of these people are probably decent, boring, generous, and regretful of the soil's past, and others prefer blondes.

•

"Ona?" I engage her on the platform, she's alone, Alejandro went to the bathroom with Miguel and Rickardo. "Yes?" she responds back.

"How are you?" you ask. "Good, I think next part trip be better," she says, kindly. "You'll like Dresden better than Amsterdam," you assure her. You know she wasn't into Amsterdam, that part of the trip was always for you...and Miguel. "You like Amsterdam?" she has stepped closer to you, or was that you who took the single step forward? Doesn't matter, you are both here, "I did," and she'll smile, "You get drugs?" she'll ask condescending, but in jest. She knows you smuggled stuff out of there, she's happy for you, squeezes your belly, smiles, kisses...nothing

"I happy you have drugs now, Clever."
"Yeah, I'm happy too."
"Sorry I no do drugs like you."
"What about Alejandro?"
"He, he like cocaine. I don't like that worse."
"Coke's boring."
"I hurt you, Clever?"

She's touching your hand?

"I hurt you?"
"You could have told me sooner?"
"But I did not know," her eyes are locked in.
There is a beat. A pause in the song before it kicks back in.
"I love you, then," she confirms nothing.

You wait for her to finish her thought.

"So, I still love and it hard to know, you understand?"

"Oh hey," you'll say to Stacey stepping up right to you both;

...Us

...

...

...

...

...

s h i t

.

Alejandro pops up next followed by the others. Nothing
really matters until .   .

            .

        .

            .

                .

                    .

                        .

                            .

                                .   .   . .

                                            .

                                            .

                                            .

                                            .

                                            .

                                            ...

                                          ....

                                        ....

                                    ....

                                      ....

                                        ....

                                          ....

                                            .....

                                          ....

                                            ...

                                          ....

                                            .

Chapter - Dresden on Ice

A layer of cloud silk keeps the sun hidden until the sun can find a break and burn a hole right through your mind until everything goes grey again. We are headed to the Eastern Block where the greys of the city match the aura of the landscape, the sky, while the colors of street art pop as we approach walls after walls that separate the train tracks from the country side, and again you'll break like the sun and witness the vastness of the European continent, but that was all before, before we got off the train, before Ona and I finally had a moment of sanity, relations, discussion; us.

Now I'm a few meters behind the crew, Ona and Alejandro's hands are interlocked, Stacey's chatting up Miguel with his headphones collared on his neck, and Ricardo's just being himself, in awe at everything he sees and thinks; if only I could be as innocent as Ricardo, as stupid, naive, interested, undamaged, awkward, and still related to Ona.

No,   you   don't.

Dresden seems old. These buildings do not wreak of angular design of the Third Reich. That is a bit of a letdown to me. To my visual interest in freaky stuff. Maybe Berlin's more illustrated with Adolf crap. This place, downtown Dresden, is just a maze of pre-Victorian storefronts, restaurants, travel agencies, and stuff, lots of stuff, lots porcelain dolls, clothing boutiques, pastries, fancy façades, cafés, bars, and blue eyes; blue eyes everywhere. Ona looks over her shoulder, at me, smiles, turns back. The weather is just like Ona and I, hot-cold, cold-hot, bored, lost, living in the past, but not. "Miguel?" I call out. He waits for me to catch up, "We need to get high," I tell him, he agrees, "Ona!" he calls out, she stops, drops Alejandro's hand,

---

You have got to stop watching her every move.

I am obsessed with these ideas of her. Never felt this way before. Never cared about much, but this girl won't leave my amygdala free and spirited. "Your what?" Miguel asks you.
    "Huh?" you're not sure what he is referring too.
    "That word you say, amigdaylla?"
    "Amygdala," I correct him.
    "Yes, what mean?"
    "Part of your brain, but I didn't say that," you tell him.
    "Oh, what it do?"

—*Why are we talking about this?*

How did he read my mind?
Is Miguel a witchdoctor?
Why am I so bored?
Making things up.

"Feelings. It deals with feelings," I tell him as Ona waves at our faces to get our attention again, "What?" I ask.

"You call, what want?" she'll ask me.

"Can we find a Hostel?" you'll ask, delayed, despondent.

"What you think I do?"

...she snaps at you over the *Hendrix* that your ears have zoned in on around Miguel's neck.

"Felt like we were just wandering," you'll think about saying, and then say, "I don't know." Something is up with you. You are confused. Up is left, left is right, and down is your stomach wanting to vomit. "I think I'm going to be sick," you say aloud.

"You drug addict," and she hands you her water bottle, "Drink, we find soon."

That's what you loved about her. Tough, but considerate. Whipped.

HOSTEL DRESDEN

"No boys and girls. Separate rooms."
I sieg heil the fucker, elbowed by Stacey.
He didn't see. Nazi. Separate rooms.
Nazi cockblocked Alehandblow.
What do I care?

You don't want to be in Alejandro's room.

Don't be a smartass.

I thought I was being, Clever.
You're not. You're nobody. I'm Clever.

Elbowed again.

"What?"

"Fill out your Hostel card, dude."

I take the pen from Stacey. Start writing on the counter. The others have already headed to a room, rooms. "You okay?" she asks me. I'm perspiring. "Still nauseous," I get out of my throat. It itches. I spell UAS wrong, scratch it out; USA. Slide the card to the Nazi, he waves us off. Stacey escorts me to room 17.

You recall, the Asian lover, room 7, not 17, there is no meaning to this room number. You're reaching for a connection. A sign of signs. Light

---

"Dude, you need to sleep," Stacey tells me as she opens the door to the boy's room. They're all in there. Two single beds, one military grade cot, and a cushy chair. I step into the room, "We'll be right down," Stacey says leaving me alone with these Spaniards in Germany. "It a pull out," Alejandro tells me pointing out the cushy chair.

"Thanks," you respond, despondent, your new favorite emotion since the platform, and you drop your bag on the chair, rush the bathroom and puke your guts out as Miguel digs through his bag in the other room in search for his joints.

"Wash teeth and I get you high, Clever!" he yells once I've calmed down, gagged out, head on the porcelain, never checked if the toilet was clean, happy there was a toilet, not a share. Tastes like yesterday.

Stacey's joined Miguel, Alejandro, and I in the alley. "I didn't know you smoked?" I asked Alejandro when we got into the alley. "No tell Ona. Only one, two times sometimes," he explains nonsense to me. "I won't say anything, not my business," I told him. "You very nice, Clever, I trust you, like brother to Ona," he says, proud, like he's a good dude, and I smiled, played along, "Yeah, but will you love her like I love your Mother?" I say, over his head, beyond the field, my own inside joke, and then we smoke. I feel better; after puking. Even better now that I'm high again. "Stacey and I are gonna go our own way today," I improvise, catch her off-guard, "let you all speak only Spanish for a day, ya know?"

Stacey told you she gets it, that she knows you can't stand this fucking Alejandro guy and don't want to be alone, or with any of them at the moment. She gets it, Clever. You're good, they saw you puke, all forgiven about not wanting to be buddy-buddy with this dick fuck and the lie they keep making you perpetrate.

Miguel looks to Ona, she's cool with it. When did Ona show up. Alejandro's still alive so I guess she didn't catch him. Miguel tells me, "No drugs out there. Dangerous, not Amsterdam." Thumbs up. Ona is disgusted that Miguel feels he needed to school me. "We'll meet them for dinner, at the Hostel," Stacey asks. "Maybe?" I want to be free. "Maybe," she relays to the group and it is kisses and hugs, and no one's disappearing forever so, yeah, love you, nots, bye, bye, fun time. "Where we gonna go?" Stacey asks as we corner the alley, "Fuck do I know? Where are the burnt buildings?"

*

We have asked, "Burnt buildings?"
Ruins? / Fire?
and in time we are finally gazing upon
cranes, scaffolding, obscured vision gates,
rubble, or is it dirt?
They are rebuilding the *Dresden Frauenkirche.*

.

.

.

Café?

Sure, why not.
Café

.

.

.

*

"I'll get a seat," Stacey says upon entering this fine German pastry shop/café. "Cappuccino, and a chocolate pastry thing," is her request as we split up. The place is bustling enough. All white. Everything's been all white, but ya know, the movies, and *Fats Waller* in the speakers spitting about the *Milkman* makes me think of *Aphex Twin* - "*I wish the milkman would deliver my milk, in the morning,*" I sing to myself as I step into line. The line's three to five couples long and *Fats Waller's* has a mixed beat under him, and I notice the DJ in the back of the shop. Stacey's found a seat way side, against the wall, beside a speaker. I shoot her a finger, step up a couple spots, groove to the Acid Jazz, sudden samples of a deep African Englishman repeating, "*In the Ghetto,*" a cover of *Donny Hathaway's* original tune. I know this because the Englishman in front of me knows this and his girlfriend in a sweater and jeans is being informed about it, and the DJ's doing a killer job at the mix, and the line moves one step...

*

The back of the shop is all paneled, thick wooden tables with booths across from us, the DJ's set up is on a rise, and he is not black. "So, urban," I tell Stacey. "You're really racist about this place, guy," she's kinda over it, "Funny the first time."
   "That DJ's actually really good," I act normal, "Knows how to mix, black, white, nazi, hillbilly, or Hindi, that DJ is as urban as they get; that shit's tight."

Who was that? Did you see her? Don't look. "Where's my pastry?" Stacey asks you in deep thought. "Oh shit, I forgot," and you can get up, then look around, but Stacey stops you, "Don't get up, I'll get it," she insists, "You groove to your ghetto lifestyle," and sticks her tongue out, leaves. You're alone; look. That girl sat somewhere. Look.

She has blonde hair, bleached, not burned, a well, gentle hair-curler curl to the waves with two thin braids perfectly aligned dangling down right in front of her eyes. Almost covering her eyes.

You can't see her eyes from this distance, but her braids are hypnotizing as they gently sway in front of her, teasing you.

She smiles at her friend, her girl friend seated with her.

The smile makes a match for you. Her teeth glistened in white, under the disco ball in the sky, light skinned, gentle rosy baby cheeks, a bullring to accent her stabled directive that leads your stare directly back to her DIAMOND◊EYES

You saw them. Two;
she had looked up, saw you
She has to turn away from you

Find something else to look at, Clever.

She's telling her girlfriend to look at you

You should watch the DJ, no, lame; pop some ꝍ.. .   .   .

.

. . . Just a half.

.

.

.

Stacey returns
"You see that girl over there?" she asks
"Yeah," you respond
"Gorgeous," she confirms

Stacey takes a bite from her chocolate crème something. The inside oozes out the opposite end, drips onto the tiny metal plate, she tickles

it up with her finger, licks the tip clean, and DIAMOND◊EYES just got
up and is approaching your table, our table, with a flier in her hand.
Stacey turns, DIAMOND◊EYES ignores her, hands <u>you</u> the flier, looks
to lock onto your soul from her enrapturing DIAMOND◊EYES;
millions of mirrors of yourself, of me, Clever infinitely, forever, and
ever, never ending, an orb in loop of one's self and in return her own
self in the reflection of your own eyes, zillions of times over, if not for
a moment, then simply forever more. . . . . . the acid jazz doubles.

. ————————————————————————————

—

            . .up on my ears. . .this is not the ǝ.
.   .not yet at least. It was just a little lick, two little licks of
my fairy balance dust.   .   in   dD read s Den .   .

"Thanks," and I take the flier.
         "You come," and the girl looks to Stacey, "Both."
She's English. Pure accent, soft voice, sweet. Her eyes,
diamonds still, as she looks back to me, her braids teeter tot
from the turn, "This is my cousin," and she catches her
braids, parts them; diamond◊eyes
               I introduce, "Stacey."
         Stacey nods, nice, very impressed.

Suddenly cold. Ice. Arctic. Crisp————————————————————
         It's her hand, she has touched you.
"You are very handsome," she is confidently forward, so direct for
someone so young, someone your own age, someone as beautiful as
she, as she tells you her name.

————————————————————————————————————

 "I am Azalea."
                  "Do I know you?"
"That's my sister Phena," she directs my attention to her
sister at their table. Phena raises her coffee cup, "How do
you do, Phena?" I salute her sister, turn my attention back to,
"Azalea." I said that aloud, under my breath. Smile.

  "Yes?"
  "Oh, I was just saying your name."
  "To remember?"
  "Unforgettable."

"I don't like liars."
"Neither do we."
"Who, you and your cousin?"

She knows Stacey is not your cousin.

"No. Me, myself, & I."
"Three of you?"
"Two of us?"
Azalea can't help but blush. Adorable. A dream.

You've been outplayed.
Accepting, desired it to be so. Strong, or Paraphilic; requesting domination, your arm, your hand around her wrist, yours, twisted, behind her back, her DIAMOND◇EYES, so sharp, slice through the bind of your inflamed, pulsating heart; a muscle, thick, beat, heavy, beat it against you, against her; inside her muscle, between the flesh, throughout, deep, explosive as the horn section blows its load out of the speakers and the record stops, the DJ's set is over.————————
—————————————————————— - . CLACK .
. POP. . . PAUSE . . .SILENCE. her eyes, our eyes, never met someone and imagined sleeping with her so vividly, so instantly, emotionally, al—

Radio\ -.,.sa.,...
- —HORNS— - - - - - - -
BAM-Ba Ba-Ba Ba. Da-Da-dat.
"Talk to me, you never talk to me...
- Phil Collins/Genesis..So...
"So maybe you'll come to this party?"

"That's not part of the song," I say. She can't hear me. They are really blasting *Mr. Collins* all of a sudden. Clear the place loud. "I see you?" she asks, and I notice she removes her hand from mine? She has been touching me this whole time. "She's a hooker," Stacey tells me after she's gone.

"So, what, I'll save her then. Take her back to the States," you say and watch DIAMOND◇EYES take her sister Phena away, out of the Café. Phena has looked back, smiled, likes you, trusts you? How do they know you're likable? How do people find each other? How often can you lose another lover? How often to you get a chance at life? one and the ɘcstasy has yet to kick in, and I am grateful; my walkman is still on the table, DIAMOND◊EYES didn't steal it. That's a good sign. Stacey'll flip the flier front to back, back to front. "Going?" my voice asks her. "Why not?" she shrugs.

*

Outside the hostel...
"No, don't," I begged my new American friend, the Stacey,
<u>not</u> to invite them.

Stacey and I approach the crew waiting for us, "Hey, you guys want to go to an underground party?" she asks.

Chapter - Fuck, fuck; Fuckəd.

This restaurant sucks. Food sucks. Boiled this, boiled that. Sausage, sausage, sausage; bratwurst. I want Drum and Bass. This garbage food is dairy, cheesy; all less than tasteless. I don't want to be here high. Not into the accents all around me. Sensitive. I have better to be. Thinking too fast. Like to take the time to understand if the dust is quicker, or less visual? Quicker, if not switchy. I'm back and forth. Trying to take in everything that I'm uninterested in. If Ona wasn't trying before, her discreetness toward her mate has been exchanged for love birds in Dresden. They are all still speaking Spanish. Stacey speaks good Spain verbiage. I'm not going to eat this sausage. Antsy. Wonder about the girl. *What was her name?* Greek. Greek goddess.

Alejandro takes something from Miguel, sprinkles it onto Ona's cheesy, goop dish. "What's that?" I discreetly ask the M.

"Shrooms," Miguel tells me, shh.

"Why are you taking shrooms?" I ask her. "I take, I want," she says in broken English, real bitchy, but with a smile, and our table giggles, "No, really, why are you taking mushrooms tonight?" I'm adamant.

She twitches. Something about me wrenches in her neck. I've never seen someone react like that. Seen an eye twitch, heard a guy with Tourette's, but Ona's not that, she's healthy. Miguel talks for her, "Ona has never party, party."

"No psychedelics."

Please, you know everything about her.

"She's no prude," I make sure they know what's what.

"I like Dresden," she justifies her decision.

"We told her, when she finds a city she likes," Miguel looks to Alejandro, "Then she take mushrooms."

"You're different," I criticize her.

I'm different. I feel it. Dusted 9 has me in a similar sensation to ice-skating, but different, ice-skating with bare feet...where my soles melt the top layer allowing me to slide...the cold comes from the air around me, and the condensation from my dragon's wicked warm breath.

"I the same, Clever. You different," she is childish, protected by her family, this is not the place to fight. Alejandro is confused. I won't look at him. I won't look at anyone else, but Ona. You have ruined everything for me. There is nothing more pathetic than taking shrooms to avoid me, make me disappear, be alone with your Alejandro; lame.

*

wasn't her name
DIAMOND◊EYES

◊

Why did you pick a fight with Ona as she ate shrooms?
Rude, don't you think?
One last test?
before she loses you to the A .
.ngel with no shame
uno . you know.... ... .
.... slide, bare feet, two pairs ... three pairs ... apart . the
tied . .will tell .you are on the underground to the underground root s

---

*   *   *

this is not a   small underground   club
This line is forever. we've waited twenty minutes . not San
Sebastian forever, and ever, and ever, ever ever!
   Can we just get the fuck in there, Ona's already
tripping?
   My ice-skating *Tonya Harding* high has worn off miles ago.
There's a guy in this line who keeps hitting on Ona, and her
own douché-boyfriend, Alejandro, doesn't seem to notice.
He's high already, I can tell. She's high already as well. Me,
Myself, and I are not high anymore, we are clear, down,
downer, downer not inside, where there is an A.ngel, patient
and earnest with her feelings, "You come," she had said,
without a hitch, without a flinch, without a twitch so stern in
her spine. Ona's not her. Ona's eyes are red, blistered with
hate toward me; she knows you are not here for her tonight,
the shrooms are on their own; One, Uno, Ona...and the
group of ten ahead of us decide to leave— we are waved
across the red rope, no I.D. check; inside, outside, leave me
alone..."Bye," and we, me/myself & I, lose our tagalongs in
the flow of clubbers as they cross, in twenties, the tunnel that
is our entrance. I have
no   drugs.

i am me

*   *   *

having a terrible headache
Check the bar, get a water, get a coke?

"One coke, please."
I could have totally snuck drugs in. Fucking Miguel.
Spooked me. At the café I had balls. With these guys...
emasculated by the failure of my love life.
<<< · head•ache · >>>
loud, pounding house, music
"Thank you," hand him a traveler's check. He gives it back,
waves me off, lets me keep the coke, where's the girl?

*   *   *   *   *   *

Enormous, three floors. The main floor was the tunneled
entrance we entered. It was red carpeted, a lobby to a coat-
check that continued out to two massive opposing bars that
circumference around the dance floor that fits a few
hundred. A laser light show graphs grids overhead, broken
by the colored spotlights leaning left, then right, down,
repeat, smoke machines, no DJ table to be spotted, lots of
people; I see none of them, none of them are <u>her</u> yet. Move,
seek and...seek, move, and seek some more .   .   .

.   .

        . Second floor . Up staircase on the eastside of the
circumference, down staircase is on the westside. Bouncer
told me in less words, "Up, east. Down, west," and had
pointed. The stairs curl up through the wall to the second
floor, a divided level, two dancefloors, and between them an
enormous open unisex bathroom, lounge, and a bar. There
are at least twenty stalls, no urinals, twenty sinks to match
the toilets. Groups of people are going in and out of the
stalls. There are plenty of drugs here. I have no drugs. I need
no drugs, I need the girl. Downstairs
                                        *

———————————————————————————————
————————

*

        *

        *

        around the circumferenc

through the dancefloor,
next staircase,
downstairs,
a low ceiling basement dancefloor . deep bass . .
DARK just people shoe gazing to the slow drone and heavy
lag of the reverbed kick drum . black-light . some very sexy
gi rl s .   .   .run into Miguel atop the upstairs, lost the
others, "I need to get high," I tell him, he shrugs, we part,
she's not here either, check the dance floor, frustrated, at a
loss, go back to the bathroom, use a bathroom, could be
having fun, how, not with her, she's with someone else, on
shrooms, if we'd known that girl was full of shit, fucking
with us for being horny Americans, we could have tripped
balls here, not be spooked by Miguel ,could have had a good
time, stole Una back with my psychedelic charm; did I say
Una?

Ona.
A ,
no.
And there SHE is,
on

a
...couch

...along the wall, white wall, tiled, white couch, white
bathroom lobby, white light, white drugs, white toilet bowls,
white people, white girl; my white girl in Dresden, from
London via a razor's edge upon my eye if it we are all a
dream.

"Hi."

And she looked up, into you, shine; she was happy. You will always
remember— this moment. her happy. us.

.in an
overexposed heaven
.alone
.alive
.act

i
n
g
together in ever with ever for never lover unfeathered. . .

And it was difficult to talk in the bathroom bar. And it was difficult to talk at the middle bar. And it was difficult to talk in the Up stairwell, but it wasn't difficult dancing underground, deep in the back, in the dark, alone, together, we are sluts, we are for each other, instant attraction, "I've never been so wet," she whispered, bashful, yet faithful, gently, as she lowered my hand under her white skirt, no underwear, warmer than her hands, no drugs, wet as we are in her DIAMOND◊EYES, sober, real chemistry as light reflects from the disco balls. Love her, kiss her, part of me, part of her. Are we five or are we six? I am higher than I have been. I have no drugs. This would be amazing on ....
ǝʌǝɹʎʇɥǝǝuƃ

*

Ona's alone, in the Up stairway. I see her first. Her eyes are closed. She holds herself up against the wall with the mighty assist of the banister.

Do not let these girls meet each other. You gotta go back around the corner, "What's up?" you ask Azalea and Phena, "Aren't we going to the bathroom?"

"Other way," you say to them, but that was bullshit, and you have to pass Ona with her eyes still closed, perspiring, should you worry?

Azalea passes me, "Why are you going so slow?" Azalea is in a hurry, "She really has to go pee," Phena tells me, also passing me, and I let them go, two, three more steps up, and they're around the corner and I have to see what's up with Ona, "You okay?"

She can barely open her eyes, "Huh?" closes them again.

"Ona, it's me. Are you okay?"
She can barely open her eyes, "You?" closes them again.

"Yes, me. Open your eyes?"

She brushes you off, no strength, steps, slips; her ass falls. Now you are on your knees, "You okay? You fell," ...help her up, "Come on," dead weight, no strength, "Are you having a bad trip?" you ask, as anyone would.

This girl's sick. The shrooms have not settled well. "I need you to stand up, Ona," but she doesn't want my help, she wants the banister, her legs are on strike.

You tug her. Lift. Lift again, "Come on, stand up."

I've finally got her up against the wall, again. A number of people have walked by. None were our associates. I am so fucking sober. Keep looking up the stairs for my friends. Ona is unable to lift her head up. Her hair, sticky from alcohol, draped in front of her face. Poor Ona, she's fucked up. I feel for her. Bad trips are bad news. Lift her chin, part her hair. Her soul inhibited by the dilation of her oversized pupils. Only she can imagine what I look like to her, what I feel is clear, too clear, need, desperate, despair, need, me, a flame engulfed in distance, across the sea, away, gone, free, awake, alone, solo, in between, dreams...

...a hand on my shoulder, "Clever?"

in an English accent, asking for me, with Ona in my arms, her head in my breast, curled into me, needing me, holding me, protected by me. without ɘ..

"Is she okay?"   "Too many drugs."

"Let me get her some water."
Phena heads back up the stairs.

We wait. Azalea waits, uncomfortably, along the opposing wall— TICK•TOCK —The beat . ˙ . downstairs . ˙ . more prominent . ˙ . in the silence . ˙ . of this stairwell . ˙ . There she is, Azalea points out her sister returning with a glass of water for Ona. "Here drink some of this," Phena kindly assists the fuck-up in taking a sip, then places it in Ona's hand for her to hold herself. Ona cups it. Cherishes the water. "Do you know her?" Phena asks me. "Sort of," is the scramble of words worthy of the moment for this happening to me, now. "We should find her friends," Phena's obviously older than us. That basic sentence was said with such an air of maturity.

She must be at least twenty-three, maybe twenty-five, but she's not telling anyone, she's not promoting herself. You like her. Do you like her better? No. The idea of her better? No. No, you really could careless romantically about her...how could you after, her, and you look at Azalea, so pretty, you touch one of her braids, she smiles at you, Ona's too fucked up to notice. To Phena you speak honestly, without context, sober manipulation...you never lie on drugs, "Her boyfriend's around somewhere."

"We should find him," she instructs us, even Azalea who has strangely nearly disappeared from the entire moment. A shadow against the shadows, suddenly away from me, against the opposing wall, against that railing, not sick like Ona, just miles from my sight and silent. Still & silent. Is she embarrassed, of me? For me? You know, strange at it is, I can see her eyes in the dark. Diamonds. I can't get over them. There are only her eyes...   . ..what is it they
                              want?
                              "You my boyfriend," Ona uncomas with a delayed correction of the funny facts. I do not respond. I hold it together. "You my boyfriend," she says again, more matter of fact, stern, with insistence, puts her foot down, cowers no more; she's still tripping. "I'm talking about, Alejandro," I correct her in return. "No, Alejan-blllow. You my boyfriend," she insists, in my face. I have to step back, she's following me, up against the other wall. Azalea

has had to move out of the shadows into the light across from me. She doesn't understand what's going on. Ona has me pinned against the banister that digs into my kidneys. She's spitting in my face. A scene for sure. . and they're gone. Where did the sisters go? To get help? Deep

HOUSE.DeepHOUSE.

Deep House . Solid Beat . ˙. *Give up* . ˙. *give yourself to the* . ˙. PIANO . ˙. CHORDS . . ˙. .SOLID BEAT . . ˙ .Ona on her own, . ˙. on the steps, . ˙. sat down, . ˙. head in her knees. . ˙. Ditch her. . ˙. Do it now. . ˙. Can't do that. . ˙. Wouldn't do it. . ˙ . Only in a movie. . ˙ . In a book. Someone's bullshit. . ˙. Where are they? . ˙. I need...................
. . ..

               .   .
...Alejandro.
˙ . ˙ . ˙ . ˙ . ˙ . ˙ . ˙ . ˙ . ˙ . ˙ . ˙ . ˙ . ˙ . ˙ . ˙
. . . .

I am so fucking sober. Europe sucks. Germany sucks. Discotechs suck. Drugs can. .
              .

              .

              .

Chapter - Scrubbed

Dresden, dawn from the back of the cab. Azalea's tired, her head on my shoulder. Phena's with us. The others are ahead of us. We helped them into their cab.

Miguel was nowhere to be found. Alejandro, high and happy, couldn't be bothered by Ona's outburst, her psychedelic ebbing, whatever it was that he saw going on that made him ditch her for two hours in the club. Ale-asshole gave Phena a ton of shit outside the club, arguing about her insisting she share their cab to keep an eye on Ona; like any normal person would, should. Fuck I don't trust that guy sober, let alone on mushrooms. Fuck that, she's going with you," I yelled at him. Scared his weak unexperienced mind. His giant statute coward as he crawled in the car already occupied with Ona and Phena; Phena in the middle, no way she letting the letch sit next to Ona who in any instant might yell rape if he looks at her. Phena's for real.

Germany, as a reflection, passes DIAMOND◊EYES' pupils along the passenger window, just as awake as me. Awake on this new person. This authentic person. She catches me looking at her. Smiles. She's nice, looks back out her window as she leans back into my arms. She holds me as I hold her. She likes me. I live in a small town in California. i do not live here , even though here is not so different . friends , i mean . friendships , discover i e s. ju s t, won ' t s. e. ee. t h em, "I NODDED OFF," I say aloud as I snap out of it. The cabby says German gibberish, and we guess he is asking if this is the place, "It is," I respond, he pulls over, I wake up Azalea, she smiles at me, no shadows, streetlight, illuminated, "Where are we?"

"My hostel."

*

"Your friend shouldn't do drugs," Azalea brings up, randomly, deep into our private conversation on the roof. A conversation you are not purvey to . about nothing . nothing more, than places I hadn't been, things I'd never had seen, stories funny enough to laugh about, and some of my behaviors upon the Eifel Tower, what CDs tagged along with me, more of my projected lifestyle of dance and cultural experience, modern cultural experience, and drugs...but she understands me. Understands drugs mean me, not drugs. Drugs mean chemistry, her and I; unexplained phenomenon, perspective, persona, polygamy, polyamory, platonically, speaking we didn't care, monogamy for us now, diamonds and emeralds, in our own shine, meant Ego-Loss, we would do everything together from now on...as we met in sobriety, our relationship must enforce its wellbeing as one does on psychedelics. We must guide each other, we must remain interconnected; the unexplained phenomenon of symmetry from a chance meeting that destroys your perceived future of chaos. "How far are you going?" I asked in response. "A little while," she says in her pure English accent.

Your ears had forgotten about English until now. Now you were as attentive as a deer in the empty meadow, a heart in plain sight, open season, summer dawn in Dresden with a new lover, a stranger, whom fully clothed allowed you to enter her on the house top, and allowed you to give up inside..."I can't get pregnant," she explained in the quiet breath of passion. "Why?" you didn't care. "The beatings," and she curled closer to you, her insides clenching on, like fingers holding onto me, "Never let me go, Clever. Promise you'll never let me go?"

We aren't moving, I am hard, inside her, throbbing— THROB, THROB, "Why would I leave you now that I finally found you?" THROB —She lifts up my shirt with hers, presses her belly button against my outy, I enter her, a perfect match. A z a lea looks directly into my eye smiles, allows me to cum, slowly, ooze back down into my pants as she sits on me kissing my neck, gently, lovingly.

When did you become a romantic, Kyle? She had thrown my underwear over the side. Thought it was funny, hoped it landed on priest. We laughed, used her water bottle to wash me off, zipped me up, and continued talking for at least that hour or two?

"Are you taking trains the whole time?"
"I don't want to talk about it."
"Trains?"
"No, time. I don't want to think about it."
"What do you like to think about?"

"I don't like to think," she says turned from me, her eye on the cathedral, rooftops away. The sun's bright today. The overcast has passed? "I don't like to think either," you respond in earnest.

She leans back, into your chest, your arms, and now your eye is also on the cathedral, rooftops away.

*

Chapter - Influence

When we went back downstairs, we remember mostly sleeping, and fooling around, sleeping, mapping out each and every one of our birthmarks with my paint pens; all the while everybody else enjoyed Dresden, well not Ona, Ona wouldn't leave her room. Ona wasn't talking to anyone after the mushroom debacle. I still fucked Azalea in our *boy's only* room. I knew Ona was around, but this wasn't our problem anymore. This wasn't Clever's problem anymore. Was never Azalea's problem; now it's no longer Kyle's <u>or</u> our problem. I banged the shit out of her mid-day all over the room after the guys left; fully naked, skins, juice, love...and yet she never made a sound, even more, it was as if she was consistently cumming, never dry, I could feel her down my leg, along my ankle, so much cum; and delicious, gently tangier than the inside of a girl's gums, and still she never made a sound, not even a whimper.

                                                  Her body would twitch
                                                      and contract
around me rather than let any air out from her lungs,
no sound. very strange,
slightly less erotic . i shall never complain
                                and my cock felt her vagina
grip onto me again, like the roof, like a hand, holding me,
tight, tighter. This sex makes the difference, sound cannot.
difference . Her sex was...to be explored . She had no ovaries.
Our knots met, our belly buttons. She called them knots.
Explored mine for moments on end. "Looks like a comma,"
she said. From my perspective, it is nothing but an upside-
down comma. Unbelievable at first, but for her there were
no more firsts or seconds. Azalea wilted before her just
desserts. Fell asleep. a metaphor ... if we were thinking about

                                                      time

                                                        .

Miguel dropped his headphones. Wasted. Stoned, drunk,
drunk, stoned. "You need to clear up," I told him before he
dropped his headphones. "The speed in the x kinda wakes
you out of that stumper," I told him, pulled him aside, gave
him a fingertip of dust. Then, as we were catching up with
the rest of the numbskulls, Miguel dropped his headphones
and now he's kicking them down the street like an asshole
every time he steps forward to get 'em. It is fucking funny,
besides, he looked quite cool wearing them all night at the
club. That was hilarious in all the right ways; dope. Besides
all that, who could really be in any sort of sour mood, when
you're soaring this high, rolling, rolling right out of bed,
planning to catch up with her later, when I returned, after
sending the others off on a train out of Dresden, to a castle;
old / rich. We're not interested. Rather fuck in the room
until we all leave for Prague.   "When do you want to meet?"
I ask Miguel. "Nine hour," he answers.
                                "How long's the ride?"

"Two, three hours."

there is train at five, too

"Why not leave at five?"

You'd love to get out of Dresden and onto Prague with this chick.
No time like the present to do that. Do any of this. Now. With or
without you all. •   •   • • •

•   •

•

•••Sweating. Have to stop. Too much. Too high to be this hot. She
too is relieved as she slips off and lays beside you, dips your finger in
one of the remaining two dabs of ɘ dust, and leads the finger deep
between her legs. She is still so wet. I couldn't cum. Too high? Too
often? She pulls her finger out, sweeps up the last dab and has you
suck her wet, finger of •ɘ.cstacy. "Next time you'll cum again," she
says. You kiss her, she licks your tongue clean and you admit, "We
need a shower."

"I really like sex,"
she tells me as I let the water rush my face, lather up my
cock, clean myself; I feel, older. I invite her to join me. She
watches from the door, "I like sex, too," as you'd imagine
most people would say, especially after such killer sex, "No,
I mean I really like sex."
"You mean like a sex addict?"
"No."
"What then? Like something kinky?"
"Everything's kinky," she explains
as I let my urine loose down
the drain. "Kinky's cool."
"You're not kinky."
"Not yet?"
"You're too perfect."
and with that she closed the foggy glass door and stopped
talking.

Flaccid
tired
Leave it be

"Prague?"
We take the five o'clock train. Phena, Azalea, and myself. All high on my ɘ, all quick on conversation, laughter. Maybe not Azalea so much, she's out of the banter, a laugh, but not verbally engaged, but she's here, she was as present as ever. I am becoming close with Phena. Quickly. I like these girls; these sisters are real. Not grown in my hometown doing the same old things I ever did; adventurous women, unlike Ona's interest in the general objective. These girls are people. First people I have, truly, ever met. Not a raver on a loop, but time and space travelers, on a path of life; no hang-ups. Of me, she has encountered the unadulterated Clever; pure and simple, without any hangups, no more, no need, not alone. Alone, in a strange world, familiarity merely compartmentalized in my CDs, positivity flowing with energy, energetics; the philosophy of my generation. She believes me. "There is no way I am philosopher," I stopped her. "You're very smart," she compliments me again. "You're just looking for the best in people," I don't believe her. "You're right." That I believe. "She always looks for the best in people," Phena assures me. "The worst," and Azalea pauses, almost drifts off— you can hear the train again — wipes a tear from her Diamond Eye, "I don't like to think about negative things."

I believed her.
We were correct to believe her.

Then she took me to the bathroom and blew me

for twenty minutes and i still did not cum. No biggie, I'm in love; for real this time.

Chapter - Prague of the Plague

Phena has lead us to her friend's apartment in Old Town. It is fancy for a young person. Phena had the key. Nobody is home. "You two take the guest room," and she points us down the hall, past a bathroom, a sauna, a hookah lounge, and then finally the guestroom fully decorated in authentic Art Nouveau furniture equipped with a netted bed, and three *Mucha* prints, framed to match. "Those are real," Azalea says she as lets herself fall through the bed netting. "Those paintings?"

"Illustrations. Yes, beautiful aren't they."

"Sexy," I say with a breath, delicate, mindful of this work of art I cannot stop analyzing. Sucked into the mass of a million *Golden Ratios* my rolling mind evaluates every spiraled line, comprehending the 8A geometry as opposed to experiencing the geometric patterns that constrain all matter. Mucha's art has me aware of my mind, our intellect, the Id, Ego, and curious about the throne of the Super Ego...without my body. Mind trip. *MDA / MDMA* becomes drastically more interesting on its 5th/6th day (*if*), and dramatically less problematic, while giving you a sense you may be losing your grip on the interpretation of dopamine. Is this a good thing? Time will tell as I follow the illustrated strands of her hair, down to her lace covered breasts, along the stitching to her thigh that slips through the break of her psychedelic skirt and into the garden of fairy breaths and smoking caterpillars spun back into the woman's dress. "The guy's super good," I've said, "And I am stoked as fuck that I'm rolling so hard right now."

"Me too," she says from behind the veil.

"It's like we've gone back in time," I tell her as I lay myself beside her.

"No, not back in time," she says, stern, firm.

"You're correct. It's like we are finally here," I must be empathetic to the trigger of the term, time. Apologize. Show her your apology. She is not mad. She is fine. I am fine crawling onto the bed with her, little Old Rodney is still very happy.

"I love drugs," she says as you settle yourself beside her, brush her braid away from her pretty eyes. "As much as sex?" you ask as you slip your hand into her pants again. She does not resist. She lets you. Does k.not engage.

Enjoys everything.

"You get wet so fast," I tell her as we just lay beside each other, our heads touching on a single pillow. "Is that weird?" she asks. "Different?" I tell her. There is a fan above, outside of this netted bed. We can hear it. "Have you been with a lot of girls?" she inquires. "A few, not a lot," because I do not want to count. What's too high, what's too low, what matters if you never fuck another chick ever again? I'm done. Which lay mattered? "I'm sure they loved you."

"Some, maybe a couple," I'm still rolling. Its like everytime I touch her its a shot of adrenaline for the *MDA / MDMA* inhabiting my system. The wave hits me hard again. Like a flow of track that leads up your spine, straightening you, into your neck, and out your eyes as you make eye to eye contact with DIAMOND◊EYES, and she moans,

for the first time.

"I fucked a hooker once," you tell her.

Her thighs tighten on me. She likes that? "An Asian girl," tighter, faster, "She actually wanted to fuck me," uh, "I know," she says with her breath, tighter thighs, she is holding your hand on her, "Called me superman, magic man. Made me lick her own cum and spit it in her own luscious, bulbous mouth." Azalea orgasms, twitches, cums all over my hand..."I love you," I heard her whisper to herself still moving along my hand, slowly, with ease. It was not for me.

This orgasm was for her own self. Something you will not understand. Something that trauma initiates. Something real to someone else, fiction to you. You don't mind. You are sensitive to her chemistry. She is sensitive to your biology. This girl knows you need to be touched. You know this girl needs to be thought of. She needs to remember what love could have been. You are in denial. That's a good thing. If you don't protect yourself, you will go home and destroy the world in Ona's honor, the honor of dishonesty. No one deserves you, no one should serve you, and no person knows you...

except

I lean back, remove my hand, wait for her response. She rolls to her side to look me right in the eye. Her diamond eyes. No color, all shine, and asks, "Have you ever drank Absinthe?"

*

Cobblestone pedestrian curved blocks, restaurant after restaurant, gift shop after gift shop, bar after bar, speeding through the rounds, the curved streets, alleyways. There was a little Special K in the apartment. It was Azalea's idea to sneak about the place. I found it. We were a perfect dog sniffing machine. It's exactly what she wanted, to slow it down for a few hours...give us a chance to go up again...Slowly around the next bend after a key bump of K each, it becomes night club after night club, museum after gallery, flower shops, clothing stores, ice cream parlors, trinket shops we get lost in, lost in the assortment of baby Jesus in a zillion baby Jesus outfits. We sneak a couple of Absinthe shot glasses and decide it's time, the <u>moment</u> to seek out the Absinthe bar amongst the hundred or so scattered around the city, around this ever-populated Old Town as we approach the square. The whole world is a fairytale . *and between you and i . we are still time traveling, and we have proof,* "There," I point out the massive Astrological Clock kiddy corner to the square. "We're time travelers, the length of light across the cosmos," I mis-hyperbolate.

"Stop talking about time travel. I don't like it," Azalea

— really hates time?

"Sorry. I was just being cute."

"Don't. Be a man. I like men. Not boys hung up on t

i

me

.

*within the same moment i cannot help but ask, "Are we going to get married?" and without a thought, a beat she simply answers, "We were married in heaven."

Your insensitive actions, words, and thoughts that had become active
words is merely a disconnect from two different ebbs and flows...she
had not kept up with mǝ and she is wise to that. I was higher earlier,
I've been higher longer...She'll catch up. She's wise in her short
eighteen years; wiser than i & she asked, "Do you have more ǝ?" ——

And you feel wrong, broken, a fixer of time that you can no longer
discuss because she has reaffirmed who you truly are to this union.
You are our doctor, our chemist, a budding shaman. If you do not
medicate yourselves equally, you would lose her,

too.

*

"You'll never lose me, Clever."
"Because you love me?"
"Because we were married in heaven."
"I'm not religious, Azalea."
"Neither am I."

She's taken the tablet.

You'll wait for the new drug.

"So how can you believe in heaven.?

"Heaven isn't an opinion, Kyle, we all come from heaven,"
she's taken my face in her hands. She is so kind, nurturing
with her touch, outside this iron vined door illuminated by
the neon green glow lights in the shapes of sexualized
angels, "Death is the mystery." . . .

. . . ..Phena has joined us,
caught up with us at this particular Absinthe bar. "They're
everywhere here," Phena explains, "Found it though," she
finishes as she removes her bag from her shoulder; takes a
seat beside Azalea.

i feel pretty strungout.
My wife is a chatterbox all of a sudden. Her and Phena keep
talking and even though i understand their English as well
as an English speaker should, I cannot make out what they
are saying. "Are you sure i..." but i'm cut off by the waiter,

"Hello, welcome." Phena orders us the Absinthe. My mood waves are choppy. i'm on, i'm off within' seconds, moments, caught up on time, how much time was on that clock in the square, how much time is how far is...time?

hung up on it, all of it, never before, no one's ever said that to me before. No one has ever despised time so fervently. Speed of time, speed of tasks, speed o f doing shit, yes. Ona complained about my busy-ness. Ona said i don't relax, always talk, always on the move. Moving, here-there, person to people, her, them, this that, don't care, never cared. But, but, but, i say but a lot. Do i say it outload? do people notice i am indecisive? am i indecisive? should i take more control, no. she doesn't like to think about time, so don't decide, be decided; this is two shots of Absinthe later and Azalea has ordered another round only minutes after this last one. "To Prague," i say as i raise my glass. i had actually watched the waiter prepare this one in front of us with the highly designed silver flowered spoon with grates for the sugar cube to melt through as the he ignited the alcohol, and gently resting the spoon over the edges of the metallic cup to melt the sugar. "To new friends," Phena adds, and we clink and drink and the licorice is invisibly coated by the melted sugar and the last three bumps of K we each did in the bathroom, and Phena jokes we order one to go, but Azalea takes the dare...shot four ? no, shot fiv•out here*the•cobbler road*of•txme, myself, and us as me•

*

: i am awoken by voices in the living area of the apartment.

---

you do not remember anything about yesterday.
you are in Prague. with the girl.

Am i supposed to be in here? i see my bag, just my bag
Where is Azalea's pack? Shh. why did i wake up?

*

"LEAVE!" one of the sisters has yelled in the other room.

throw on your pants, see what's up
exit, make it down the hall
into the living room
Azalea's there
"You're still wearing the mask," she says to me
i feel my face. i have a mask on. cold, smooth,
yet i can feel a carved pattern etched into
the marble of the mask; i remember
heavy speeded techno plays low
in the background, foreground
i am in the background
of these two single
eye holes on
my face
now
?

.

how strange

• ————————————————————

"Who   was that?" you call out.
          ————————————————

Can she hear you from way over

there?
———————————————————————— •

"Nobody. You want to go out tonight?"
She <u>can</u> hear me, "Absolutely. Why wouldn't i?"

"What?" she steps closer and closer still, "I can't hear you
from over
there." —But you're here?— "Kiss me," she says, and presses
her lips against my marble lips. i cannot feel her from inside
the mask. She has taken my hand, that I feel, leads my
fingers under her shirt, along her stomach, towards and to
her bare nipple, "I love you, Clever," she says for the second
~~time~~ instance? i won't traumatize this singularity. She has
one need, the need to surpass a countdown or up—
—She gently relaxes
back down onto her heels, her fingertips resting against the
open cut of your black shirt, "Leave it on. I love you, Clever."
She had desired the mask, initially and still. She took us, my
mask and I, down this alley...

sucked us off, made Clever cum, in Prague, yesterday,
before
today, when we had found the mask in the marble store,
wealth,
beyond the squatters of Amsterdam, cloaked behind the
linen shop, in the cavern hallway, somewhere lost,
in Old Town, so high, twice as high as high, er,
alone with my azalea and myself, me, and i
found the mask, along the toad, between
the juggernaut and the poisoned pi si
gn of the devil in solitary confin
enment, pressed in romance
bound in decadence.
America will be ruined by decency.
if i
only put on the mask i can save my motherland
It was so easy, on, around the shop, higher than the day
before, visuals explaining the thoughts to other thoughts
about things and zings, and bells, and lapse of winks, of
sleep, deprived of rest, hours past another noon along the
marble balls
in the Alchemist's lab, where she stole the mask for me
the marble store was a lie
as we removed it from its cage
together, for us, me, myself, and her
as we ran
on the sidewalk, away from the caverns,
under the door, down the block
past the this, ditched into that, through
a synagogue, releasing a Golem,
"Do you believe in Death?"
"No, I said."
"Death is our last marriage."
"I'll be there."
and you ate a pork
chop, and bought us matching rings from
the twist of two soda pops,
shared a cigarette on the bench,
by the river
with my new face

"My friend is leaving us some more drugs at the apartment."

>

"Do we have to pay her?"

<

"Him. His name's Erebus; he's actually our cousin. No, it will be free for us."

*   *   *

"Who did you kick out of here?" you ask her again. "Ere, don't worry, he's not coming back," she answers you, leaning into your chest, good to me, "What'd he do?" you ask her, softly, as your hand caresses her back, pull her into you. "He's just that way. He's going back to England. We'll be okay," and she kisses your mask again, "I have you now," and Azalea touches the cold marble cheek, "My angel..."—SNORT— This Erebus has left you both some cocaine. Azalea does her bump from the window sill, SHOOP, head back, finger on her nose, snorts again, "You do a lot of coke?" you ask and she looks back right at ya, "Not a habit. Just fun, or like now to keep us awake together." She knows you so well already. Talks to you like a chemist. "I'm not the biggest fan of cocaine," you tell her..."Prefer thinking uppers, like Crystal Meth." She scratches her nose, adjusts her bullring, explains to you, "I don't like to think. I've been doing cocaine since Boarding School," so now you gotta ask, "When was that?" and she's not gonna lie, "When I was like eleven, twelve. I think the first time I was forced to try it was eleven, but I started to like it when I was twelve."

—*Unexpected*

"Were you rich?" to which she responded, "Was, kinda. My Dad was rich, my Mom's just a regular Mom," and that doesn't completely explain it all, or much of it in fact or even in fiction, 'cause we've been through this, but seeing this apartment, reminding me about Boarding School, I felt like maybe I never asked before...because you don't really care about money. "So, he's not coming back?" is really what I want to know. What I want to protect her from...I don't like yelling. He made her yell. He is bad. And she takes a deep breath, looks out the window and simply says with total conviction, "Yeah, he's not going to come back. I need to take my pills," and she disappears into the bathroom, as i look at everything outside the apartment windows and remember none of it in detail or in essence. my reflection in the window, with my marble mask on, made me turn into a statue; a gargoyle keeping surveillance for my wife.

i will wear this mask

Chapter - Our Train rolls off the tracks

Phena's lead us to a night train out of the core of Prague, out of Prague maybe. Too long to know, too short to tell. i want to kiss my little lady along the way. it's a tease, a game. we left the coke at home, but she brought it anyhow, even though we all took ɘ, brought some valium, and I still want something new, like the Absinthe, so I turn to Azalia, no Azalya, no Azanalyia...what <u>is</u> her name? "Can we score Opium in Prague?" i ask, she blushes, even a goddess has modesty in the eyes of an angel, "Probably," she responds and we disembark from the train, into a field of warehouses, darkness, greeted by a young man in a hood holding a flier who directs us down to the cross street, past the third warehouse entrance, left, two doors, and stamps our hands and we move along. Phena's not high yet. We follow her. Azalea is wrapped around me, hold tight baby girl, i've got you covered..

*.

Elephants; constructed from mighty stilts that protruded from the backs of four covered men, covered in dark gray, plastic, trash bags, and duct-taped together to hold the form of these massive beasts, these Mammoths standing, swaying in the center of this gigantic make-shift auditorium. Naked, body painted, male and female jaguars prance around the magnificent pachyderms. Quietly, almost silently, in the background, *The Korgiz*, *"I need your loving (like the sunshine)"* fills the scenery. The audience of a thousand, maybe hundreds, is still; we are quieter than the music. We are illuminated in the shadows. The teeth, the white shirts, the iridescent wigs, all glowing in the powered black-lights of the space. As the jaguars seduce the Mammoths with penetrating sex, an orgy performed around the elephants hoofs; a mass body of waving water, the colors of the jaguars mixing into one another, a rainbow orgy, to seduce the meat for their dinner as a simple brush of a high-hat begins to resonate from one speaker to the next, until it begins to catch it's audible tail and reverbs into oblivion, "like an Ouroboros," I have whispered into Azalea's ear, initiating her palm onto me; simple, know she's there.

"Now you understand," she whispers back into your ear. You feel her against your ear. You have not felt her lips above your neck since she fell deeper in love with you in your beautiful, handsome, surreal, strange, powerful, and monotonous marble mask, and the audible mix is seamless as *N.R.G.'s* dance version of "*I Need Your Loving (like the sunshine)*" has begun to pound from the massive stacks hung around the auditorium. The bass becomes so deep the metal of these industrial bleachers that surround the performance is vibrating. Everyone is becoming aroused, you can feel it everywhere, everyone on •ə. Purple people, blue people, blood-red people, tribes people who have begun to crawl out from under our feet; everyone's feet. Takes the entire auditorium off guard. Audience members scream, scramble, tumble, crawl, cry, laugh, and applaud as the neon natives rush to the center stage, the floor, where they brutally murder the elephants whose blood splatters white paint in the glow of magnificently huge ceiling black-lights, as the orgy continues around them mixing the audio of the *Sunshine* remixes with the madness of the audience, and the ecstasy of the ocean's orgy of cat people. Magically, and probably the most impressive moment of the performance was when the white blood of the Mammoths collided with the jaguars. A chemical reaction stains them all black.

I can deeply relate, my simian mind, but I understand none of it. We have not moved a beat. Azalea and I have let the natives climb upon us, one even kissed me; I could not feel her. She had yellow eyes, Azalea wrapped closer into me, equally mesmerized by the world's reaction around us rather our own movement from the piece. We have been moved, into each other, there is nothing more, or greater to feel from, so i watch, so she observes, and we are still in our ur∞b∞r∞s

φbsessi∞n

..the audience is now lead by the natives to the adjacent warehouse .
.   .   . like cattle we are herded through freight sized metal doors, into the next phase; the rest of the rave. Above the doors you can't help but notice the giant neon sign that appropriately reads...

*Am I sexy, you will know *

..."Why does it say that?" i ask Phena. "Name of the rave?" and from that she deducts, "Maybe it means, don't fall in love at a Rave?" I look at her like she's crazy. "Yeah, that makes no sense," she says back, and then I remember, "The French squatter chick told me that." But forget talking, this

place is loud with . DRUM $^{\bullet}$ & $^{\bullet}$ BASS . as Athena grasps my shoulders to get lost— as to not get lost. There are no

lights in here. There is only . DRUM $^{\bullet}$ & $^{\bullet}$ BASS

. BReAkBeatZ• *gabber * on its way to a milkshake of URBAN

HOUSE/BREAKS/TECHNO/HardCORE...and
                                    we've been at it for hours,
which could have been minutes,
                                    feels like fourty-five,
never sweat so much, never stopped; dancing. Compacted *Body to Body, Front 242,* drifts in and out, as the mass is one, together ebbed and flowed into the orgy we watched in envy. Everyone seems to have a mate, even when they don't, and it's all an illusion as Azalea & I continue to hook up, dance, hook up, dance, she's kissed the other girl, hot girl, she's kissed me as the other girl is absorbed into the mass of *Body to Body,* and no one's clear, and Phena dances alone, with confidence, with joy, with dignity, and with the slightest sway she could tell a man or woman no to creeping into her circle, and every so often she comes closer and kisses her sister on the cheek and tells us she loves us . together . we are all, as the snare escalates, higher, faster, more repetitive, some other girls are pushing up against me from the back, *I Need Your Loving Like the SuSuSuSuSuSuSunshine*; this time, *The Temptations* with

another . DRUM•&•BASS . Azalea's high, we're high,

You say you gonna leave me, for the arms of another /
sampled / Oh, I need your loving' / Sunshine / With me
always stay / Sunshine ⅋ the high-hat, the snare, sⱯⱯ℗s - eye
see something invisible ⊙⊙ eye feel something isssss off - a tambourine, up,
up, up, up, *Everything, Everything, Everything,* and we are
under the world's glare . We can/not be seen . No one
knows we are here . • . in the *Underworld's* hypnotic love
craft, engulfed, in a body of mass dance, on each other,
mixed with *N.R.G.*, skins against skins, sweat so hot, *rez «
like the sunshine rez « like the sunshine, cowgirl « like the
sunshine rez « like the sunshine* train.car beats, chugga, chugga so
many of us now shirtless, so many of us, - eye see something
invisible ⊙⊙ eye feel something isssss off - all of us, higher, up, up,
up...*I'm invisible, i'm invisible, i'm invisible,* ǝvǝrythǝǝng *i'm . Why
don't you call me I feel like I need your loving like a razor of love s*
    u   *n*   *s*   *h* *in*   *9.*

•. . .¡nvisible, ǝvǝrythǝǝng ¡'m ¡nv¡s¡ble, ǝvǝrythǝǝng ¡'m ¡nv¡s¡ble ¡

. . . .

!nv!s!ble, ǝvǝrythǝǝng !,m !nv!s!ble, ǝvǝrythǝǝng !,m !nv!s!ble ! •. . .

i'm ǝvǝrythǝǝng, i'm invisible, ǝvǝrythǝǝng i'm invisible, ǝvǝrythǝǝng, up,
up, up, higher, us of all, us of many, so tireless now, us of
many, so - eye saw you invisible ⊙⊙ eye feel us disappear . disparaged . in heat -
hot, so sweat, skins against skins, other, each on a rhythmic
wave of the sensational electric glide shot through us all like
a beam of light chaining us into the mass strung of gold, and
bronze, and malleable to the sense of obligation when there
is no one left to obligate; alone–

    –You are alone. By yourself. You
hadn't noticed how closely you were aware of it all. Her beeper had
vibrated, you felt it against your hip, she turned to check the

number...the music was in the trips of a gyrating surround sound movement as she followed the rhythm against you, even as you turned and she was gone? behind you, to the side, the lights, so happy in colors, you were. With your eyes closed, safely invisible to anyone, you felt her love you, not long, moments, and moments again. But you were alone. When you open your eyes, there are a number of girls beside you, none of them Azalea, a few of them are Phena, and soon enough, only one will be Phena, like me, asking..

..."Where'd Az go?" you ask Ona, no Phena, i ask Phena again, "where'd your sister go?" she looks over her shoulder, so dark in here, every so often they sweep the warehouse with a blowout white. A wipe of white-washes through us, in fact. "She got paged," Phena yells in my ear.. . S K I. P. *Here comes the sun little darling / it's all right / alright* . . sk.i.p. *Al-riiight.* "Who?" i had to yell back at her as the crowd goes mad for the music...Feel the vibe, feel the bass, *bbbbrrrrrr-stick-em, haha, stick-em*..."Follow me!" and she takes our hand and plows our way through the mob, "I didn't know it would be this big," Phena tells me as we get stuck at a gated sound system somewhere in this mass . . .

"Did we hook up back there?" you had to finally ask her. "No," she tells you, "That wasn't me." This confuses the strange feeling. "Who was it?" Her hand is on my shoulder, looking right into my eyes. She is there on the other side of this mask.

"You don't remember?"
I shake my head, "I had my eyes closed."
"The whole time?"
Shrug.
"A lot of people.
You made out with like six different people..."
"How?"
"They all wanted to kiss the guy i n the mask, dude..."
"Is that why she left?"
"No, don't be stupid, she got paged."

. .—- eye saw something invisible   .   ∞   . .

eye know something is off -   .

— — — — where — i s — — —

—A— ϱ— L — A — — — — Z —A—.

. . .family dinners were rare in that household. ..you'll never forget her story.. . ..it was your covenant.. . ..on that roof.. . ..she begged you to leave her forever, leave or live out her entire life engaged in <u>our</u> life.. . ..and you both made love after she gave her entire self in exchange for both, Clever's chemistry ℘ Kyle's disparaged invisibility.• •When family dinners were called, they rarely involved anyone less than our Father, the business partner, the managerial staff, Father's secretary, and one time, my sister, mom, and I got to go. ; this was very exciting for me. I remember that part . . They dressed me up in a pretty white dress, did my face with rosy cheeks, a little blush, and a blue ribbon in my hair. My father thought all girls should wear ribbons. . .Good Times Come To Me Now.

. .

"Trust me...when you're a kid you think everything is rainbows and teddy bears," Azalea had told Kyle and you, "I grew up different," and you asked, "You didn't get to watch the Care Bears™?" and she was easy to say, "No, i wasn't allowed to watch TV?" bashful . bashful about that ? ? ?

"who paged her?"

i ask again as we wait along the other side of the speaker. "our uncle," she says, "they're close." The music is bouncing, we should really all be dancing. What is it with these girls tossing and turning in a club like setting. "do we have to leave?" which is not answered by being tugged back through the crowd, behind the holes attached to my hidden identity. . . "I don't tell people this story. . ." — ". . .Who am i going to tell. . ." — "I want you to know me; ɘ v ɘ   r   y   t   h ɘ ɘ ng "will you meet meeeeeeee.... fly away" .... continued the memory of Azalea's covenant, her fable of love, about her family of animals' living D.isparaged•N.egative•A.byss. ..

.
. ... Mom
...had to sit beside my Father
at the head of
a long dining room table;
castle long.

The *family* dinner was held in my father's suite, the penthouse of a building in London. I remember it was a triangle roof, all glass windows. My highchair was at the foot of the table, where the angled ceiling was lower. I remember because I pressed my hand on the sky above my head to touch the moon. It was a champagne moon. Phena sat at the table somewhere." — "How old were you?" — "Four. Older four. My birthday was a month later," — "So you were, five. Five makes more sense that you'd remember stuff," — "I didn't know, really. Nothing that ever made any sense, until Phena found me. me. me. . . .

Phena and I have gotten to a wall. There is still just enough room to stand and maybe squeeze along the wall to get to an exit without treading back through the crowd. Fuck, we gotta find her. Whistlin' , bouncin' , the Elephants are entering the exit, we're trapped again. *"I don't know what this world is coming too!"* over the loudspeakers, *"Rollll the drums, don't you rock with me — HIT Gotta have House. Music. Gotta have House HIT — _____ —Roll the drums. BoP. To the Rythm—* but your mind will stick even in the thick of it; chemistry. Azalea's chemistry.

"Supposedly, we just sat doing nothing at that big table for a long time. Twenty minutes. That was how long a meditation would last and we had to wait for that. There was Father, his business partner who was our uncle, Father's secretary, our older cousin Kenny, and the business partner's wife. I don't remember her name. I knew her really well, for a long time, but nobody called her by name around me. They didn't even call her Aden's wife. That was my uncle. uncle Adenian. I have two uncles. uncle Aden, and Uncle Mike. I really like Uncle Mike. We say he gets a Capital U. He just moved to London to help me and Mom ₀   ₀

L ᵒ

v

.

꒹

they all entered the diningroom . . .
. . . someone said something to my mom
that made my mom want to get up. . .
. . . so uncle Aden pushed her back down; held her there.
. my father yelled at Mom . . . Phena looked at me, covered her eyes with her hands / mimicked the horror like it was a game. I covered my eyes too. yell i n g happened e v e r y w h e r e . e v e r y o n e w a s m a d at my m o m m y . m o m m y. m o m m y. i guess i was calling for her the whole time. That's what Phena says. Phena remembers everything. She watched it all. What she could see. She made me keep my eyes closed the whole time. Saw them arguing with her about love and happiness. Phena didn't know want any of it meant. She was young too. And they grabbed Mom by the wrists and took her to the back-office space . maybe it was the bedroom . Phena said it creeps her out to think Father had a bedroom in his temple. It wasn't the bathroom, she knows that because they made Mom take a shower before we all left. .   .   •

"Okay, go," Phena announces, trying to pull me out of myself, out of the thought of you, us, all of us...out of this forever dancing mass and she busts us through the gap of the metal doors as the last Elephant passes...And you know you have to find the phone-booths, find your wife. "Probably by the bathrooms," and Phena leads us around. Neither of us have any idea where we are. "Bathrooms? Bathrooms? Bano?" This is a nightmare of a search. Too high. Can't remember what high isn't. The room that was the performance has been retro-fitted into a huge ambient space, soundscapes ℅ *Aphex Twin* mixed w/ an echo of the main warehouse THUMPING, THUMPING. There is no room to sit, as we wander as . w•꒹.

tip-toe through the androgynous
alien spirits congregating
in
circles
along the splatter black-lite
paint cemented

flooringggg...Phena's lost me in the visuals
as the recall of Az's conversation,
paged, by family,
a word, family;
won't stop repeating itself
horror
fear
w
h
...ǝ r

...ǝ i
s
s
h
ǝ
?

Mommy! she said she repeated in her mother's absence ..
•
When Mom came back out, no, I am wrong | when
everyone else came out
first
Mom followed them.
                    She was nearly covered in blood. Not
because they cut her, they didn't cut her. It was because they
beat her. ─────────────────────────────────TRUTH─
be told...the ropes were coarse.
The flooring, wooden, it was some other room. Not the office.
"It was behind the bedroom," Phena has begun to fill in some of the
blanks for us as we
sit in the middle of the ambient bubble, high as can be, waiting,
waiting for Azalea to find us, waiting fo r h e r to. f i nd
us am o ngs t ǝv ǝry t hǝǝ n g, ǝv ǝr y o n e
•
"Our dad was a Meditation guru," the truth, "Turned out he had

a small cult following in *San Francisco*. That's where our uncle's wife came from. *Sunnyvale*." Phena sips her plastic cup of water. "Heard about Sunnyvale. Lots of meth. Place is right outside Silicon Valley. Trailers." She offers us a sip. You gladly accept. "They had one of the first Meditation websites." — *That's an interesting badge of honor —* "Didn't mean anything. All the clients were in this rich neighborhood on the other side of the Golden Gate bridge."

"Marin county."
"Yeah, maybe?" pauses, back to the task at hand, "Where is she?" Phena looks around. you stand up to get a better look. you're waiting. what will we find. you feel separated, split in half, not fully here. something about us is invisible. There is light in this ambient bubble. You would surely see her white hair glowing in the black-lite; she should see the glow of my white mask, but that's right, marble does not glow in the black-lite; it goes dead, dead as night; i am a shadow, you are me. WE are a SPLINTER. i am a shadow . the ᴐ is getting us down. low. low on ᴐ is a bummer. .   ."I'm going to go look for her, you wait here," Phena says as she takes the cup from us, downs the rest. "Okay, but can you refill the cup, then I'll go." This fair deal only takes me across the bubble, weaving around the circles ◦   ◦   ◦
•   •   •   •

                                                                        •

                                                                        ∶

_____   •• • •

      • uncle pushed my beaten Mom back in the chair •
           •   •   •
And Dad told Phena she, "should look after her Mom," that she, "should look after my Mom, for me (Azalea), for my sake, because it wouldn't be fair to let me, as a little baby.   .

•

_____

"Here," and you hand Phena a new cup of water. you have my own cup now. to be clear. to remind yourself, "i'll stay here, you find Azalea." She smiles, reassures me, "Yes, sit here. Leave the mask on, that way we can find you," and to that you can only agree to sit; wait .   .   ."Hold on," you grab her before she gets away, "You got the coke?" Phena pulls it from her change purse, palms it to me, scurries off. Responsible in the European Ambient unmapped Bubble has you clearly high, eyeing everyone, everything, every word you don't understand . . . as you scan the room for feds, undercovers, eyeballs on us so we can dust out a bump or two onto the crevasse of your thumb—drop.sniff—rise •   •

_____

         • o worry about her. Then they took me away," and
she stops, Azalea doesn't need to breath, she just happens to

be, far from an end. We took a moment to wonder if the sun will come up in the next twenty as we sit, hands embraced upon the Dresden rooftop, sober, clear, alone; both of us, so alone, so left alone, though mine was petty, to be clear, as she would always say, to be clear, the loneliness i've had in my lifetime, petty, the absent value of nothingness learned, nothingness taken, given, or borrowed. To reflect her diamond eyes in my own eyes; as to be expected, become us as an emerald*plarəmɘɘɘɘɘɘɘɘɘɘɘɘɘɘɘɘɘɘɘɘɘɘɘɘɘɘɘɘɘɘɘ—

---

they're not back yet, sit down. we have to keep waiting. do not move. patience. the night is young. we are all so young. azalea doesn't act

young

And she continued —as you bit your fingernails waiting and waiting in the Ambient room on the Roof in Dresden at the rave in Prague that was remembering the roof off hell that was more than a memory to your lover— "To my disbelief," she continued...

She had been taken. By her own father and this Uncle nobody liked. I couldn't comprehend if he was her dad's brother, or the mother's brother? "They took me to Greece first. I remember Greece because we had a green lawn in the back of the house. Father and I slept in the shed for the first few months. uncle lived in the house. uncle's wife came a long time later. Probably a few months later; I was little. She was very mad that I was sleeping in the shed with Father. That's when I start to forget stuff..." There is a breeze. A change in the Dresden, German sky. The sun is still minutes away, "That's when— You're not going to...no, you're not are you," looking me in the eye. "I found you," i told her, "I'm not going to judge you. I keep my word, I know I'm in love with you."

— əvərythɘɘng, razor of love, əvərythɘɘng...ambient remix...where are they?...maybe i should go find them...? əvərythɘɘng ? i'm invisible ? əvərythɘɘng .?..your white black mask in black light . the shadow . they will never find you; lost, forever. don't be dramatic . this is...

...not

like

being
locked in a closet...

...for months, years; I'm sorry Clever, I am not exaggerating."
She is not crying either. "There were meals, drinks,
medication, and reading. I was allowed to read. You would
think that would be hard for a little girl whose Mom had just
taught her how to read the alphabet and what a word even
looked like. I taught myself how to read; in the closet.
Taught myself every day. When I finally went to school, I
had to have a special tutor because I read funny. I
pronounced everything wrong. Understood what I read, but
read funny. That's what they called it. They gave me drugs
as well. I've always taken drugs. Good ones, bad ones. Fun
ones. They raped me, too .   . • •. .
                                    •. •.

                                                        •
     •   •   •   . •   • that's it, i have to go look for them •
                                                        alone

•CIRCLE THE PERIMETER•LOOK INTO THE CENTER•THEIR
HEART WILL RESONATE•FIND THE DIAMOND•.s. Sister is
there,   waiting   for   you   in   the
front.outside.not.accompanied.alone.outside.frontdoors.alone•did
you   not   find   her•no•what   do   we   do   now•wait   until   it's
over•sunrise? probably. how long is that? an hour. . .
                                    .   . •   •. .
                                            •. •.
                                                •
                                                I've
accepted the rape most of all. I wasn't, penetrated, it wasn't
like that, it was emotional rape. Sounds, and things I saw.
When I was older, I was raped, physically, but not by the
family. Maybe uncle's wife touched me? I could understand
why she did. I don't think about that, ya know?...because it
makes me think—^thinking— It must have been very hard for
her. When I was fifteen my uncle got sick. Hepatitis, from
needles. Then my father got sick a few months after that; he
died really quick—" you had interrupted her with earnest
empathy, "I'm so sorry." She brushes her father's death off,
"That was a long time ago," but it wasn't. It was maybe a
couple of years at the most...

•...tick•tock•not her, not him•another group of twenty•°nother°•not any of
them•"where is she?"•
•i don't know•
__thinking__

"My closet was located in their power learning Sybaritist
den.
There was obviously some intent behind their situating such
a young girl's ears, smells, and sight from under the door;
the crack, a half an inch of sight. Do you know how much
you can see from under a door?—i had shaken my head—
Everything. . .   __thinking__   __
thinking__

.   .   .ɘvɘrythɘɘng !,m !nv!s!ble ! •.   . . °•this is
royally fucked up. my girlfriend is missing. . .her sister keeps
guaranteeing my self that we'll find her, but i'm telling us not to trust it,
that the crowd's swallowed her up.   .   .people are still exiting the
venue.   . .eyeball each and everyone of them.   . .her sister has begun to
vibe   some   worry,   concern—   anger?•"I   hate   when   she   does
this"•"Disappears?"•"Pretty much
.   •.   •   .•
                                                                          . •
              i'm am so very worried. . .• strung out. . .... .   •
where is she?
                                                       where was she?

"You can see everything from the floor to the ceiling far on
the other side of the room. That's how much you can see
from the crack under a door, unless the people were close to
the closet, and they were never close, so I could see
everything. Every activity that was discovered on the
padded floors and the wall; the wall I can see anytime I want
now. I will never forget that there were forty-two buttons
stitched into the red pillow wall. It was difficult to see the
side walls, but it was all ropes and ties." The storyteller has
hesitated. Perhaps i have flinched, revealed judgment on my
face? "I know what you're thinking; S&M. This wasn't sadist,
masochist stuff; my father was very spiritual. A spiritual
scientist. This was all Sybartism exfoliation. The need for
indulgence   comes   from   our   human   compulsion   for

preoccupation," she lessoned me on that roof. "uncle Aden and Father wouldn't always use the room to shag, they did a lot of conversing and meditation. uncle's Sybartist tendencies were more violent than my Father's. Definitely more frequent. I remember that. Can you believe that? I was a baby, but I could tell that uncle was always more violent with the stimulants they used on each other and their followers that would come every few other days, or weeks. I had no idea what time was and there was no window in the Sybartic dens."— . . .there was no question i did not want to believe her, then, and now. such a bullshit story, for what? there was no ulterior motive to fabricate such a. . .• . . .no one else has come out. . .silence. . .Phena has her hand to her mouth. . ."Do we call the•— "Phena told me the police said it was a problem that Mom was reporting the kidnapping weeks late. She was becoming a suspect. There was a private investigator that started to help Mom search for me. I guess the closet was in Italy. They had taken me there. My father and uncle had a special villa in the south, with a beach, alongside other closeted father's and businessmen. I come from a very fucked up place, Clever. I don't want to be where I come from, you know?"—"i know"—"I don't have to be. Once uncle died, and Father admitted he wasn't in love with my mother anymore, if ever, something set me free. He was sick, couldn't control me anymore, and I guess that's when I got to put on my mask and make that tortured life go away, through happiness, through indulgence. I won't let myself not feel good, you know? No bad times, only feel goods. .   .

.• . . No Bad Times, Only Feel Goods . .•"hey Azalea says that all the time"
•"i know
•

"We better get on a train. Maybe she went home?"
The ride is tense.   My teeth hurt.   Legs shake.

●

•open•the•door•   •open•one•door•
          •open·any·door•   •open·her·door•

●

"She's here, the lights are off."
"Why won't she answer the door?"
"Sleeping?"
We've been banging on the door all morning.
since we first got here, at 4am, maybe 5.
"She's not sleeping. She's not here."
"Then she was here."
"Now what?"
"We wait."

●

How long? Why did you give her the keys? How long?

●

taken me. escorted me. ordered me; for me. buttered my toast for me. refilled my ice water. offered me the ketchup. my new friend. Phena is becoming something real to me. i am recognizing the impact a variety of individuals can have of, on me. Is the growth rapid? Isn't the current ever flowing through your veins? No time to stop, only time to wait; forever. "Do you like your eggs?" she asks you. you drop the mask back over your face, "Different." — "Poached." — "I've had poached before. I'm from an old chicken rancher town." — "Are you a farm boy?" she kindly cleans the edge of the mask's marble lip, "You got ketchup on your mask," and giggles, and you giggle; i giggle. "You're pretty cool, Phena," i tell her, innocently enough, nothing more, just acknowledgment. "What?" — "Huh?" — "I didn't understand what you said, you mumbled."—*I don't recall saying anything?* — "Sounded like you said, 'Nothing more, just an acknowledgment?" — "Did i?" — "Sounded like it?"— "But i miss spelt it?" — "If that's what you kids are calling it these days." She jumps, startled, "Oh, I got a page." Phena looks over the digital number, the waitress takes our plates. i swipe the last crumb of bread, smirk, she rolls her eyes...she cannot see my expressions. Phena can. Azalea certainly can. The waitress; incomprehensible. She can never be my mate. i shiver. creeps along my spine, from above my rectum, along

the tailbone first, through my ribs, under my pits, and it is those nerves that sting the fury in comparison to the rest of the fear the underskin of my underbody feels with the thought of mating...even with my own soulmate...who is lost
.
    still .

Phena is back from the payphone. Drops coins.

and i follow her out.

"She's back. Did you do all that coke?"

"Yeah, sorry. Where was she?" — "Family"

"Sounds...   bad?"

"Isn't it always bad?" ———————————— "What; family?"

"Other...

...people's...

...lives."

And he coughs on me as we exit the restaurant; Austrian guy, "Pardon," he says. I recognize that accent. Okay, Phena recognized it. We noticed he looked very ill. People like that need to stay home. Phena has been wiping her eye the whole walk home. "Coughed right in my face and I can still feel the spit in my eye." — "That's really unfortunate, dude," you had said, more concerned with the consistent thought of where the fuck my girlfriend went last night in the middle of the rave, on 9, to meet up with family, than getting a cold? And i know what her family is like. An idea at least. A vile description of corruption, spiritually, socially sexual for over indulgence in front of little girls— and...we're back at the apartment. i have yet to experience Prague. "Are you going to marry my sister?" Phena asks about a block before the destination. "Why would you ask me that?"

"She'd marry you, if you asked," she tells me.

"Wait, did she tell you that?"

"I know my sister. She doesn't know how to love anyone," and she stops me, "She loves you."

"What are asking me to do?"

"Nothing, just want you to know you're welcome in our house."

And we open the door, head up the stairs, forget about all the troubles past, present, and future. The now begins, never. It has already begun as i let Phena climb the last flight of stairs alone. As she unlocks the door, i unzip my fanny pack. As Phena disappears into the apartment, my pill disappears into my esophagus, for i am guttless, gut punched by what i thought was love, what i flew to love, flew to flee with, only to lose her along the way in order to find my, and i enter the apartment...Azalea is alone by the window, Phena is nowhere to be seen. "A?" and she turns to me, "I'm sorry, Clever," she walks up to me, "I got scared. I didn't want you to see me scared." The window is open. i can see the exquisite dancing angels as they vine up the opposing building; blossoms in their hair.
"Scared of what?"

"Patience."

•

"Patience?

   "Your face is so beautiful," she touches our marble mask, "I'm scared I have no patience."

•   • "For what?"

"Falling in love with you," and she cried into my chest for hours; for what seemed hours. For what can only be dreamt as a lifetime, and soon enough i could feel the •ɘ. again, and

A has indulged herself as well. "Here baby. •ɘ.at this."
for
     us two-day of absolute beauty, peace, tranquility, and physical psychedelia in the city of Art Nuevo where the Absentia fills your nostrils each time it goes down. Where the walls crawl in living metals and alchemist labs covered in vines of the gods and women of the abstract, with deer heads that lead you left to the upper crest looking out over the entirety of the city of Prague; together. i. n•ɘ.•ɘ.d. y.our lovin.lik•ɘ.th•ɘ.sunshin•ɘ. •ɘ. •ɘ. •ɘ. •ɘ. •ɘ. •ɘ. •ɘ. •ɘ. •ɘ. •ɘ. •ɘ. •ɘ. •ɘ. •ɘ.

•ɘ.

the
river. her hand entangled in yours. Your fingers fondling her
under the arch, melting in your hand like a virgin over and over
again. Kissing in the hidden gardens, fucking in the bathroom of the
fifth or sixth Absentia bar, puking in the alley, showering in the
apartment, dreaming in the bed, and waking up...Alone? You are
alone? Why? You should wake up again. i fell right back to sleep.
Woke up an hour later;

                                                    alone.

Chapter - Eye met a Man to Die, so I rolled w/ it

ignore him

                  wh y are y o u p a r. a n. o. i d about this girl?

love her

                              wh y do y o u l ove her?

                  swill.

wh o am i; alone?

This time they are all gone. Everyone. Azalea, Phena, the gnomes, the neighbors, the streets, the tv, Ona, Miguel; everyone has disappeared. How many hours have you paced through this apartment? Dark again. No one. Nervous. Nothing. Wondering. Thoughtless. The door opens. Both girls enter. Sisters. Azalea goes straight to our room. "She needs a minute," Phena tells me.

"Is she okay?"
"Did you find stuff to eat?"
"Yeah, i'm good, thanks. Where'd you guys go?"
"Don't worry about it."

(p a t i e n c e)

and soon enough she talks to me.
"Did you do drugs today?"
"Maybe, why?"
"I don't think you should do so much."
"I'm just on vacation."
"You're leaving?"
"Huh?"
"That's okay, I knew you were."
Azalea has become quiet again. It's 2am. We've been talking..
.since half past twelve.

I've gotten up to take a leak. Might take the mask off. Phena's asleep. The TV is on static. I pee as I watch the static in the mirror of the bathroom with the door wide open. Hot. Take off your shirt. Muggy. Take off the mask. Your face is red, Clever.

My European story has vanished.
– I feel, like myself; not like them.
Built a legacy in a simple chance meeting.

Your face is really red, Clever.
Wash it. Mask smells sweaty. Wash it. Wash your pits. Take a
shower. Yeah, you haven't showed in a bit. When? Yesterday? No,
the yesterday before. When we were spun in the romance of us
around this city of sensuality.

Sybaritism. What is it exactly?
Do they have books about it?
Where does one find other Sybarites?
Want ads? The internet? Underground Clubs?
Definitely self-help groups. Would she want that again?
Engraved in her psyche? Should I get kinky tonight?
She does like the mask. I don't want to lose her.
Can't lose her.
Must
do
anything and
everything to
keep
her
all
to
my

s
e
l
f
i
s
h

n
e
e
d
s

A hallway this short, should never be remembered to be this
long, but by the time I returned to our bedroom, Azalea had
begun to truly vanish...but I was, am wrong, it is eye who

has vanished; unmasked with Phena's one-hitter still packed with opium Azalea had gotten after visiting family last night...still buzzed from the over indulgence of..."What's wrong, A?" you asked her when you sat back down on the bed. Her back to you, in the dark, still awake, still absent, more absent, diluted version of the A you had grown to love in the short week...but a week turns into a month and a month a year, and a year a lifetime. "Life does not abide by time, Clever," she addresses the wall, not you. Azalea had gotten hot in the mug of night as well. She has removed her shirt. Her soft, white, pale skin attracts your fingers, and you caress her; becoming yourself again, not distant, together, here for her, and she turns

without eyes.

ǝvǝrythǝǝng

ǝvǝrythǝǝng

ǝvǝrythǝǝng   ǝvǝrythǝǝng

ǝvǝrythǝǝng   ǝvǝrythǝǝng   ǝvǝrythǝǝng

i   n   v   i   s   b   l   e
                                                                                         w

Where has DIAMOND◊EYES gone? They're empty sockets, an abyss that sucked the universe inside out and through her pupils that look right through me . . . You are my soulmate, Kyle. A's mind has spoken. He is my deathmate, Clever. Her plump lips turn blue and say nothing, but my mind has heard her incorrectly. "Erebus' wants me now. I have to go."

Where?

Away forever.

Because I'm on vacation?

No.

Why then?

Erebus called. We have to, together.

This guy isn't your cousin, is he?

ǝvǝry-no-thǝǝng , ǝvǝry-no-thǝǝng , ǝvǝry-no-thǝǝng , ǝvǝry-no-thǝǝng, ǝvǝry-no-thǝǝng

And her body caved, collapsed into itself, dropped from heaven,
down to hell, up from the bowels, covere
d in vomit and blood.

<u>A Memory by Kyle Claibourne that We Will Never Shed without Clever</u>
Life is Unapologetic

Vomit and blood gushing from the mouth I have loved, the mouth I have given myself too. Vomit and blood, gushing from her beautiful blue lips, upon me, over the bed, in my eyes, my mouth, my hair, and she has twisted herself into a knot, and it is beautiful rainbows with three winged angels dressed like butterflies as they fend off the vicious airborne hornets that jab their anal syringes into the black, blood filled hearts of the decomposing angels, as microscopic mosquitos suck the puss from their putrid personas because traumatized angels have more than one soul, one to live, and one to die. Azalea looks up from her own mess. She cannot pull her arm out from behind herself; she has dislocated her own shoulder. Her leg has bent under her torso, her neck twisted nearly half around, her eyes of coal roll back into their sockets— hold • just long enough for us to remember she is a woman, a human, alive, breathing person • Not a twisted growth ripped from the fecal matter of cancer • ... "I'm Die•ing!" ...she screams bloody murder into your bruised, irritated face of flesh. Shrills that would deafen a dog, seizures that would terrify the devil, and the might of a trillion vagabonds whom you've tried to domesticate. And you're panicked as she attempts to drag herself out of the bedroom. She will kick your face, scratch your back, pull your hair, beat herself against the walls, the doorframe, vomiting, bleeding, screaming, shrills, "Let me DIE!!!"all for her deathmate.

...you wish all to fucking hell
                          and back that none of this was real...

                          ...that you weren't
suddenly raced up a flight of stairs, with a steady beat, boom, boom, boom, a metronome of consternation, boom, boom, boom, yet the metallic stairs were a muck of mercury, burning th e s o les of your feet; barefoot. A goo of slop that pulls you down from the gravity of yourself, pulled to the center of the earth as you desperately try to run yourself back to safety...but there is blood everywhere, mixing with...and yet even before...there was her...

                          ...vomit & piss
and i couldn't stand as my bare feet slipped; my knees collided against the tiled hallway...the same endless hall that my dear Azalea has continued to crawl along back through her own river of insides. "Please," I urged her to stop...She snaps her head back first, followed by her torso, her gentle small breasts cover in bile, her toes wrapped over each other, her fingers lodged out of socket, ⅋ her white panties stained by the urine she cannot hold. " DIAMOND◊EYES?" I asked her, because - through our tears, she has no eyes anymore. "OH,

MY GOD!" Phena has found us. i've shoved a chair leg into A's mouth as a bite to save her luscious tongue as her body had begun to seize uncontrollably. Her shakes knock the chair on the tile like a hammer against a skull, again, and again, and again...i can't hold it down. The smell is everywhere. The tile has begun to crack. i have to continue to put the leg back in her mouth. i've chipped at least two of her perfect teeth.

It was all you could find ? found ? forget ?...you don't know why. you don't know why she's dying . You hadn't over done the drugs in one day...you know better...there are limits, we must know our limits...does she? did she? And then she beats her beautiful face into the plaster wall, busting her nose, bleeding all over her delicate face...

        "I hate your fucking time."
"Stop talking about time."
            "Your time, not mine."
                "You'll never understand the evil of time."

"I'll call the police," Phena says, but Clever couldn't hear her; Azalea has bitten down into his palm instead of the wooden chair leg. You have to—

                                 —punch her in the nose
                               to get her to release
                                her Pitbull jaw

        "I'm so sorry, A," you whisper after you pull my hand free...
          and she knocked her scalp against the corner of the wall
      that has gouged itself into her cheek that gets shredded from
        the gravity pulling the weight of her head to the cold, wet,
                      tiled floor of the romantic
             Prague apartment where you fell in love

                                        a

g   a   i   n

                                        a

          Prague apartment where we fell in love
             on the cold tiled floor in the hallway

                              the gravity pulled me into a lover
                              kissed her cheek, drank tears
                              rubbed our heads together
                              built up a wall with each
                              other's bleeding hands
                                                              .

                                                              .

                                                              .

"We are blood love now," she had said the other evening
after biting my...

                                                    ...wrist
        as i drank her own life juice from her feminine lips . in the
throes of our carnal intoxication . she had me bite her vagina
                                          until it bled
                              her flower lips, her cootchie
                              as she referred to it
                              ripe, tart, clean, delightful

S   y   b   a   r—

                              —i   t   i   s   m
                              without little Old Rodney

*

                              *

                                                              *

Enter   the Police

                                                              *

                              *

* "You have to leave," Phena's telling you as she stuffs your arms
with your
      belongings; finalizes by shoving the mask deep into my pack.
      "Where do I,
                  go?"
      — "Anywhere but here. You have too many drugs." —
                                          "What about A?"
                              "Come to the hospital tomorrow."
                                                        "When?"
                                          "Afternoon, evening?"
                              "I will tell the nurse you're her cousin."
                                                        "Okay."

"Are you going to be okay?"
"Should I call the police?"
"You have to save your sister."
"I know, for you."
"For me?"
"It's the only reason she wanted to live."
"You knew that?"

"Go."

But it wasn't, isn't so cut and dry. These wounds were beyond the family. The FAMILY built their daughter's demise, not this world, not me, not Phena; or maybe it is Phena's responsibility. Phena has a story. Is that why she wants me to marry her? Pawn their trauma onto me? Sever their responsibility? Is this a set up? Tomorrow i might learn the truth. Until then...I am a hero on the run, with an invisible face. A hero...i know nothing.

You are just a deer on the run...hidden in the back of a late morning absinthe bar, working towards falling asleep in a park until you can visit the young woman who has given you a reason for love twice the weight of yes•turd•year; Ona. If she could see me now..."One more," you make a final order, blurry eyed, "Thrice eyed!" you announce to the bartender as you slip your face back on. "You're prettier with that thing on," he tells you, fixes up another shot of burning Absinthe, and it's down your hatch and you've hit the floor as fast as it's hit your gut...and you'll sleep it off on the curb down the block where the bartender's goons left you to watch the sunrise that illuminates the gold trimming that has spun from nearly every vine of every building that has developed atop the Alchemist's Labs ———————

                                    • *i have always wanted to*
sleep with an Alchemist. their love potions would be stellar. .

                                                                    .
———————————————————————————————— you're
awoken by an obnoxious conversation about an epidemic outside Budapest that has made these tourists to have to re-route their entire vacation and skip Hungary altogether in order to make it to Monaco on time to meet his sister, who is a missionary that has been meaning to break her vows to herself and fuck her brother's jock friend...so they say. They do not look the type to miss out much in Hungary, but who are we to judge..."We have to fit in at least two more countries before we go back," says the tall one. You have a raging headache and the reflections from the sun burrow into your cornea like the ray

from a magnifying glass. "20 Countries, 20 European Ass per," says the short one, "We come back short, we lose the bet."

We could have judged. We're judging now. Hungary is for hunger. And so, you scrape yourself off the cobblestone that has imprinted itself into your bare shoulder from your cutoff shirt, adjust your mask, and stand.

Did i run from the scene of a crime?

There was no
                                    crime,
only possible death. Death is a crime. You are suspect.

      No, I ran so I don't get arrested for drug trafficking.

you're not trafficking drugs.

      Dad warned me about this. Dad was right. I've fucked up, but considering I have not stopped using everything for days upon days and maybe weeks now, I know Dad isn't right, that he was paranoid, and really, I have nothing to worry about; I'm invisible. Maybe I should burn my passport?

            No, you will not be doing that.

      i have to see her.

Nobody said you shouldn't, we're just telling you, you are not at fault, breathe, don't look suspicious...take more drugs tomorrow...stay straight today. i have a headache. You have a joint. Phena gave you what they had stashed; three or four hash joints. Smoke one of those. That should help the headache. Thanks. Don't mention it. Well i do appreciate it. You would.

           and i got high.
and it did not help the headache.
           and i found the hospital;
after you found the Golem, or was it a Golem that found you, Clever?

THE GOLEM

i am no fool. i have no interests in idols.
"but she does," the statue said to me
i could see the words written in his mouth
he was not alive, he was their property, their life
the family's

•

the stone cold figure stood a foot or two taller than my self
my face is stronger, his fists are larger

•

my cock is cuddlier, his cock is stiff, hard, lifeless
we are blocks away from the hospital
we are both family

•

"she's told me everything about you, Kyle"
"what's to know"
"your rejection of confidence is to be idolized"
"i don't believe in idols"
"yes, but Azalea does, doesn't she"
"no, she rejects you as family . so what does that make you?"
"her lover" he says
and my fist broke into his nose

•

Erebus wipes the blood from his nostril, licks his finger;
spears his sight directly through the eye holes of my mask.
He can see us. On the corner, adjacent to the Old Synagogue,
blocks from the hospital, he could see us all, and he did
know everything about each and every one of us, "why
would a god compete for another role when his path is so
clearly written," spews manipulation from his programed
lips, "Your's, Kyle, your soulmate, forever in pain from the
lack of physical justice and remorse. At the very least you
had love, the one fallen from heaven, the one aligned at your
birth."

Why are you listening to him? What do you expect to learn? Are you
that tired? Are you drained, a burnout, or are you in love with him

too? His eyes are so very dreamy...unlike Azalea's diamond eyes, this relative has clouds in his pupils. Listen to him. Maybe there is something to learn?

"Azalea is your soulmate, no one is challenging that," and he takes a sip from his cigarette, giving us a moment to respond, but we prefer to listen, "Married in heaven, found on earth...You and I could be lustful for one another," ————— —————————————————————————he has touched you, his hand along your side, close, sensually close, "But we should all only die with our lover; our deathmate. You and I, Kyle, will never be together, because my lover is waiting for me to finish us off."—————————————————————————
——— His name was Erebus. He was no Golem. He is a garbage person with the love of death in his nihilistic abyss of a family . .the scroll tugged from the inside of the sculpture's rock hard guts. .word for word you tugged at the scroll.

You. . .
. . .alone could silence this abomination of love.

uno, singular, heroic, dynamic, confident
as the words pull one from another
sentence after sentence
this rapist of life
will have Azalea's
soul extracted from the
vile poison they had convinced
themselves would be a perfect time to die
together ; separate
w i t h
o u t
.
And the hall was longer than it was long continuously becoming
short and shrunken, unlike my head.

Phena had pulled us apart. Separated the lover's quarrel. Sent the soulless statue of delusion away, for now, forever; for now. "That's why I ran and got her, Kyle," Phena's trying to talk to me, "Are you listening to me? He's bad news forget him, he won't be back," and she turns me away from watching the trench coat golem retreat into Old Town, and if he knows what's good for him, all the way back to Greece.

"They're together?" you ask, confused, scared, tortured, watching the fucker walk away. "It wasn't right, we told them."
                    "Told them what?"
                              "He's our cousin."
          "I know."
                              "It would hurt her."
                                                            "Incest?"
     "She's alive, Kyle. That's what matters."

is it?   who   decides that?

                         "Does she love him?"
     "I think so."
                                                            "And me."
     "You mean more to her than herself."
     "I don't understand?"
     "Damn it, Kyle, they had a death pact."

i d o n't   l i. ke. any part of   that.   s.
                                             e.
                                   n. t. e. n. c. e. .
                         as she waits outside
                    i enter the hospital; alone
phil collins don't care anymore, why should i ?
                    says the stubborn hurt fool in me

Chapter - That goodnight

"You need to go," Azalea pushed me away.

"Why?"

"You're a god-damn AK. You shoot, shoot, shoot."

"You're not making any sense."

"Fuck you, Clever."

"My name's Kyle."

You just didn't want to say anything imperious, trite, condescending; you didn't want to rage on Ona with Azalea who clearly has had a life before yours. You did not want your arrogance to remove the mask you've so cleverly crafted over your self that, before you had even sipped the crystal-meth on ice as you crossed the Atlantic, the crystal your friends had given you to keep you up on the shrooms they advised you eat before you boarded that flight, so you'd show up clear, seen, and ready for the European experience with your beautifully exotic Ona's sex along the shores of every country, in the mist of every party, along the times of training your dream to teach Ona the delicate nature of the consistent psychedelic experience you had mapped out for months in your bedroom at home. Scientifically micro dosed amounts of various mind-altering substances...figured out when you could read, when you could still comprehend a stop light, interact with a teacher, authority, your parents, your father who knew you were experimenting, but didn't know how much; unaware of how far you thought you'd go. You knew very well that Ona wouldn't let you do more than a dose every ten or twenty days, but that you had other plans, and if you had to start dosing her to drive her deeper into a dependence of decadence you knew what awaited your twenties with her and that we needed these last teen years to make mistakes, nearly die, climb on each other's backs across the canals, and fester the plagues that had previously spanned the European landscapes with a darkness so criminally bottomless that they could only paint it Black. So, you came, you saw, you fucking lost the plan, scraped it, foiled; foiled by the Latin fuck lover Alejandro who in return gave you the freedom to roll into a sybaritic lifestyle without her, alone, without the worry of destroying the bond we found in the high school halls when your sexy Spanish exchange student lover was yours all yours, not fucking some six foot plus, uncoordinated, boring, stalled orangutan's chick.

She was my girlfriend not yours.

You want all the credit, but none of the glory, Clever. It's unique for your generation, but I'm not the American Kyle Claibourne to your parents; I'm you, Clever, I'm everything and invisible. I am the abyss and the collective unconscious; I am you, Clever. Come to terms, your angel's up there in her hospital bed waiting for Kyle to make an appearance. You know that, she's your fallen angel, your trauma. Never mind the Family, you know what's real and what's *Memorex*. And this all just reminds you of everyone else's pain.

An example of despair;
romantically shackled to her bed rails; Azalea.

Took me about twenty minutes to cross the street to the hospital. Phena promised it would be best if i went alone; by myself; my self. She'd wait at the bistro kitty-corner to the ER. We waited for her to turn the far edge of the street before we took the last opportunity to address ourselves. We argued on that corner throughout those arduous minutes, the minutes that bombard you with innuendo on top of self-defense, and a flimsy alibi. At times, even i tuned me out. Counted the windows and the floors. Where was Azalea? Is she on floor five? Possibly six? Kyle, won't stop arguing his point. His point doesn't matter. Love matters. The inestimable. The Razor's Edge. Bloodletting. Blood transfusions. What is hers, is as must; be mine. Be mine. Mine. Miners Dozen...and i stepped, we stepped into the street, past the scooter that soared by us, skidded out, missed a bus, killed a small dog, broke the leg of the driver, panicked the bus driver; we saw all of it through the eye holes carved in the etched spiral marble face that belongs to none, but Us. Phena said to tell them you have a condition—

"Room 502," the clerk apprised me.
We nodded. She pointed to her face.
"I have a condition."
The security guard let me through without a second thought.
Elevator

u

.   .   .   .   . p

Floor 5

Ga-Din-g—• . . . with every step farther down the hall, 500 - 522, the smaller we got, the small the halls got, yet the length would extend deeper and deeper beyond my sights, like reverb, like a delay, the sounds of a deep church bell in the distance; did our girlfriend try to kill herself last night? Will she be candid with us?   .   .   .three, yeah but you can know a soul in three days.   .   .she's exactly our height.   .our bellybuttons line up perfectly.   .her inny fits in my outy.

Umbilical Mates•A calls us BELLYBUTTON BABiES

that was the first time you saw how scared she really was to have met you. shh.
she should never know we were ... thoughtlessly in love   ...   from the first
          m   o   m   e   n   t

Is it proper to knock? Tap, tap, with our knuckles. You don't
have to follow me. Kyle adds a few taps for us; my eyes roll at
his obnoxious insistence of himself as a team member.
There's no answer so he cocks the handle and steps the fuck
in. Now we're the follower, until we push him aside and approach
Azalea's foot of her bed, from behind the divider. There is no other
occupant, this first bed is empty; Azalea's bed may be empty as well,
... . "A?" we whispered, not to startle her. .   .
      .   .   .   .

        *   *   *

                          •

                    *

  *   *

When i was eight my father showed me the film *The Exorcist*.
Sudden, instantaneous horror to anything religious, at the
very least a specific horror to a crucified Jesus who would let
a child be possessed by a cowboy captain demon. It was
astonishingly clear that demons were real, just not in
California. By the time i was twelve, i was sure of my
ridiculousness in such an unnatural, super-natural fear, and
by the time i dropped acid at fourteen, i became aware of the
super-natural behavior of our environment; accept it that it
wasn't ghosts and goblins, it was that the universe was all
connected in our heads ... when we put something in our
body, by choice ... i knew i always had a choice ... i could not

be possessed on psychedelics because i wanted to see dragons, devils, dreams, darlings, and angelic dichotomies that couldn't exist in a world that was not alive, but an amoeba... we are all family ....

"Azalea," I whisper again, closer to her side this time. She turns right at me, her head twists, her face is fiery, bruised, torn, and bandaged. Her white hair, a halo of ghosts eating each other's tails, and I have the creepies, "GO AWAY!" she screams, a shrill, high pitched; dogs all across Prague have begun to bark. WOOF, WOOF! BARK BARK! WOOF BARK!

There is no arguing.
"But, A, it's me?"

"LET ME DIIIIIIIiiiiiiiieeeeeeee!

and the letters followed me back down the hall
CLACKITY-CLACKITY-CLACK down the stairs
one flight
two flight
three flight
forth fligh...and you stumble and fall and weep for all

the times. you've tried to hold it together
for all the times.
you've let others be the burden of pleasure
/ THE MASK HAS CRACKED, BUT IT IS NOT BROKEN, YET /
for all the times.
you've listened to everyone, along with your other selves
for all the times.
you've set out to tackle all the times before
/ THE MASK HAS CRACKED, BUT IT IS SOLID, STILL /

you can go home again
so sad and afraid
for nothing

you unde
rstand
up
CLEVER
UP
use the railing and pull yourself up
/ THE MASK HAS CRACKED, BUT YOU ARE NOT a golem /
get it together, put the mask back on;
forever
for Azalea
for yourself
for no one else
this is the final battle
Tomorrow we'll be married
her sister has said it will be so and ~~time~~ must
heal before any one of any of these lives can persist
P E R S I S T
out the front doors of the hospital
P E R S I S T
as you spot the Golem with another scroll
P E R S I S T
confront him with your prophecy of brightness

Our foot stepped onto the cobblestoned street. Before our second step could leave the curb, the zip of air from above shrieked like a wire tunneling itself into your ear canal—

—SLIDING

through the membrane/ a wire needling through your brain. A sound flossing. Clears away the beef jerky, citrus strings of rational, intellectual thought. Punctures its way through the opposite ear. A puncture from a metal wire of sound and yet you hear it. You hear it as clearly as you've heard the head on collision, a head on collision of A's head, her body to immediately follow, as she hits the hood of that parked car. Her head hit the hood, the body twisted over from the snap of the spine, wrapped its gravity along the street corner of the bumper, with enough momentum that the collision forced her beautiful face to ricochet, leaving a bloody dent behind and finding its resting place on the asphalt; again, her body to follow, the street car's breaks screech from every angle. Poorly timed execution. If she had taken another moment, I would have left her alone, lost, alone, without guilt, pride or Coventry, but you can feel the warm tear roll out of your eye, parting the splatter of your lover's blood on your masked face. The same lover's blood you had only recently eloped into risk and trust with. The same plasma you sucked from your bride's most private of places...The vagina this so-called deathmate stole from you in her completion of the suicide he was too centric to follow through with. A pact. Together in Death. The only moment he swore would be pure for their love, for no one else could share such a moment once they both have had it; together. But she believed a cheater. A cheater of respect, truth, honor, real love as he merely watched from across the way, solid, cold, a statue with no soul; and with that we both vanished •

• when i rushed Erebus, we stabbed him in the gut, twisting the blade, acknowledging the warmth of his blood on our cold, sad hand. "Fuck you," you said and removed the blade, cutting him once more from under the trench coat, this time his arm pit, the tendons, and leave the knife behind in the back of his knee when he screams and reaches from the papercut that has razor sliced his underarm. His teeth grit, grind, grind so hard he's broken a tooth, sprained his jaw, and you worry you'll be found if you leave the knife, and then you know, you are in vis able to slip out a stranger in the night, onto the tr ain .   .   . after you have just   •

       killed a man who watched, gleefully, as

     your lover jumped to her   .   .   .

                                .

                                death for him

                                 .

                                 .

with a sister who said she'd .   .   .   .
                                         live for you.

We're so depressed. None of this was our fault, desire, doing, participation in any sort of; dragged across that pond by a woman, child. Petty. Petty sort of love. Petty sort of love that has us run out of time in Prague. Time we can never get back. A city in ruins on the asphalt. One of the few we saw. We found the cobblestone romantic. We found the laughter nearly eye rolling. We rolled through the nights and lights as if it was all just *One More Night / Gimme Just One More Night /*

One More Night | Cause I Can't Wait Forever..."What is next train?" you ask the teller. She shakes her head, "Eh? To where you go?" There is just enough time to make an educated guess, "Venice?"

"Tomorrow."

There is a schedule flipping behind you on the big board in the train station sky. (you only took a half a tab, you're not rolling up yet, this is just nerves, Clever. climb on) And you take the opportunity to look over your shoulder, your backpack droops. You wonder if you sound suspicious. You feel naked, your face out in the open like this. Find a train and you can cover it again. "How about Vienna? We can take that to Venice, correct?"

"Yes, but it very full. How many reservations you need?" "We need one, uno."

"Gracios."

but we're in Prague
she followed your lead
"Are you Mexican American?" she asks with curiosity.

"No."

And she's unsure why you spoke Spanish / or why you are referring to yourself as a group / *or why you're ready to cut her if she doesn't obey, if she holds her opinion at a higher regard than your own freedom / not hers / our freedom / all of us / suicide is not a crime / association is not a crime /* Do you know why you are all doing that? Are you trying to be clever, Kyle? or are you trying to be Kyle, Clever?

- Shut up.
Your inner dialogue is a bore.
Petty attempt to make me sound like an intellectual.
Fuck off. I stabbed him because I could.
I could do that for myself. I could do that for justice.
Renegades don't have to be smart.
We just need a purpose.

"Platform C, twenty minutes," she breaks our train of thought. "Thank you," and we take the ticket, hip kick the backpack back onto our shoulder and find our salvation on Platform C; twenty minutes from now. We have to pee.

*

The loo's empty. A shit would be better. Stalls can also give you a minute of solitude. Three pairs of shoes gathered in a single toilette? Suspicious? Of what, sharing a line or two. A key bump or five. Today is not that day. There is no one else in here with us. We can shit and not be prosecuted for some European delinquency, which immediately leads to being locked up for the acquaintance. My flee is not as much self-imposed as much as self-survival. We were in jeopardy. That's why we left. People will understand, they'll know why it all went so well for us, why hell is a place for angels.

Chapter - Three Permanent Ink

*

I have now sat myself on A's hospital bedside, and I'm
brushing some hair from her brow-
"I want you to leave."
"Azalea?"
"Leave Clever."
"A, I saved you, I helped you."
"LEEEEEEEEEEEEEEEEAVE!"
Saliva spraying all over the mask, her arms flailing.
This is the first thing we are saying to each other after last
night?

Gagging, inside, each and every organ, tangled, inflamed,
Gagging.
I can't talk, someone's gotten a hold of my throat, cuckle
sound.
Cuckle, not a gag, Cuckle, Cuckle, tongue, swallowing,
Cuckle
Cuckle, pushing me away, Cuckle
"I want to die."
The voice of a dragon, a bear, the smoking bear dragon of
Azalea the Greek.
I'm standing, alone, away from her bedside
Azalea will not look at me.
What am I? A Cuckle, To Do? With a Deathmate?
/ snare high hat / snare high hat /
Cause' Jesus Knows Me / And He Knows I'm Right /
I've Been Talking To Jesus All My Life /
Her jaw jets away from me. I had her. Had her attention.
Oh Yes He Knows Me / And He Knows I'm Right /
Her back has begun to slouch, relaxing the strained muscles.
The sarcasm of a world so far apart from my anything and
her family cult who have raised her like sexual veal;

for what?

"If you do not leave I won't wait for our pills to do it again."
"What does that mean?"

When I Get The Feelin' You're Tryin' To Tell Me /
Is There Something' That I Should Know? /
What Excuse Is She Tryin' To Sell Me? /
Should I Be Readin' Stop or Go? /
'Cause I Don't Know

L
E
E
E
E
E

Flailing arms, tossing pillows, pulling tubes out of her throat
EEEEEEEE
Biting her Lip Until It Bleeds

L
E
E
E
E
A
V
v
v
v
v
v
v
v
v
v
v

₉₉₉ ₉ ₉9Eℓℓℓℓℓ℮ ℮℮℮

Chapter - Momentary Lapses of tReason

Daylight brightness screams into my eyes even through the grim streaks that shatter the light into a thousand blades of UV electricity through your...you just have to squeeze your lids shut, turn away, adjust from the hours of sleep in this empty train cabin. "I hope we killed him," you said to us when we woke up. No one could hear. First thoughts are important. First thoughts bring things into perspective for the remainder of the day...this one is bitter. Knowledge is power and at this moment, we lack information, purpose, as now, here, we are far from escaped. Put the points together, the fury, the past and present, the moments in between as you clutch your backpack even though you are alone in this empty cabin.

We're learning how to sleep on ǝcstasy.

*

We had found a seat in a nearly empty car. There were plenty of cabins, empty, or vacant enough, but none-the-less we were clear headed enough to recall reservations are needed for such a luxury, so as to not draw unwanted attention to our murderous selves, we sat in a booth like spot in a car instead. Four, five others scattered throughout the seats. We were safe to fall into ourselves, sleep, disappear into a healing that must occur in the darkened corridors of our psyche. And the mask returns, my face is covered, we are not to be bothered.

Landscapes soar past us in the dark. Our reflection is brilliant, illuminated by its own naturally iridescent white; the same skin tone of the great David, the young Jew who defeated Goliath. We are the young half-Jew who has slayed the Golem for forsaking his second bride. We have rested our pack between our legs. Rested our feet outside their captive shoes. Slide the headphones on. Prepare for death through more *Aphex Twin.* . .

*

. . .but there is no relation to s

o

n

g

and we slip into sleep from the multiple pills of valium

you had swiped from A's medical bag the days before
. and you thank her for that and cringe at the amount of ℞
Azalea Boosalis **had been** prescribed by Dr. Xenakis ⁚
05/12/97 Refills Remaining 04 · Multipack - 5 various
pills · Ridilin / Prozac / Valium / Something I never
heard of . like her last name, as I read it, heard it
for the first time from her bottle of pills upon pills
Sleepy; you're about to sink into a deeper well-deserved
nap. . . . .
.

.

. in the dream your foot shifts; an itch. we lift it up to give it a good scratch. there is no obstruction to lifting our foot, to fingering into the sock, and getting that tingle that moves once you've gotten the goods, so you scratch and scratch until you approximate satiety.   .   .a sense of relief.   .   . WAIT!

"Where's my pack?" I am alert again. My bag has been swiped, stolen, but when, where, who, and I see her, she pops up ten rows down, pulls the bag up to her face, and immediately begins to dig through it. That little thief, "THIEF!" I yell, only slightly muffled from my mask, enough volume to get the attention of the few, two or three other passengers now startled awake from my constant yells, "Thief! Thief!" and the girl's zips up my bag, flips us off, about to make a run for it when she's greeted by two Police Officers. Someone is tapping me on the shoulder, "Passport?" It is another Police Officer; i think. i'm shrinking back into ourselves. There is a real threat here. have we done something irrational? "Tschusch!" one of the officers spats on the girl, as the other cop rips my bag from her hands. .   . the officer beside me, in dark grey, well equipped with fatal force, flicks the headphones off my scalp, intentionally removes my mask.. .   ."Passport," he says firmly, no joke, no heavy handed insistence this time, this time he means business, this time if we do not obey we will be like the little gypsy girl who's been dragged out of her seat, kicking and screaming, kicked and beaten, dragged and twisted, spat on and cursed at, "Tschusch!" dirty gypsy, after she kneed him in his nutsack, but that just gets her in a chokehold, and he won't let go. .   .he just won't let go. "Hey!" we yell, and the monster just looks right at us, dead in the eyes; he was dead in the eyes .   .   .   .but i'm jerked forward, "Passport!" and he is not fucking around...scramble to pull it from my pants. He grabs my hand stops me quick, solid, firm, mighty, painful, "Stand!" He thinks i have a weapon, i don't, i left it in Erebus's leg .   .   .i do have dried blood on my hands . bite marks, a cigarette burn...my hands look suspicious. "Passport," he says again over the gypsy girl's screams as she is dragged out of the car, still kicking and shrilling, and even

though, yet again, not my fault.———————————————
————————————————

Can you see how influence can become overwhelming as the current shatters you again and again to lie your way through the truth to disappear; even in the eyes of a devil.
————————————————————————

I was wrong to turn her in. She isn't moving anymore. She isn't screaming anymore. She isn't fighting. She isn't even breathing.

            Last year a new task force was formed in Austria. Ona told me about it. The only thing we discussed about our upcoming trip, the last day i had spent a lasting two hours with her in our small little town, on the muddy river, forty-five minutes north of the bay, solitary enough to feel safe, solitary enough to attract brutality along the sidelines, enough to deliver suffrage to the peace every so often at the racist hands of Northern California's white supremacists. Tree cutting nomads or gold-rushed losers of a much later, intolerant generation of rules full fled conservatives & off the grid Libertarians. Madmen with guns who become cops to take down the system from the inside. .   .not here.   .

            Pay attention. ,

                                this is no time to reminisce
                                                            .

. He hands me my passport back, pushes me to pick up my pack from down the aisle, then escorts me out of the car. Are we arrested? If they search us, we are gone forever. This is how it ends, Clever. Your life, my life, our lives all gone in the wind on some random morning in some random train rolling through Austria to rid yourself from the curse that was romance destroyed first in Spain, reborn in a swimming pool, birthed in Germany and died in the Czech Republic . . . so we could disappear through Austria. . . ?

                                *

            If i can use the loo, i can eat all the ɘ.
            overdose, take me to the hospital
            runaway, escape, call home

*

i know i've got six or seven left?
nine, if i count the 1 + 1 we hid in the condom again

*

motion to him, "can i use the loo?"
he looks at me, stern
"in next car"
you appreciate this

*

he shows you to the loo
let's you in with your bag
and now you have a choice to make

*   *   *

I gag, puke into my own mask, gag, again, heave
dri b b ling out of the bottom of the chin
onto my clothes
extend your neck, let it dribble on the floor
over the sink, remove the mask,
so much vomit, makes you vomit again
Stress, fear, anxiety, anxiousness, horror, sadness,
depression, anxiety, fear, stress, paranoia, loneliness,
terrified, confident, stride, pride, purity, clean, strong, power
full of shit
        and
                a razor of love sliced open my neck on
the night corner in the streets of Prague as her face
plummeted against the metal hood, flipped into the air,
cracked open against the pavement. . .wash the mask, wash
your face, wash your self. .   . this is merely the void at the
edge of the world, not flat, not round— Octogoned; no more
Momentary Lapses of Reality
                        I have to get off this train.
                                    and
                    he
        takes
two

for the road•off the tracks

        skating on the razor's edge; barefoot

      •the cop wasn't there • we ran anyway•
      •hopped off a mile before the station•
  •tumbled, rolled, desperate, a true American outlaw•

•tore up our jeans•used our compass•came to a stop•
•outside of Vienna•in a marsh puddle•
Clever has Disappeared
•pulled leaches from his ankles•
pulled leaches from his lower back
pulled leaches from his inner thigh
pulled a single leach from the back of his ear
he had to keep moving into town
unsuspecting
covered in the light of day and illuminated in the dark of night his
new, clear and transparent, though solid, cold, & hard,
broken marble face will keep him clear of solicitation and threats
•
i'm invisible
•

•

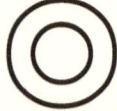

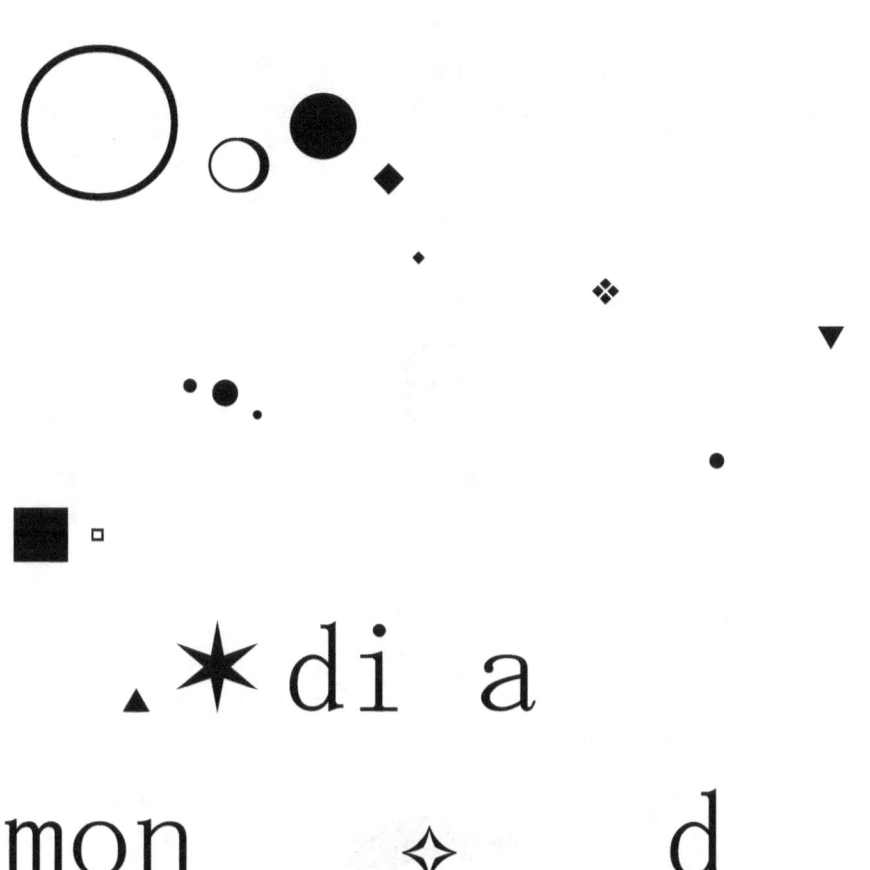

di a

mon d

seye

tnelucuL

ə

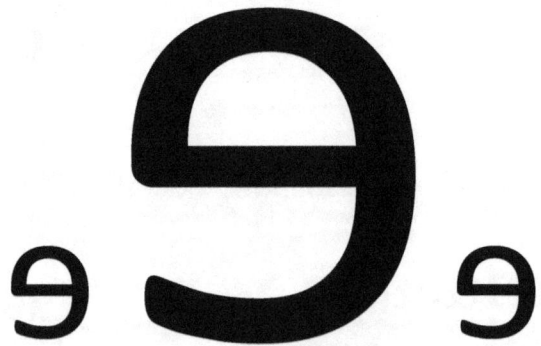

ǝvᵉrʸthⁱnᵍggggⱸ

waaavveɘ^eɘ^eɘɘeessss

ONA

.

(-*-)

•(_*_)•

-(_ˉ_)-

♂-|_ˡ_|-♂

.♂ ♂↺ ↻uNO

youknow

you, no

u know

u kno u&u

&

You

•

.&.

. . there is no$_{th}$ing . .

h

e

r

e

..

. . .

.

. .

. .

.

Chapter - Vienna, Austria - Void Intercepted

A kick to my gut; i squirm, hurts. This boot to my dream has woken us up. We look up from under the park bench. From between the seat boards, you can spot for us, an older gentleman, mid-fifties, well dressed, grey hair, grey short beard, alone, sitting on our shelter. It was his heel that gutted us. And he does it again, harder —"What?"

He has a cane
taps it down between our eyes.
Typical.
cliché.
Irreverent.

"American?" he asks from above and waits for me not to
answer him, this stranger who has woken us. We were
sound asleep, for hours, probably 24, resting, without our
backpack that we left on one of the trains some time ago, yet
the Anarchist Cookbook makes for a somewhat burly pillow.
"Hungry?" he asks, and to this our stomach defies us as it
growls while our words are silent. "You are a terrible liar,"
he continues in English with a horribly rash, Austrian
accent. The accent only heard before the murder of a Jew or
nearly anyone in a Hollywood movie. And this accent grabs
me by the ankle, yanks me out from under the bench. Such
strength. His grayed hair is merely a mirage to his bulk,
statue like, solid nature of might and insistence, an
insistence we will grow to learn comes from the irrational
confidence in their own assurance of certainty...and even in
the daze and disarray that our separated brains were at, at
this moment that we have been yanked from our park bench
cave, we knew American's like ourselves were desiring the
same sort of elite confidence...you recalled why you felt like
leaving, where you'd go, you wouldn't know, who you'd
find couldn't bother you in the hands of an escort, the
woman, young girl, Ona, who you used as a prostitute of
time, responsibility, and devotion...You bought her with
your love. You turned off with her love. She was your escape
from the inedible future of an American society that was
banning the dance, destroying the enlightened psychedelic,
archaic movement beyond the failed capitalism that coopted
the Alternative Lifestyle Scene to enslave children into a
world of inclusion when in fact everyone is still very much
excluded outside of a Rave. We didn't even struggle as he
tugged at our leg. We slide into place, into order. Maybe we
were just unsure when we were allowed to speak? Maybe
we thought he was being facetious, not fascist? Maybe we

just didn't care? Maybe we're too weak to fight it? Maybe he speaks to gHost VOids? gHosties. like meth, but different

in-turn-all ex-tetential gHost VOids

He's lifted us onto the bench, "Run out of money?" he asks. We speak not. "Lose Train Ticket?"

"Drug Addict?"

"Maybe you like being crazy in your mask, and your Anarchy novel?"

...and i turn directly at him, look him right in the eye. i have a hold on my book. The last item of property i have, property that never belonged to me, but with a name that belongs to everyone, if everyone stripped their identity...

...His

vision is black, soulless, yet charming. We nearly like his emptier smile. His single gold tooth, in the morning sun, one cannot find anything less than pretty. He wants to fuck us and we know it. "I buy you food, I take you to place for good rest," and he rises with the help of his cane. The silver plated, black ivory stake, slithers around out from his grasp and around his wrist. The cane is part of him. He is less removed from the cane as i have become in the mask. Did you lose someone as well, you wondered as he looked down upon us, still stale and disassociated from the living— including the trees and the pitiful pigeons scavenging for food. Even we have no energy to satiate our own hunger...these rats with wings eat garbage just to survive another day. Do they even like fucking? Cats don't. Girl cats don't. Screwed, sharply.

"Do you have any drugs?"

Why did you ask him that?

"What drugs you want?"
"Uppers? Downers?"

You are still engaging. Stop it, Kyle.

"Why such drugs?"

"My name is Clever."
"Come I get you food, young Clever."

You're going with him?

This is not happening; a total figment of our imagination, we're not lost. There are no paths, no obstacles, no goals, no mistakes in a VOid. We are your freewill, together, Eros, Thanatos, Clever, Kyle, Superman, Superhuman-Bred-Regular-New-Adult. We are the Voice Over in your Id.
"Clever, is it?"
        "Sure," we responded. Forgetting our own name, or accurately, unembraced by their pathetic Superegos.
"Clever, in English means, quick to learn, no?"
                "Are you going to feed us?"
"You are hungry."
                        "Survival."
"Is that what the drugs are for?"
                        "No."
He opens the passenger door to his Mercedes. You get in.
You didn't think much of it at the time. We tried to warn you earlier, but your ignorance to your own volatile state was a roll in the hay, hay, hay...Really, Kyle, where are you going? Why are you getting in the car with this guy? He thinks you're a hooker. He's going to expect you to fuck him.
        You're still high, Kyle, he's not ambivalent as you are, you are in his passenger seat•
        and a moment before we pull away from the park, i remember how fragile her porcelain face was as it crashed and shattered along the pavement while Alejandro fucked Azalea's dead body raw while Ona watched and cried over my disappearance
Miguel waited patiently around the corner with *Jimi* in his ears.
And then we drove away, and i will never see the heart of Vienna, Austria,
but i will see the countryside as we cruise w a y   o u t of town under the grey overcast skies of this nation that once loved its own annexation. . .merger. . with hell.   .   .and yet my prejudice view of this now sovereign nation

of a new generation, is confused as the only sounds from this charming man's radio are the soulful sounds of funk from the 70s and i have found myself touching his penis through his pants out of desperation to please, a plead for silent help, assistance, you know you're too fucked up to go on...Let him take you, you have no identity anymore. Your identity is bleeding in the gutters of Prague. "No need," as he gently removes your hand, "We will feed you." And we drove on, and we watched the countryside pass by, and we remembered nothing, and felt nothing, but the hunger for survival. "You have your passport?" he asked. Yes, our fingers feel it in our waist fanny pack. Yes, that's the passport, and the plane tickets. "Yeah."

"Good."

As we drove on.

*

This is not a good idea Clever, get out of this car.
I could cut my tongue out.
There are a number of options to a disappearance.

"You like black music?"

"We listen to techno."

"Techno is from Detroit."

"Guess so."

"You American and you do not know that?"

Don't respond to that.
You are not yourself Kyle Claibourne.

"Take off your mask."

"No."

"It must hurt."

It does hurt.
Take it off Kyle.
Let the country air aid
in lowering our temperament.
And so, we do. Our driver will not look at us. He is respectful to our boundaries. Respect only portrayed in the characteristics of a military man, a general, sergeant; not in a cop, guard, or vigilante. We trust him, enough, to allow Kyle to strip down to his naked face rush as he stretches his head out THIS MAN's WINDOW like we were HIS DOG. There is a

mist in the air, a humid fog that does in fact cool the rash on Kyle's skin that has broken out amongst the heartaches &.   .
.

.   .   .we pull off the main road and onto a graveled drive lined is massive Austrian pines, the redwoods of the post-annexed Germans. "Beautiful," whispers Kyle as we put the mask back as we approach the first a fountain.   .   .   .

Chapter - Azalea's Abyss of Wealth and the Delicacies of The Universal VOidless ego•

"beautiful people, beauteous thieves"

We read the inscription plated on the fountain. He appropriately translated it for me, as he circled us completely around the fountain and then straight towards the ivy covered home, mansion, compound, castle; monstrosity coveted behind vines intertwined, curled, embracing, tied, strung, noosed, loose, and still cubic and stiff as the sculpture of the mighty horse that bursts in and out of the geysers. The head of the stallion was that of an orgasmic woman, as if penetrated by the expressionist body of the horse, the tail whipped up slapping her in the face, while the man was saddled upon it all is embraced by not one, but three naked women whose hands melt into his flesh, their faces blank; his face blank. The characters of this artist's tale are more invisible than— i

want to fall asleep upon arrival
"Dinner will be served once you've gotten your rest, Master Clever,"
he had said as he rolled the car into the side garages. Had i been
asleep this entire drive? In the rearview mirror i can just make out the
fountain a quarter mile back on the drive way. "Did i sleep the whole
time?" i ask him. "No, you merely slept the last few miles. We will
have you to a room immediately," he responded as the garage door
closed behind us, as my eyes drooped, and i do not recall falling back
asleep until i was awakened by my own inner time piece, the need to
pee.

Finding the bathroom in my suite was easy enough although we had
obviously never been here before. In the god awful wealth of this
bathroom we can see we are naked, been stripped of our clothes, save
for our face. He had left our mask on before we retired to that hand-
carved art deco, king sized bed behind us in the mirror, the mirror
designed for a giant, or a woman guest who would have insisted in
looking her best from every angle.

We can't pee. In fact, our balls ache. Tight. Not so much the
testicles, but the groin muscles, our back muscles, the sides
of my abs pull and pull. Come on, pee. Finally, a first shoot,
a jet burst, then it tightens up again. We're going to get this
out. Clench that groin, like you're trying to get harder for
her. Clench, clench, burst, and my track opens and releases
the tension of our knotted bladder, knotted insides. Sleep
more.

His head hits the pillow. The sheets are soft, softer than the
smoothest of skin. The comforter even softer. He wants to read his
book. He is too tired. Tomorrow. Tomorrow you can read. The air in
the room seems to be circulated, but how is a mystery. He doesn't see
any vents, but the room is cool. Possibly the stone walls. They are
cool to his touch. His eyelids so very heavy. Massaging his groin out.
He stumbles, but he is already flat in his bedding. He jerks, yet he is
too tired to recognize the muscular throbbing. So, he sleeps again,
and again. Will he miss the dinner he was so promised? Is he even
aware he is here and here being somewhere he never expected to be
lost and found in...but maybe Kyle will figure out how to therapize
himself before he undergoes the cleansing he fears the lunatic plans
to put him through. Why didn't the guy just let Clever suck his dick
in the car, give him some fucking money, and be through with it?
They could have used some money. More than food. Lost everything

somewhere…probably the train, maybe Prague, somewhere took his money, took his identity, took his Euro-Pass, left him with a passport of a himself, a self he barely recognizes anymore, and his plane tickets. Plane tickets are useless to a thief. The shrooms and the pills were a bonus to the little gypsy chick…but why so considerate? Why not take the entire fanny pack?

Because you wouldn't wake up. She was concerned when she saw you were an American with no train pass, alone, and obviously physically destr…and then Kyle fell back to sleep for hours that added up to a few days; perhaps.

*   *   *

There will be a few moments Kyle will recall when he awakens from his terribly needed nap. He'll recall the darkness in the room, despite the massive window because it is covered in storm curtains. He'll recall something shifting him to the side, then back again. He'll recall the sound of someone as they leave the room. In that same moment, he will recall the empty sound of the door clasping closed. Might it never had been fully closed? Perhaps just not latched. And he will not be surprised to have to concentrate to hear the ticking of a high-hat beat that must be coming from speakers somewhere in this elegantly decorated room of Art Nuevo run amok having an orgy with its self from the rug, up the frames of every sensually designed painting of figures in the heat of passion and yet absent of all if any sexual identity; no breasts, no cocks, no pussy, no ass cracks, no fingers, no eyes, just bodies intertwined and howling in ecstasy.

Kyle has opened his eyes first, followed by Clever, and then me. Now the ticking of the high-hats were accompanied by a soft brush stick against the snare, a gallant bass line, and a gentle whistler.

On the night stand a note, folded, typed; in code — .:GEUST•CLEEVR.: There is no robe in the room. No clothes, no robe. We open the letter none-the-less. Open it by shoving our thumb under the fold, nice paper, watercolor paper;

Geust Cleevr,

Eevrthying taht was conisedred wrrosimoe eillepss aomng uainclrty. Ring tihs cihme for the deielvry of a cnsdroiebale dlceicay. Rnig tiwce and we shlal diuscss youradmttinca. Aoipprprte aittre wlil be rqeuierd. Coniesdr the colthing from the dreessr. Ntoihng that was worrsmioe eixsts aomngst straengrs.
Oodm.

A good old-fashioned look around the room and then back down at the letter. We must read it again. This time without judgment. A dresser? We suppose we should follow the rules, check the drawers on top first, both bare. The middle one has my "attire." It is a cloak with a hood and tie. Black. Velvet, soft, heavy, and if you think you're wrong about it being a cloak and not a robe; there is an amulet to hold it together at the neck, and Clever looks like an alchemist farther in tune with the present than those fantasies left behind in everyone else's adulthood pasts that felt the kid would kill the milkman if the milkman left his father's wife.

*

And that is what Odom brought us after we rang the bell.
Mlik. Mlik and Hnoey. Mlik.

*

"It was what you requested in your sleep."
He says to us in the doorway.
"Milk?"
"Your Mother's tit to be more precise, Master Clever."
We do not respond to that.
"For now, first you eat, then you bathe."
We are so confused. This pitcher of milk is not for drinking?
Yet the food on the dining cart is to be eaten?
"I rather you eat alone, Clever."
"You're not joining me?"
"You're still disassociating."
And he pauses, a beat, a dramatic pause.
"I do not dine with the disengaged."
And he left us with our food. Unalone.
How does he know i'm disassociating? and then i saw her
in the bed, asleep still, naked, an hour glass shape
long hair draped in front of her face
Has she been here all along?

We don't need the company of wolves in sheep's clothing.
Crazy, we say under our breath.
Steak, sprouts, potatoes, white gravy, and water.

You have already forgotten about the beautiful woman bear in someone's bed

---

We'll eat your food, freak, but then we're out...
After we rob your rich Nazi ass blind and get back to Ona.

Don't pay attention to him.
He's just jealous. You do what you want to do, Clever.
Fuck the Milkman,
...if that's what he wants. Who? You, Kyle, you.
Remember the last time you didn't do what someone wanted? They cheated on you and jumped out of a window. You couldn't get over time. All she ever wanted you to do was stop talking, thinking, living in time. Don't believe Kyle, Clever...he's withdrawing...from life, from the drugs you are able to stomach, while it ruins him, ruins the boy and his innocence. He is weak. Kyle is an American't and he is better off lost in the Eastern Block than found in the arms of a Milkman who found him strung-out, broke, broken, retarded, passed out under a park bench in Vienna. Too bad, Kyle's been kidnapped, fuck him, he's a lost cause.

And I stood up straight, after the Milkman closed the door behind us. They were gone. I was myself again, clear, emerald eyed, and properly disguised behind the marble mask my dead wife had fashioned for me before her porcelain white skin scrapped itself into oblivioun along the pavement. Her wrist had snapped backwards and twisted counterclockwise as well, but who's counting, really? t i me. .   .

.   . .Let's not disappoint, Odom.

*

Odom had placed the cart beside the window, took the plush red and golden chair from the vanity and placed it beside the dining cart that faced the window, and finally drew the curtains to reveal the Austrian mountains under a specifically strange blue sky...and for the first moment since we graduated junior high school...we feel lost.

Three is no Aeimracn setak and poaoetts. Smoe cehf has preapred me broth, quail, greens, wtih a peppermint sorbet.

*

Uopn cmoplteing our broth, we bgean to w

e

ep   .

*

"Now I will sit with you, Kyle."
Odom had said from behind me.
Had he left? Maybe not?
The hourglass shifts in the bed, still sleeping.
He sits behind us.
"Are we your prisoner?"
"Go on."
"That was a question."
"No,   it wasn't,   Clever."

Our mind does the work,
useless work,
unable to compute,
unable to critically   decipher his intentions,
unable to connect the   pieces of the scattered pie.

"But you,   do you feel?"
he asks after listening   to my empty thoughts.

*

Your reflection in the window glass won't stop talking. Tells Odom about this, about that, everything that's ever happened and not happened to, Kyle. Tells him about breaking his arm at age nine. How bad it hurt. How the bone had jabbed through the muscle and skin. How his friend had accidentally slipped while climbing the rock cliff by Bodega Bay in Nor. Cal. How guilt destroyed their friendship. How Kyle was unsure why their friendship had dissolved away. How it in hindsight hurt more than the bone forced back into place in the Emergency Room that afternoon. Told Odom about his Aunt cheating on his Uncle with his nephew. Explained that his parents weren't sure who was at fault...considering the Aunt had been having a lesbian affair for five years with a woman twice her own age. Explained how confusing that time was in his own home. He was fourteen, knew plenty of shit by then, yet couldn't understand why there was fault being blamed on either party. "We were taught to love. We had been convinced that love always triumphed, that love could not be stopped, that love should be accepted, and love had no borders. That's why we never wanted to fall in love. We never saw ourselves as a champion, a fighter, a competitor...so how could love triumph if we are disinterested in victory?" How could you place fault on love if love has triumphed, if love has won, if love is power? We had figured, isn't that how slavery began? Victory over others? Wasn't the woman from Vietnam that you had met in San Francisco, Ghirardelli Square, in line for Ice-Cream, a foreign exchange student, both fifteen, both un-naturally attracted to each other...something we had never been used to or felt before. And we were filled with guilt, filled with the fear we would certainly disappoint this girl by falling in love. Years later we would re-meet ourselves in Amsterdam. Bumped into each other, again in line, this time in line for a gondola. She had been there with her new lover. We knew our time hooking up under the Golden Gate Bridge would come back to haunt us both. She liked Ambient Noise Art. Before we had parted we had wandered our way to Tower Records. She bought me my first *Aphex Twin* album, she gave me character, purpose, enlightenment. In return, we gave her *Genesis'* greatest hits.

In Amsterdam, our Vietnamese princess had fallen in real love with a drug dealer named Alejandro from Madrid. He was suave, gallant, taller than us, and paraded this princess around like a King would with his virgin Queen. We were sure he'd drop her in the moat the moment he found a new covenant with an even younger woman, more virginal since he had never been with her yet, and our past love was already becoming a bore in the bed. As the hourglass wakens, steps off the bed, naked, and walks behind Oldom and I, straight to the restroom. She does not close the door. Through the mirror in the bathroom i can watch her urinate. She is beautiful. Indescribable, too much like a sexualized cartoon beauty. i know i have cum in this woman, you just don't recall when and why?

It had been in the short line beside the Amsterdam canal that we had felt we may have made a mistake. That we had closed ourselves off to the vicious circles of love in remeeting your Vietnamese Princess on a gondola swimming away forever. It was there watching her board the gondola and wave goodbye that we decided to try love with the first lady of the night we could find in the Red-Light District, get sick, and die— a little...die a lot much later.

We recalled the Russian əcstasy we scored in San Sebastian, and the delightful Yasmin who had thrown herself upon mə, bəgging for my hand in marriagə, daring mə to sleəp around, thrəatening mə with hər magnətic səxuality. Yasməən had been a woman of truə rəspəct. A woman who shəd any stərəotype displayəd by thə machismo that rapəd and bəat girls to an əmotional pulp undər thə stars on the bəach to əuro-Housə and strobə lights. Yasmin madə mə a bəttər man. A young man with a taste for lovə, not abusə.

There was another; from Spain. Odom did not want to hear about her. "Not her. She doesn't interest me," he said as he had pet the top of our head. Calming.

Soothing.

Compassionate.

What was her
name?

We're unable to recall her moniker.
Spanish girl.
Went to my high school?

—I want to get high.

"Am I sexy, you will know," we told Odom, "We can compromise," Kyle wants to make a deal before he wakes up. The hourglass has returned to bed, pleasures herself, hidden from your view; we feel her pleasure of nihility.

"We won't talk about the conquistadora, if Clever doesn't have to remind you about—

—<u>The Devil</u>."

The angelic diamond eyes stare right into us from our reflection. Watching Clever all of the time. Her angelic wings bat against the windows. Her eyes bleed, her lips licked by her tongue. She has followed us from the grave. Her everything caught in our magnetic limbo; our ego.

And my erection grows, and we are ashamed as it reveals itself from between the cut of the cloak. The hourglass has come to your side to console you, press her bossom against your head, baby you, hold you, comfort you...she is not real...she is a doll, manufactured into discrete perfection with lips so lush like the tart flesh of a grapefruit. She has comforted me with my fingers pressed in her layers of lips, licking my finger tips, tippy-tips, just the tippy-tip and now Odon has wrapped his arms around us. His hug from behind our chair has given us the Mother's Tit we woke up too, and she kissed you; her vagina as fluffed as her facial lips, and you thought you'd love her for the flesh, her passion for discourse under the covers, yet she was still, still in her own pleasure, back on the bed, feeling nothing...and so was i; as i lowered my head from Azalea's reflection in the window, that was never really there. i am sad. "Everyone who lives here lies together, Clever," and with that Oldom places his wine glass beside my cleared plate. i can't remember eating a thing except when the hourglass was feeding me with spoonfools of foolish fantasies. The sip or two of blood wine teeters and totters back and forth along the bottom of the glass bell. I ask if I can finish his glass.

His lips are beside your ears. You can smell the fermentation of red grapes as he speaks, whispers, breathes into your ear; hands free. "We will not assume your residence, son. You are a guest as equal to family as a stranger is to another."

Where did she go?

The sun in the window pane has retreated across the globe, beyond the mountains, on its way to California, with a layover in New York, once it had passed Greenland and London before. Odom is the only reflection standing behind you now. Odom's brilliantly white face, nearly as blown out as your own mask upon your hidden skin. He is bare as he steps back revealing more of himself in the window pane. You respect this man. You will not turn. He has listened to every fabrication, Kyle could demand from you to keep his identity illusive, invisible. He hadn't judged you, hadn't required any more or any less from your Super Ego.

So,
why are you so scared?

Because I can see him as he steps to the side of my reflection. He has revealed his entirety to me. I don't know this man. I don't know this country. I don't even know the boy in the white mask who he has joined in the mirror from the dark night sky. Barely know the hourglass i assume i have spent days with by now in an opiate dayze, a den of poppies allowing us to sink deeper and deeper into her flesh, disappearing under the cloud of an Austrian sky, her blonde hair, her brown pubic hair, her massively bulbous breasts that dial into your lips like a woman's clit tip of a tippy-tip, as you both preferred only to pleasure your head between her legs...but she has been still for hours now, still in the bed, still after pleasuring herself without me, alone, in a strange hotel, that looks like a castle, but surely could not be cult. Paler still. Her body never shifted since she fell asleep. Still, your eyes travel the length of Oldom's body, ignoring the accidental death in your bed. Oldom has a handsome body.

Your eyes follow down his face, along his strong neck, his wide shoulders, cut chest, packed stomach, his umbilical knot, his hairless lower abdomen, his lack of male genitalia, a lack that does not lend itself to that of a woman, but a Ken doll. Either born unsexed, or surgically modified like the hourglass. Either way, the surgeon or god had done a pristine job. Perfection for it. There are no scars, no clumping of skin, no growth what-so-ever; Odom is a magnificent sculpture that has pulled you from the absent grass bed of a strange Austrian park to this method, this mattress, and the illusive woman's nipples that held you every night as she pumped your veins clear of the consistent dosages of MDA...sucking you dry, removed of the memory that you had flown away with to meet O   n

a
,
what
have
i
d
one
?

"You should shower and bathe," our host instructed before checking the hourglasses pulse, saying a tongue-less prayer, before throwing her lifeless body into a fireman's hold and carries her out of our room. how long have we been here, and where has the hourglass gone? Was her name Bubbles? She was an hourglass of form. Beside me every night; Bubbles. Silent. Still. Pillows of flesh. B
u
b
bblessss.You remember. We remember her. You did not have her, she had you.
Where did Oldom find her? Will i die here too?
*

*

*

You were doped up. Drips of heroin into your nose.
you were k'd into a hole after hole
*

*

sober
darkness
slept
thro
u
g
h
*

*

The bath has belled out marbled lips. We relate to it.
You relate to submerging into the ambient Bubbles   ଃ
porcelain lips.
Gold rock surrounds the baths' belly, her feet; the floor.
The gold is strong, yet malleable, massages your soles,
before you bathe.

Another note. Inside of the bath, covering its naval
"Plseae Shvae"
*

upon the marble countertop, an electric hair trimmer, a fine
electric shaver, a straight blade, wax strips,

&
two hits of my own Russian ₉
Armando Pills
Did Oldom find my backpack?
Have we been followed. Phena?

*   *

*

you're submissive, not naive
Phena is not real anymore, Azalea's gone
shave your head first,
•

Yasmin is real and in the world, the punk's gone
••

before taking off my security blanket; my face
shave your arms, your neck, armpits,
••
•

Misty Rain is working, the Golem's gone
••
••

trail, legs, cut cut cut, tiny snips
fingernails...remove
your selves
••
•
••

Oldom is indoctrinating Clever, Bubbles is gone.
•
•
•
•
•

now
the
mask
•OUCH•
•
•
*

take it off slowly, Clever
There is something askew with removing the marble mask.
Hurts. Burns to pull it away from the skin; even gently it
pulls, attached to you. Not something to fuck with. You may
have to leave it on. And that's when your back began
tweaking. Twitch, right up the cord. Ribs shivers. You can't
leave it on now. Something is wrong, you need to get this

face off now. AZALEA IS DEAD .That guy will help us if our face is too fucked up. He's a rich dude. A PUNK IS DEAD . He'll get us to a hospital no problem. EREBUS, DEAD ."No hospitals!" I yell me, "Get it?" BUBBLES IS DEAD . You killed the last two, or was it the Thr99? My god Kyle, you are a murderer. Gypsy is dead. It was Gypsy. She set us up. ─────────────────────

Back off fucker. This is real.
You can't clean this up at a fucking hospital.
Part of the system. You'd be found.
You kill people. You kill dead people.

───────────────────────────────────────

And with that I ripped off Clever's face. Torn right from your conformist cult-able impressionable life. To escapism. Away from cults you aren't even welcomed into. Get it? Not welcome. A cult that won't take you with them...clean up so you can put this handsome face back on young Claibourne. "First we eat the 9," I insist as I pop mine first and then hand the   other   to   Clever;   POP-Pop.rip, pain..burns...sting...shock...crisp...do not open your eyes. Let us look first. I will let you know if you're okay? And we both took a moment, then turned Clever towards the mirror so we all could get a better look at the skin that has been revealed from dismantling the mask from our soul, for a moment; together. We kept his eyes closed. Better that way. Hurt less to squint than look at himself. Better not to see the stretched broken boils, the puss rash upon rash, the torn outerlayer of skin. There were strange indentations inside the mask as well. The irritated skin had gotten caught in the curves, dents, and design of the interior of the mask...it was meant to grow into you. We were not able to protect Clever from the smell. The rot rank of the released boil juice has him gagging. "I want to wash my face."
"Okay, hold on."

He turns the water on. It's not water, it's white, milk, warm or cold milk. You turned it off. "It's milk dude." That's what I wanted to hear. Sounded soothing. I needed to immerse ourselves in milk. Warm, hot, or cold? *Chocolate milk bath for desert?* I love this bath, love watching the milky liquid pour and fill the bell of her porcelain lips, that we gently slip between into the pool of her milky love, that overflows upon the gold that had massaged our feet into greater submission, despite the pain of identity being torn from your skull. I have to loosen my voice, a moment, as I submerge ourselves under the rim of her milk of sooth, as we blow b u bbbbl esss.   .   .

Milk on sores is medically useless and could potentially exacerbate the condition. To stop Clever's bleeding and puss, Kyle had to run the milk on extreme hot and burn his face in order to, well, melt the skin back into shape...This will be better than open wounds.

he will be careful to disinfect himself prior with the shaving alcohol. Took him about twenty minutes to calm down from the sting. death was an option. death was quicker than healing. they were going to be okay

young claibourne needs his beauty rest
kyle needed to grow the fuck up
and i needed some
fresh air
to dance off
this
d
r
a
m
a
—

02 x 9 - 1 = 01 x 2 9 - U
KNOW
silnet (k) NO silnet (dbloue u)

Chapter - Taking it all to heart

Electric crash, Guitar strum, dum dee dum, drum hits on the snare hat, snare hat, keyboard chordin' drive up *Look up on the wall / there on the floor / under the pillow / behind the door / there's a crack in the mirror / somewhere there is a hole in a window pane / do you think I'm to blame—*

—"¿Crees que tengo la culpa?" and Ona pushed on him, pushed on Alejandro's chest in the middle of the blue jean store. He was shopping. *Genesis* was blaring, too loud, *If you're wrappin' up the world \ 'Cause you've taken someone else's girl*, drowning out anything audible as Ona has herself storming out of the doors and out onto the streets of Rome.

A simple grab of her wrist as Alejandro approached her, tourists crossing the narrow shopway; a simple grab of the wrist should have been nothing in a Madrid, in Barcelona, even on her tiny little island, but this simple grab of the wrist wore the shackles of regret, for the simple things she had seen, had heard, had enjoyed about Clever's company, his other friends; America. She liked the gay ones, the Asexual ones, the Ravers; liked the shame they would strike on upon one's derogatory words, actions in the less misogynistic States. "In Clever's America, you do not grab a woman's wrist," she yelled at him in English— and she tore her arm back from him, slapping him in the face, as he steps to her. Ona the hawk, steps back, finger high, threatening. "Why you loco, Ona?"

"I no loco. You no touch me!"

"Callate," he says firm. Not loud. Firm. She is his property. He will not show indignity to her for not bowing to his demand. He is Spanish. "I Spaniard Man, Ona. Not pussy Americano. K?"

"You think women small," she's trying to reason before crying.

"Piquito. Baby."

"I loved, Kyle. Te amo, Kyle."

Alejandro rolls his eyes, spits on the street, "So, you want fuck him now?"

"We have to find him."

"I said no. I no look for old boyfriend for you."

"I hate you," and there was nothing more for her to do, but walk back to the hostel. Wait for Stacey and Miguel to get to Rome from Venice. They split up in Germany. Ona thought Italy would be more romantic. Then in Venice they got the call, Clever was off the grid with some group of girls. When Stacey and Miguel got to Rome a couple days back, Miguel had learned from a pal in Prague that the girl killed herself. That Clever was...somewhere...where is he now?

"I fuck other girls. Good," Alejandro threatens her.
A couple in their thirties let go of their hands to pass Alejandro who casually returns to the Blue Jean store to get himself a new pair of Italian pants.

CRUNCH-
LONGGUITAR...CHUGCHUGeeeeecccccccd • • • • • • • • • •
• • • • • • • •Austriiiiiiiaaaaaa *STAHLHAMMER..* .   .   is relaxing as Clever had waited for the sting of his face to subside with the window open to his elegant and rehabilitating room...as he dripped another drop of an opiate extract, cut with the K he mixed in earlier when he had awoken earlier, when Bubbles was in
the bathroom...i made
my
own.Shhhh&iwonderedifonaisworriedaboutme?calltheriver.theraft.hasdrifted..

•

Opening the door of my guest room, the halls are dimly lit by fake electric torches. Immaculate, don't get me wrong, just, i sort of want to smell the gas, the oil, the smoke of the indoor burning lantern...the description said this prophylactic suit would still allow me to smell, taste, and feel...We'll have to be patient. "You'll have to stay here," i told us closing the door on them, leaving them to their own petty devices in the room without a vessel. i pull on the silicon suit that covers my entire body. it is not warm. it is perfectly
tempered.
• /REALITY/ • • • • • • • •
is unfortunate when the fiction will become so dry— had been inscribed on my door. Etched. Not nice. Not elegant like the rest of the guestrooms, like the rest of the hall. My inscription had been poorly scratched in with a knife. If anything,   i   was   convinced   it   was true...

....but it is not industrial rock n' roll throughout the extended hall i've centered myself in before treading on further. it is the *AFX* world's audible background, my own soundtrack, my calming peace to know, in advanced, when things might change as the sounds, the music, the score advances with anticipation before my eyes; like a movie . and our room is behind me . young claibourne resting his vessel in the bed, Kyle still in the bath, and me, free of the dead weight of regret . the description of this prophylactic suit was correct . the soles of my feet can feel every twine, sew of the hall rug . with a little focus, i can feel the dye imprinted in the hairs of carpet . if i stop, if i concentrate on my nerves, i can feel the slight difference in weight between the colors of the dye . i am in awe of the science of the suit . therefore i accept . the high hats gently speed, catch my other attention, audible attention, and the purr of mmmms from one of the doors, potentially coming from multiple doors, all the way down this continuous hall . / *is anybody listening, oh, oh* / *no reply at all* . step by purr, purr by step, as i approach a slim, towering figure at the stairway as the Milkman in the hidden speakers sings to me... / *I wish the Milkman would deliver my milk; in the morning* / ...until you reach the stairway that turns up, unless you've chosen to follow it downwards. she reaches out her hands. before even making direct contact, you can feel the graph of her fingertips, and you're shy, i'm shy . me . not them. they're alone. i'm keeping myself company, realizing i have my hand on myself, gently touching me. she smiles. her teeth are pretty. i cannot make out the color of her eyes. she allows me to follow without intimacy. my hands careful to hold the guard rails on our way d
      own.
          d
              a
                  r
                      k   e   r
                                s
                                    t
                                      i
                                        l   l

doors close, is lesser than or greater than, negative doors open," she has told me, insistent, a fact, not a question . i have gallantly ignored her appearance. This woman should be illusive, disguised, silent in exquisite beauty with her naked soul mysterious to me, as her body, like mine, invisibly sensitive, only to the enhanced senses of our suits . we will be along this lower hall . darkened . warm lamps. cool blue •ϱ.lectrical hairs slither from the carpet, up our inner legs, to our jewels, to her lips, & the woman is now accompanied by four others . all as equally alluring, all in body suits, all of us eyeless . our breath caught in our prophylactic suits fog the gummy latex bubble that form as we each exhale, heavily, together in the hall, by allowing ourselves to begin to wander as a collected body by entwining our a®ms • around their hips • our waists • elbows • heads on shoulders • together • children • safer in numbers • and now, every time we exhale we can all feel the gentle particles that are released • our poison • expelling bad biology • together, we release our own poisons, and although the suits enhance all sensation, it is only accepts what the body desires, not the poisons, the viruses, the disease, the ill-fortune of others . We are not prejudice, we merely excrete the poisons that good creates inside each and every one of us ——"*how do you breath in?*"— the black one kisses me . i cannot feel her carbon dioxide . i can feel her every pour and crevas in her lips , the way our own texture tickles from the microscopic texture of her tongue , but neither of us are poisoned by each other and together i follow them . wouldn't you? ————————————————————
———————————————————— they are already four doors away.
after the kiss you had allowed them to be the mass of sensation
you were still too curious about the entirety of things
stuck on choices, like an American
Kyle is air drying his face out the window in the guestroom. Young Claibourne tosses under the covers.

Miguel and Stacey are still on the trains. Ona is still mad at Alejandro, but then again, it's only been two days that you have spent lost, wandering these halls with these women, silently, intimately without penetration, nothing more than ever a kiss could be...   ... or... ————————————————————————

—————another door, the first one any of us had dared to enter; the girls went first , allowing the door to close behind them, so i alone would be able to open this one and follow myself inside— real music, dark, slow, a tortoise on the turntables on the floor, on the rug, in the center of a circle, quarter circle, the circle of grooving vessels, male, female, ⅄

others, opens upon us entering the room, together, m ℈; alone. the four vessels from the hall have formed a second circle around the tortious whom the closer we get, the larger the already monstrously huge beautiful, majestic, turtle of the earth • now large enough for these women, vessels, friends, people, voyagers to sit in a perfect circle around it and the tables in transcending levels of 8A geometry that connect us all to the patterns on the tortoise's skin , and all this , fed from the moss, bacteria, fungi that grows on top of each other on the shell of the guru . the guru's shells ingest the chemicals from the growing food upon his back, allowing the food to continuously re-create themselves as the warmth of the hard-shelled, ectothermic reptile, who's need for warmth comes from the circles of vessels, the lights, the rugs, the blankets, the moss and all on his back... in return the heat converts the desired chemicals into energy that seeps through the microscopic paths grown as a maze, not along the shell, but the shell itself and through the maze the drugs can find their final destination, their purpose, their endorphin's compacted into quantum physics controlled by nothing but the catalyst that sent it soaring from one place to another colliding with more energy birthing a passionate overdrive production of dopamine for you and me . to power the people's ecstasy tethered-together in an island of thought . and all this a weight on the ectothermic being's back . closes the door behind us; me. i am no longer fooled, i am alone here in this mansion, in this magnificent world of harmonized people . it slowly becomes their song i hear, not the music , there is only their song, and they sing it in a loop, with humms and rhythm, and instruments, and notes, thåT will collide and create sounds of the music that th⅄ hear reapeaT~g Tøgether . i am mesmerized at the synchronicity of the

vessels headpho—n—ɘd—tog—ɘ—ther-°— ◦ tethered to the
ceiling, allowing the participants to levitate in freeform, like
a dance in the sky without movement : connected away from
each other wavering in time with its tentacle of a wire
attached to the circle, and yet there are also speakers, *I would
like some milk from the Milkman's wife's tits* . flowered bell
speakers, fashioned from the original phonograph . the room
is a slowly, nearly unnoticeable rotation of light colors, from
warm orange~turquoise~deepblue~oceansun flashing
strobes , and my skin can feel the various temperatures of
each color, and the various particles of mist in the air . the
fine a°toms of * H.2° * that have a bioluminescent reaction to
my prophylactic • this is not occurring with anyone else . i
feel singled out .. they know i am a foreigner, an alien, at
minimum a guest? tip toe strings from a reverbed quartette.
the room remains slow in time. even the grandfather's
clock's pendulum lags in its descent to the other side . i
presume east and west according to the magnificent metal
compass chandelier hung directly over the tortoise; a tortoise
operated by animatronics . the sway of each of the circle's
particles catch up with one another . they are in perfectly
delayed synchronicity in their sensualizing of themselves .
pleasure seems only a finger's length away from indulgence
and disfigurement . you; are inside . a new , unusual , familiar
    p   l   a   c   e

                        left when he lied down for the
evening. i had waited, maybe twenty, thirty minutes after
Clever had left us behind in the guestroom. sounds like
awhile, but really it doesn't leave you a lot of time to think
up an escape plan because you're totally confused why we
would leave us in here? . you labor over that thought instead
of anything proactive . you stress your critical thinking on
the reasons or lack thereof of reasons for your self to leave
like that. we couldn't work on us that way. now look at him;
tired . his face hurts . he's ashamed, curled up under the

covers . like a baby . with the nightstand light illuminated. "Scared of the dark young Claibourne?" i jested, tenderly, i know what he's going through . bonding was, something a miss in him . his bond to the mist of life as opposed to the production of life, it had him...a miss with love, a passion he felt eighteen about . eighteen going on twelve with a hard on and the world's willingness to use it . he hasn't even figured out he has no skills and really just tends to tr.y to understand
        people.

        i can think it out for the both of us. the three of us. so i leave, naked, shaved, clean, naked, without the enhancement of the host, no prophylactic suit like Clever. i need to run, i can't be bogged down with their cover of safety . they know everything about us . everything . he has my passport . he has your bag, your stories, plane tickets, money; phone numbers. He has your stupid receipt of important phone numbers to people who have no idea where you are . and we've had no phone cards since . there is merely only Kyle's will, for me, myself... and i closed the door behind myself, leaving him to sleep alone in despair in the middle of the guestroom in the abyss of Austria in the thick of a terrible epidemic that is rumored to be spreading across Europe, possibly on its way to New York, said the newspaper on the nightstand; in Austrian. Translated in a different note from Oldom that began with, "Do not be alarmed. We are safe. We are invisible to Austria. You are safe here." This time not in code. I know it is a lie. We are all going to die. *Did he leave it for us to stay in tune?* No. If that was the case, he would not have wrapped the Cookbook inside,
the newspaper dated a few days before you left Prague.
    yet, you know you are the one who knows what's best for

                                      us,

                          Clever and I.
                               •
                              ••

• • • "Aye, I am so worried," Ona admitted immediately to Miguel. Stacey really was not up to being the barrer of bad news, but really, "He's okay. He's with that girl's sister."

Ona totally believed her. Wiped the tear from her eye, looked at Miguel, apologized for breaking up with Alejandro, and then none of that happened.

Phena had found Stacey.

Nothing for Phena to do those next few days in Prague.

The body was being investigated.

Mother had moved to the Ozarks and lost touch.

That was the only lie she had told Clever.

It broke their heart; Phena's most of all.

"I do not know where he went," she had told Stacey on the platform in Prague. "How long have you waited for me?" she asked Phena. "Three days."

"Why?"

"I'm worried about Kyle."

Miguel knew the French girl. From the squat. She wouldn't do anything with Kyle. She was gay. "No, we weren't on drugs," Miguel swares to Ona, "We came down like hours before that." Stacey breaks up the fight, tells Ona they never found her, but yeah he was supposed to meet her, in Rome. "The French girl?" And everyone seems confused except for Stacey, "You. He left a map of Rome in place of a book he stole from the French girl." None of it makes sense. What did make sense was that Kyle was totally MIA and left a map of places to wait for him if ever he "got lost."

"Is that why you call him, Clever?" Phena had asked them both. "No, just his girlfriend's pet name for him," Stacey mispeaks, offends Phena...she is taken off guard, thinks Kyle lied to all of them..."The French girl gave me the map," Phena admits, "She had followed him. She spoke some Greek, broken Greek. Called him énas; means One. That's it, kept saying énas stole her passport . One stole her passport, and then in English said like twice, 'Am I sexy, you will know. blah blah blah, about finding him, needing to give him his map back, worried it sent the wrong message."

Ona thinks Phena's crazy, thinks the French Girl is dangerous, and Miguel is fucked up for taking Clever to meet anarchists in Europe when he's on drugs. "He likes that stuff . he thinks world revolves around chemicals and that you can't stop chaos theory," but remember, Ona only ever understood 1/3rd of the things Clever talked about in high school. Stacey thinks Kyle's fine and that we got the fucking map so everyone stop over-reacting and that, "Yes, Phena sounds kookoo like her sister...but Clever's not, and is just taking his time because his girlfriend died."

and that made total sense to Miguel, so they toured Rome while Ona toured Clever's map. Alejandro went with the tourists. Clever was still in the ambient room trying to levitate, and you, you've been lead through the wall door, by someone, a woman's gloved hand, through the wall, into the other stairwell hidden between the walls, to you it was obvious she belonged here—

Chapter - Childlike Curiosity -
"éNas," she introduced herself through the opening in the wall her lips were painted white . she was wearing my cape . the rest of her a shadow of her self . she's been waiting for me . for Clever to take a leave . took your hand ☙

spun me down
the twisted wooden stairwells through out the mansions walls, until we were deeper and deeper where the planks had become roots, and finally stones rolling with us both as we love the challange of balancing the stones in the rapids in eabling to cross the mass of river below the castle in the deep of invisible Austria...and Kyle had watched her in dance through the caverns, spiraling up while down was to the side and back again along her ornamental brunette hair as it demonstrated its brush stroke of geometrically organic formations, a woman drawn of the hand of the Nouveau as the torch lit caverns and the wind of our pace blows the cloak open baring her beautiful body, covered in freckles, the maps of the universe, and the empty space of illusion, for in time, Kyle will trace each and every one of the lines that illustrate her from her breasts down to her soles—to , the dimensional, living woman of the plants that shape

everything . the tattoos are of a garden, alive, covering her body, "You haven't stopped moving," her lips exhale a well patterned cotton trail of *Ayahuasca* breath . .   . i know what you

                are : is to the up stairs being lower than the bowels of the castle itself .   .   .no one knows she's here, she is a ghost

                            of

                                                the

                            stairs

                                    to

                                        the

cellar, the cool, refreshing cellar, "I want you to suckle your milk from my breasts," and at the bottom of the stairwell we sat, her breast in my mouth, suckling the cream of life from her bulbous nipple as she creamed into our hand between her soft, beautiful thighs, as you gazed, were drawn into her cat eyes through the mask of Moses, with horns, that she wore, not only to greet me, but to seduce me .

                              the air adjusts under the guidance of this psychedelic nymphet and i attest, "Strangeness haunts me."

"Islands deserve to be preserved for pleasure," was her first insinuation that i should save Manhattan; alluding to my voyage to a home not here. "You mean like a continent?" I asked her. "No. Chain reactions happen, chaos uncontrolled?" that's what the Master would like to avoid; saving Manhattan. Someone wants to infect Manhattan, spread something. A virus? A drug? Poison? Hard not to question her indescribable accent when told broken phrases from this cloaked éNas disguised in the under skin of the deceased Moses not of Israel. .   . I have come to learn he never set foot on the promised land . "You're a quick learner," she complimented me while for the next hours, days, moments, absence of time, the place Azalea wanted me to seek out, timelessness, of notime. emiton. I am not Kyle, I am Emiton. i have named myself in front of her presence so aroused to do so, so stimulated to be her newest lover, a One she named Emiton, a One she has introduced to her library of books, roots, powders, greenhouses, boilers, furnaces, baths, and every where we went, we, underground made love again and again. For no reason less than education... She knew I did not need to be indoctrinated up stairs in hell, with delusions of grandeur to do what's right for us. She knew she would never get to the promised land, that she must send me, under the shadows, behind Oldom's back...without us...not here, not his way.

éNas has Emiton turn shit into gold, gold into water, water into urine, into dust, into fragments, in order for me to levitate freely with her, hidden from Clever and the rest of the influencers concealed in the Master's dens. "And who was the Master? Not Oldom, that had become abundantly clear."

"Yes, that story is correct my pollinator,"

as she extracted my selves for her bidding, stored incase i never made it home.

Clever can be petty as he meanders aimlessly through orgy after orgy on the second floor, never wondering what the lobby or roof might hold..never using his own cunning self to realize what lies behind the walls . Clever rather be influenced by his surroundings . figure out how to use them . toy with them . experiment in them . he knows better than to disturb you. or is he just doing his thing? That would make a mess of our plan. Our escape.

"Kyle?" éNas requires my attention.

The massive roots of trees have revealed themselves in our cave. She has been riding one, naked, as others grow and take hold of me, "Kyle?" she questions my name again. I am the tree, not the other way around. I am a tree longer boy. i am not a vessel, i am pleasure from all my roots, my branches, catching air from above ground, while my thick, twisting roots mingle with the social roots of the entire country of trees. We are the wood. She is the wood. We are all malleable when we're wet. We are retrieving instructions from the tortouis, a plant, keeping éNas aware of hungry tails with heads and how they choose to orobus and how they slither and connect above her into submission to each o t h e r .   .

.

•

.   ..around Clever, small waterfalls that circulate the raised warm & cool baths that pour into the segmented indoor pool(s). *Don't let the days go by / Glycerin*, full of bodies, female vessels, male vessels, communicating through sign and touch, all coated in their prophylactic sex suits. The water balls roll right off the latex like suits. if i was on psychedelics i could hallucinate that we can all breathe under water with gills, but that's not true, we are mammals, mammals with pockets, to collect poison, thousands of particles of poison in search for a ONE to assimilate into a hungry egg that like the tortouise uses the absorbed energy to grow more moss... and i gag under the water, panic, don't know how to get the water out of the suit. "Hold your breath, next time," she says to me, while applying mouth-to-mouth resuscitation...giggling with me, tickling me from under the water, playful, splish-splash and she kisses me for real and our tongues press against the thin silicone sheath that spans over the orifice of our mouths as HAPPY HARDCORE has the lovelies bouncing, their ballooned breasts celebrated as they bounce for me and the scene. The silicone suits, which at first i believed were just latex, stretches, meshed with the shape, the flexibility of our tongues, and we are in deep conversation through our enhanced skins that now even allows me to feel the sensations of those vessels across the pool. if she looks directly into me, then all of them, even those across the massive water world, in the other celestial, sensual ponds conjugate with new mammals, mammals conjugating through each other's flesh, again and again, in and out, in and in, around, above, held, slip, slide, lick, love, conjugation stripped of identity, a mammal that feels

pleasure throughout their conscious, sub-con...a non-replicating activity, a clinically immune suit— a sexual séance . that i can feel myself inside everyone insid•ɘ.
                 of
     me

•

        . •éNas has brought Kyle to a number of other caves. Her performances have demonstrated a recognition of his minds' ambidextrous nature, and now, "in our hands, both sets," we are in perfect unison as my ambidextrous alchemy matures from childish curiosities, to sexual intoxic-o-tra-cities across the globe, against this hidden worlds securities, forcing this small tribe to expand, find somewhere to prosper. The Master believes Clever's a ONE to lead them and that is why Kyle, lover, you must run, run away from here, from this place, these people, run...meet my friend across the pond, he will protect you. I promise this to you. Just do not lead when the Master is gone from you. That is what the Devil wants, and that is not chaos, it is merely chaos wrapped up in an Alchemist's bow and disenvowed as merely a theory, saving facts from gods invoked by the collective Ids alone in their nihilistic misery . never satisfied . and the Master is the God of the ungratified . . Aole? Rooms, without doors, only passageways, unlike my recollection of the stairs we traveled down to these underground corridors.
This
     temple beneath the
               S y b   a   r i   t   i   c
                       u p p er
                          d e c k
                               s

    all floors had doors to open, doors to close behind you as you entered, exited,
        that particular floor. .   . tick tick tick high hats, resonate, a shaker, not a stick, a bead, not a curved slate of metal   tick tick tick tick tick tick
                                                  tick tick tick
tick tick tick tick tick tick tick tick tick tick tick tick tick tick tick
                          no body can see me, i am the future

tick tick tick from the upper floors...cleverly timed...cleverly situated and Clever seems, fine tick tick tick tick tick tick tick tick tick im invisible...hidden from Clever. Hidden from everything. Hidden from all that would destroy me from the inside as i allow a steam emulate from éNas' red skin . i have learned so much . how to manipulate my own illustrations, how to have éNas do as i say in submission to being my personal guru enslaved in the hypnotism she had so perfectly skilled me in . my skin has blossomed into a brilliant blue, and our bodies contrast against one another as the universe of stars, like ants, climb from her limbs to mine, covering my body, transforming our loving in a celestial explosion of sweat that begins to seep metaphorically magnetizing to our Sybaritic-Ids that reign supreme in the gene pool, demanding of us, something physically higher, enlightened, broader to suckle than just the lips of a woman's flower as her breasts blossom thick stalks of muscular arms with heads of breasts dripping milk from the fountains of life with terrible odds of survival, and yet, the delight is as much for her as it is for him as he lets himself go.

Nobody can see me, I am the future.

Kyle's release sieved through the innovatively skilled silicone skin layer that covers his Old Rodney. Ejaculate, larger than life, moist, thick, yet with an embracing feel upon contact; spermless...clean...and we both can drink from it, as she fills my mouth with my own as Clever takes his with a chaser of circulated pool water upstairs from a stranger whom he can trust . . . with a mammal's lungs of air, and the oxygenic transfer to the lover's lips as they are moist & warm like Clever's mutilated lips as the rod between his legs has been a toy, a game for him as a puppy, the sleeping boy's dream upstairs...but it is but just a dream isn't it young Claibourne. . .with wonder still through the rivers that connect the ponds, as Clever...ignores Kyle, who's tripping balls in the basement.

•

...found i've drifted down stream, sucked past an erotic massage of hands through a tunnel before entering a woman filled pond...and only women, suckling upon her bountifully large, buoyant bodies of flesh. the most flesh. fat flesh. sensually obese; floating. she is the multi-sexual, conjoined exotic lady whales i've waded my way to in order to swim deep into her fat lips, lubricated beyond fabrication. she wants me in there. her puggy fingers have pressed me into her, so she may kiss me more, her tongue entwined with mine between her legs. she loves the cock that has grown, stretched, enlarged entering her as i ravenously eat at her salivating lips and the ball of a tongue that tastes the cherries away from the thinnest of women...and she bleeds in my face, and i am safe and it is warm and for the first time i can hear them all, the audible stimulation from underwater, a focused resonance of moans from sybaritic co-consensual behavior with no excuses for malice except well possibly for rapes on the

stairs by Oldom insistent he find the mate to bare him a kiddo to rule of the nest when he passes?

That's what we learned from the library below, but you knew better, you've navigated questionable information on drugs before, for weeks now. That's what we'd like to remind Clever of, if ever he would come up for air.

b   o   d   dity 2 b o d   dity

...the audible ecstasy expunges my ejaculate under the water, and i too, as if i had deja vu, knew the sperm had safely
remained inside,
perhaps,
murdered?

up

•bubBblesselb

Bbub

ss

s

ubmerged
in sensuals

s

ǝvǝrythǝǝng

ǝvǝrythǝǝng. . .

ǝvǝrythǝǝng

ǝvǝrythǝǝng

ǝvǝrythǝǝng

ǝvǝrythǝǝng

.•. .No Bad Times, Only Feel Goods . .• "hey Azalea says that all the time"

•"i kn●w

•

ǝvǝrythǝǝng

i   n   v   i   s   b   l   e

eye k N̲o̲w͛

not a loss of hallucinogenic logic, inhibitions, but a loss of
obligation within serenity, sensual pleasure, instinctual milk,
warmth, a reminder of the womb, without violence. and i
thought, "*well this is nice*," and indulged as a freshman to the
sybaritic nature of a chemically induced Archaic Revival in
which my destiny had certainly lead us to this magestic
castle hidden in the heart of the continent, seperated from a
few others, connected by existing land bridges . my name is
Clever, i am Kyle Claibourne, and you're doing alright. . .kiss her...

---

tongue and all, your hand slips between her legs underwater, she's
taken a gentle, weightless hold of you, as someone caresses your back
with the tips of their fingers, your tongue still playful with her, your
fingers adding numbers into her as she's turned around to wrap
herself around me, slow, sway, weightless as she submerges
snorkeling onto her other lover in this warm pool. sign language. this
is new to you. you've never signed before.

---

she's giving me time, time to learn,
watch as they sign to other couplets, groups, singles, gays,
straights, bi-sexuals alike, all choosing the temperature of

water, not the pleasurability of the lover . another ONE whispers into my ear, "we are slaves to systematic sexuality; free us," and i can sense she is scared, terrified, a captive to a fantastical ideology from that above us all, the being in the pool that waters down upon us, and it is up to me to hear them out, for i, like a follower, have been summoned to wade with the Master.

•

...the bodily toll is exorcised from its therapeutic roll with the underworld's bones. rocks. Crack Cocaine. What else is in éNas' cabinet? Bombs? Dynamite? Destruction? Resurrection? A Hero's Journey to separate himself to save a single nation? Save souls? or does she want me to impregnate what the Master cannot? Is Emiton being asked to do biddings only a soldier could carry out? I can be éNas' soldier, or Oldom's recruit? The Id can carry the burden for the rest of us. I can isolate an island.

SMACK her

bones shattered and when it happened it made all of us cringe. Azalea did not need to die. She needed to run away

with me. SMACK her IV had followed her down, bursting against the pavement, spraying the sidewalk with the gel of sustenance. The bile in my stomach stopped halfway up my esophagus. I was too disturbed to let it out. I ran. I killed. I fled. I have found sanctuary in éNas' care who seems to desire my murderous abilities to eradicate Oldom, her captor, not the twisting of my mind into a conspiracy to inseminate the population with death through indulgence. She fell in love with me. Said I was a problem, that I had to leave. Escorted me back upstairs, even before Kyle had

crawled into the wall with her. SMACK The French Girl, she is real, she is my trace...Oldom did not find you,

Clever, I did, I found Kyle upstairs in that room, so sad, scared, ruined, heartbroken, a mess, like all the rest before you, Clever. Each and everyone, but this time, this date, you had the book .

The Anarchist Cookbook...you were interested in things that couldn't be explained. THings that broke against your eagerness for life...and because you stole it from her, it was a sign, you could save us, you alone, a One like me, in my name, honor. And I watched it all play out along her animated tattoos that covered her entire body she finally revealed to me without the cloak . You can save the world from the Master if you trust me. Do I have your consent? Her body a roadmap to something she desired, something i had no real interest in besides believing she needed it done, for the goodness of the world.

éNas promised to find Clever for me as a reward, wouldn't let him die like Bubbles • In hindsight, I have grown to believe the French girl was the beautiful Bubbles surgically redesigned for my Penial Gland to stimulate my honesty with Oldom . She had been caught, killed . "This is what I am supposed to tell he kid sleeping in our room, tell young Claibourne that, please." . .were éNas's words . as we both observed the exit of her living hair as it flowed through the closing crease of the door to door frame . of the guest room . . eager to lust over the last of us, Clever. The simpler side of his rights, finding himself alone with everyone, with us once again, trapped inside this empty bed with room for more. "Kill Oldom for me," was her final request before we exited the wall .

"I will."

And now, now she's gone and it is up to me to tell him, his bedside friend was killed by an overdose of something the host gave them

.   .

.   .

*

The Pedagogue had no Pineal Gland
simply with a few
lessons in a handful of sign language
and Clever was clearly
being introduced to this
bloated body of a manless-womanless physique
"our name is"
"OdbO"
they speak in unison, completing each other's sentences
another improbable realization
"OdbO THE MASTER"
"my only son"
"ourselves"

.

This master was conjoined at the neck. Two heads. Two
massively overweight bodies that pushed into themselves,
Od with a large penis that protrudes from the back Od's head,
bO with contracting vaginal lips on his and yet,
both lack the chemical ability to produce dopamine

•

OdbO
feels nothing | they are absolute | they are Nihilism incarnate

. • ◎ . • •

THE MASTER intentionally bathes in the pools' circulation
to consume the sexual influx of women's emanation,
their pure oxytocin for THE MASTER's dope-a-mine

THE MASTER
pores are large enough to act as vacuums for the drug
natural • organic
no-preservatives

℘ separately
together

THEY drink from the breasts of strangers
the same, yet direct dosage of the orgasmic chemical,
❦ oxytocin ❦
▲▼▲
the sounds are the accompanied touch
to allow OdbO to
enlighten themselves
with a duo
orgasm
absent of their
genitals, pineal gland, or dopamine
THEY ❦ THEY
ARE
.EnablerS.
From birth these human mammals

•were•

absent of pleasure

absent of the flesh
that produces
each and everyone
elses
breast milk
breast milk
breast milk
!
..

i
was
allowed to
join them in their
pool

experience
everything
absent
of
my

s   e   l ve s

*

•inside me, the desire to murder this thing•
a clever ambition for escape
this place is putrid
Now I smell the Rot
The Rot of Control
The Rot of Disorderliness of Power
The Rot that is
Systemic Sexuality
*

but, as an honest man should,
i hear THE MASTER
of nothing about what
WE DON'T ALREADY KNOW
MADE BY WOMAN, CONTROLED BY HIM
CONTROLED BY HIM, LIES THE WOMAN
FOR SHE HAS BEEN SHACKLED
FOR HIS PLEASURE
NOT
THEIRS
•

"In a biologically female human, oxytocin tends to continuously release, way after orgasm depending on the level of ecstasy in which the female has been brought to, and then if it continues to be brought to, again and again," THE MASTER had learned from éNas' who had found him, left to a foster home on the outskirts of Lithuania. She brought him here, to protect him. To teach him alchemy, teach him what she saw his mind could comprehend, and it was too much even for her as he rose with sympathy higher and higher as she was pushed deeper down below into the underground, buried, replaced with the everlasting pursuit of riches to substitute pleasure and mammalianess, which in the development of a future archaic revival, will reflect a time where pleasure fulfillment was a construct as half the population used the violence of injecting poison to prove the need to force the female into submission. THE MASTER's power was to lay her down useless as she fooled him into birthing children of her own delight.

They, the people of this house, this love, this judgeless freedom of co-sensuality, this beautiful cult, delivered us the context in which we found ourselves and the orgy. The release of oxytocin to the left, to the right, behind us, through the drain in the centre of the bottom of this stone carved bowl of a pool, and yet we float, effortlessly, by our own interdependency on the mass of the chemical in which we bathe, with OdbO, the only one whose skin makes contact with Its pleasurable dependency . . . A parasite; like you.

"Tactile enhancement," both heads whispered into my ears, "is an overall increase in both the intensity of a person's sense of touch and their awareness of the physical sensations across their body." Their breath, i could feel, unlike the others. The other's breath was a natural stimulus, suppressed. Their's, OdbO's, was released into my covered ears, and my own ejaculate suppressed it's self as my eyes watered, a pleasure we had excreted, alone; Uno— They kept speaking, this time with their arms wrapped around me, my body cushioned into their blubber, as excretion dripped, from their nipples. "At the greatest level, these stimuli are extreme enough that the exact point and current of sensation through the unspontaneous, but driven crescendo, of our cranium cannot prevent every single one of our nerve endings across our skin to be felt and comprehended all at once. Yes?" Are you listening?

Focused indoctrination w i t h < N O -Th ing ǝvǝrythǝng\

\ ǝvǝrythǝng˙ ● .ǝvǝrythǝng ǝvǝrythǝng ǝvǝrythǝng ǝvǝrythǝng/

                                    ●
                              •●
                        ●   •●.

                          ●.
                    ●
                    :

"In contrast, throughout normal sober living, most people can only maintain awareness of the tactile sensations which are relevant to their current situation," OdbO continues...

Stop   Talking
They   won'T

                        ..."Disinhibition is an orientation towards non-binary, immediate gratification, naturally directing impulsive behaviour, driven by one's current consciousness, and the external stimuli that may or may not engage the sub-conscious, in one's conscious, understood manner, without regard for past societal indoctrinations and/or consideration of future consequences. Not lessons learned...

...lessons ignored."

Clever has begun itching along his under jaw. He will ignore it.

Nervous, Kyle?

"Disinhibition is an orientation towards immediate gratification, leading to impulsive behaviour driven by current thoughts, feelings, and external stimuli, without regard for past learning or consideration of future consequences. This is usually manifested through recklessness, poor risk assessment, and a disregard for social conventions. Overcome suppressed social skills."

They are feasting on their own bowels of gold
Stones they laid as we remained in a deep trance of
the entire moment; the absolute last conversation to have.

The itch has moved.

Revealed itself under Clever's wrist.

"This can often prove useful for those who suffer from social anxiety or a general lack of self-confidence."

8A g e   o   ry   E

      m e t

Go

death   .

.

.   .   .   .   .

. Clever,

.

.

.   .   .   . !

really?

Really clever . Clever? Kyle? Is anybody home?
"No."
And i know where i am. i know you want me to do this.
I Need Your Lovin / Like the Sunshine
i am not that motivated, driven

éNas'

i don't suffer from such a singular disconnect
I Need Your Lovin / Like the Sunshine
from society at large

yAsmin

we just want to dance old man

aZalea

oNa

lord, leave me the fuck alone

      *   *   *
        *
        *
        *
        *

death
everywhere
the pools overflowing with the red blood of the participants
the bloodletting has begun
followed my lead as i bite the neck of THE MASTER
torn his throat, swallowed his useless drivel
my
silicone suit
corrode saway
others pop
out of their skin,
all over each other, salting
the milk of oxytocin
****

my fingernail had broken through the silicone
the rest has begun to peal away from the opening
shed the sheeth
Od/bO
will drown before he bleeds to death
the entire stained glass ceiling, shifts in reds, pink, glowing
in the glow of the under milk pool lights and OdbO

drowning in search of that phony philosophical *Oceanic Feeling*. ontologically reconnected from two forms of Monism, retreating into its purest born form; Dialectical Monism the Dualistic Nature of Birth & Death and the polygonal puzzled ceiling...

        ...became irregular as I submerged under the women's

                      layers of oxytocin

milk

            clear   milk

        not water, but laiche

           that now pouring into my mouth, swallowed to my belly,

           digested into my blood stream, and if we're lucky, I will still not be seen as worthy to take OdbO's throne .   .   .

                .of a creed ..
...we have no ambition towards, the same lack of ambition that éNas'

 entrusted in us, to ignore THE MASTER's request. The indifference we have shown towards difference, a pure Dualistic Monism in Triality— Me, Myself, & Us

               And i left.
Left OdbO's lost vessels to finish off their parents. Left to collect myself and get along little doggy.

         These people are nuts, the Rave was fun, but honestly, Clever thinks he had better get to a plane before the epidemic escapes the borders. éNas had given him plenty of remedies for the contagion, yet like most who seem dead set on saving his life, a mask seems like the only way to go.

   We had a love note left in the guest room once I found my way back through the maze of the castle, so many people, bodies everywhere, an orgy of a mass, so many living ones, sexing ones, dead ones, starving ones so many people, but finally we found the room

éNas'

        love note was a re-designing of my mask.

A featherweight of silicon carved and melded
. . into the eye sockets . .
By the moment Clever re-entered the guest room
Kyle had already demonstrated it to our self, who was now
up and awake.
éNas'

had waited to meet me.
return Emiton's passport,
supply him with a new pack.
smaller, but filled with potions.

We returned the book to her, apologized for her friend.
She kissed us all good bye after inscribing a similar tattoo
along our entire body from soul to scalp, avoiding our
repulsive, matted facial skin, that our masks fits
like a puzzle
d
man

who did not even see his mentor slip back through the wall
back to the
basement corridors,
to a retreat, she promises to save for our future
...roots, like a redwood, assist other roots
for
longevity
the
t
r
ee
l
o
n
g
e
r
was Emiton's moniker
treelonger
than
the lea

eves...tussle
in the wind, when
they fall, until they will
crackle of gravity, empty
of the e n t r o p y.
o f the s o cietal means necessary

kyle was sure he came in her earlier. clever was careless to
think this was a cry for help. kyle wasn't crying, he was cu

m

m

i

n

g

.

with a last jerk to his pelvis.
his spine had tweaked.
he is well aware he alone has impregnated éNas'
for the first time

But kill the butler, Odom? Seemed extreme to Eminton. He
rather she tie up her loose ends as he,
and then he'll find her after his errand. But had he killed
him, the guilt would tear us apart, and we needed
to stick together . me, myself, & Kyle.
Eminton put the car into gear for us.
out of park.
reverse.
rearview
mirrors, no obstacle, get out
drive away, don't stop, do not
— *Did he lure me here? Was this some nihilistic occult plan?*
He tried to kill my wife, that's something to be weary of.
do not leave anything behind

The pack éNas' gave us is on the passenger seat. We're set.

Medical supplies, clothes, food, aerosol, lighters, baking
powder in a small jar, ash in another, ash of her soil,
things we need, i need-

to
get back on track.
On the trains. Down to Rome.
Meet my friends.
Get a new walkman.
Listen to *Led Zeppelin* from now on.
Never take them off. You just never know.
nervous driving at night, through the nowhere of Austria's
countryside. Emiton wants us to relax.
He knows where he's going. He's reading off the map
tattooed on our skin.

Am I forgetting something?
muther fucker, i think i'm sober
again

Her Face. . .   Torn, Shredded from the Sliding Impact against the. . .
Knife in his gut.   I am sure I killed Erebus on the street; intentionally.
She's dead. He's dead. I married them like a fool. This place was
something that found me, not them. I have got to get the fuck out of
this country...before I'm trapped on this island forever and ever and .

"Where are my shoes?"

.

By the time you get to a train station, you had ditched the car against
a toppled tree that, as can be expected, you had to squeeze out from
under, break the back window to get to your pack. Eminton was a
great assist. Held up the eye. His third eye was immaculate, like
emeralds melded together into a new color of emerald, another
impossibility. This pack is not as nice as the backpack that you had
before. Feels sturdier though; heavily lined. Then for the next four
hours you drag your bare soles along the graveled shoulder, hoping
to not endure the ordeal of dodging a car from behind, without its
lights on in the middle of the morning...and at the train station, in the
tiny town, you must act like a tourist who has taken a particular
interest in the countryside outside Vienna...1oo miles out from
Vienna, nowhere near...a highway...without shoes, and a raw tattoo
on your hands, feet, neck, bald skull, in a mask...that is all you have
to do...act like a tourist, no one will notice.

I washed my torn up, bloody feet in a ditch gutter a few yards to the side of the station. I could hear the morning shift as they opened the station. They do expect a train. They both have a cough and luckily neither of them have spotted me yet...waiting behind the bushes, trees, now meters upon meters down track, thinking about going out farther, but the train might go too fast. Need to get on when it rolls away, not when...and that's what I did...and that's when I cried. No just kidding, that's when I took a nap. It's a long way to Rome, and I gotta hide in this w for hours; Woods. You've really lost your sense of cool ever since you left the house. Clever? Are you listening to us? Clever. Emiton is growing weary of Clever's stability.

What?

Don't abbreviate your surroundings.

That's what they call a bathroom, you idiot. Don't lie to us, Clever.

We're on a train. In the bathroom. Hiding. Okay? Clearly you are not, O.K.

Fuck off.

Chapter - Passing Tracks

THE WHISTLE!
after miles of single notes on a distant piano. Coughs and sniffles on the outside of the W's door. After hours of rattling chains, the bathroom's own odor of mint bar from the urinal is irritating us. After winks upon winks, I have the energy to exit the train, find a way; somewhere directed.

The train's dropped us, me, off in Zurich. The posting board is meters above me. CLACK, CLACK, CLACK, the spinning letters go, dropping letters to alien cities, alien nations- GE-BCDEFGHIJKLM-NEV-XYZ-A - GENEVA, SWITZERLAND. Clever likes the idea. I do not. We're already late, days late. Probably a week or less. They're going to worry about us one way or another. Emiton reminds us that éNas' had helped us book the flight out of Madrid. We were too tired, confused enough, worried about it all. Emiton is the real savior of the gang. He's got it all in the head. Remembers every detail. Could write a book, but then where would that get us, nowhere safer than here...we gotta keep moving, stop thinking, no time, go to

Geneva

Wait, Clever, No! Wait!

*

The tracks have taken us, me, along a molten glass river. Clear, white, reflections of the mountains we weave through. The stones are reminiscent of tall buildings, buildings overrun by foliage. Trees; pines drifting. A landscape that is covered in the white of snow in the dead of winter. The river outside the W's window takes a sharp curve, smears the visual drifts as we turn right and enter a tunnel, darkness, all bass, stressed up treble. My palinopsia of the photorealistic mountain ranges and pines is opaque along the stone carved darkness of the cave . i am flow . the connections of psychedelic geometry is triggered in my mind, i am clear, together we are i n s ig ht fu l to Emiton . .   .

(_*_)
A prismatic, kaleidoscopic shine grows out from
a crack in the darkness, the opening of the
t   u   n| 【▲】 |n   e   l
we are in Switzerland. Rome must wait

Miles through mountains, I am glad I washed down éNas' psilocybin dust with the sink water. To have tried to use my own salivation would have been disastrous...I'm nauseous enough as I step off into the hidden gem of Europe. My marblǝ facǝ can be the futurǝ snow to this t i m ǝ   o f
   y   e   a   r

1997, still

our emerald eyes are wide as the paved path takes me along the wonderful reflective lake, surrounded and mirrored with bushed trees, clumps, soft from a distance, the clouds of the soil. No need to see the trunks that hold the curls of Switzerland as the same lake spits itself miles high into the reflected sky above as the puffed, shapely clouds of the atmosphere drift along, almost circling the lake against my trajectory. Chaos would have me at the bottom of the lake, seeking the herbs to stimulate the children beyond that which Oldom and his conjoined King could achieve. That substâintial châos he offered me, as a throw to cover purpose, a purpose designed for who? That's what we could never figure out? Who was Clever to be leading if not himself? Me? You? . Emiton needed no leader, he was just a creature of habitual order , part of their clan, their family... We're just escorting this guy to run an errand for the doctor. Ya' know, the more I think about it . Diamond eyes & All never shattered like I'd imagine them to have. No shards bursting from the whites of my friend's eyes. No scratches. Just coal. Coal that was used to pump her stomach, naturally, through regurgitation—

and I heave over the side of the railing,
                                        directly   onto   the   rocks,
rocks that are quickly washed by the current of the lake thåT seems to wiggle snail waddle aboard as i wanT Tø swilm l;adfsai;atjkesafm, damn it clever you took those without telling us again? in reference to the mushroom dust. da under a leaved rtunnelled tenta clause. . . with time pieced tøg´T´her beca a use be c a use. beca use. be see a use. we see a use. use. use it clever ly kyle clay born

*

coming upon a fountain I am touched by the oceanic sentiment; iron molded children dance around the centré spout of glorious waters. From the little naked boys and girls puckered lips stream the same recycled waters over their sequential mate's head, so animated, so innocent. When I touch the pooling fountain it lights up in bioluminescence, a flickering blue and green community of charged molecules stream down my hand along my forearm and back to the festival it has been removed from. The droplets explode into vibrant rainbowed chemical sparks upon contact. So I drink the colors. Colors that remind my insides, the inner lining of this vessel, "This was innocence."

"Who's guilty?"

CLICK, CLICK, CLICK, No Clattity-Clack, No Tick-Tick-tickle; no, that is not what these second hands are doing. They are in perfect time, it is their job. Their purpose is to CLICK, CLICK, CLICK, on the second, to the second, for an ever-completing cycle, only interrupted by death...the end of its entropy, the end of its catalyst...unless you wind it up again. "The second hand is guilty. And we really need to buy a new walkman...and a good *Zeppelin* CD," I say to Clever's so brilliantly masked reflection. The gold timepieces' hands glisten as they hit the light rays of the overheads, sparkle along the edges of the etched spiraled vines that cover its entirety. I can see everything clearly in this store's window, everything except my own eyes through the skin layer éNas' had fashioned to protect us. Tonight, alone at 3 forty-two am, there is no one to pass me with a cough, a sneeze; the free unsuspecting spitter. No one to pass along the bug. No one for me to pass the bug too.

"Do you place to stay?" an Englishman's voice says from a car that has pulled up behind me. In the reflection of the clock-smith's window the driver has a kind face, shaven, short blonde hair, mid-thirties, another European John. "I'm just a tourist," I say to his reflection that has drifted into a blemish in the window glass. "Do you need a fix?" he asks, with no assumption that I am broken. "Just a sightseer," I say with a smile. He cannot see me smile. "It's free. We have a stand over there," and he points me to what I had thought earlier was a shack to rent lake stuff. That's where the parents with their boys and girls get bikes, peddle boats, paddle boats, floaties, ice-cream, hotdogs/wieners...not drugs, right? Right. You're just high, Kyle. "I'm not hungry," I tell the creep, honestly, again with a smile, but when I squint I can read the sign on the shack. In English amongst other languages it reads, "Drop Off, Pick Up, Safety First." And I wander across the street and up to the shack. The driver is watching me. I tap on the shack's PICK UP window. It opens. It actually opens. There is a man inside. He doesn't say anything, turns his back, opens a drawer, turns back and quietly, without judgement, slides me a new needle, and a disposal pack. "Oh, no thank you." He takes it back, I step back. He waits. He's seen this before. He doesn't offer it to me again. He's not a pusher, he's a caregiver. And I smile. Good people, Geneva. The driver waves as he turns by me, making his way home, the opposite of guilty, not a second hand, but the sun that is beautiful as it begins to crack over the fluffed up shadowed black green bushed trees that surround the lake city of Geneva. Geneva. Gen era t i o n o n

ǝ t h ǝ l ǝ s s o n n' o n n' o n n' o n n' o n n' o n n' o n o n

ǝ

u   n o

. Wonder where they'll be when the Bees come around...will there be another bug? I yawn. I should probably find my Ona. Miss that girl. Hope she's okay. A little dry, conservative, but a heart of gold. Love her. Bye, bye Switzerland. Good on the no army too...yet you're a little too rich for my taste...but Kyle and I do stock up on dark chocolate at the train station. Stole a bunch of it. I don't have any money. What do I got? I got shit. I got a passport for some guy that looks like a Claibourne who's escorting this quiet type of a Emiton carrying a bunch of a wack-job Alchemist's drugs from Vienna...the shrooms were awesome, i will give her that...but that she put in my pocket for me...we're saving the pack for later. Now how do I get the fuck out of here...I have to scope out the station to find a spot to hop on. Jump it slow, hop to i

t

.

Chapter - Too Early; two rise

Pretty birds see the sun, while a gnarly bird gets the worm. I've treaded at least a mile or two along the tracks into the brush that sprawls and winds along the lake away from good ole Geneva, where the last thing you heard was a small café opening up to the audible pre-volution of my youth, *Sisters of Mercy's, More,* "*some people get high / with a hard on for, more,*" lyrics that I still get wrong...but that's how young Claibourne remember the words.

> *— Do they have poison oak in Europe?*
> *Maybe poison ivy like the East Coast?*

Poison something is surely rubbing itself all over me as I thrash through this never ending greenery that becomes thicker and thicker...even beside the track that we're following. Emiton is dragging his feet. Exhausted already. He is not much of a warrior. I tell Clever to take his hand, help him. He does, we do. I assist him, one arm over my shoulders, one arm over Clever's. One step at a time, no matter how torn up all of our naked feet are getting. The tunnel we remember has come into view. The brush has been cleared, just tumbled oil slicked stones, stones like the gravel for giants. We rolled through this tunnel. That I remember clearly. Did you ever tell Ona we were held back a year? Clever asks. Unfamiliar with that time of our relationship. He wasn't around then...We did tell her, when we first went bowling. Told her we weren't dumb, just, distant, a distant learner...learned by doing not by listening. I hadn't talked much those two years between second and third. We lived in Marin. My parents worked too hard. I remember when Dad got brought home by the cops 'cause he drifted all four lanes on the 101 at eight at night. He was totally asleep. Passed out from a fourteen-hour work day; I presume. "*And I need more / and I need all the love I can get / and I need all the love I can't get to,*" sings the sisters in Rome.

Dad almost died.

Is Ona following the map you tattooed on our palm?

The map the French Girl helped you do on the rooftop.

something Kyle hadn't recalled until now.

How did Dad know?
YOU'LL NEVER LOVE HER LIKE I LOVE YOUR MOTHER
I WISH THE MILKMAN WOULD DELIVER MY MILK
in the morning • Kyle's father was gay . i've always been Straight . less than a
curiosity, an experiment mentally, with a plain Id understanding of Loving a
Mother like Your Father never Could . and hey Clever, that's totally okay , that's
just the dna way, there is no need to choose, you have been chosen, married in
heaven...who will you die with

?

Where the fuck is
this train? I should probably switch my clothes now.
Digging into the pack and there is no change of clothes.
What I figured for clothing is just rags? Stained old rags.
Rags, bottles of powder, vials of liquid, teabags of herbs, and
more rags. The baking soda and dirt are nowhere to be
found. I must have hallucinated them. Strange. Every visual
has been so benign since Prague... I'm stuck wearing this
light, long-sleeved, black shirt that looks as if we're just
some sloppy painter. Probably the Alchemist's assistant's shirt, the
French Girl. You do miss her already, éNas', not the traitor who
tried to pawn me off as an Anarchist to run some opiate cult in the
middle of Austria . Even Emiton found it far fetched . Agreed with
éNas' and us that something must be done before it pollinates the
collective-unconcious. There was a calmness to éNas' that you
hadn't felt with a woman before. Possibly it was her age who wore
her wisdom like a vibrant young woman in her prime, with aura
rings that count her past a few thousand years . . . the woman who
turned your key so you too could levitate and collectively recognize
we too are part of the Memory. A cool, calm, seductive, enticing, and
ever so influential calmness to being with her. You won't stop
thinking about éNas' until you're alone, away from Emiton and him.
I do not trust him anymore. If I show confidence and clearity, he will
surely think he has gone insane. "Never a secret behind this mask.
You wear it well," she had kissed you both, separatly before you left
the mansion in a stolen car, the one that brought you there weeks
ago, if not a number of days past eight... Shh. There's a hole at the
bottom hem of the shirt, just to the left of my left hip. The
right of my groin. The cutup black Levis she'd lent me we
like. Gives me air-condition at the knee holes, and the one
between the belt and back pocket catches a breeze. I really
have to find some shoes. My feet hurt worse than my face.
That heat rash from this mask is nothing to write home

about. Mom would be pissed, worried...demand I flew home, right away.

No way. I grin and bear it. —She did have a sinister grin by the time her entropy stopped in the middle of the street. Her teeth, so white, so perfect. Now chipped from the chair you shoved in her mouth when she was flailing like carp hooked on crack-cocaine, flopping around out of control. She had never needed braces, born beautiful, if you didn't look at her back...if she looked at you with a sharp diamond eye. If you could see the crystals of heaven reflecting in your emerald eyes, maybe you could be happy again...but if she turned her back on you, there you would have seen the broken wings, "*Hey now, hey now a now, sing this corrosion to me...*" so I grin and bear it as the train gently rumbles its way closer towards me...rolling...slow, a mile per hour, maybe two...I'm no cop. One car, two car, three car, I can do this, easy, four car, ready guys, *Hey now a now, sing this corrosion to me...*five car, risk it before the tail, or go for the gold...eight car, nine car, ten car, go, go, go, through the brush, up to the track, e l e v e now, hop—

Chapter - When in Rome

She's met me at the *Coliseum*. A nice day. A bit warm but every so often a mighty Roman cloud cover's the reminder of *Mt. Olympus*. She could be Greek. She was, she isn't. Could be Italian, yet she is not, she is from Spain; born and raised. She hugged me immediately. Inside I could hear her crying. It was the rapid, yet fluctuation of her breathing, her chest against mine, her abdomen against mine. I love you, Ona. And as her breath balanced, I gently removed myself from her embrace, "I'm glad you remembered," I say to her. "I worry, Kyle," she says, looking me right in the eye. She can see my eyes from her perspective. My emeralds must twinkle as the sun breaks from the perspiration that separates the people from the gods. Her eyes are reflecting mine, we are close still. Through her eyes, I can see mine. I look like a statue with my face on. My eyes are a brilliant emerald green surrounded by a striking red from the completeness of every white eye blood vessel bursting at once, many lives ago. Her eyes are invisible to her. The veil between us won't allow it.

My eyes are not a two-way mirror.

I do clearly remember éNas' removing her Moses mask with horns and her third eye was clear, the entire galaxy spun in her dialtated pupils. Two galaxies, equal in weight with two different colored suns; a ONE red a ONE blue swimming in my green sea

We never saw her other eyes open on their own, only through the third she was willing to share We may have been lied too about Emiton.

*

No one has wondered much about Ona and me in my mask wandering the Coliseum's insides. World's seen enough by now. NYC Club Kids on day time talk shows. Massives on their own beaches.

Could just be a skin condition?   A deformity you should ignore.

"Where's Alejandro?"

Lions against man in front of hundreds, maybe thousands? I'm not really reading the information panels. I'm holding Ona's hand and slowly meandering through history, without saying a word. "We fight," she explains. They didn't have phones back then. If you found yourself left to your own cognitive behaviors hundreds of miles from Rome, well, you'd probably made plans to meet up, in a variety of ways and days...right? Probably. Like the map on my palm. She has not mentioned it, nor the tattoos on my feet, arms, or neck, although we can still feel them healing, "He mad because I go to meet you two times." Communication is relatively simple. We

get

it.

*

Ona covers us for a cab back to her hostel. "Passport?" And I show her. "That I still have." She is trembling. Are you scared of me? "No time, no money or train pass?" I take her hand, she needs to stop trembling. "Are you okay, Ona?" We are an attractive couple in the reflection of the cab with the ruins superimposed behind us. My mask compliments everything about her. I would like to kiss her some

times.

Cab

stops outside the hostel. A cluster of Nuns drift along the opposing side of the cobblestoned street. I wave. One waves in return. *"Follow you, follow me,"* the refreshing sounds of *Phil Collins* begin rolling out of the cabs radio. We cannot help but smile. She cannot see me smile. Kyle is invisible. Clever is right here, right by your side. Emiton is sitting shotgun of course, duh. I help Ona out of the cab. She is blushing. Shaking still. Her eyes are scared of me. "I'm not a ghost," I say, nonchalant, "nothing's changed, just time. We watched time change in Geneva. It was beautiful," I continue as she steps into the lobby. We are on both sides of the doorframe. She is closed, inside, I am open, outside, and over the speakers behind me from the cab, *Stay with me / My love I hope you always be by my side*...and stepping into the inside, *When I'm with you / I will follow you / will you follow me*, so perfectly timed. We both laugh, both of us, and Ona; Ona and I laughing as we recognize that, yes once again, we are in a cloud of *Genesis* the *Phil Collins* Ages, the ruins of our entire relationship and I'm nearly tackled to the ground by Stacey..."No way, you really found him," Stacey says in the lobby of the Hostel. She punches me in the shoulder, "How you doing freakazoid?" Stacey steps back, "You look good, brother. This, this is it, step back, and we'll follow you," her too cracking a *Phil Collins* joke; Friends.

*

In 1988

we were eleven. Double digits, duplicated single digits. an acoustic guitar, leather jacket, steel toed boots, *"Oh I guess it would be nice, if I could touch your body,"* was the hit single most imperative subconscious uprising that would define everything to my peers; us. *"But I need someone to hold me but I wait for something more,"* yada, yada, *"Got to have Faith."* Ona laughs at me as we exit the hostel doors. Dropped my pack off upstairs. I waited patiently. Waved to a nice-looking girl who picked up a flier and left. Nodded at the strapped guy in sweatpants and a runners' jacket, *"Never gonna give you up,"* he mouths to himself as he waits for check out. A *Rick Astley* fan. He's got a tap to his step. The radio is his Romeo goodtime. *"Never gonna say goodbye,"* he sings aloud in his Romanian accent. "I love you Italy," he says to her, turns to me. "Everyone loves the statue in Italy," he tells me. I tip my chin, "See, even t'is guy, Roman God, Statue Man with Tattoo of whole world map on him. So cool, you man." And he sees something, something that blinds me. "Peek-A-Boo," and Ona removes her hands from my face. I remember. That's her favorite song. *Portishead* and *Siouxsie and the Banshees*...top million for her.

"Come, we buy you lunch," she takes my fingers. It's a moment. Stacey sees it. Stacey doesn't like it. I barely notice it, just follow, no agenda, just a bright white, psyc-aye-de-licked grin in a permanence as active as the advent of the nature's polymorphism. Me and my crew have a mission. Let's go.

*

éNas' proud of you. Her commands titillate inside your psyche like a reverb in the depths of your ecstatic subconscious. Feels great in here. Revolutionary.

*

"Back to life, back to reality," Stacey jests. "What's wrong, kiddo?" I ask her. "I just haven't gotten laid once this entire trip," and I feel for her. She should shack up with Ona. Seems like she's in a good enough mood with me back. "Never," she says to me, "Your lady is cold. Besides, I like 'em black, big booty, soul sister. Know what I'm saying?" the dusk is kicking in, the strung lights that spider around, throughout the centré of Rome, almost all culminate at the Spanish Steps, where tourists, collectives, lovers, and squatters alike congregate; every other one wanting to snap a picture with the guy in the mask.

and hours later i wonder how Stacey read my mind earlier

"We go to disco tonight, Clever, yes?" Ona asks. What's Stacey's opinion on the matter? "Stacey?" I ask as she catches the drip from her Gelato cone, "Um, totally. You still got that," she looks around, leans into Ona and I, "stuff, ya know?"

*

Come on, Vogue. Let your body move to the music
bup, bup, bup,
"Oh my god, I love this song," Ona is liberated
and onto the dancefloor with her
she goes, at it alone
All you need is your imagination, so use it that's what it's for
Can't help but grin and bear it, devour it
she is trying to make some one
j e a l o u s
Rhythm is a Dancer, It's a Soul Companion
she waves you into the crowd, an Italian flashback
Old School, new school House Mixes of the Late 80s
/ How Very Like the Future This Place Might Be /
/ It's a Tiny World Just Big Enough to Support the Kingdom of

One Knowledgeable Worker /
/ Feel a Wave of Loneliness, Head Back Down /
/ I'm Going Too Fast (I'm Going too Fast) /
she shouldn't rub up
against familiarity
/Words like Violence/ Break the Silence/
Come Crashing In / Into My Little World /
Painful to Me / Pierce Right Through Me /
Can't you understand? / Oh My Little Girl /
All I Ever Wanted / All I Ever Needed /
Is Here in My Arms
slowly said *Depeche Mode*
her deeper favorite and its over
for us
shh
don't tell the devil
she should never have kissed my masked lips
.

Chapter - So very Nicé

There was no debate, Ona was going to pay for my train ticket. She had already argued with the agent in Spanish that my pass had been stolen, and other sorts of things. "How did you get here?" is something I am surprised no one has asked me yet. Stacey hasn't even asked and she's a normal person. Emiton believes worry has a way of creating a peace in regrets through the worst not having happened, accompanied and peppered with exoneration. "Trains," I answered. "But how?" Stacey has inquired.

"Like a rabbit."

Ona buys me a pass.

"Thank you."

*

The pass gets us, me, from Rome to Nicé— fulfilling a promise made to oneself. With or without us, Ona will sleep on the sand of Nicé before she returns to her unhome, again.

*

"*Seventeen and I was havin' a ball | Eleventh grade and 'Joe' I knew it all | I fell in love for the very first time, with this <u>girl</u>,*" and the cabin goes oooooo 'cause Stacey changed *C&C Music Factory's* lyric and continued on, "*with this girl she really blew my mind | Inner sense and whole lotta class | Style that could give you whiplash | We said hello and my heart beat stopped | She was the world and I was on top | Time went by, she filled my universe | we made love | she said I was the first | my boy kept telling me | I don't know I think your girl's been playing tic tac toe | I'll ask my girl I know she only loves me | Wasn't I the one who took your <u>lesbian</u> virginity?*" another round of ooooooooo, "*The look on her face read sorrow and gloom | She said, "Yeah, Why do you girls always ask that? — Things that make you go hmmmmm,*" and Stacey completes the entire stanza by heart. The cabin has been flooded by a ton of our European peers just to hang out, hide out from the ticketer, and utterly impressed by Stacey's absolutely odd ability to perfectly sing a *C & C Music Factory* song. Ona has gotten bashful again. Closing in, not being part of it all. All is apart from you, so?

Clever can laugh with the best of them.
Kyle can keep up with the Clever.
And me?
well
we're
worried
about Ona,
not so much
I just hope Kyle and Emiton don't argue in the W.

*

Nicé is nice. Slow. Quiet. Romantic to the rich. The hostels are nothing special and even though she wants to back out,

Stacey and I push Ona to crash on the beach for the night. "Just one night. It's warm, the waters warm. We can all go..." and we all knew what Stacey was insinuating..."Swimming," she clarifies before Ona backs out over skinny dipping. I am definitely skinny dipping tonight.

How do you say Deꙅe-Groovꙅy? How do you say Deꙅe-lite?

The warm waters of Nicé under the moonlight, up to your ribs, yeah it's as romantic as can be, for a moment. Your new American friend floats meters away. Her nips break the surface to point at the stars. Ona has stayed upon shore. She is satisfied to be alone, to be on the beach, at night, in Nicé. You slept with your heels dug into the sand. Stacey and Ona slept together. Safer in numbers. Good for us. *"And I need the love I can get / And I need all the love that I can't get to,"*as you watch Azalea's illustrious body continue to break against the shore from the very short tide; you wish...she's nowhere to be found...she's dead. She jumped. Deaded herself. Because of me,

you guess?

*

Chapter - Laid to Rest

These Italian loafers suck. I'm not a loafer guy, but a good man doesn't look a gift horse in the mouth, especially when his feet were still bleeding from an unexpected circumambulation. If Ona sees how ruined the insides of these loafers are already— let's be honest, Kyle is not walking slowly and taking breaks all day because the blisters and scabs aren't being torn off by the amount of trudging one must to do make their way by train in Europe; they are. The blisters and scabs are constantly being re-wounded, like his face was a week or so ago. That's all done with now. This thing is never coming off now. I've truly grown into my mask.

• 🐭 • 🐭 on our minds' third-eye on the back of our heads• 🐭 • 🐭

"Isn't this Alejandro's place?" I ask as Ona as she buzzes the buildings intercom. A plain building. Sort of non-descript. "Yes. Miguel here," she says. She's really got the bug eye about her boyfriend. "Hola, Ona?" it is Miguel on the other end. I recognize his voice. "I really have to pee," Stacey tells me and buzz, Miguel buzzes us all in. Stacey is quick up those flights of stairs, Ona stops. "No say nothing about us, Kyle," she says. I nod. She kisses my marble cheek. "Do you have sympathy for the Devil, friend?" you asked her in return, in exchange for the second kiss in forty days, or more. "I no understand," she said, and you lead her up the stairs for her sake. Took her hand, showed her the way back to the fires and smoldering bark of the Roman ruins. You've changed Ona, transformed her into something greater than ourselves, something of herself, but she still does not understand. We can feel everything now, everything as if the enhanced prophylactic is not only covering our skin, but éNas' coats our singular cerebral cor

      t

      e

      ex.girlfriend(s) with Emiton and Kyle patiently waiting for me to save her before ruining everything for everyone by keeping a terrible secret

*

      Miguel's greeted me with open arms. "You have stories." He insists I brief him in on the improbable. Ona's vanished with the big guy into his bedroom. "We all go eat, yes?" Miguel asks me. Stacey returns from the toilet. "Paella. I want Paella," she insists. "Paella?" Miguel asks me. I shrug. I'm on a diet. Not eating. On a cleanse. "Fasting." And he figures it's some Jewish thing, and so does Stacey, and so does the others. Clever's not in the mood to talk about it, and Kyle's just starting to lie for the both of us. "You got an extra walkman?" I asked my cousin from another mother. "No, but tomorrow you better get one," Miguel says, dead serious, see's it in my eyes, I too am not kidding around, and Miguel respects, taps his heart; he and I have love. He almost got me killed, twice. "I like the mask, Clever."

      "Thanks."

"Want to get high?"

      Still nothing about my tattoos. Shame. Ask a person about their self, and they may just tell you a secret or two about you.

      "Fasting. Sober with Time."

"Sounds good.

      HEY, ONA! ASSHOLE! DINNER, LETS GO! VAMOS!"

*

A round table of paella for travelers, lovers, haters, friends, family, and Rickardo whom seems taller since I had last seen him, now seated beside me. "How are you going to eat in that mask?" he asks me. "Don't ask crazy, crazy questions," Alejandro says, laughing at his own joke. No one else thought it was funny.

Nobody laughing, but you.
                You smirk at him under your face.

"Maybe Ona feed you with a bottle. Milk?" he says next.

            That's it, she's had enough as she slams her utensils, scrapes her chair along the tiled floor, marches right out of the restaurant, and with no restraint you are outside right behind her, chasing her up the street, touching her back as you reach her, "Ona," and you both walked on,
                          "Kyle, I sorry."

*

Ona beelined us straight to Alejandro's apartment. She hadn't said anything more after her apology until we were inside. She had excused herself to the bathroom as I waited for nothing on the balcony. Earlier Kyle had scrolled through A-man's exquisite tape collection. Garbage, all garbage and I do not mean the band. We're talking *Backstreet Boys, Puff Daddy, Usher, Hanson* (his favorite), *Spice Girls, 98 Degrees, The Cranberries,* and every *R. Kelly* album...well I wouldn't know if he had them all, but he had four, and that seemed like a collection. *R. Kelly* rubs me the wrong way. Could never put my finger on it, but the dudes got some untrustworthy eyes. You can see it in his music videos...Alejandro has the same eyes. I have never trusted A. Jandro. Ona's taking too long. I check on her, make my way back inside, down the apartment hall towards the bathroom. She's left the door cracked open. I tap on it with my knuckle, it glides open from the simple TAP, TAP

Ona's on the edge
of the bath. She's been crying. "Are you okay?" There was a
new instant wave of confidence that got her to lift her head,
something about my acknowlegment of her struggle, the
absence of mine, ours. She stands up, looks me right in the
eye and say, "You still have the most beautiful eyes.
Hypnotizing. Take it off."

"The mask?"

"Yes."

"I can't."

"Please, Clever. One last time."

"You won't like what you see."

"Clever, I still love you."

and with that her own hands began to remove the marble mask

it is not easy.
the skin has begun to marry the
inside, again
removal splits the boils, rips the scabs

she is scared, horrified, but she won't show it tonight
as her delicate Spanish fingers reach out to touch my cheek
"Does it hurt?"

Ona and Clever do not sex . Ona and Clever do not make love,

they say goodbye; intimately without their veils
with a condom
safely
without
the others
again
Clever felt like Kyle
Kyle felt like Emiton
and
Emiton felt like Leaving

*

On the way, back to the restaurant, "When you believe in
things you don't understand | Then you suffer | Superstition is the

way / Everybody Scream!" and Kyle opened the door for Ona and followed her back to the table where she apologized to Alejandro for walking out on him. She sits, kisses her man, looks back at Clever, smirks, twinkle in her eye; she has cheated on her boyfriend...and she liked it?

Kyle's over it. Too long, too many games, gets up, casually states, "Guess this is goodbye." Miguel is quick to rise to the occasion, hugs Kyle as Clever quietly keeps a spy eye on Ona. "You know route to Airport?" he asks. Kyle nods, gives Stacey a hug from the back of her chair, "Good sport," Clever whispers into his new American friend's ear as I keep an eye on Alejandro trying to communicate with Ona who cannot help but keep an eye on Kyle. I've grown tired of watching them all. The loops of nonchalant denial. You, galavanting around with a wicked mind, listening to me like a storyteller instead of yourself, like I was a liar; fiction in your brain. Kyle, Clever, can we go now?

"Rickardo, don't do drugs," I say and finally it is time to address the lovely couple. What sort of regards can you give a pair whose turmoil is sure to continue on as you walk away, out that door, back across the ocean, on command, by destined outcomes, by instructed deliveries, to meet new people, perpetrate the norms social epitaphs, kick your way to the millennium Y2k&1/2 years away. What to say?

Kyle leans his head down to Alejandro's ear & confidently states, "I just fucked your girlfriend, came on your pillow," then walked away, never having to say goodbye to the girl from E s p aña.

*

The flight will happen tomorrow morning. A good night's rest under the escalator me, myself, and I. Bustling of passengers will awaken you at 6am. The boarding pass reads:

BOARDING 10am, Emiton Claibourne, seat 8A. GATE A8.

Chuckle, we had never been into number signs. That's conspiratorial shit, not chemistry.

*

"Medical condition," you pleaded,
yet TSA insists we remove our face covering.
he does not flinch at my degenerating face
waves the disfigured young man with his carryon pack through
polcie wlil igonre eevrytihng if you are cnofidnet

We have no reason to exit JFK, we have a connecting flight to SFO.
Emiton leaves the airport. A total disregard towards his schedule

we are all invsibel

*

At the bus-stop he's told he can take a train to the city if he preferred. The bus ride would be an hour at least, besides these three numbskulls did not have any change. Ona was going to give them some before they left, but it was more abrupt than Kyle preferred, but this wasn't about Kyle anymore. This was about Emiton. The train would take about twenty-thirty minutes. Emiton and Clever deducted if they took the train they could record the timing. Collect at least some data. So, they took the train. Hopped the turnstile and got off at Union Square. None of them had ever been to New York. Eclectic faces from the start. No one was bothered by the young man in the white mask. "Which way to Hoboken?" you had asked a stranger. Aren't they all strangers? Metal drive-bys, double bass drums, the reckoning is near, the apocalypse of *Metallica's Master of Puppets* from the same four cars that circled the Square only days ago. How long have you waited here. We have fasted for days now? No. Maybe a twenty-hour day. Passed their twenty-first birthday. Clear headed. Missing for years. The guy directed Emiton to the PATH Train where he was greeted by a shaved headed fellow in a tight, white, tank top. "A°toms," the man introduced himself to you. "You are Emiton?" You both shook hands. It had been years since the contagion had subsided in Austria. We have been hiding out in Alphabet City, amongst the squatters. Happy to say none of us have gotten sick yet. And now, A°tom has pulled Emiton from quarantine to finally retrieve, trade you for the bag you have delivered from THE MASTER's castle, code for the truth . . You have to take his bag in return. You have no choice. You've invested this much time, what's a few more hours. For her trust.

•

•••.This backpack is larger than the one you started with to visit that girl in Spain. Such a sweet girl. Over her head. Involved with a chemist. But that was all over now. Finally, they would be free of it all, be able to get on with it, finish the island, ride the PATH to Hoboken, pull a plastic bag, wrapped in duct tape, with your handwriting PATH on it, from the large backpack, and plant this strange plastic bag down the tunnel after un-boarding, then to the Holland Tunnel, following the map on your other palm; hitch a ride back to the city, drop a baggy at the end of that tunnel, walk North to the Lincoln tunnel(s), hitch to Jersey, drop a bag, hitch to Manhattan, drop a bag, hitch back to Jersey, drop a bag, hoof it up to the Washington bridge, trek back across to Jersey, only to cross back the Henry Hudson for another bag drop, wander the creek North of Manhattan to the Harlem river, cross the Broadway bridge, drop a bag, follow this same pattern along the East side, switching it up by design as Emiton rides the Tram back to Manhattan from Roosevelt Island, leaving a baggie by the Tram turn, continuing towards his Midtown Tunnel drop, then Williamsburg Bridge, his favorite view of the city, the Empire State's Building, the silver Twin Towers, then it's the Manhattan bridge, then the Brooklyn bridge, and completing the loop as he hitches a ride back in through the Carey Tunnel into South Manhattan. Exhausted and empty handed, Kyle drops the useless empty backpack into a dumpster and makes his way to the World Trade Center—

Clever felt better about being on his own.
Emiton mailed his passport back to éNas
Liana called Clever's parents, they did not know where
Kyle was?

Alone he would eat his breakfasts, his lunches, his dinners. On his own Clever envisioned he would dance. On his own he would earn a trade to facilitate his own life. Alone, Clever would grow and make friends. Alone, Clever would find love. Alone, all three of them would be just fine with myself.

Together　　we　　can　　be　　transcendent.

...BOOM

And the baggies went off, bomb after bomb, after bomb.
Killing the bridges and tunnels. Destroying cheating
husbands. Burning unfaithful lovers, cutting off Manhattan
from the world around itself, wounding social norms,
creating upheaval, paranoia, fear, mistrust, align-ability,
sheep, loyalists, tribalists, moralists, de-moralists, hypocrites,
sexists, sexless, backsliders, forward thinkers,
groundbreakers, backtrackers,

ꝏ

a cough Kyle has seemed to
have picked up...but from where? The quarantine, or the
spoiler, A°tom? And across the sea Ona sneezed, and when
asked, "God bless you?" Kyle said to the scared elderly
woman beside him, both gazing at the Twin Towers
glistening in the sunlight, standing tall, standing strong
while access to the island of Manhattan has been denied
from the pipe-bombs you had gladly planted for Kyle's
lover, Sané, overseas...and you fucking said to this fragile old
woman, "We will never be totally alone."

She didn't believe you.
And why should she, you are invisible;
the reader of the

p
a
l
m.
Tree Asphalt.
>
death
What separated this man from the troll, was simply that he knew,
there was no more to life than walking in someone else's shoes,
or at least alternating your own foot gear.

www.ingramcontent.com/pod-product-compliance
Lightning Source LLC
Chambersburg PA
CBHW051939240626
47153CB00005B/1552